The Virgin

a novel by

Hannah Blue Heron

Order this book online at www.trafford.com
or email orders@trafford.com

Most Trafford titles are also available at major online book retailers.

Note for Librarians: A cataloguing record for this book is available from Library and Archives Canada at www.collectionscanada.ca/amicus/index-e.html

Printed in Victoria, BC, Canada.

ISBN: 978-1-4251-4938-3 (soft cover)
ISBN: 978-1-4251-4939-0 (eBook)

Trafford Rev. 07/27/09

www.trafford.com

North America & international
toll-free: 1 888 232 4444 (USA & Canada)
phone: 250 383 6864 • fax: 250 383 6804 • email: info@trafford.com

10 9 8 7 6 5 4 3

Also by Hannah Blue Heron

- Memoirs:
  - That Strange Intimacy
  - Growing Tall in Colorado
- Collection of essays, poetry etc.
  - Self Portraits in the Nude

ACKNOWLEDGEMENTS

Many thanks to the Southern Arizona Womens Writer's Group, who listened to all of it and especially Jeanie Marion, who carefully edited the entire manuscript and Margaret Moore for her continuous support and valuable suggestions.

NOTES FROM THE AUTHOR

It was the summer of 1959, the second of five I spent at the University of Notre Dame in pursuit of a Masters Degree in Theology. The humidity of the Indiana summer was intensified by my nun's clothing patterned after that of a well-to-do woman of the sixteenth century. The only parts of my flesh that were visible were my hands and a portion of my face.

I am certain that my jaw became somewhat slack as I listened to the lay professor of the Old Testament, informing us that the harlots inveighed against by the Prophets, considered themselves as virgins in the service of the Goddess. Their primary duty was to bring their male clients into ecstasy with the Goddess right in the confines of their temples.

One lost her status as virgin by giving herself over to pleasuring one man only, thus bearing many offspring for his household, for which she received food, clothing and shelter.

Being a professional virgin at the time, I could hardly help from comparing this version of virginity with my own i.e. the Church's, which was entirely one of deprivation in the service of a male God, for which I also received food, clothing and shelter, but without the pleasures or pains of childbearing.

I soon forgot about this interesting bit of information until thirty years later, when divested from my habit and dispensed from my vow of chastity, as well as those of poverty and obedience, these zesty facts presented themselves as the catalyst for the novel which you will discover between the covers of this book.

Preface

Around 3500 B.C.E, the agrarian civilizations of eastern Europe were being invaded for the second time by Kurgan warriors from the north. The warriors belonged to nomadic tribes seeking grasslands for their herds. During this second invasion, some of them traveled on down the coast of the Great Sea (Mediterranean) and infiltrated the port cities of Anatolia (now the southern coast of Turkey). These invasions were cultural as well as territorial. The warriors replaced the existing egalitarian societies and their fertility goddesses with their hierarchic social structures and warlike gods. Similar hierarchic and warlike tribes of the Semites were advancing from the south. Thus began the patriarchal oppression that persists to this day.

It is not until 3200 B.C.E. that this tale takes place, when the wheel, which has been used primarily by potters (the potter's wheel) for the past three or four thousand years, begins to be used in transportation, a great step forward in the evolution of humankind.

ANATOLIA
Al-Rah Montah
El-Raspell
Et-Huyuk
Al-Rah
Et-Bann
Et-Toll
Et-Ray
Al-Labah
Tel Dann
Zaphir
Tel-Phar
The Great Sea

Prologue

The tall, dark-skinned woman pulled her shawl in tighter to keep out the winter cold. The shawl completely covered her black, wavy hair, but her rich brown eyes could be seen peering out from under, as she carefully picked out the path leading to the hut of Clara, the Virgin High Priestess of the village of Al-Rah. The young woman was shivering, not only from the cold, but because of what she had to tell the crone. She called out to let the old woman know she was coming in through the small entrance of the cone-shaped hut. The acrid smell of burning wood assailed her nostrils, but comforted her at the same time. She was hardly able to make out the tiny figure huddled by some coals which were barely glowing.

"May I put some wood on your fire, Mother?" she asked, as she retrieved some tinder from the supply, put it on the coals and blew on it until tiny flames appeared.

"Thank you very much, Kasha," the crone quavered.

Then Kasha obtained a couple of logs, and added them to the fire. As the fire blazed up, both women relaxed in its warmth. Then Kasha shivered again, as she tried to formulate her message.

"Mother Clara, I have not bled for the past three moon cycles, nor have I been able to eat in the mornings."

"Well, my dear, I would say that you are with child, young as you are."

"I know, Mother, but I say to you, truthfully, that I have not completed the act with a man in the temple, in order to conceive a child."

Clara sat up straighter when she heard this and peered intently into Kasha's eyes. "Are you quite certain? Sometimes it becomes difficult not to... to..."

"I am positive, my Mother." Kasha gazed right back into the priestess' eyes.

It seemed to Clara that the young woman was telling the truth, but to become with child without the help of a man was rare. Clara had heard of it happening, but had never experienced it with any woman before. She finally spoke. "Get my shawl, then, and we shall go to the temple and hear what Inanna has to say."

As they slowly walked through the village to its edge where the temple was, Kasha noted how infirm Clara had become and put an arm around her waist to give her support, as well as warmth. Although snow rarely fell this far down in the valley, it could get quite cold in the winter.

No one living in the village during Clara's time had helped in the construction of the temple. It was a round building, sunken about waist-high into the ground. At ground level, slate rocks, mortared with clay, formed the upper wall, which extended well above the heads of the women. The interior of the wall was covered with a thick coating of mud plaster, on which were painted images of the Goddesses. The thick plaster also served as insulation. The roof was made up of heavy branches, attached to a center pole, in which many thinner branches and long grasses were thatched once a year.

As the High Priestess and Kasha went down into the temple, they inhaled the pleasant odor of crushed sweet grass, which was spread over the floor every few days. Then the smell of hot oil from the taper burning in front of the clay statue of Inanna, opposite the entrance, also seeped into their nostrils. Inanna was the Great Mother of All and the protector of the temple in Al-Rah. The paintings of the other Goddesses could hardly be seen in the dim light.

The High Priestess walked up to the statue, took a sprig of sage and held it in the flame. Both women breathed in this simple incense with pleasure. Clara was energized by it and she began to chant her request to Inanna. "Oh ancient Mother, we greet Thee with our love and and also with a request. Enlighten our minds as to the thing which has happened to Thy young servant Kasha." When she finished chanting, the two women knelt in silence, waiting for a sign.

Kasha was, again, shivering with anticipation and dread. Then she felt a change in Clara and turning towards her, saw that her back was arched and her eyes were staring upward. The young woman edged away in fear, but then realized that the High Priestess was in a trance, during which she would receive an oracle from the Goddess.

Clara's mouth opened wide and the Oracle came forth in deep, strong, sounds, which echoed throughout the temple. Nevertheless they evinced nothing but kindliness. "Kasha, hear me, for you have been doubly blessed. You have received a child directly from me, without the help of a man. You can be certain that the infant will be a girl. You have nothing to fear. Not only have you been blessed, but your entire village is blessed."

Kasha was astonished that the Oracle spoke to her directly, although she was relieved by the affirmation of her claims. Clara gradually relaxed into her normal state, turned and embraced the young woman, whom she had been training to take over her duties as High Priestess. With this confirmation of Kasha's claims, Clara felt certain that her choice had been wise.

The two women slowly returned to Clara's hut, just as the sun began to rise, and the sight of the dozen or so conical huts, which were home to the various members of the community, was reassuring to them. However, both of them continued thinking about the Oracle's message. When they arrived at Clara's home Kasha again replenished the fire and then left for her own dwelling.

When Kasha had become aware of her pregnancy, she was not afraid that she had lost her Virgin status. In those times, a woman lost her ***virginity,*** when she gave herself over to having sex with only one man. Most often she went to live with him, but, whether she did this or not, she lost her status as a Virgin of the Goddess, as well as her temple privileges. Deciding to conceive a child with a man in the temple, in this way serving the Goddess in the highest way, did not endanger her status as a Virgin, but enhanced it. Often the man never knew he had fathered a child, although when the child was a boy, and had lived for seven sun cycles, he was returned to his father or "adopted out" to another man.

Kasha's infancy and childhood had prepared her in strange ways to begin her training as the next High Priestess of Al-Rah, even before she had finished her thirteenth sun cycle. As was true for most of the Virgins of Al-Rah, she had lived with her mother in their own simple hut, built much like Clara's. Her mother, Bella, was filled with an abundance of energy and an obsession for pleasure. She would often take her child with her to go foraging for food, but if they came upon a meadow sprinkled with flowers, she would forget their original purpose and spend the day making garlands to wear in their hair and, dancing the day away with her little girl. It was often Kasha who reminded her mother that they needed to take time out to eat.

During the spring of Kasha's third sun cycle, after the women had finished with the rituals for the feast honoring Inanna, the children were sent to bed, as usual, while the women remained to play their drums and flutes and dance throughout the night. Bella danced harder than any of the others, even those much younger than she. Long after the musicians had stopped playing, Bella continued dancing to the music in her mind. The others, used to the woman's erratic behavior, had fallen asleep. She danced on and on, unaware that the moon had set and a glow could be seen on the eastern horizon. She was also oblivious to the sharp fist-like pressure between her breasts, when suddenly, she let out a piercing cry and fell to the ground.

The High Priestess, Clara, ran over to her. Seeing the staring eyes and the completely inert body, she nevertheless knelt down and listened for a heartbeat. Hearing nothing, she cried out, "She's dead! She's dead! She has returned to the bosom of the Great Mother!"

Clara's cries shocked the others awake. They crowded around the fallen woman and could see that the High Priestess was right; Bella had, indeed, joined with the Great Mother.

Clara took Kasha into her hut, since her own daughter, Orana, had reached menarche and was already building a hut of her own. The Priestess tried to make the little girl feel better by describing how happy her mother must be, dancing in the Great Mother's bosom, but Kasha simply couldn't believe her mother would be happy anywhere but with her.

The High Priestess was very busy training Orana to be a Sibyl* like herself, teaching her how to make the potions that would open her mind to the oracles sent by the Goddess for the enlightenment of the Virgins. She also needed to train her daughter to take over her duties as the Virgin High Priestess of Al-Rah. Neither woman seemed to notice how devastated Kasha was at the loss of her mother, nor did they have much time for her at all.

One day, soon after, Kasha wandered out into the forest, vainly hoping

---

* A female prophet

to find her mother, when she ran into the healer, Sylva, who was gathering herbs.

"What are you doing in the forest by yourself, little one?" the crone asked. Kasha looked directly into the old woman's eyes, letting her see the pain in her own. Sylva held out her arms and Kasha threw herself into them, sobbing out her grief. After comforting her, Sylva began talking to her about herbs and healing. When evening came, the child refused to return to Clara's hut. Sylva went over to tell the High Priestess that she would like to keep Kasha in her hut, in order to teach her herb lore to carry on the tradition. She assured her the child was willing. Clara was actually relieved and quietly handed over the little girl's few belongings.

Shortly after this, Orana moved into her own hut and after several sun cycles decided to have a child. The child born to her, whom she named Gennah, was singularly endowed with flaming red hair and bright blue eyes, both features rare in Al-Rah. She quickly informed Clara that she couldn't be the mother of such a singular child, be the village Sibyl and also take on the duties of High Priestess. Clara tried to persuade her daughter to change her mind, but to no avail. Gradually she understood that such unwillingness would make for a poor High Priestess, a most important role in the village, and she began to observe the other young women to determine who would be suitable. Kasha had barely reached menarche, when Clara realized how unusually mature she was and also how devoted she was at the rituals. Not long after, she approached Kasha and began her training. The young woman was surprised to be chosen, at such a young age, but in her heart, she knew she would make a good High Priestess.

After having informed Clara of her pregnancy, Kasha danced, for the first time, with the beautiful Virgin, Neelah, at the festivities celebrating the return of the light, after the longest night of the year. Neelah had long, black hair and surprisingly contrasting blue eyes. As they danced to the drumming of the women, their bodies seemed to flow together in perfect symmetry and it wasn't long before they were embracing. Kasha led the willing Neelah to her hut, where they spent the night in each other's arms. The next morning they decided to live out their lives together in that very hut. Neelah was delighted that Kasha was pregnant and looked forward to mothering the child along with her.

Not long before Kasha's infant was to be born, Clara came to her hut, one evening, saying, "I am ready to return to the Great Mother's bosom, my child. Please help me down to the temple and be with me to begin this journey, although I know I must make it alone." Kasha had noticed the increasing weakness of her mentor, but felt unprepared now that the crone's end had, indeed, come. She got up at once and helped the old woman go down the hill to the temple for her last visit. Neelah followed close behind.

In the temple, kneeling before the statue of Inanna, Kasha held Clara in her arms, and the two younger women sang all the songs to Inanna and the other Goddesses that they could think of. Suddenly the crone sat up, looked deeply into Kasha's eyes and said, "You have been a better daughter to me than my own and I thank you." Then her eyes opened wide with ecstasy and she cried out, "Oh, Inanna! Oh, Great Mother, I am coming!" Thus, she died peacefully.

Neelah left the temple to get the rest of the villagers, so they could all sing the petitions to Inanna that she would receive Clara into her earthly bosom, even though it looked as if the Goddess had already done this. Then Kasha instructed Orana and Neelah to carry Clara's body to a cave high up on a hill above Al-Rah, which had been used as their burying ground since before any of them could remember. They sang the litany to Inanna as they wended their way far back into the huge cave. As skeletons from the past came into view, Kasha stopped and chose a place to put the shrouded body of Clara. Again, each woman prayed to Inanna to take Clara into her earthly bosom and then continued the litany as they slowly returned to the village. In this way, Kasha assumed her place as the new Virgin High Priestess of Al-Rah. She had barely completed fourteen sun cycles.

Just before the spring festival, in honor of Inanna, Kasha began to experience the pains of childbirth. Neelah helped her with the birthing right in their own hut. It turned out to be a comparatively easy birth and the new mother was delighted to see that her baby had wavy black hair like her own and, although her eyes were a very deep blue, it was evident, even then, that they would be turning to a deep brown. Together, Kasha and Neelah named the child, Ashannah. By purposely ending the name the same way as Inanna's, they dedicated her to the Goddess.

By the time the early harvest festival was approaching, towards the end of summer, Neelah was suffering from a high fever. She not only regurgitated any food she tried to eat, it got so that she couldn't even keep liquids down. Kasha tried everything she had ever learned about herbs and healing from Sylva, who had also returned to the Great Mother's bosom some years before. She prayed ardently to Inanna for help. This continued for many nights and days and Kasha asked Thesta, who had a son Ashannah's age, to care for Ashannah, in order to give her more time to care for Neelah and also to protect her child from the illness. In spite of her ministering and her deep love for the woman, Neelah continued to lose weight and to shrivel up right before Kasha's eyes. One afternoon, Neelah cried out, "Hold me, Kasha. Oh, hold me tight!" Kasha rushed over to her and did as she asked. Soon after, Neelah died in her lover's arms.

Again, Kasha had to take over the duties of seeing that her partner was buried in the proper manner. First they put her body in front of the statue of Inanna in the temple and sang to the Great Mother to receive her. Once more Kasha had to lead the women to the cave, where they carefully placed Neelah's body by Clara's. It was almost more than Kasha could manage, her devastation was so complete.

Ashannah had not even completed her first sun cycle.

Chapter One

She watched in awe as a brilliant light shot through the sky. "It's a falling star!" she exclaimed, but she was not afraid. It was as if she were lifted up into the very arc of light the star was making. She felt the air swish by as she rushed through the earth's atmosphere with the star. When it went out of sight, she continued on her flight. It seemed as if she were caught on a stream of air, floating endlessly. She had been one with the star and now she was one with the night sky, lovingly sustained by the cosmos.

The voice of her mother calling her name brought her back to the familiarity of the hillside, near the temple, where she had been lying on her back when the star had appeared.

"I'm here, Mother Kasha!" Ashannah called out and got up from the ground so that her mother could see her. Then she ran over and hugged her.

Kasha murmured, "These nights, when there is no moon, are truly beautiful in their own way. The stars show up so clearly."

"Oh, yes," the child agreed. "Did you see the star rushing through the sky?"

"No, I didn't, but I'm glad that you did. It must have been wonderful!"

"Yes! Yes! That's what it was!" agreed Ashannah, with delight at her mother's understanding. "It just filled me up with wonder!" She laughed at her little game with the word and with the pleasure which the memory of her experience with the star brought her. Kasha felt a deep tenderness towards her child, and they looked deeply into each other's eyes, mutually enjoying being together.

★ ★ ★ ★ ★

Ashannah spent much of her day in the village garden. She loved the familiar odor of damp earth as she took her digging stick and prepared little holes for the seeds, saved from the last harvest. The expectation of another crop in a few moon cycles kept her from noticing right away the inevitable ache in her back. She would stretch herself, relieving the ache, and lie down right where she had stopped, filling her nostrils with the odors of the soil and of the wild cinnamon nearby. She soon entered into a state of blissful oneness with the Great Mother.

One day, early in the sixth spring after her birth, Ashannah had been working in the garden for a short while, when she sensed someone approaching. Believing it was one of the village women, she continued working. She was quite shocked when she suddenly found herself down on her hands and knees, from having been pushed from behind. As she twisted around, she saw it was the boy, Eetoh, the only other child near her age in Al-Rah.

"Why'd ya do that?" she demanded of the laughing intruder.

"I dunno," he replied. "Just wanted to see what you'd look like all over the ground, I guess," he answered laughing.

"And how would you have liked it if I had done it to you?" she asked.

"Maybe I wouldn't have liked it, I dunno." he replied, the laughter having stopped as soon as he perceived she was quite angry. Then he turned himself so that his back was toward her. "Here. Now you can give me a shove."

"It would hardly be the same when you're expecting it!" she cried, beginning to feel exasperated.

"Well, shall I say I am sorry?" he asked.

"Not unless you are," she quickly retorted.

"Well, I am sorry if I've made you not like me," he said. "I was really just wanting to play with you." His mouth spread out into a wide, jagged-toothed grin.

Ashannah stared at him, taking in his sandy-colored hair and strangely green eyes and finally relented. "I'd like to get some more seeds planted. Then maybe we can play." She had noticed how he was often alone. He was the only boy in the village.

"Show me how and I'll help you," he offered.

"Well,... boys don't usually come into the garden," she stammered.

"But I'm here, and I'd like to help," he insisted. "Besides, what other boys are there?"

Ashannah couldn't think of a reason why he shouldn't help, so she got him a digging stick and demonstrated, making a small hole, dropping in a seed, and carefully covering it by pushing the dirt in with the side of her hand. Finally, she gave the damp soil a few pats to discourage the birds from digging up the seed.

The boy charged right in with the work, hurrying so they could play. Ashannah had to tell him not to make the holes so deep, and to space them so that there would be plenty of room for growing. He seemed impatient with having to be so careful, but finally managed to please her. However, he quickly tired and began to entreat her to stop so they could play. She knew this reluctant energy wasn't going to be helpful to the new plants, so she acquiesced.

Eetoh led the way to the river that ran along the sunset edge of Al-Rah. As Ashannah followed, she realized she had not spent much time playing and wondered what they would do. Upon arriving at the river, the boy ran right out into the deeper water.

"C'mon, Ashannah! It feels great. It's nice and cool!" Eetoh shouted.

Ashannah slowly put in one foot and quickly withdrew it. "Ooh, it's so cold!" she exclaimed.

"Just hold your breath and come on in," he insisted. "You'll like it, really!"

Eetoh seemed to be having so much fun that she gritted her teeth and waded in. The water was barely up over her ankles, when she slipped on a rock and fell fully into the stream. The chill took her breath away.

"How can he stand it?" she wondered, but by the time Ashannah was able to stand up again, she realized that the water no longer felt so cold and that it actually felt good. She waded on out to where Eetoh was standing, and they spontaneously began splashing each other. She looked into his eyes and knew she had never seen him so happy. Embarrassed by this unexpected intimacy, the boy began to splash harder.

In the meantime, Kasha was standing on a knoll, looking down on them. She savored the feelings the sight of her child stirred in her heart. She noted the little girl's ready smile, her large, dark brown eyes, the small nose, all in a frame of wavy black hair. These things reminded her of herself. She felt blessed.

"It is good to see Ashannah enjoying herself," she thought. "She is such a good child, that sometimes I forget she is a child." She was sorry that there were not more children in the village, so they could play together. "Well, at least now she has Eetoh," she sighed.

Besides Eetoh and Ashannah, there were only four girls who had not reached menarche, but they were all four or five sun cycles older than the little boy and girl. Kasha knew the reason for this diminishing of infants being born in Al-Rah, but she didn't understand it. There were fewer and fewer men coming to the temple to achieve union with the Goddess, and some women were leaving Al-Rah to go live in Et-Ray, sharing a hut with a man. That these changes in their lives were threatening to the future of Al-Rah was not lost on her, but then Kasha remembered Beyla and Zolah, the two infants, who had been born in the past sun cycle. She stood up straighter and decided to plant in the garden awhile.

Ashannah and Eetoh began to spend more and more time together. Eetoh's imagination motivated Ashannah to discover her own. They would spend hours thinking up game after game. If Ashannah did less work, Kasha did not mind working a little more herself, realizing that her daughter was developing in wonderful ways.

"Some day, though..." she thought with concern. "Well, when that day arrives, I will help her face it."

After a time, Ashannah began to miss communing with the Great Mother. She gradually realized that this did not happen except when she was alone. She did not wish to hurt Eetoh's feelings, but finally told him that when she was working in the garden, he should not come in. He would watch her from nearby and when she would stop working, stretch and lie down, he would be amazed that she could remain there so long without moving. Somehow, he knew she was not sleeping.

"What were you thinking about for so long?" he finally asked her one day, when she had rejoined him.

"Oh, Eetoh! It's so wonderful!" she assured him. But when she tried to describe how it was, he became puzzled and quickly bored. She was equally mystified that he hadn't seemed to have had any similar experiences. Sometimes during one of their games, she would point out some little thing of beauty to him, hoping to lead him into that amazing state, but it just didn't happen. She gradually gave up trying.

At other times when she was feeling especially close to him, she gazed into his eyes, as she did with Kasha, but Eetoh always looked away, or even ran from her. In spite of these differences, they were together often and grew closer and closer.

One afternoon, far into Ashannah's tenth sun cycle, an adult male came to Al-Rah. He asked to see Thesta, Eetoh's mother. Thesta spoke with him briefly, and then called for her son. This time it was Ashannah who wasn't asked to join in. Thesta left Eetoh alone with the man. Ashannah noticed that the man's hair was the same sandy color as Eetoh's and wondered if his eyes were also green. She watched intently as the two of them engaged in animated conversation.

She did not know that the man was Eetoh's father. She did not know who her own father was, or even that she had one. None of the children of Al-Rah knew their fathers. Ashannah had probably never heard the word father. Fatherhood was limited to the confines of Et-Ray and was only slowly coming into recognition.

"What could they be talking about for so long?" Ashannah wondered.

Finally Thesta brought the man and Eetoh a meal, and, after eating it, they got up together and left Al-Rah. Eetoh did not even say good-bye. Astonished, Ashannah watched them walk down the path leading towards Et-Ray. Her eyes stung with tears as she realized that Eetoh had become so engrossed with his new friend, he had entirely forgotten about her. Thesta saw the stricken look on her face, and walked over to her.

"He needed to be with his own kind, Ashannah. You must have seen how different he is. Yes, the two of you enjoyed playing together, but some times you had to put yourself apart from him. I know. I had to also. That was very painful for him. Even when we were worshiping the Goddess, he felt left out, even abandoned."

Ashannah stared hard at Thesta, as if seeing her for the first time. Her hair was almost as dark as her own and she, too, had brown eyes. She didn't look like Eetoh at all! Yet, she was his mother. In fact, Eetoh didn't look like anyone in Al-Rah! Then she saw that Thesta's nose was short and turned up like her son's.

"Well," Ashannah thought, "maybe because he looks more like the man, who came for him, maybe that's why Eetoh went away with him." Then she suddenly realized, on a deeper level, that his differences were more than how he looked and she spoke aloud. "Yes, Thesta, you're right. He needs to be with his own kind. But I will miss him very much."

Later that evening, when Ashannah was alone with her mother, she hardly said anything and avoided looking at her. Kasha sensed her pain and finally broke the silence, saying, "You will heal from this, daughter. I believe you will soon begin your moon bleeding, and will be very busy learning new rituals in the temple. The Goddess will shower blessings upon you in her joy at receiving another daughter."

Ashannah looked over at her mother, smiling with anticipation.

But there would be long hours during the days when she would miss Eetoh. She wondered what he was doing with his new friend and if he missed her, too. She became impatient for her bloods to come.

It was shortly after Eetoh left, that death visited Al-Rah for the first time since Neelah had died. Now, eleven sun cycles later, Della, the mother of Zolah, became ill with much the same sickness that had taken Neelah from them. Again, Kasha applied all of her healing powers and potions, but with little result. While Della was ill, Beleenda persuaded little Zolah, who had barely completed her fifth sun cycle, to come and stay with her and Beyla.

When Della died, the women placed her body in the temple, according to custom, while Kasha and the others prayed to Inanna to take her daughter into her earthly bosom. The children were not required to be there, but Zolah wanted to see her mother and Beyla went along to give her comfort. When Zolah saw the glazed and staring eyes in the emaciated body, she could not believe it was her mother and ran screaming from the temple. Beyla, also screaming, was right behind her. Ashannah was stunned by their behavior, but she knew at the same time, that if it had been Kasha, she would have acted in the same manner.

During the next sun's journey, the women carried the body to the hillside cave where they had buried Neelah. It had been the village's burying ground for as long as anyone could remember.

After Ashannah and Kasha had returned to their home in the village, Ashannah tearfully approached her mother.

"Will you look like… like Della some day, Mama? Will… will I? She began to sob.

"We all return to Inanna's bosom some time, Ashannah." Kasha replied, taking her daughter in her arms.

"But… what's it like in Inanna's bosom?" the child persisted.

"No one knows, little one," her mother honestly replied. "No one has ever returned to tell us." Then, after a long pause, she said with assurance, "But after all, she is our Mother."

Ashannah had just ended her twelfth sun cycle when she began her monthly bleeding. She was in the garden cultivating, when she felt something trickle down one of her legs. Kasha had thoroughly prepared her for the event, so that she was not in the least frightened. She quickly glanced down and upon seeing the blood, leaped up and ran out of the garden towards her home, shouting out to Kasha with delight, "My bloods! My bloods! My bloods have come!"

On hearing her shouts, every woman in the village came running, wanting to rejoice with Ashannah and her mother. For three sun journeys they celebrated, giving Ashannah many little gifts and speaking of the temple mysteries into which she would now be initiated. In spite of her comparative youth, the women now considered her a woman like themselves.

If Ashannah was put off a little by the ways she was taught to pleasure men into union with the Goddess, she didn't let on. It was of more interest, when they instructed her on what to do when she desired to conceive a child of her own. But they did not urge her to do this, and she quickly decided that it would be some time before she would want that responsibility.

Ashannah wondered if Eetoh might come to the temple when she was on duty. Would she even recognize him if he did? It was quite dark in the temple, the only opening being the entrance, which was covered by a heavy mat, woven from reeds. The small dish of oil burning in front of the clay image of Inanna did not shed much light.

The day finally came when the women decided that Ashannah was ready to take her turn as Virgin of the Night. In spite of the careful preparations, she was somewhat fearful. As she entered the temple, her nostrils were assailed with the familiar odor of sweet grass on the floor. Walking towards the image of Inanna, she became aware of the mustier odors of the earthen floor and felt as if she were in the very bosom of the Mother. Then, she noticed how quiet it had become. The thick plaster covering the walls kept out the sounds from the village and the nearby forest. In this silence, she drew into herself and began praying, kneeling before the Goddess, arms outstretched, as she had done since she was a child.

"Receive me, Oh Ancient One," she prayed. "I am your loving daughter and wish for nothing more than to please you." Inanna showed her pleasure by filling Ashannah with ecstasy. It was almost dawn when a man finally entered the temple. Ashannah knew at once that it was not Eetoh. He was much too large. She administered to him as she had been instructed. He groaned and pitched with pleasure, calling out to Inanna in gratitude. Ashannah was relieved that it had been so easy. After he had rolled over on his side to sleep, she carefully covered him with the special blanket kept in the temple for that purpose. The sun was just beginning to rise, and she was free to leave.

After Ashannah had begun her moon bleeding and the feast in honor of Inanna had arrived, she was excited, because after the ritual, she would be allowed to remain with the other women for the singing and dancing throughout the night.

She dressed carefully for the event, putting on, for the first time, some bracelets of shells, given to her for the occasion. As she approached the temple with the other women, they found Kasha, as their High Priestess, at the entrance ready to greet them as they entered.

"My sister, what do you bring to the circle?" she asked each one, but to Ashannah she said, "My daughter, what do you bring to the circle?"

Ashannah was surprised to find tears burning at the edges of her eyes. "I bring perfect love and perfect trust," she managed to answer. It was the traditional response, but she felt it from the depths of her heart and a smile spread all over her face, replacing the tears.

After entering the temple, the virgins stood in complete silence, each woman holding an unlit taper made of the lovely smelling wax of bees. Kasha walked up to the oil lamp, keeping vigil with Inanna's statue, and lit her taper from it. There she turned to the nearest woman and lit her taper. That woman lit the taper of the woman next to her, until everyone's candle was glowing. Suddenly all of the Goddesses, whose images had been painted on the plaster walls, were made visible by the light emanating from all the candles.

It was then that the women burst into song, singing the praises of Inanna and the other Goddesses. Afterwards, Kasha called out to the four directions, inviting the spirits from afar to join with them in their celebrations. Ashannah was filled with great joy, as she felt the presence of these spirits as they entered the circle. The women closed in together, joined hands, and, as they slowly lifted their arms, they toned. Beginning as low as they could, they raised their voices, at the same time raising their arms, until they could not tone any higher. Reverberations of the sound filled the air and the women trembled from the energy just released. They dropped their arms, feeling immersed with the blessings of the Goddess, and opened themselves to any messages she might send.

After a time, Kasha said, "Let any woman who wishes share her vision."

As was often the case, it was the sibyl Orana who spoke first. Although she was small in stature, her very presence evinced so much power, no one perceived her that way. Now her voice rang out in its oracle's tone, compelling each woman there to listen as carefully as she could. "We have a new Virgin among us," she announced, and walking over to Ashannah, she placed a hand on each of the young woman's shoulders. She focused her piercing black eyes on the new Virgin, transfixing her to the spot. Every woman present was equally transfixed. No one could remember any other new Virgin being singled out in this manner, not even Gennah, Orana's daughter. However, not one woman there envied Ashannah. No one wished to be the subject of one of Orana's oracles, least of all Gennah.

"You will become a healer and High Priestess, as is your Mother, but more importantly, you will lead us over a mountain to a new home," Orana announced. "The journey will be so long and arduous that … that some of us … will not make it." Orana continued to stare at Ashannah, who trembled with fear, but at the same time felt a strange exhilaration. Mostly, she found it difficult to understand what the Oracle was saying.

This will not happen until many sun cycles have passed," Orana continued, "but you must not shirk this responsibility, when the time comes."

Suddenly Ashannah felt very much like the little girl of a few moon cycles back.

"How could she lead them over the mountain? How would she know the way?" she asked herself. Then, abruptly, her mind became clear with understanding. "If this is the wish of the Goddess, how can I not obey?" she calmly replied.

"Wisely spoken," Orana replied approvingly and, looking at Kasha, commanded, "Let the circle be opened."

Kasha quickly dismissed the spirits and did as Orana had ordered, even though this meant the ritual was made much shorter than usual. As she did so, the benevolence of Inanna lifted the burden of the Oracle from the memories of every woman present, including Ashannah.

After the women had departed from the temple, they gathered at the large fire pit in the center of the village. The new Virgin found herself hardly breathing as she watched Beyla and Zolah reluctantly leave, since they were still too young to remain. Someone began to beat on a small hand drum, while another woman started playing on a bamboo flute. The women slowly began dancing sensuously to the music. At first they danced by themselves, but gradually they began to pair off, continuing the dancing, as they gazed steadily into their partner's eyes. Gradually some of the partners began to separate themselves from the group.

Gennah, Orana's redheaded daughter, danced over in front of the new Virgin.

She smiled at Ashannah, encouraging her to join in the dancing. At first Ashannah stiffly imitated Gennah's movements, but then she closed her eyes and let the music take over her entire being. Her body began undulating with the ancient rhythms. When Ashannah opened her eyes, she was amazed to see how beautiful Gennah had become. Her slightly parted lips seemed fuller, her cheeks were flushed, her hair shimmered in the light of the rising moon. And her eyes ... the gaze emanating from them filled Ashannah with an excitement she had never felt before.

Gennah, who was small in stature like her mother, raised herself up on the balls of her feet. so that she could reach up and put her arms around Ashannah's neck, as she continued to sway to the music. Ashannah's body became inflamed as she felt Gennah's breasts moving against her own. The younger woman felt her nipples stiffen, as if reaching out to Gennah's. Their embrace tightened and Ashannah felt the other woman's mons rubbing against hers. The new Virgin's thighs and vulva began pulsing until it became unbearable and she pulled Gennah down on top of her, wrapping one leg around Gennah's hips, her other leg becoming entwined between her partner's.

Gennah laughed and exclaimed, "A wild woman we have here!" and she stroked the younger woman's buttocks, letting her fingers trail enticingly close, but not quite reaching her vulva. When those fingers finally found and caressed the small pulsing organ hidden within the labia, Ashannah felt her entire body explode with joy. She cried out in rapturous surprise, gazing at her lover with adoration. She wondered if Gennah was also in that incredible place. She saw that Gennah was looking at her with expectancy and sensed at once what to do to bring her into that euphoric haven. As one, they embraced, rocking on to their own music. The ecstasy was complete. Ashannah wanted it to go on forever.

It was the rising sun shining in her eyes which awoke Ashannah the following morning. She found Gennah smiling at her, and they kissed each other slowly, as if in a dream. Then they rose and walked, arm-in-arm, down to the river to bathe. The cold water would help them return to their daily tasks.

Just before departing, Ashannah looked deeply into Gennah's eyes and asked, "Was it a dream? Or was it real?"

"Meet me by the garden tonight, and I'll show you whether it was real," the older woman promised with a smile.

Tonight seemed like a long time to wait, but Ashannah went to her tasks full of dreams. It had never been like this with Eetoh, she thought. She wondered briefly if the comparison was fair, but her days of missing the boy's companionship were finally over.

Chapter Two

Similar scenes of love making filled Ashannah's and Gennah's nights and sometimes extended themselves into the daylight hours. But Ashannah gradually noticed that whenever she told Gennah she loved her, her lover looked down or looked away and, sometimes, simply walked off. Ashannah would be filled with pain, wondering what had caused the coldness. Slowly she realized that Gennah never spoke of loving her.

One day, Ashannah finally asked, "Do you love me?"

"What do you think?" Gennah replied tersely, as she started to walk away.

This time Ashannah pursued her, crying out, "I don't know what to think! Most of the time, I think you do. You make me feel so good, so happy. And then … like right now, you don't seem to want to hear me say that I love you. You don't seem to want to say it to me."

Gennah stopped abruptly and turned to face her young friend. "You're right! I don't want to hear you say it, and I don't want to say it! So just be quiet!"

Ashannah was devastated by the rejection. Tears flooded her eyes, but the taste of their saltiness, as they ran into her open mouth, helped her to find speech and she gasped, "But why? Why?"

Gennah's eyes also filled with tears, but, again, her anger flared, "Can't you just be satisfied that I make you happy?"

"Well … well I … suppose so, if that's the way you want it. But … don't I m-make you feel good?"

"Of course you make me feel good! In fact, you make me feel wonderful!

Maybe that's it. You make me feel too wonderful!"

"I ... I don't understand!"

"Well, maybe I don't understand either!" Gennah gasped and began to sob.

Ashannah put her arm around Gennah's shoulders as they walked towards the garden. There was a fence of bamboo plants surrounding it, serving as protection from animals, as well as providing shade and shelter from strong winds. As they were about to go through the opening, Gennah stopped abruptly and cried out, "I don't want to go in there! Oh, Ashannah, I know you love the garden, but I don't! I ... I know you won't understand, but I want to move to Et-Ray and weave and weave and trade my baskets and cloths for things from other places; for beautiful things from places far away!"

All Ashannah could manage was a startled, "Oh!" She did not understand. She not only loved the garden, she loved living in Al-Rah. She treasured the varying rhythms of the days and nights and of the seasons of the year and how they affected her life and the lives of all the women. She had no idea that any of the women felt differently. She remembered that Eetoh seemed dissatisfied, but not any of the women! Then she remembered Rootha and Angah, who had both moved to Et-Ray within the last sun cycle. Rootha wove baskets, had taught Gennah her craft, and Angah worked with clay, made beautiful pots from the very soil near Al-Rah. Ashannah admired their talents and loved their baskets and pots, but did not understand why they couldn't make them in Al-Rah. Then she remembered that it was the men coming for their wares and bargaining with the makers that the women of Al-Rah did not like.

"But could ... couldn't you take your baskets and cloths to Rootha to trade for you?" Ashannah asked.

"No!" Gennah exploded. "Rootha is a wonderful weaver, but she is not good at trading at all! In fact, she has me trade for her. And besides, I like to do the trading myself! Maybe if you come to Et-Ray with me some time, you would see how wonderful it can be! And I ... I ... well, this man, Ator, wants me to come and live near him. He wants to take all my baskets for trading. He says mine are even prettier than Rootha's. He says he can get many beautiful things for them."

Ashannah was astounded. Gennah's baskets were prettier than Rootha's? She hadn't even thought to compare them. Then she felt the hot breath of jealousy, something she had never experienced before.

"You mean ... you love Ator more than you love me!"

"Oh, don't you understand, Ashannah?" Gennah said impatiently. "He doesn't begin to make me as happy as you do, when we're making love! But ... but he does understand how much I like to make baskets and weave cloth. Why, he's even shown me different ways to weave ... ways he's learned from going to other places and seeing what other weavers do. And then there's wool. It's the hairs from an animal called a sheep. He brought some to show me. Women take this wool and comb it and then spin it into yarn and weave it. It makes a good cloth that's very warm, warmer than the cotton or linen we have here."

"I have heard about it," Ashannah said, "but what do the sheep have to say about it?"

"They don't kill them like you would to use their hides. They just take the hairs! Oh! I don't know how they do it, but I know they don't kill them!"

It came to Ashannah that they were getting off the subject. Yet, were they? She slowly began to realize how important weaving was to Gennah. It was just as important to Gennah as working in the garden and gathering herbs was for her.

"I ... I think I'm beginning to understand a little," she admitted. Again tears welled up and she gasped, "Well, maybe I would like to go to Et-Ray with you some time. I guess I'd like to see it, to see what it's like."

Actually Ashannah had been to Et-Ray several times with Kasha to help a couple of the non-virgins with childbirth. They even went once in answer to a request for Kasha to apply her healing powers on one of the men, who had been wounded during a hunt. But they had gone straight to the houses involved and had quickly left, as soon as Kasha was finished. They hadn't seen any other homes, nor had they gone to the market.

"Gennah wants me to go to Et-Ray with her to see the market and to meet her ... her friend, Ator," Ashannah announced to Kasha the next day. Kasha heard the pain in her voice and began to surmise the problem facing her daughter. She did not reply at once. but searched Ashannah's eyes intently. She saw the pain was deep.

"Do you want to go and meet her ... ah ... friend?" she finally asked.

"Welllll ... I g-guess I want to see why she likes Et-Ray so much. She wants to build a place there to do her weaving and ... and probably wants to live there some day." At this, Ashannah broke down and began to cry.

Kasha took her daughter into her arms. After awhile, she murmured, "I know that you love her very much."

"Oh, I do! I do! More than she loves me, I guess!" and, again, Ashannah began to weep.

"It's a mystery to me, Ashannah, but some of the women seem to prefer ... being with men," her mother counseled.

"But she likes to be with me better than him! She said so! But he takes her baskets and cloths and trades them for things. Beautiful things, she says. Things we don't have here and I guess things that she wants."

"I see."

"And he shows her different ways to weave from people he's watched in other places."

"Well, that must be exciting," Kasha said.

"Maybe its her weaving she loves more than she loves me!" Ashannah gasped at the idea.

"It does sound like it," Kasha had to agree. "You see, she is older than you. You haven't chosen a particular work that you like doing."

"Oh, yes, Mother! I want to work in the garden and gather herbs and make potions to help people heal themselves, like you!"

Kasha couldn't help being pleased. "Well, I think you will be good at it. Plants seem to respond to your care, and I'm certain that people will, too."

"But I d-don't know if I'd rather do that than be with Gennah!" Then Ashannah became angry. "Why do I have to choose between them?"

"Perhaps you won't have to, daughter. I think you should go to Et-Ray, as she has suggested, and see how it feels." Kasha's voice broke a little as she considered what this might mean for herself and Ashannah.

Ashannah gratefully hugged her mother, and went into their hut to get the basket Gennah had made her for gathering wild plants. Gennah had even made a lid for it, with hinges made of the rushes. Swinging it by her side, she walked out into the woods. It was late spring and there were still many plants available, both for healing and for food. The concentration it took to search them out would keep her mind off Gennah and Ator.

First, she found some small white mushrooms that would add flavor and sustenance to the greens they would eat at supper. She was delighted when she found some of the ferns with curly tips, that tasted something like almonds. Finally, she gathered some broad-leafed plantain, which, after chewing it awhile, would soothe skin rashes. By then it was getting late enough that she should return to the village. As she approached the cone-shaped hut that was her home, she felt a fierce pride in it and a great gratitude towards Kasha. When she walked in and smelled the drying herbs hanging from the roof and saw a pot of vegetable stew above the coals in the center, she was beside herself with joy. When Kasha came in shortly after, she was surprised at the vehement hug Ashannah gave her. Then the daughter prepared a festive salad from her gleanings. The two of them ate in silence, filling themselves not only with food, but with the comfort they gave one another.

The next day Gennah invited Ashannah to go with her to Et-Ray. She was eager and ready to show her the town, but she was fearful at the same time. Gennah was afraid that Ashannah would never consider living there.

It took them about a hand's span of the sun's journey to walk there. Et-Ray was not all that different looking from Al-Rah, except the cone-shaped huts were closer together and instead of a temple on the edge of town, there was a large building in the center, devoted to trading. It was built of slate, like the temple, but was rectangular in shape and was entirely above the ground. One of the longer sides was left open. This place had no statue nor paintings, and when Ashannah saw it, she thought it was ugly. Gennah defended it by describing how it was when it was full of men and women trading their wares. "Maybe there will be some trading going on before we leave, Ashannah." she hoped aloud.

They went to Ator's hut, but to Ashannah's relief, he wasn't there or anywhere in the town. They found Rootha weaving baskets in front of her hut and Gennah greeted her teacher warmly, as she sat down beside her. Ashannah noticed Rootha's chestnut colored hair, with gray streaks running through the heavy braids, and thought it was quite beautiful.

"Let me see the basket you have there, Gennah," the old woman growled.

"It's for you, Rootha," Gennah said, as she handed it to her. "It has some barley in it, since you like it so much."

"Indeed I do, Gennah. Thank you. You take good care of old Rootha, don't you!" She gave Gennah a tight hug. "But you are still not pulling it tight enough, girl!"

Gennah blushed and responded defensively, "It's as tight as I can pull it, old woman. But don't you think it's better than the last one I made?"

"Well, yes, perhaps it is," the crone admitted.

While they were conversing, Ashannah noticed that Gennah's baskets were more beautiful than her teacher's, but saw that Rootha's were sturdier. The crone turned towards Ashannah and, as if she had read her mind, said, "Yes, Gennah knows how to make her baskets pretty with beads, shells and feathers, but mine are stronger. She needs more strength in her fingers to pull them tighter." She resumed working on her own basket.

Ashannah blushed at the old woman's perception and said, "I can see that Gennah's baskets won't hold water like yours do."

Gennah quickly acknowledged that this was so, and Ashannah smiled when she noticed that Rootha was blushing. She also saw how large Rootha's hands were and how firm muscles stood out in her arms, as she pulled on the rushes.

They left Rootha and walked over to see if Angah was in her hut. She wasn't, but Ashannah went over to look at some clay pieces she had drying on one side of her hut. "Look, Gennah! Look at the fox Angah has painted on this pot. Why, it looks just like her!"

Gennah rushed over and, upon seeing the fox, laughed, "Why it does look like Angah! I hadn't realized how much she looks like a fox! The slanting eyes, the pointy nose and wide grin!"

Ashannah carefully replaced the pot, and then Gennah asked, "Would you like to see the place where I'm going to build my hut?" Before she got an answer, she was leading the way. Ashannah noticed, at once, that it was right next to Ator's hut, but she knew better than to say anything. However, Gennah noticed the sadness in her friend's eyes and suggested they begin their way back to Al-Rah.

As the early harvest festival in honor of Ninlil approached, Ashannah was so busy helping Kasha prepare the festive dishes for it, she didn't have time to think about Gennah or Ator. Since the barley and emmer (an early type of wheat) were both in, the two women made a lot of breads. But first they had to grind the grains.

Behind their hut were a number of flat rocks indented enough to form a shallow bowl, into which they poured the grains. Besides these were long, round stones, which they rolled back and forth, bearing down on the grains, so that they broke down into flour.

When she had barely finished her fifth sun cycle, Ashannah had begged Kasha to find a small rock and stone grinder, so she could help with the work. As Ashannah grew, Kasha found stones a little larger. Ashannah persuaded her mother to leave the smaller grinders there, so she could see how much she had grown.

After they had made the flour, they mixed enough water in it to form little loaves. They carefully placed these on large, smooth slabs of rock, where the sun would bake them. For this particular festival, Ashannah made her loaves different by adding sage or other herbs to give her loaves added flavor. Kasha was proud of her daughter's inventiveness. They also made stews of squash and beans, flavored with herbs and spices.

Gennah came by to taste some of Ashannah's dishes. "These loaves with herbs in them are really delicious, Ashannah. I never appreciated before how much work you put into preparing food, as well as planting and harvesting it. And this stew is wonderful!" Embarrassed, Ashannah answered by plying more food on her friend.

At the ritual, Ashannah surprised Gennah again, as well as all the women present, when she was asked to call the spirits from the different directions. Instead of speaking, she sang her invitations.

After the ceremony, the women began to dance. Gennah and Ashannah danced right over to the forest where they had established a trysting place. They could hardly believe that almost four moon cycles had gone by since the first time they had made love. Now they gazed at each other in the light of the full moon and soon were wrapped in the ecstasy of lovemaking.

"Oh, Ashannah, you are so beautiful tonight!" Gennah exclaimed. "I want to be with you forever!"

That was exactly what Ashannah wanted to hear. She pulled back her head to look deeply into Gennah's eyes. Startled, Gennah buried her face in Ashannah's bosom, thinking, "Do I ***really*** want to be with Ashannah forever?"

Chapter Three

The next morning, Ashannah awoke to find Gennah at her side, smiling in her sleep. She leaned over her lover's face, slowly approaching her left cheek, until she was close enough to flutter her eyelashes on the soft skin. Gennah opened her eyes and said, "So that's what it feels like when a butterfly kisses you!"

Ashannah laughed, "I'm a pretty big butterfly, don't you think?"

"You're a pretty one, for sure," Gennah replied, looking deeply into Ashannah's dark eyes.

"I love you, Gennah," Ashannah murmured, and then fear gripped her heart as she remembered Gennah saying she did not want to hear those words.

"And I love you, Ashannah," Gennah answered and kissed her with exceptional tenderness. "I have not been good to you, lately," she admitted, "but that's going to change. I know now, for certain, that Inanna has gifted us with one another."

"Oh, Gennah, I believe so, too. Blessed be Inanna for all her gifting, but especially for giving us to one another." Ashannah embraced her beloved. Their bliss was interrupted by Gennah's stomach growling loud and long. They both laughed and got up to search out something to eat.

As they were eating, Gennah looked directly into Ashannah's eyes and said, "Ashannah, I still want to finish my place in Et-Ray, so I can be working on several pieces at once and also keep in contact with the market. But I want us to build our own home, here in Al-Rah, one large enough for you to store your herbs and a loom for me. Weaving cloth doesn't take as much room as basket weaving," she explained. Before Ashannah could respond, she added hastily. "As soon as we finish eating, let's go find a good place."

"I'd like that, Gennah," Ashannah responded, much relieved. "I ... I have actually discovered a good place already ... that is, if you like it. It's on a slope that faces the winter sun, which would make it warmer. There would be plenty of room for a garden of my own, and it's downhill from a spring."

"Why, that sounds perfect!" Gennah exclaimed. "I'm finished eating. Are you? Can we go see it?"

Ashannah hurried with the last of her mush and got up to clean their bowls. Gennah waited impatiently, but said nothing. Finally, Ashannah was ready to take her to the spot. It was farther from the village than any of the other homes, but Gennah understood why Ashannah wanted to have her own garden. Nonetheless, she couldn't see a level place for their hut, so she asked Ashannah about it.

"Listen! See how this sounds," Ashannah quickly answered, her excitement evident in her voice. "I'd like to dig a flat space into the side of the hill, so that the back of the wall will be in the hill and part of the sides, too. That will also help keep us warm in the winter. And besides that, I want to collect some nice smooth stones from the river and line the inner walls in the hillside with them. The rocks will absorb the heat from our fire in the winter and keep us warm through the night. Also, they should help keep it cooler in the summer, like it is in the temple. How does that sound?"

"Well, I'd say you've been planning this for a long time. It seems like a lot of work, but it'll surely make it warmer in the winter and cooler in the summer, like you said. You've got some good ideas, Ashannah," the older woman concluded, admiringly.

"Thanks, Gennah. I'll work on it by myself, until you get your place finished in Et-Ray. In the first place, you've already got a good start, and also, ours is going to take longer to build with the rock wall, and all. In fact, I haven't figured out how to dig a flat place for the floor! It would take forever to do it with digging sticks and my hands. Even shells wouldn't help much."

"So, how will we do it?" Gennah asked. She thought a moment and continued, "You know, Ashannah, I think I remember Ator speaking of some kind of thin, flat things, made from copper, like my knife. They make them down by the Great Sea. They are much larger than my knife and you can scoop up dirt with them. I think he called them shovels. Maybe we could get one."

Ashannah wasn't too sure she wanted Ator's help, but it would make her plan more possible.

"Do you think the metal would be good for the earth, Gennah?" she asked.

"The earth is where the metal comes from, Ashannah!" Gennah quickly replied. Ashannah couldn't argue with that.

After Ashannah thought about it more, she had to admit that she wouldn't be able to build their house, as she had planned it, unless Ator could get one of the metal shovels. Unfortunately, he was away, and Gennah wouldn't be able to ask him about it until he returned. Trusting that he would get one, the two women went ahead and picked out the exact spot for their home-to-be. When she wasn't working in the garden or foraging, Ashannah carried rocks up from the stream, so they would be ready as soon as they got the walls dug out.

Gennah began spending much more time in Et-Ray, so she could finish her hut before the winter rains set in. First, she had carefully drawn a circle on the ground and had dug holes all around it about a foot apart. Then, she buried the large ends of the branches Ator had cut for her in the holes. The branches were all about the same length.

She complained to Ashannah that she didn't even have time to weave, so the younger woman began going in with her to help. They gathered the tops of the branches together and tied them to form the familiar cone-shape of the other huts. Next they wove in grasses between the branches for the walls, leaving a smoke hole at the top. Lastly, they gathered some of the large leaves of catalpa trees to weave into the grasses. These would make the little dwelling almost waterproof.

Just before the first of the rains, the two of them finished putting the last of the catalpa leaves on the outside. Ashannah stayed in Et-Ray that night, since it was too late to return to Al-Rah before dark.

When they went outside to cook some barley the following morning, they discovered that Ator had returned the night before. He was very surprised to find that Gennah's house was completed. When he learned that Ashannah had helped, he became a little more friendly. Nonetheless, Ashannah didn't feel like she should ask him about the shovels, although they were much on her mind. She sensed that Gennah was getting uncomfortable being with the two of them, and after they finished eating, she reluctantly returned to Al-Rah by herself.

Later in the day, Gennah also returned to get her weaving materials. Ashannah had offered to help with the move, but Ator was waiting at the edge of the village for that purpose. Just as they were about to leave, Gennah whispered to her friend, "I won't forget to ask him about the shovel."

Ashannah felt a little better, but she experienced definite pangs of jealousy when Gennah didn't come home that night, even though she realized that it would have been too dangerous for her to make the return trip in the dark.

Ator had brought Gennah a new style loom that would make her weaving easier and would facilitate putting patterns into her pieces. He had traded most of the baskets she had given him for it. When he began hanging around her work place, wanting her attention, it seemed that he didn't want her to work on the new loom or on her baskets. He felt that she had lost interest in him, which was close to the truth. When she faithfully returned to Al-Rah every night to be with Ashannah, this made him even more demanding of her time. Gennah sensed that he wanted to make love, but she no longer had any feelings of desire towards him, nor did she feel that she owed him anything. After all, she reasoned, the baskets had been an even trade for the loom. And besides, she thought to herself, lovemaking shouldn't be done for things, but simply from one's feelings for the other. However, she remembered that she had made love with him before because of the things he had brought her.

Finally, after a handful of days had gone by, he confronted her. "Gennah, how come you go back to Al-Rah every single night? We haven't made love since I've returned. I want you woman. You stay with me tonight!"

When Gennah understood that he wasn't even asking her, but demanding what he thought was his due, she stared at him speechless.

"By the joys of Inanna, don't you want to love me?" he asked. "I'd hate to think I carried that loom all the way from Tel Phar to Et-Ray for nothing! Or did you think I'd wait until it was your turn in the temple? You haven't made me do that for a long time!"

Gennah stood before him, saying nothing, but her stance let him know she wasn't eager for him. Still, she realized that everything he had just said was true. Perhaps she did owe him a favor for transporting the loom as well as for bargaining for it. At the same time, she also felt she would be disloyal to Ashannah, if she made love with Ator in Et-Ray. She knew he would not understand her only wanting to make love with Ashannah. Then it came to her how she had jeopardized her standing as a Virgin by making love with Ator outside the temple. Still, although she had considered it for a time, before she became lovers with Ashannah, she no longer wanted to leave Al-Rah and move in with Ator in Et-Ray, which would definitely cause her to lose her Virgin status and take away all her temple privileges, although she had made love with him several times before in his hut in Et-Ray.

Gennah found herself faced with the dilemma of choosing between learning the new techniques in weaving that Ator could show her, or being lovers with Ashannah and remaining a Virgin of the Temple. Ator definitely wanted her sexual favors in return for his trading and the knowledge he could acquire for her. While Gennah stood there in confusion, Ator lost patience, grabbed one of her wrists and pulled her towards his hut.

"Stop, Ator! You're hurting me!" she cried out.

"Well, are you going to love me or not?" he wanted to know. She simply could not make up her mind. She wanted Ator's assistance with her craft, but she also wanted to be true to Ashannah and to remain a Virgin. She reluctantly followed him into his hut, hoping that somehow, she could have it all.

During that winter, the temple was unusually busy, because the rains were heavy enough to keep the men from hunting or traveling much. A couple of mornings there had even been a little snow on the ground, which was not usual down in the floor of the valley.

Just before the shortest day of the year, Ashannah went on duty as the Virgin of the Night. A young man came in, prostrated himself before Inanna and waited for her services. Ashannah sensed it was Eetoh, her childhood friend, right away and wondered if he would recognize her. Then she realized that this was his first time in the temple and gently instructed him on what to expect.

"Is that you, Ashannah?" Eetoh asked as he recognized her voice. She could tell that he was relieved and embarrassed at the same time.

"Well, you're not really supposed to know who I am," she laughed, "but I guess you know, anyway. I really don't think Inanna will mind."

Slowly and tenderly she brought him to ecstasy with the Goddess. She left before he awakened, but she quietly decided that when she felt ready, he would be the one to help her conceive. Since it was the method all the women used for becoming with child, she did not feel in the least unfaithful to Gennah. When it was time, she would tell her.

After Ator helped Gennah set it up, she was very excited about the new loom. She would now be able to weave much wider bands of cloth and began on a piece of very finely spun linen, which she had dyed an azure blue. Since it was her first attempt at weaving in a design, she limited herself to three bands of a contrasting color at each end of the shawl, leaving the flax for the stripes their natural color.

Because she had spun the flax so fine, the piece would be the loveliest she had ever made, but it would take most of the winter. Ator appreciated its fine quality and was certain he could find someone who would trade it for a shovel.

After making himself a new quiver of arrows and re-fletching some of his old ones, Ator began to be bored with inactivity. On clearer days, he would go outside of Et-Ray and hunt for rabbits to satisfy his craving for meat, but he still had too much time left over. He began demanding more and more attention from Gennah. Out of loyalty to Ashannah and the desire to retain her status as a Virgin of the Temple, she avoided Ator as much as possible, but this was difficult since her hut was so close to his. Also, since Ator always insisted on completing the intercourse, she was afraid of becoming with child. Now she was relieved when she was unable to go to Et-Ray because of the rains, even though it kept her from her work. She definitely did not want to have his child, nor any child, for the time being.

Late one afternoon, when Gennah was working at her loom in Et-Ray, taking advantage of the last light of the day, Ator came bursting into her small hut, very unsteady on his feet and shouting loudly. She had seen him this way only once before and quickly realized he must have been drinking fermented barley juice with some of the other men. They were doing this more often as the winter dragged on.

"C'mon, Gennah! You're my woman and I want to love you! And I mean right now! What do I care if you ever finish that stuff! Anyway, it's getting dark and you're liable to mess it up."

"I'm not your woman!" Gennah cried out. "I belong to Inanna!" But she knew he was right about the light getting too dim to work. Realizing he was likely to grab her and pull her up, she quickly stabilized her shuttle and stood, in order to more firmly hold her stance.

"So, now, are ya' comin'?" he asked, thinking she was going to comply.

"No! No! I don't want to love you when you're like this! You smell awful, and you'll hurt me!"

"Well, I'll hurt you more if I have to make you!" he threatened.

"Get away from me! I don't want to be near you!" she screamed.

Never before had she heard the names he began to call her as he grabbed her right arm and dragged her over to his hut. After he pulled her inside, she could smell how filthy it had become. She wondered if he ever changed the grass and pine needles on his floor.

He threw her down, roughly spread her legs, and entered her. She felt a sharp pain, as if she had been stabbed. He began pumping furiously. Gennah kicked, bit and scratched Ator, but she was not strong enough to deter him. He pinned her arms down and pumped on. Gennah blacked out briefly and then became delirious with fear, thinking she was going to die.

She screamed with all her strength, "I -n - a - a - a - a - a - a - na!!!"

Fortunately, she didn't realize the scream was all in her head. Not a sound passed her lips, but Inanna heard anyway. At that very moment, Ator spent himself and fell on her. Her breath was momentarily knocked out as he slumped down on her, and she realized that she was trapped by the weight of his utterly relaxed body. Suddenly, rage filled her, and with that strength she was able to work herself out from beneath him.

She painfully crawled out of Ator's hut and groped her way back to her own place, where she dipped a piece of cloth in a jar of water to staunch the flow of blood. After she sobbed out her anger for some time, she lay limp on her floor in a state of shock.

However, she was unable to sleep, and after what seemed like at least a cycle of the sun must have passed, she noticed light rising in the east and forced herself to stand, finding the strength to do this with the thought that Ator might come for her again. After leaning against the door sill in order to steady herself, she slowly began her way down the path towards Al-Rah and the safety of her mother's home. Whenever she started to sob from the pain, she would bite her lower lip and continue on, stubbornly putting one foot in front of the other, knowing that each step brought her closer to home and further from Ator.

She began silently chanting the litany to Inanna to keep the horrible memories of the night from taking over her mind. She had barely gone half way, when she realized her throat was burning from dryness. She dragged herself over by the stream in order to slake her extreme thirst. She slipped and fell on some grass, wet from the morning dew. Sobbing, she crawled for the short distance left and gulped down some of the water, which was icy from the melting snow in the mountains. This revived her, and after carefully bathing her bruised labia and the insides of her thighs, she pulled herself up with the help of a sapling sycamore tree and continued on towards Al-Rah.

By the time she reached the village the sun had risen, and she could see that the women were out getting their day's supply of water. She hunched her shoulders, hoping to make herself less visible, as she made her way to her mother's hut. She especially did not want Ashannah to see her like this.

As she entered the familiar dwelling and smelled the usual odors of her mother's cooking and of her own rushes waiting to be woven into baskets, she began to cry.

"Oh, my daughter, what has happened to you?" Orana exclaimed, taking her child into her arms. Only then did Gennah notice that her simple tunic was torn and bloodstained and that there were bruises all up and down her right arm. She could imagine that her eyes were red and swollen.

"Oh, Mama!" she cried out, and throwing her arms around her mother's neck, she sobbed out her anger and disbelief at what had happened to her. Orana held her close, her own tears mingling with Gennah's, as she listened to her daughter's tale.

When Gennah had been born, Orana was certain that her unusual coloring promised that her daughter's clairvoyance would exceed her own. As it turned out, Gennah was not only without any such talents, she was deeply embarrassed by the way her mother looked when giving an oracle. She had no desire to emulate her mother in any way. In return, Orana had often expressed disappointment in her daughter's lack of this gift. Now, in Gennah's urgent need, both women forgot their differences, and Orana became a caring and loving mother.

When Ashannah came over a little later to see if Gennah had returned home, Orana met her outside the hut. "Ashannah! A terrible thing happened to Gennah, last night! She came home early, just after the sun rose. Oh, Ashannah, it was truly horrible!" Orana began to cry, but she continued to block the doorway.

"Well, let me in so I can see her, Mother Orana!"

Since the woman was small, Ashannah was tempted to push her aside. Orana sensed this and gave her a sharp glance, keeping her from doing so.

"Not yet, Ashannah! Not yet! She has just fallen asleep and that is what she needs most."

Ashannah reluctantly agreed and turned to walk away, saying, "I'll come back later, then."

"Yes, oh, yes, Ashannah, do come back and ... and bring Kasha with you. Gennah will need her healing powers."

Ashannah clearly heard fear in the woman's voice and, once again, she wanted to push Orana aside and go to her beloved. Tears of frustration filled her eyes, and terror gripped her stomach.

"I'm going to get Kasha right now, Mother Orana. The sooner the healing starts, the better it will be."

"You're right, Ashannah. Yes, go get your mother, now."

On their way back to Orana's, Kasha persuaded her daughter to let her see Gennah first.

"You can wait right outside their hut, and I promise to call you as soon as I have determined what needs to be done for her," she said.

Ashannah acquiesced, but was beside herself with unanswered questions. Why had Gennah decided to come home before it was light? Had she been attacked by a wild animal on her way back to Al-Rah? She had no inkling as to what had actually happened. Such a thing was unheard of. When Kasha finally came out and told her what had occurred, she was aghast.

"Ator ... Ator did that! To Gennah?" Tears flooded her eyes, and intense anger filled her heart.

"Her body will heal," Kasha said, "but I am worried about her spirit,"

Ashannah ran over to Orana's hut. She stopped short at the entrance, feeling Orana's intense protectiveness.

"Please let me see her, Mother Orana," she pleaded. "Perhaps I can help heal her spirit."

After a brief pause, Orana led Ashannah over to where her daughter was lying. Ashannah lay down beside Gennah, gently easing one of her shoulders under her head. She began to stroke her hair and to sing softly into one of her ears. Gennah cried a little and then gradually gave herself over to the healing.

"I saw some purple crocus, today," Ashannah finally said.

Gennah smiled and sighed, "Spring, at last!" This had been the longest winter she could ever remember. Nor would she forget it soon.

Chapter Four

Ashannah hugged herself against the early morning chill, but felt invigorated by it at the same time. She noticed that daffodils were joining the crocus and she started towards the garden to listen to the early morning birds and commune with Inanna, as was her habit. However, the anxiety she felt about Gennah held her to the path that led to Orana's hut. When she arrived, she was amazed to find the mother alone.

"Oh, Ashannah, Gennah is feeling much better," Orana assured her. "She went out for a little walk, but she'll be disappointed that she missed you."

"Maybe I can join her. Did you notice which way she went?"

"I think she was going down by the garden."

As Ashannah approached the garden, she saw Gennah already returning to the village.

"Ashannah, I'm so glad to see you!" Gennah called out, as she ran up to embrace her lover.

"Ummm, and am I glad to see you!" Ashannah exclaimed. "It's good to see you walking again."

Gennah pulled her close and began to cry. "I'm so fortunate to have you, my love!" she gulped between sobs.

"We're both lucky to have each other, dear one." Ashannah stroked Gennah's cheek and continued, "Kasha left when I did. She went to visit Grenda, whose baby will be born soon. Why don't we go to my house for awhile? I'm pretty sure we'll be alone."

"I didn't know Grenda was with child!" Gennah exclaimed as they walked on. "I guess I haven't seen her lately."

"I guess not," Ashannah laughed. "She looks pretty ripe!"

"Could we go a little slower?" Gennah asked.

"Well, at least it's not far," Ashannah consoled, as she slowed her pace.

"I'm surprised at how weak I am! I didn't walk far, at all."

Ashannah put her arm around Gennah's waist to give her support. "Here we are," she announced, as they came upon her hut.

"Could we lie down for a bit?" Gennah requested, after they got inside.

"If I get to hold you."

"I'd love it!"

Ashannah began stroking Gennah's hair behind one ear. Turning towards her, Gennah said, "Ashannah, I need you so much! You're making me feel better already!"

"That's what I'm here for, Gennah, to make you feel good."

Gennah pulled back and looked deeply into Ashannah's eyes. "I feel so close to you, when we look into each other's eyes, like this. It's ... it's almost like making love."

"It is, Gennah," Ashannah readily agreed, but her groin was aching with desire. She firmly ignored those feelings, and to assure Gennah, she said, "It's wonderful just to have you in my arms again. Blessed be Inanna for gifting us with one another."

"Blessed be!" Gennah affirmed as she snuggled down into Ashannah's arms. Then, she sighed deeply and confided, "The worst part is at night. I can go to sleep, but I have these terrible dreams about ... It's like it's happening all over again!"

Once more Gennah began to cry.

"Oh Gennah! That's awful," Ashannah said, holding her lover closer. "When Kasha returns, perhaps she'll know what to do."

As soon as Kasha walked in, Gennah told her about the dreams. The healer quickly came up with a plan. "Ashannah, could you go to Et-Ray and get a small lump of clay from Angah? Or better yet, I know where she gets her clay close to here. Go to the far side of the temple and then walk towards the sunrise until you come to a small spring. You'll see where she has dug for clay. All we need is a lump about the size of your fist."

Ashannah left right away to accomplish the task, but she wondered how a lump of clay could help Gennah be freed from the evil dreams. When she returned with it and expressed her doubts, her mother reminded her, "This lump of clay is part of the Great Mother … of *our* Mother." Then turning to Gennah, she instructed, "When you go to bed tonight, hold the clay in one of your hands. The Mother will absorb the evil images. In the morning, come to me with the clay and I'll tell you what to do next."

As she prepared for sleep that night, Gennah prayed to Inanna to take away the frightening dreams. Upon awakening the following morning, she felt lighthearted and free of the evil. She hurried to Kasha's in order to complete the ritual. Together, they went to the stream and Kasha instructed her to loosely, but carefully, hold the lump in one of her hands and to put that hand into the stream. She was to hold it there until the last of the clay had been washed away by the moving water. The water was icy cold, but Gennah kept her hand in it until the last of the clay melted away. The dreams did not come back, as Kasha had promised.

When the other Virgins heard of what had happened to Gennah, they were shocked. Never before had a man forced a Virgin of the Temple to give her services, much less to complete the act with him. Anger stirred them into action, and they planned to go to Et-Ray to mete out some punishment on Ator.

When Kasha heard of this, she gathered them together and reminded them that Ator had not done this to Gennah in the temple. "It was not right for him to do this any place, but … I believe Gennah had … pleasured him in Et-Ray, before."

As the women slowly comprehended that Gennah might no longer be a Virgin of the Temple, they stood there in silence.

"Still, no man has a right to force himself on any woman!" Orana cried out in defense of her daughter. "And besides, she has learned her lesson well!"

Kasha put her arms around her friend and instantly agreed with her. "I don't believe she had decided to give up her place in the temple. In fact, she had probably refused to pleasure him outside the temple again, when he … forced her! She was and is still a Virgin of the Temple. But if we go to Et-Ray and … well, I'm not certain that we would be well received by the other men. I mean … they might defend him … and who knows what they might do to us?"

"Yes, Kasha's right," spoke up Mirah. "They have bows and arrows, with which they kill animals. Who knows what they might do to us?" Mirah was barely a sun cycle older than Gennah, but the women had already learned to value her opinions. She had long chestnut-colored hair, but it was her unusually large eyes, the color of a mourning dove, which seemed to affirm the women's belief in the good sense she made whenever she spoke. "But I believe some of us should go to Et-Ray and tell them what happened," Mirah continued. "I am certain they will not want Ator to trade for them any longer."

"Yes! Yes!" Orana cried out. "It is mostly the women who have things for trading. That is the best way to ... let him feel our displeasure."

Mirah, Ashannah, Kasha and Orana set out for Et-Ray the following day to let the women of the trading town know of their plan. It was a hand's span after the sun had reached its meridian when they arrived. They went to see Rootha first, since she was so close to Gennah. She became livid when she heard what Ator had done and promised that none of the women in Et-Ray would have anything for Ator to trade.

"I will also tell the men who make things for trading," Rootha promised. "They, too, will be disgusted with his behavior, I'm sure."

Gennah healed rapidly with Kasha's care and Ashannah's love. One afternoon, when she and Ashannah were sitting at the site of their future home, she said, "Ashannah, I'm feeling much better. I'd really like to begin weaving again."

"You mean you want to go back to Et-Ray?" Ashannah was shocked.

"Oh, no! I'm not ready for that, yet. But ... but I was wondering if you could go get my loom and yarn, so I can finish that linen piece, and we can get the shovel and begin working on our house."

"You mean you're still going to have Ator trade your things!"

"I never want to see that man again!" Gennah assured her. "There are other men who travel and trade, but I'll need a finished piece before I can ask one."

"I'll be glad to go get your things, Gennah, but I do wish your house wasn't right next to Ator's. I think I'll ask Kasha to go with me."

"That's a good idea," Gennah said. "Although I don't think Ator would dare do anything to you, I know he wouldn't if Kasha is with you."

That afternoon, when Kasha and Ashannah arrived in Et-Ray, they were relieved to see that Ator was not around. As they came out of Gennah's, loaded downwith her things, Rootha came up and told them that Ator had taken all of his things and departed. The two women hurried back to Al-Rah to tell Gennah, who hurried out to meet them.

"Rootha told us that Ator packed all of his things and left Et-Ray a few days ago," Ashannah announced jubilantly. "Not one woman or man gave him a thing to trade."

"Was … was he angry?" Gennah asked, her voice trembling.

"Why, I don't know. Rootha didn't say," Ashannah replied.

"Well, I'm sure he was," Gennah continued. "I hope he doesn't … doesn't try to …" She couldn't say what she was thinking.

"We won't let him harm you, if that's what you're thinking," Kasha broke in.

"He wouldn't dare come near you, now," Ashannah agreed, as she hugged her lover tightly.

The following day, Gennah began working on the linen piece.

"See, I'm just about finished," she said, when Ashannah came over later in the morning. "I think it will make a lovely shawl, don't you?"

"Oh, yes!" Ashannah cried out. "Why it would be beautiful enough to use in the temple. It is the most beautiful thing you've made so far. I love the stripes! I knew you would be able to figure out how to put designs in your weavings!"

"Do you really think it's beautiful enough for the temple? Well, this is my first attempt, so I'll probably be able to make something even more beautiful next time. I'm going to weave in three more stripes at this end, and then it'll be finished," Gennah said. "I believe I can finish it in two more journeys of the sun. There is an older man, En-dor, who does a lot of trading. But he doesn't live in Et-Ray, and who knows when he'll be through again? I do trust him, though"

"Maybe Rootha or Angah would come and get us, when he does come through," Ashannah suggested.

"I'm sure they would," Gennah agreed. "I do hope he comes soon."

Two days later, Gennah completed the shawl, as she had foretold, and felt strong enough to walk to Et-Ray. She asked Ashannah to go with her.

"I suppose I'm being foolish, but I'm still afraid to be alone outside of Al-Rah. Who knows … .?"

"I want to go with you, Gennah," Ashannah interjected. "And I agree, you shouldn't be alone, at least for awhile."

They left early in the morning, so that Gennah could rest before they returned in the evening. As soon as they arrived in Et-Ray, the women gathered around Gennah to see how she was doing. As the others gradually returned to their work, Rootha remained.

"I … don't know how to say this, Gennah, but I really think you should be warned," the old weaver said, concern showing in her eyes.

"What is it, Rootha?" Gennah asked, her heart racing with apprehension.

"When that … that evil man was leaving Et-Ray, he said that he was going to get even with you, as if it was your fault that we refused to give him things to trade!" Rootha exploded. "I don't know what he might do, but I thought you should know."

"So! You were right in not wanting to be alone!" Ashannah cried out, as she put her arms around Gennah.

"But what would he do …?" Gennah stammered.

"We won't give him a chance to do anything!" Ashannah exclaimed.

"The men took his hut apart and we women took the branches outside of the town and burned them," Rootha explained. "We didn't want a thing left to remind us of him."

"May Inanna bless all of you," Gennah said fervently, tears welling in her eyes. "That will make it easier for me to use my hut again, but not right away."

"What's in the bundle?" Rootha asked. Curiosity was evident in her eyes.

"It's a shawl I just finished," Gennah answered. "Would you like to see it?"

"Why it's the loveliest thing, I've ever seen, Gennah!" the old weaver exclaimed, as she held it out. "It's even beautiful enough for the temple! You may not be strong enough, yet, to make really fine baskets, but this shawl is … is truly beautiful!" her old teacher exclaimed, as she examined the piece closely.

"We are hoping to give it to En-dor to trade for a shovel," Ashannah said. "Gennah thinks she can make something even more lovely for the temple."

"What's a shovel?" Rootha wanted to know. "It must be something you want very much, to give this up for it."

"It's a kind of metal tool, which will help us build our house in Al-Rah," Gennah replied. "Ashannah has thought up a new kind of hut, which will keep us warmer in the winter and cooler in the summer, but we definitely need a shovel in order to build it."

"We could send one of the little boys to Et-Toll to get En-dor," Rootha suggested. "It's not even a full hand's span of the sun's journey from here."

"Is that where he lives?" Ashannah wanted to know.

"Yes," replied Rootha. "Why, I do believe I see Eetoh standing outside the marketplace. He would be happy to go get his father."

"His father?" Ashannah thought. "En-dor is Eetoh's father? What does that mean?"

As if he had heard them, Eetoh began walking towards the three women, grinning broadly.

"Ashannah!" he called out. "What are you doing in Et-Ray? I thought you never left Al-Rah."

"Oh, I've been here fairly often, lately," she replied, "but Al-Rah is still my home."

"These women have a favor to ask of you, Eetoh," Rootha broke in. "See this fine shawl Gennah has just made. They would like your father to trade it for a … what did you call it, Gennah?"

"A shovel." Gennah replied. "It is a metal tool for scooping up dirt."

"I know what you mean," Eetoh said. "I'm sure En-dor will be able to get you a fine shovel for this lovely shawl. I don't believe I've ever seen one so beautiful!"

"Do you go trading with your … father?" Ashannah asked, unwittingly changing the subject.

"Yes I do, and I like it very much," he answered.

"Would you take the shawl, then, and tell him what we want?" Gennah asked, a little impatient with the interruption.

"I'll be glad to," Eetoh answered, still looking at Ashannah.

"Do you know when you'll be leaving?" Ashannah asked, uncomfortable with the way he was looking at her.

"Not for a few journeys of the sun," he answered.

"I just remembered that Kasha and I have some herbs and spices to trade, in exchange for a knife, larger than the one Gennah uses to cut her threads. We need one for cutting branches for our home."

"Either En-dor or I will come to Al-Rah on our way to Tel Phar and give a low whistle by the temple," Eetoh planned. "Then you can show us your things."

Ashannah's and Kasha's harvest had been unusually large the preceding fall, and Ashannah had come up with the idea of wrapping the dried herbs and spices in bundles and sending them with Ator to be traded, either for foods not available in Al-Rah or some small tools. Long before, Ator had brought Gennah a small copper knife with which she cut her threads and rushes. This made her baskets and cloths much neater than when she had cut them off with shards of flint.

Kasha thought this was a good idea and helped Ashannah make bundles from pieces of woven hemp. Being stronger than the cotton or linen, it would give the herbs more protection.

After Ator had ravished Gennah, they had given up the plan, but as she and Gennah were talking with Eetoh, Ashannah realized that he and En-dor might trade for them, also.

One hand of sun journeys later, while she was working in the village garden, Ashannah heard a low whistle. As she approached the edge of the village, she saw that Eetoh was with the man who had come for him many years ago. She noted that not only did he have sandy-colored hair like Eetoh's, but slanting green eyes as well. She quickly achieved a deeper understanding of what being a father meant.

Ashannah got right to the point. "Kasha and I had a large harvest last fall, and we wondered if the people of Tel Phar would be interested in trading for some of our dried herbs and spices?"

"What kinds of things do you want in return, Ashannah?" En-dor asked.

She briefly described the house she was building and explained the kind of knife she would need. At his request, she left to get a bundle of the herbs.

After looking through the herbs carefully, En-dor said, "I'm sure the people of Tel Phar would be interested in these fine herbs, as well as the spices. They can't grow many things so near the salt water. However, it would take more than these to obtain the kind of knife you want."

"Oh, there's more!" Ashannah assured him and went to get the rest. She gathered the little bundles together and then put them all in a large piece of woven hemp, so En-dor could carry them more easily.

As she handed the large bundle to En-dor, he said, "I was wondering how to carry all those little bundles, Ashannah, but you figured it out for us. You're a smart woman."

Eetoh instantly agreed. Ashannah smiled her appreciation, but quickly left them to continue her planting.

About three hands of sun journeys later, Ashannah and Gennah went to Gennah's hut in Et-Ray, so that Gennah could work on some baskets and Ashannah could weave some things from hemp. They had barely settled down when Rootha came running towards them, waving a shiny new tool in one hand and two smaller tools in the other.

"Here are the tools for building your house!" she called out. "En-dor left them during the sun's last journey."

Gennah took the tools from her teacher and turned to show them to Ashannah.

"Oh, Gennah, they're beautiful!" Ashannah cried out with pleasure. "I didn't know they would be so shiny!"

"Well, at least for awhile," Gennah laughed. "My knife was shiny like that when I first got it, but it isn't any more."

"See how firm the shovel is," Rootha demonstrated. "It won't bend as easily as our copper knives, because it's got tin in it, too. They call it bronze. And this cutting tool they got for you, Ashannah, is called a hatchet. It's also made from bronze. That was a wonderful idea to trade some of your herbs and spices for tools."

"It will surely make cutting the branches for the front walls of our house easier," Ashannah commented as she examined the hatchet. "And I thought we would only get a knife for our herbs," she said with delight.

Ashannah and Gennah left at once for Al-Rah to try out the new tools. As they approached their site, Ashannah began jumping sideways, crying out, "Let's hurry and see how the shovel works!"

"Wait!" Gennah cried out, laughing at her friend's impatience. "Remember when Rootha showed us these two little loops at this end of the shovel and told us that we should find a branch, about as long as one of our legs and thick enough to fit tightly through the loops, for a handle?"

"Oh, I remember now!" Ashannah said. "That will help a lot! And we can use our new hatchet to get the branch."

They were unable to find a stick the right size, and, since the sun was close to setting, Ashannah suggested, "Let's try the shovel without a handle, for now. We can at least get some idea how it works."

They hadn't worked a full hand's span of the sun's journey, when Ashannah straightened up and groaned, "Whew! I can see how a handle will help. My back is already aching!"

"Mine, too!" Gennah admitted. "I guess we'll just have to wait until tomorrow to get much done."

They hugged each other with excitement and each returned to her mother's home, Ashannah carrying the shovel and Gennah the hatchet and knife.

The following day, they were relieved at how much easier using the shovel was, after putting a handle on it. They had worked for two hand spans of the sun's journey, when they decided to stop and rest.

"Let's curl up together, right here, where our new home will be," Ashannah suggested. Gennah lay down by her and, looking into her eyes, sighed, "I love you very much, Ashannah."

Fervently returning the gaze, Ashannah replied, "And you are my heart's only desire." She took Gennah into her arms and right away felt her trembling all over. She searched her lover's eyes. "Are you … are you afraid of me, Gennah? she asked, her voice breaking with emotion.

Gennah burst into tears. "I don't know what's the matter with me! Whenever I think we're going to make love, I start shaking all over!"

Ashannah stroked Gennah's arms lightly, wanting to comfort her.

"Maybe I could just love you, without you loving me back," Gennah offered.

"But Gennah, I can feel you loving me, right now, as I am loving you. Can't you feel it?"

"Why, yes!" Gennah agreed. "Yes, I can. And it's so healing when you love me like this!"

Ashannah continued to stroke her, ever so tenderly, avoiding anything that might frighten her. Gennah gave herself over to the massaging and finally fell asleep. Ashannah curled around her. After a few minutes, Gennah suddenly awoke, stretched herself and then asked, "Are you asleep, Ashannah?"

"No, but I thought you were."

"I think I did sleep a little," she murmured. She rolled over to face Ashannah. "Thank you for loving me, even when I can't … can't …"

Ashannah gently kissed Gennah. "Don't say any more. You know that I love you, and truly, I know that you love me." Then she got up and as she pulled Gennah to her feet, laughed and said, "It will be much better when we have finished our house. This ground is pretty hard!"

When Grenda had told Kasha that she hadn't bled for three moon cycles, tears of joy ran freely down the priestess' cheeks. She embraced the young woman, saying, "I was beginning to wonder if Al-Rah was ever going to hear the cry of an infant, again." Then she stepped back, looking

Grenda over, and said, "And you're a strong healthy woman, so I feel certain that Al-Rah will soon have a new baby to cheer us up!"

"I truly hope so, Kasha," the young woman replied, smiling.

Kasha decided that there should be an extra large celebration for the birth of Grenda's baby, hoping to inspire some of the other young women to have a child. But deep in her heart, she knew that it wasn't a lack of desire on the women's part. It was becoming quite rare for a man to come to the temple.

It had long been the custom for everyone in the village to participate in a birthing, and since it had been eight sun cycles since Zolah had been born, the women were ecstatic as they sang and danced outside Grenda's hut, while Kasha, with Ashannah's and Mirah's assistance, delivered the child. When she came out and announced that they had a new daughter for Inanna, the women gave a great shout of joy. Several days later, Grenda named the little girl Leah.

Chapter Five

Later in the spring, just after Ashannah had finished her fourteenth sun cycle, she and Gennah, with help from Kasha and Orana, had finished the excavation of their new home. On the day of Inanna's festival, Ashannah and Gennah had gathered branches and had finished putting the frame up. It would be the largest dwelling in the village. Only the temple was larger.

That evening, after dancing, the two women put several armsful of pine needles inside their unfinished house and lay on them, looking at the stars through the frame. The dancing had been wonderful, as usual, but Ashannah sensed that Gennah was still fearful of making love.

As if to confirm her thoughts, Gennah exclaimed, "Oh, Ashannah, I know that you want to love me and I certainly want to love you ... but ..."

"It's all right, Gennah, really," Ashannah broke in. "I wouldn't want to hurt you for anything!"

"I know you wouldn't! And ... and it is feeling a lot better down ... down there, but I'm still afraid for some reason! Anyway, I want to kiss you, ... you're so beautiful, tonight." She embraced her lover and kissed her deeply.

Ashannah couldn't help responding as Gennah kept kissing her over and over. By the time she was approaching Ashannah's vulva, the younger woman was moaning with anticipation.

As Ashannah began to climax, Gennah cried out, "I'm ready, too, Ashannah! Oh, yes, oh, yes!"

Euphoria quickly embraced them and soon they were as one.

★★★★★

Both women kept very busy for the next few weeks. Gennah was spinning some extra fine linen for a really fine robe for the High Priestess. She hoped to weave in a design of almond leaves going down the edges of the opening. Ashannah was busy packing in the stones for the back wall of their house. When it was time to start weaving in the walls, Gennah wanted to do it, so Ashannah began collecting long grasses.

By the time of Ninlil's feast, they were ready to cover the structure with catalpa leaves, and a new robe was ready for Kasha to wear at the ceremonies. Gennah had dyed it an azure blue, and the daisies at the edge were a bright yellow. Kasha and the other women were in awe of its loveliness.

"It is the most beautiful robe I have ever worn!" exclaimed Kasha. "In fact, it is the most beautiful I have ever seen! I know that Inanna is pleased with it, as well."

In the meantime, Ashannah had discovered that the dirt from their excavation would make fine loose soil for her garden. Then she realized that she could build up the garden bed with this soil until it was level, so the water wouldn't run off before it had a chance to penetrate. At the downhill end of the garden she reinforced the wall she had formed with more rocks from the river.

One day, when Ashannah went up to the spring, to begin digging a trench to carry the water to the garden, she thought of digging a large hole, where the spring came out of the ground, as a storage place for the water. She dragged the soil from the hole down to the garden in the shovel. Later, she lined the hole with rocks to keep mud from mixing with the water. Then she realized that they would be able to come here for their drinking and cooking water, instead of having to go to the stream to get it.

When she was finally ready to begin the trench, she knew she would have to find a way to block the water from running out of the hole into the trench, until she was ready to water her garden. She and Gennah were able to find a rock large enough to do this. When Ashannah was ready to release the water into the garden, she found she could do this easily by using a large branch for a lever to push the rock aside. She was also able to return the rock in the same manner.

One day, early in the afternoon, Ashannah was walking by the spring hole on her way to gather herbs, when she stopped to admire her work. She knelt by the edge and looked down, only to see another woman staring back at her. She jumped up and ran down to the house shouting, "Gennah! Gennah! There's a woman in the spring hole! Come and look!"

Gennah was so intent on her weaving that she hardly heard her.

"C'mon, now! She might go away!" Ashannah insisted.

"What do you mean, there's a woman in the spring hole?" Gennah asked, as she reluctantly put aside her weaving.

"C'mon and see for yourself!" Ashannah repeated and hurried back to the spring. "Hurry, she's still here!" she called out.

Gennah knelt down beside her, finding it hard to believe what she was hearing. But when she looked down, she saw two women! And one was Ashannah!

"Ashannah, it's you!" she screamed. "But who is that woman beside you?"

"It's you, Gennah!" Ashannah yelled.

"She does have red hair like mine," Gennah exclaimed. "Oh, Goddess, what's happening?"

The two women began laughing heartily, as they began to understand what was occurring.

"Is that what I look like?" Ashannah asked, as she peered, again, into the hole.

"And is that what I look like?" Gennah echoed.

They looked back and forth at each other and at their reflections, laughing with pleasure. They turned their heads from side to side and watched as the two in the hole did the same thing.

"Let's see how we look when we kiss," Gennah suggested. They nearly fell in, as they tried to kiss and, at the same time, lean over the hole to watch their reflections.

"Let's go get Kasha!" Ashannah cried out. "I wonder if she's ever seen herself!"

After they had described their experience to Kasha, she laughed and told them there used to be a pool at one side of the stream, where this would happen from time to time.

"Well, let's go!" she exclaimed. "It has been a long time since I've seen myself!"

By the time they returned to the spring hole, they could barely make out anything.

"I think the light has to be just right," Kasha explained. "But this will always be a good place, because the water is still. We'll probably be able to see ourselves tomorrow."

She was right. Soon all of the women of Al-Rah were coming up to

Ashannah's spring hole to see what they looked like. They laughed uproariously as the women in the hole mimicked their every movement.

Al-Rah seemed to be going through a period of prosperity. The gardens had yielded more than ever and they had gathered more than enough herbs for trading. Best of all had been the birth of Grenda's little Leah.

However, while Ator's behavior of the past winter began to recede from most of the women's minds, Gennah continued to fear that he would return and try to harm her in some way.

As the nights became longer and colder, Gennah wove a heavy mat of reeds for their doorway. While they were hanging it, Ashannah admired it, saying, "This is a really fine mat, Gennah. I've woven quite a few things out of reeds, but it never looks like this."

"Yours would probably keep the wind and rain out as well as mine," Gennah insisted. Then suddenly she burst out, "Oh, how I love our little home, Ashannah! Thank you for finding such a wonderful place and for making it so beautiful!"

"Why, Gennah, it is you who have made it truly beautiful!"

"Really, Ashannah, we both have, and that is the most beautiful thing of all!"

They slowly embraced and were soon making love in the intimacy of their own home.

Before it got too cold, Ashannah went out to cut bamboo for her garden fence. It took her several hands of days to put up the entire fence. She was already thinking of the many things she would plant in the spring. She wanted to try transplanting some of the wild herbs that she and Kasha used for healing. In that way, she would be more certain to have a plentiful supply.

Because her garden was at the opposite end of the village from the temple, Ashannah decided to build a little shrine to Inanna right in the center of it. First she made a fairy ring from colorful stones she had been collecting, and then, on one of their trips to Et-Ray, she spoke to Angah about making an image of Inanna out of clay.

"You want to put it in your garden?" Angah asked. "Even if I painted it completely, I don't know how long it would last, after a few good rains. Let me think about it."

A few days later, Angah came to Ashannah and said, "I've found a wonderful stone that looks very much like Inanna. I don't know if the two of us will be able to get it up to your garden, though. It's down by the river."

"Wait until I get the shovel, Angah. If it isn't too big, we can put it on that and drag it up."

When Angah saw the shovel, she knew at once that it wasn't large enough. "That's all right, Ashannah. I think we can roll it up."

Ashannah was excited at the thought of having such a large image of Inanna in her own garden. As she followed the older woman, striding towards the river, she watched Angah's gray braid bouncing off her back. Ashannah had to stretch her long legs to keep up.

When they reached the river, Angah showed Ashannah the stone she had in mind.

"Oh, Angah, it does look like Inanna! But it also looks very heavy."

"But see how round it is, Ashannah. I really believe we can roll it up to your garden."

They tried it with some success, but it was very strenuous work. Then Ashannah thought of cutting two long, sturdy branches and using them for levers to make the rock roll more easily. This also helped, but it was still arduous work. The difficulty lay in the fact that the rock was much narrower at one end, which made a nice head for the image, but also made it more difficult to roll in a direct line. When they had it about half way to the garden, Angah said she would have to stop in order to return to Et-Ray before dark, but she promised to come back the next journey of the sun.

The following day, as the two women struggled to get the heavy stone up to Ashannah's garden, Angah muttered, "What we need is one of those carts I've seen in Tel Phar."

Ashannah was astonished. "You ... you mean you've been to Tel Phar!"

"Didn't you know? I went with En-dor and Eetoh last spring, when they got your shovel and hatchet. En-dor wanted me to see the wheels potters use to make bowls and vases. You can make things a lot faster with them, once you learn how."

"But, what's a wheel, Angah?" Ashannah asked.

'Well, I'm not surprised you don't know. I didn't either, until En-dor told me about them, and I really didn't understand what he was talking about until I went to Tel Phar and saw one for myself."

The conversation had left the two women standing with the two levers braced under the stone, waiting to be pushed.

"Let's finish this push, Ashannah, and then I'll try to explain," Angah suggested. Since they were fairly near the garden, they decided to finish getting the stone up there before talking more. After the sun had finished another hand's span, they finally pushed the stone into place and hefted it up on the large end.

"Oh, Angah, it's beautiful! Thank you so much!" Ashannah said, as she brushed the dirt off the image. "I've got some emmer buns we can eat. Why don't you go on up to the spring hole and we can eat up there in the shade."

"I'll do that, Ashannah. I could stand a long, cool drink of that wonderful water. Then I can tell you more about the wheel."

It didn't take Ashannah long to get the buns, and when she arrived at the spring hole, she found Angah lying on her stomach and laughing at her reflection. She was admiring the contrast between her white teeth and the darkness of her skin.

"Look, Ashannah! I'm kissing myself."

Ashannah leaned over the spring hole to join in the fun, again noticing Angah's pointed chin and almond shaped eyes, reminding her of a fox. Finally, Ashannah pushed herself up from the spring, saying, "I'm really hungry, aren't you?"

"I am! I am!" Angah laughed as she sat up. After they had eaten, Ashannah reminded the potter that she was going to tell her more about the wheel. "If you have to start back to Et-Ray, I'll walk a ways with you, while you tell me," Ashannah suggested.

Angah agreed and they began the walk towards the town. "Well, a wheel is round, but thin and flat at the same time," she began. "It's something like a barley cake, but it's made of wood and is much larger. It has a hub in the middle and you can put it on an axle, so it will spin around fast. I told you it would be hard to understand, Ashannah," she laughed, as she looked at the perplexed look on her friend's face. "The best thing would be for you to come to Et-Ray and see mine. Then you can see what I mean by a hub and an axle."

"And round, but thin and flat, too," Ashannah continued, joining in on the laughter. "So, you were able to get one for yourself? I'd love to come and see it.

Maybe Gennah and I will come in the sun's next journey."

The following day, Gennah and Ashannah were amazed at Angah's wheel and what she could do with it. Ashannah noticed that it was made of three wooden planks, held together by copper pins. The planks had been rounded off so that they formed somewhat of a circle. A copper band ran around the edge to ensure that it would stay together. She wondered if she would be able to make one. The first stumbling block would be to know how to make the planks.

"But wait until I show you what a cart is and what it can do!" Angah said, as she bent down and began drawing a picture of one on the ground. "The bronze bands on these larger wheels have spikes on them, which dig in the dirt and give the cart more balance," she explained, as she drew them in. "They put a kind of basket, to put things in, between the handles. The baskets are made of wood or bronze, rather than from rushes." She pointed to the handles and drew in the basket. "You can load whatever you wish into it, and then pick up the handles and push. Once you get going, the wheel makes it easy to take the load from one place to another. Besides that, you can get more in the basket than you can carry."

Ashannah's and Gennah's eyes were wide open with wonder and admiration. "Just think of all the things we could do with one of those!" Ashannah exclaimed. The two younger women left for Gennah's hut, so Gennah could work on some baskets. Ashannah felt her head was literally bursting, as she thought of the many ways she could use a cart. She finally had to speak out. "I wish we had a cart, Gennah! Why, think how much easier it would be to bring things here from Al-Rah or to take things there from here!"

"Maybe we will, someday," Gennah replied.

It was nearly the Longest Night, as Ashannah made her way to the temple, since it was her turn to be Virgin of the Night. There was no moon, but the sky was glittering with stars. Ashannah drew in the crisp, winter air just before she entered the temple. Shortly after she had greeted Inanna, she was surprised to hear someone come in. As she watched the figure prostrate himself before the statue of Inanna, she realized it was Eetoh.

"Now! It's ***now*** I'm going to become a mother," she thought. It was as if someone within was guiding her. She thought Eetoh had probably been to the temple many times since their first encounter, and she was appreciative of his gentleness. Some men with experience were rough in their treatment of the Virgins.

As they lay there, side by side, Ashannah purposely recalled the many happy times she and Eetoh had, playing together as children. These scenes filled her with tenderness, and she turned towards Eetoh and began stroking his hair. Eetoh turned to embrace her, but Ashannah resisted, wanting to extend her preparations as long as possible. Then Eetoh started to say something, but she interrupted by kissing him with all the tenderness she could, yet keeping herself from becoming passionate. This was not possible for the man, and he returned the kiss with much fervor. Ashannah relented, opening to him and guiding his stiffened member into her vagina.

Even though Ashannah had been warned about the pain experienced the first time a woman completed the act with a man, she was taken by surprise when she actually felt her membrane breaking. She sucked in her breath and reached down to slow his thrusting until her own juices would have a chance to do their work. After the pain subsided, she and Eetoh came to a wonderful climax. Eetoh cried out his gratitude and a little later fell asleep, with his head resting on one of Ashannah's breasts. Ashannah was drawn into a mystical trance in which she saw fish being spawned in midstream, then flowers opening their petals and releasing their fragrance, so that bees would be drawn to fertilize them. Finally, she watched, again, as Grenda gave birth to Leah. Smiling, she stretched, covered Eetoh, and went to her garden shrine to thank Inanna for blessing her womb. She was certain that she was with child.

After three moon cycles without bleeding, Ashannah told Gennah that she was with child. "She should be born around Ninlil's feast. That will make her a good gardener," she laughed.

"Then she'll be born around the time I will have finished four hands of sun cycles, but I'm no gardener!" Gennah argued, and then exclaimed, "Ashannah, a mother! I can't believe it!" But she knew her lover would be a good one. "And I'll get to help with her, without go … . without …"

"Without going through the pain! I know what you were thinking, Gennah! But Kasha says the pain is worth the joy of having a baby in your arms and I believe her. But you're right," she added smiling, "You will get to help mother her without going through the pain."

"Are we sure … are you certain the baby will be a … her … a girl?"

"Well, pretty certain," Ashannah replied.

"Oh, Ashannah! It has to be! I would really have trouble loving a boy!"

Ashannah was surprised at Gennah's vehemence, but understood where her feelings came from. She said no more, but thought to herself, "When the time comes, I'm sure we will love it no matter if it's a boy or a girl."

After work in the communal garden was finished in the spring, Ashannah began planting her own garden for the first time. It was there that she felt the first stirrings of life in her womb. She began laughing aloud with joy and went over to her garden shrine to give thanks to Inanna. There was a single crocus blooming at the Goddess' feet. Ashannah understood it as a sign of Inanna's blessing and ran to their home to share the event with Gennah.

After hugging one another, Gennah said, "Now I know why I began warping my loom for a new cotton piece. It will be a soft wrap for our baby!" Ashannah's eyes quickly filled with gratitude and she embraced her lover tenderly. After making love, they went out into the woods and picked more crocus and daffodils to make coronets for the clay Inanna in the temple and for the stone image of her in their own garden.

The rains had been abundant during the last winter, and Ashannah's spring hole was flowing over. The seeds in both gardens took and were peering through the soil. The Goddess extended her blessings to Ashannah, who grew round like a plump melon. Together, in the early afternoons, when the light was right, Ashannah and Gennah would go to the spring hole to take in the changes. Ashannah not only grew rounder, but her face seemed to glow with light and love. Gennah also became more beautiful, as if Ashannah's happiness poured itself into her. That spring Ashannah had completed three hands of sun cycles.

Kasha had been ecstatic when Ashannah told her she was going to be a grandmother. She felt that Inanna had certainly answered her prayer that the Virgins once again would hear the voices of little children among their huts. As she watched her daughter become rounder and more beautiful, the healer became impatient for the birth to take place.

In midsummer, just before Ashannah was to deliver her child, Beleendah surprised Kasha by admitting that she had not bled for three moon cycles.

"But Beleendah! You already have two little girls in your hut!" Kasha exclaimed.

"They actually aren't so little, Kasha. My Beyla has just completed two hands of sun cycles and Zolah is just about to finish one hand plus four. And ... well ... I didn't really plan it. It ... it just kind of happened!" Beleendah was blushing, but giggling as well. After controlling herself, she added, "Anyway, I firmly believe it was Inanna's wish, so how can I complain?"

After embracing the woman, Kasha went directly to the temple to thank Inanna for blessing the little village three times in one sun cycle.

As Ninlil's feast approached, Ashannah entered into the preparations with her usual zest, but, being so large with her baby, she simply did not have the energy she usually had. Gennah had finished weaving a number of pieces for the baby and felt free to help Kasha with the foods.

During the ritual, Ashannah was singing to the four directions when her water broke. The women considered it a great blessing for this to happen during a celebration. Kasha and Gennah made a "chair" with their arms and carried her home, with the rest of the women following, singing. After Gennah, Ashannah and their mothers had entered the hut, all the Virgins encircled it, singing and dancing.

A little later Kasha announced she could see the baby's crown. Again, there was great rejoicing. Kasha directed Mirah to make a fire and heat some rocks. After the rocks were hot, they would place them in a basket of water, so it would be warm when they cleaned the new baby and mother.

A short while later, Kasha had Orana and Gennah squat down, side by side, facing each other a little. She told Ashannah to sit on their thighs and brace herself by putting her arms around their necks. This would leave her free to catch the baby, as it came forth from Ashannah's womb. As Ashannah was pushing and groaning to help the baby through, the women outside joined in, groaning and grunting right along with her, raising a wonderful cone of power.

Kasha deftly caught the infant and placed it in Ashannah's arms, announcing for all to hear, "It is a new daughter for Inanna. Blessed be Inanna!"

"Blessed be Inanna for all her giftings, but especially for giving us a new daughter, through Ashannah!" the women replied and, again, began singing and dancing.

Kasha showed Gennah how to cut and tie the umbilical cord and together they helped Ashannah expel the afterbirth. While Gennah remained inside, cleaning blood off the mother and infant, Kasha scooped up the afterbirth into an old basket, and, holding it aloft, went outside to the cries and cheers of the awaiting women. Then she put it in the hole already prepared for it, where they would plant a seedling catalpa tree.

Meanwhile, Ashannah lovingly rubbed precious oil all over her daughter, exclaiming ecstatically over the infant's tiny hands and fingers, the perfect little feet and toes.

"And look, Gennah! Look at those precious little ears!"

"And her tiny little mouth," Gennah continued, "and a nubbin for a nose!"Gennah finally took the baby outside so that all the women could praise her beauty. When she went back inside, she gave the infant to her mother and lay down beside them. Only moments later Kasha found the three of them soundly sleeping. Her heart filled with joy, and she quietly left to join the other women, who were finishing the ritual in honor of Ninlil.

During the night, Ashannah was awakened by her little girl's cries as she thrust at her breast. The mother guided the nipple into the infant's mouth, and, as the infant began to suckle hungrily, she caught her breath, saying, "Easy, little one, easy!'

When she sat up, the throbbing eased after a bit, and Ashannah was filled with pleasure as her daughter continued sucking. It was truly wonderful, being a mother, as Kasha had promised.

Several days later, when Gennah and Kasha were watching the infant as she lay nursing in her mother's arms, Ashannah suddenly sat up and announced with certainty, "She shall be called Elissa. I have just received this name from Ninlil."

The other two women responded together, "Blessed be Ninlil for this beautiful name! Blessed be Elissa now and for many sun cycles to come!"

Kasha left to go tell the rest of the women.

Gennah looked deeply into Ashannah's eyes and said, "Oh, Ashannah, now I want to have a baby, too! But … but I don't know … if …"

"You will, Gennah, you will," Ashannah assured her.

Chapter Six

As she walked along the path towards Al-Rah, Gennah enjoyed the fall odors of crushed leaves and burning wood. She quickly strode through the little village towards the place that was truly becoming more and more her home. In fact, it felt more like home than her mother's hut ever had. She was eager to receive Ashannah's embrace and she anticipated the joy that would spring up in her heart, as little Elissa reached out for her.

When she arrived, she found Kasha sitting against the wall holding Elissa and crooning to her. Suddenly, Gennah realized how much the older woman missed her daughter's presence in her own home. She was not nearly as close to Orana, as Ashannah and Kasha were.

As Ashannah got up to greet her, she noticed how much her lover resembled her mother. She saw that as Elissa matured, she was taking on the physical characteristics of her mother and grandmother. Wavy black hair graced all three heads. Elissa's eyes were already losing their baby blue and she was also blessed with a generous mouth, which often formed into a wide smile. Besides that, Ashannah and Kasha were taller than the average village woman, and judging by the length of her limbs, Elissa was going to be tall, too.

"Will she be a gardener and healer, as well?" Gennah asked herself.

Gennah loved her mother and they had grown much closer during her healing after Ator had injured her. Nevertheless, their new bonding didn't approach that of Ashannah's and Kasha's. Sometimes she envied Ashannah's closeness with her mother. Then, remembering how tender and sympathetic Orana had been during her healing and how much she had helped Ashannah and herself in building their home, Gennah cut short her negative comparisons.

After she received the enthusiastic embrace of Ashannah, Gennah settled down by Kasha. The baby was sleeping soundly, so she did not ask to hold her, but enjoyed her infant beauty from where she sat. As the sun began to set, Elissa awoke and hungrily reached out towards her mother. After Ashannah had the baby happily suckling one of her breasts, Kasha rose to leave. As if she had read Gennah's thoughts, she gave her an especially tender hug.

As the Longest Night was approaching once more, a man called Fenn came through Et-Ray from Et-Bann, a small village north and west of Et-Toll, with a bundle of raw wool. Rootha went to get Gennah, as she knew the young weaver was interested in weaving some of this material.

When Gennah entered Rootha's hut, she was assailed by the pungent animal odor emanating from the wool. She was barely able to keep from showing her disgust and when she touched the wool, she was even more repulsed by its greasiness.

As if he had read her thoughts, Fenn explained, "It's the grease that keeps you dry when it's raining, and, truly, there's nothing that keeps you as warm as wool."

Gennah was tempted to reply that perhaps it didn't get that cold in Et-Ray, but she realized that jackets and leggings of this material would be welcome during the winter months.

She knew right away what she had that would appeal to Fenn so that he would want to trade the wool for it. After telling him that she was interested, she left to get an especially large basket she had recently woven. It had firm handles on it and would enable him to carry his wool much more easily. After they had agreed on the amount of wool coming to her, there wasn't much left.

"Here," he said, throwing the remains on her pile. "You might as well take it all. Then I can go back home before the winter snows come. I have a new wife waiting for me," he added shyly.

Gennah was momentarily puzzled by the word "wife", but she quickly dismissed her curiosity, wanting to concentrate on the matter at hand. She decided right away, that she would card, spin and weave the wool in Et-Ray, not wanting to inflict its odor on Ashannah and Elissa.

It took her several weeks to learn to spin a firm and even yarn from the wool and by the time she had woven a small covering for the baby, it was past the Longest Night. To her amazement, she discovered that as she worked with the wool, the oil made her hands smooth and soft.

When she finally took the baby blanket home, she was not surprised when Ashannah wrinkled up her nose with disgust. She quickly convinced her of its warmth and showed her the change it had made in her hands. Ashannah rubbed the oil from the blanket on her own hands and admitted that it felt very healing.

After a time, they grew used to the odor and Gennah decided to make a blanket large enough to cover them all. She taught Ashannah how to spin the wool, not only to hasten the work, but to give Ashannah's hands the benefit of the oil.

There was barely enough wool to make the blanket large enough, and Gennah hoped Fenn would be through with more wool in the spring, not realizing that he had to wait until the weather was fairly warm before he could sheer his sheep.

The winter was comparatively mild, and Gennah, Ashannah and Elissa often went to Et-Ray to weave baskets and mats of hemp. Gennah found a way to fold the baby's blanket, so that by placing a corner over one of Ashannah's shoulders and putting the opposite corner around her waist, they could then tie the ends together, thus forming a sling in which to carry the baby, leaving Ashannah's arms and hands free.

Sometimes Ashannah would take Elissa over to watch Angah work her clay with the new wheel. The baby was fascinated, becoming mesmerized by its continuous motion.

As Ashannah watched the wheel, she dreamed of the wonderful things she could do with a cart like the one Angah had described to her. In spite of her dislike of Et-Ray, she began to wish that they could go to Tel Phar. She had been told that it was much larger, noisier and filled with many more strangers than Et-Ray, but she longed to see the wonders Angah had described to her and somehow acquire a cart. She also knew that the women of Al-Rah could use another shovel.

On the way home, one afternoon, she confided her dreams to Gennah.

"Oh, Ashannah! I'd love to go to Tel Phar! But ... I guess I never thought that you would want to. Yes, we could surely use another shovel in the village, and how wonderful it would be to have a cart! I'm certain En-dor would let us travel with him. Do you truly want to go? I would be afraid to go without you."

"I truly want to go, Gennah, but I can't until I get my garden in."

"I'll help you all I can. In the meantime, we can spin and weave things for the shovel and maybe even a cart! I wish we had more wool, but I guess cotton and flax will have to do."

"Do you think I could help you spin cotton and flax, like I did wool?" Ashannah offered. Gennah accepted the offer immediately.

When it was warm enough to begin planting, Ashannah built a small, temporary lean-to in the corner of her garden, as well as one in the community garden. In this way she could lay Elissa on a blanket under the lean-to and be free to work and watch over the baby, as well as to take out time to nurse and play with her. Elissa would sometimes grab hold of a fist full of dirt and then try to eat it. Ashannah was certain that this was a sign that she would become a gardener.

It was about then that Beleendah gave birth to a son, whom she named Ran-dell. Not one woman showed the slightest disappointment over having a boy in the village. They were too delighted at having three children born so close together, after so long a time without any. Beyla and Zolah were thrilled that they would have a new little playmate.

Gennah and Ashannah had spent most of the winter working at their weaving, and some of the village women gave them items to trade, as well. By the time En-dor arrived in the early spring, they had actually produced more than they could carry, especially since they were taking Elissa along. Even when Kasha volunteered to go along with them, they weren't able to manage everything, and En-dor felt that they would need it all, if they were going to get a cart as well as a shovel. Carts were a recent discovery and, therefore, scarce, leaving the cart maker pretty much in control of the bargaining.

Ashannah sighed and said, "It seems like we need a cart to carry everything we need in order to get a cart."

"I'm afraid you're right, Ashannah," En-dor sadly agreed.

"I have an idea how we could make a kind of cart, one without a wheel," Gennah broke in. "It wouldn't be as good and probably won't last long, but I think it would get us there with what we need. We'll have to gather three or four long branches and weave them together with smaller branches and grass, like we do the sides of our houses, leaving handles at one end. Then we could tie our things to it and drag it along behind us."

"Why, Gennah, I think you've solved our problem," En-dor said with admiration. "In fact, I've seen hunters bring in a kill that way."

"And we can use our hatchet to get the branches," Ashannah said, ready to begin at once.

With the improvised travois, Kasha didn't need to go. She was relieved, since she hadn't wanted to leave the village without a healer. In two more sun journeys the travelers were ready to leave.

At first, Ashannah and Gennah took turns carrying Elissa and also dragged the travois at times, to relieve En-dor. The baby began to get restless from being confined so long in the shawl. Finally, Ashannah stopped and said, ""We'll just have to rest more often and give Elissa a chance to eat, as well as to move a little."

"You're right, Ashannah," En-dor agreed. "Let's stop for awhile, right now."

That evening, En-dor built a big fire in a circle of rocks that had been used for that purpose before. The women put some flat stones in the fire, and when it had burned down to coals, they heated some of the food they had brought on the rocks.

"You two know how to make food taste good, even while we're traveling," Endor said, as he ate with relish.

"What do you do when you're not trading, En-dor?" Gennah asked, a little embarrassed by the compliment.

"Why, Eetoh and I have a hut in Et-Toll. It's the next town along the river above Et-Ray. We don't even have a village of Virgins nearby. Et-Toll is made up mostly of men who are hunters and traders, although we all do a little of both."

"Don't you have a garden?" Ashannah wanted to know.

"No, we don't. The few women who live there do a little foraging to go with the meat, and we trade for grain so that the women can make buns. We also trade for clothes, since there aren't enough women to weave clothing for all of us."

Neither Gennah nor Ashannah asked why the men couldn't weave or make bread for themselves, but they were wondering, nonetheless. Every woman in Al-Rah had her own small loom with which she wove her own clothes, and as long as necessary, her child's clothing. Neither woman could imagine a life so dependent on others.

By the third day, the trees and other vegetation were growing scantier, and oaks and pines were giving way to juniper and cypress. Ashannah would have liked to stop and do some foraging, to see what new edibles and healing herbs she could find.

By the end of the day, the food they had brought with them was gone, even though they had supplemented it with a little foraging. En-dor knew that the thought of eating flesh was repulsive to the women, but he tried to persuade them to eat some fish, which he could catch without spending a lot of time. By the end of the fourth day, they were hungry enough to agree to this. En-dor carefully wrapped his catch in some catalpa leaves and placed the little bundles over the coals of their fire. Hunger aided the women with the first few bites, and they quickly appreciated the warmth of the food,as it filled their stomachs. Ashannah began to imagine how its flavors could be enhanced with certain herbs.

The following evening, Ashannah began setting the fire, while Gennah placed Elissa in a shawl and went in search of larger wood. En-dor left for the stream they had been following to catch some fish. Ashannah was bending over some tinder with her flint and rock, when she heard footsteps approaching from the opposite direction En-dor had taken. Before she looked up, she knew it was more than one person. She raised her head and saw three men walking into the clearing. Their hair was shaggy and dirty, and their bodies were scantily covered with untanned hides.

Ashannah felt their hostility right away, but greeted them in the usual manner, simply because she couldn't think of what else to say.

"May the blessings of Inanna be upon you. Welcome to ... to the warmth of our fire."

"Are you traveling alone?" one of them asked.

"Why, no, I am with two companions." She was wondering when Gennah would be returning from gathering wood. With relief she saw her entering from one side. The men turned upon hearing her.

"Well," said the leader mockingly, "another woman with a babe. I guess we won't have any trouble taking whatever we want." Turning back to Ashannah, he continued, "You have a fine load there. Just what we need. We'll just take it and leave you in peace."

Ashannah was astonished when she realized their purpose, but she was grateful that they thought the baby was her second companion. As they approached the travois and Gennah comprehended their intention, she stepped up in front of it. "You can't take our things! Why we've worked hard all winter to trade them in Tel Phar."

The men, surprised by her boldness, stepped back. Then the leader drew a sizable knife from his belt and said, "If you won't try to stop us, we won't have to hurt you, but we are taking your things. We're traders, too!" The three of them burst out in boisterous laughter. When Gennah didn't give way, the other two men drew out knives, as well.

Ashannah stood transfixed, her mouth agape, as her mind slowly took in this different way a knife could be used. The women of Al-Rah had been using knives for nearly three sun cycles and had sometimes cut themselves from carelessness, but she had never considered how knives might be used to purposely injure someone. Then she realized the danger her baby was in and ordered Gennah to step aside. When Gennah couldn't seem to move, Ashannah screamed with all her strength, "En-doooooor!!"

Again, the men stopped their advance, as they realized she was calling for help. Seconds later, they heard En-dor crashing through the bushes, as he ran towards the camp. When he broke into the clearing, his bow set with an arrow directed straight for the men, all three turned and ran from there as fast as they could.

Ashannah broke into tears of relief, but she also gasped in horror. "Were ... were you going to kill them?"

"Well, I guess I didn't have to, did I? Besides, what do ya' suppose they would have done to you? They may have killed you, or at least injured you enough so that you couldn't stop them from taking our things. But they knew their knives wouldn't help much, when I could shoot an arrow from where I stood."

Ashannah had nothing more to say, but suddenly she was afraid of this man, who would not only kill animals for eating, but would injure or kill people, as well! Yet, he had been protecting them. She was filled with bewilderment.

As if he had read her thoughts, En-dor stated, "I have never killed another man and hope I never do, but I had to save your lives, didn't I?"

Ashannah burst out crying, but as soon as she regained control, she thanked him. Nevertheless, it took all of her will power to calm down enough to console the crying Elissa. En-dor went to retrieve his cache of fish, but neither Ashannah nor Gennah were able to eat anything that evening.

En-dor began pacing restlessly. "I should have known that carrying all of these things would draw the likes of them to us. It's going to be worse, the closer we get to the city."

The three of them had already been keeping watches at night, to keep the fire going, so preying animals would leave them alone. En-dor doubted that anyone would threaten them at night, but he slept with his bow in his hand and his quiver of arrows by his side.

The next morning, it was obvious that none of them had slept much. En-dor caught some fish and insisted that they eat something before continuing on their way. He had no idea how stunned the two women remained from learning that men would injure or even kill one another for things! They looked at their own knives with a new respect, but also with a certain loathing.

When they set out, once again, for Tel Phar, they began meeting other traders, all of them men, some going towards the city, others going in the way from which they had come. A little later they saw their first cart, loaded down with more things than they had on their travois. It renewed their desire to have one, too, but they were wondering if it was worth the dangers they were facing.

In the early afternoon, they came to a fork in the road, and although all of the traders ahead of them had taken the left fork, which was wider and obviously more traveled, En-dor led them onto the right fork, which was hardly more than a path, saying, "This will take us to the village of Al-Labah, where only Virgins, like you, live. I want you to spend the night there, with our things, while I go into Tel Phar and find some of my friends to finish the trip with us."

"That's a good plan, En-dor!" Ashannah exclaimed.

Gennah was instantly relieved that they wouldn't be going into Tel Phar yet. She hadn't even confided to Ashannah, that she was terrified that they might encounter Ator there.

Chapter Seven

The sun was just beginning to set as the four travelers approached the village of Al-Labah. The reflection of the sun made it seem as if the little conical dwellings of the women's homes were made of new and shining copper. Lumps of unshed tears filled Ashannah's and Gennah's throats. It looked so much like Al-Rah! The terror of their recent experience fled from their minds and hearts. They felt as if they were at home and safe, once more. As they drew nearer they saw some of the women were coming out to see who they were.

"Gennah! I believe they are afraid of us!" Ashannah gasped.

"I'm afraid you're right, Ashannah!" I can actually feel their fear.!"

"I think that they believe that we've come to harm them!" Ashannah gulped.

"After last night, I can see why," Gennah said.

"You two go on," Endor whispered, also aware of the women's fear. "I"ll wait here with the things, while you go tell them of our wishes."

Ashannah and Gennah noticed how the women relaxed a little as they approached without the man.

"May the blessings of Ninlil be upon you and guide your steps in peace," one of the women called out.

This told them that the temple and the entire village of Al-Labah was under the protection of Ninlil.

"And may the blessing of Inanna be upon you and everyone in your village," Gennah replied, letting the women of Al-Labah know that they, too, were Virgins in the service of the Goddess. "We come from the village of Al-Rah, under the protection of the ancient Mother Goddess, Inanna, and the guidance of the High Priestess, Kasha Al-Rah." Gennah continued. "We request that we might remain in the safety of Al-Labah for the duration of the night and perhaps another night, as well, if we may.

The woman who had first spoken walked up to Gennah and looked directly into her eyes, "Your coloring is strange, but I perceive that you do not wish us any harm. You, your Virgin companion and her babe may remain, but not the man."

"As you speak, so shall it be," Gennah assured her.

"I will get our things," Ashannah announced and walked back to where En-dor was waiting. Again the women of Al-Labah grew tense, but no one said or did anything. As Ashannah returned dragging the travois behind her, and En-dor headed back towards the road leading to Tel Phar, the women of Al-Labah relaxed once more.

"I am Tornah Al-Labah, the High Priestess of our village," the tall, stately woman announced. Gennah noted her beak-like nose, piercing eyes and gray-streaked hair.

"I am Gennah Al-Rah, a weaver of baskets and cloth. And this is my companion, the Virgin, Ashannah Al-Rah, and her infant, Elissa. Ashannah is a very fine healer and a beautiful singer."

Ashannah, blushing over the introduction, was relieved to be able to bow low to the High Priestess, hoping in this way to hide her embarrassment.

"And I see that you are much beloved of one another," Tornah observed with a smile.

"Spoken truly," they both replied, noting that her fomerly austere appearance had now softened.

"Let us go into our temple and give thanks to Ninlil for delivering you safely to our village." Tornah raised her voice when she said this, so a lot of the women could hear.

As they approached the temple, Ashannah noticed that it was somewhat larger than theirs. Instead of shale, the upper wall was made of large stones like the ones from the stream bed she had used in their home. She couldn't see the mortar well, but it seemed different from the clay of their soil.

Upon entering the temple, tears again filled her eyes as the familiar odors of hot oil, sweet grass and damp earth filled her nostrils. The taper burning in front of the image of Ninlil was the only light, so she could not tell if the walls were decorated with paintings.

Tornah and the women of Al-:Labah began to sing a litany to Ninlil. The Virgins' responses were enthusiastic and powerful. Ashannah and Gennah felt great gratitude to the Goddess and to the women. They had no idea that it was their presence that had filled the women with strength and joy.

Just before leaving the temple, Ashannah took one of her bundles filled with mugwort and laid it on the altar before the image of Ninlil. She took a pinch of the herb and threw it on the flame burning there. As its pungence filled the temple, the Virgins all sighed with pleasure.

Then Tornah led them towards the center of the village, where a large fire pit had been formed.

"Leenah! Estah! Quick! Get some wood for a fire before it is dark. The rest of you get what food you can, and we will have a feast in honor of our guests."

Ashannah and Gennah were most appreciative of this, as they knew that at this time of year the village provisions were somewhat diminished. The women of Al-Labah were grateful for the herbs and spices Ashannah offered to make the food more tasty.

"How long has it taken you to come here from Al-Rah?" inquired a short, wiry woman with a raspy voice by the name of Gannah.

"A handful of sun journeys and that many moon journeys," replied Ashannah, holding up four fingers. "Dragging our goods and carrying the babe slowed us down some. We brought many things to trade for a cart and also a shovel."

"A cart would require many things, indeed," Gannah said. "They are very useful, though. We have two in our village."

Ashannah became very excited by this news and wished it were still light so that she could inspect them. Gennah, however, couldn't restrain a yawn.

'We have an empty hut near here, where you may sleep," Tornah said. "The weaver looks as though she might fall asleep here by the fire."

Somewhat embarrassed, Gennah acknowledged that she was very tired.

At this point, two little girls, one near menarche and the other probably two or three sun cycles younger, came up to Ashannah.

"May we … may we see the baby?" asked the oldest girl.

Ashannah was pleased to show off the sleeping Elissa. She bent low so they could see her. "Her name is Elissa," she whispered. "You may see her again tomorrow, when she is awake."

The following morning, a woman with very long, yellow hair, almost the color of the sun, came with some bowls of porridge, similar to what they made in Al-Rah. Ashannah got out some cinnamon to put on it. As she sprinkled some of the spice on the woman's porridge, she noticed that her eyes were a bright blue like Gennah's.

When the woman tasted the porridge with the cinnamon on it, she exclaimed, "I've never tasted anything like this before!. It's wonderful!" Ashannah insisted that she keep one of the bags, which she had brought for trading.

"I don't seem to remember your name," Ashannah admitted.

"It's Leenah," the woman replied. Ashannah noted how Leenah tied her long hair back with a piece of linen and wondered if she ever sat on it. It seemed long enough. She watched as the woman automatically swept her hair aside as she seated herself.

As they were eating, they compared the herbs, spices and wild edibles the women of each village used. Suddenly Leenah blurted out, "Your lives are much like ours! Why are you endangering yourselves by going to Tel Phar?"

"Why I … I guess we didn't know it was dangerous!" sputtered Gennah. "One of the women from Et-Ray went last year. She didn't speak of danger."

"Where is Et-Ray?" Leenah asked.

"It's a trading town a hand's span of the sun's journey from Al-Rah," Gennah explained.

"Well, maybe if she lives in a trading town, she wouldn't think it was dangerous. But for Virgins of the Temple, it is very dangerous!"

Both Ashannah and Gennah were sitting rigidly by now, wanting and yet not wanting to hear more.

"The men of Tel Phar don't want people to honor the Goddess anymore. And they especially do not want their men to come to our temple. They took Ninlil out of her temple in Tel Phar and put their God, Enlil, in her place."

"What is a god, and who is Enlil?" Gennah interrupted.

"Leenah laughed. "Can you imagine such a thing as a god? A man being so honored? As if a man could have children and people the earth, but they think that Enlil is the father of us all!" As she finished, she was no longer laughing.

"Why I haven't heard of a "god" before," exclaimed Ashannah. "Do you mean that they think their god is like the Goddess, but is a man?" She paused a moment, but finally continued, "Well, they don't have a temple in Et-Ray! Only the ugly ... er ... only the market place." She hoped Gennah hadn't heard her word describing the market.

"All right, Elissa! I'll put you down for awhile," Ashannah exclaimed to the struggling child. With her mind still on the conversation, she placed her baby stomach down. The infant curled up her knees, pushed up on her hands and actually crawled for a few paces.

"Did you see that, Gennah?" Ashannah cried out with excitement. "She's crawling!"

Gennah stooped towards the baby, holding out her hands. "Come here, Elissa. Come to Gennah." By then the baby's strength had given out, and she was flat on her belly again. With Gennah's coaxing, she tried to get up on her hands and knees. Ashannah gave her a little boost, and the child was able to crawl a few more paces. When Elissa's strength gave out again, Gennah swooped her up in her arms, shouting for joy, "What a big girl you're getting to be!" The baby was laughing along with her. Gennah put Elissa down on her stomach, holding her up a little, while the infant, again, curled up her legs and pushed up on her arms. This time she was able to crawl the entire space, in order to reach her mother.

"Well, we'll always remember Al-Labah as the place where Elissa began to crawl," said Ashannah, twirling with her laughing daughter. Then it became evident that the child was hungary as well as tired. Ashannah offered her breast, which Elissa began sucking eagerly.

In their excitement over Elissa, the disturbing conversation about Tel Phar and the god, Enlil, had been momentarily forgotten.

Gennah took it up again, saying, "You mean the men aren't coming to Ninlil's temple anymore?"

"Oh, there's a few faithful ones," replied Leenah. "But they don't dare come by the main road. They sneak in through the forest. They're the ones who trade for us. That's how we got our carts."

"Oh, could we see your carts?" Ashannah asked, perhaps unconsciously changing the uncomfortable subject once more.

"Why not?" replied Leenah. "They're probably down by the garden."

"Oh, I'd love to see your garden, too!" Ashannah exclaimed.

Leenah laughed, "Well, as soon as Elissa's finished eating ..."

"She can eat while we're walking," Ashannah assured her, as she and Gennah got up to follow her.

"Al-Labah is a lot larger than Al-Rah." observed Gennah.

"Unfortunately, many of the huts are empty, what with so few births and some of the women choosing to go live in Tel Phar."

"But I thought you said Tel Phar is dangerous," argued Gennah. "Why would they want to go there?"

"It's not dangerous if you give yourself to a man. He will be sure to protect you. To own a woman, or many women, gives a man importance," she explained.

"But who would want to be owned by a man?" Ashannah exclaimed.

"Well none of us who have stayed here," Leenah vehemently replied. "But perhaps it is safer, now, to be owned by a man."

Both ashannah and Gennah were speechless. As they were approaching the garden, Gennah noticed three huts that were in very bad repair.

"Did something happen to those huts?" she asked, finding it hard to believe that the women would allow them to get in such a state.

"I'm afraid so," admitted Estah, a younger woman who had been working in the garden. She was in direct contrast to Leenah, having shiny, tightly curled hair, the color of a raven's wings, and dark brown eyes. "Some young men from Tel Phar came one night, not long ago, calling us whores and threatening to destroy the whole village. At first we couldn't believe what we were seeing and just stared at them, but finally Gannah ran towards them screaming and threatening them with a hatchet. We quickly joined her, waving shovels, knives or anything we could get hold of quickly, and they ran off."

"This is Estah, my lover," Leenah interrupted shyly.

"What is a whore," Ashannah interrupted, hardly noticing the introduction.

"I"m not sure, but they think it's something terrible," Estah replied, as she kissed Leenah on the cheek.

"So you … you aren't so safe here," Gennah said.

"Well, we're not just waiting for them to come again," Estah cried out. "There's not a woman in the village who doesn't have a knife,shovel or hatchet to protect herself and the village, too, if necessary. It would surely take more than three or four of them to do much harm, now that we're ready for them!

Again, Gennah and Ashannah were aghast, but they knew they would do the same thing if Al-Rah were in danger.

"I've been looking forward to seeing Tel Phar for so long, but now … I don't know," Gennah stammered.

"Gennah, we can't go back without trading our things!" Ashannah cried out. "But … . I'm afraid, too!"

"Well, if you just don't let on that you're Virgins of the Goddess, you'll probably be all right," Leenah said. "None of them know you like they do us."

"It has just been during the last twelve or thirteen sun cycles that this has been happening,." Estah explained. "At first, when a couple of boats came down the Great Sea from the north, full of men with metal tipped spears and bows and arrows, preaching about the superiority of their god over Ninlil, everyone laughed, but after awhile more and more of the men began to listen to them. They definitely want to destroy the Goddess and replace her with their god."

"But how can they do that?" Ashannah broke in.

"By now in Tel Phar, there are more who believe in Enlil than there are believers in the Goddess, especially among the men," Estah continued. "They call us, Virgins, terrible names because we refuse to belong to them. Some of them even say we should be put to death. Any man who stands up for us is punished and if he doesn't promise to worship Enlil, he is finally killed. So you see how dangerous it is for the men who remain faithful to Ninlil and continue to live in Tel Phar. But there are some who are not only faithful to Ninlil, but take risks in order to help us. We are very grateful to them."

Both Ashannah and Gennah stared at the two women in disbelief.

"Just look at those huts," Leenah exclaimed, "if you don't believe me!" They did as she said and tears filled their eyes.

"I think you should go to Tel Phar and see for yourselves," Estah counseled. "But don't say anything that would give you away as Virgins. Act like you belong to the man who came with you."

Ashannah and Gennah wondered if they would be able to do this convincingly. Then they saw two women approaching them with the two little girls who had been curious about Elissa the night before.

"I am the Virgin, Fannah Al-Labah," the older of the two introduced herself. "And this is my daughter Meldah. She would like to see your baby." Fannah was of medium height with light brown hair and hazel eyes. Meldah looked very much like her mother.

"And I am the Virgin Deenah Al-Labah," the other woman announced.

The women from Al-Rah were astonished to see that she had hair almost as red as Gennah's. Her little girl's hair was brown with reddish tints. "This is my daughter, Nella. She would like to see your baby, too."

"I remember you from last night," Ashannah said smiling proudly. "It's too bad you weren't here a little sooner. Elissa started crawling for the first time. Right now she seems pretty sleepy. But you can see her better than you were able to last night."

The two girls crowded up close in order to see the sleeping baby. They were obviously disappointed that she was asleep, but they observed how much she looked like Ashannah.

That evening while the women were eating Elissa again showed off her new ability to crawl. Nella and Meldah were ecstatic.

En-dor returned early the next morning. Remaining outside the confines of Al-Labah, he gave the low whistle that he and Ashannah had used in Al-Rah. The two women were ready to join him and quickly went out to meet him, dragging the travois behind them.

"Where's Elissa?" he asked.

"We thought it would be easier to leave her here, although that does mean we'd have to come back here before going home," explained Ashannah. "There is a woman here who has enough milk for her baby and Elissa, at least for a journey of the sun." She didn't mention their fear of the city, itself.

"That's a good idea. You could come here while I finish up my trading. I should help you today, since you have never traded before," he observed.

Gennah started to say that she had traded many times in Et-Ray, but stopped herself, realizing, by now, that Tel Phar was quite different from their little trading town.

"We're really grateful to you, En-dor," Ashannah said. "We definitely want you to stay with us while we're in Tel Phar."

When they got to the main road leading to the seaport, a man came towards them greeting En-dor. He was at least a head taller than their friend and very muscular. His eyes were dark brown, almost black, the same color as his tightly curled hair. His beautiful dark skin was the color of mahogany.

"This is Da-nid," En-dor said. "I had hoped to get Sa-dor to help us, too, but he doesn't seem to be in Tel Phar, now. I'll lead the way. Ashannah, you and Gennah come next with the supplies, and Da-nid can walk behind. That way, I don't think anyone will try to take anything."

Perhaps the two women had looked at the huge man with some misgiving, because as they took their places, he assured them that he was a believer in the Goddess and respected her Virgins. Reassured, they felt doubly protected seeing that a thief would not be so ready to challenge such a large man.

"From here on out, though, we had better be careful of what we say," warned En-dor. "It is better that they think you women are our … our … I can't remember what they call the women who belong to them."

"Wives," prompted Da-nid.

It had taken half a hand's span of the sun's journey to get back to the main road, and it would take them another full hand's span before they began to see the buildings of Tel Phar. The two women were becoming excited, but were also fearful, especially Gennah, who was still wondering if they would meet up with Ator. They continued on until Gennah suddenly stopped, exclaiming, "Ugh! What's that smell?"

"Well mostly it's the salt and the fish from the Great Sea. Also, it's spoiling food and people's waste. It isn't as clean here as it is in Et-Ray and certainly not as clean as Al-Rah or Al-Labah," En-dor said. "There are many, many people besides those who live here. People come from other cities along the Great Sea, as well as Tel Phar. There are big dwellings here for those people to stay in while they are here. The people who own them have many fine things for putting up these strangers and feeding them. Every time I come here, Tel Phar seems to be larger."

"Do you stay in one of those places?" Gennah wanted to know. She was on the verge of tears, because something about the odors had reminded her of the way Ator's hut smelled when he had dragged her in there.

"Oh, no," En-dor laughed. "I don't have enough to trade for something like that. I just find a place to sleep somewhere on the edge of the city. But I think you and Gennah better return to Al-Labah before it gets dark, even if we haven't finished with your trading. They … they don't seem to respect women very much … women who aren't in their own homes, anyway. Especially at night."

Ashannah was noticing how much warmer it was in Tel Phar than in Et-Ray. She had already noticed how damp her skin felt in Al-Labah. As they began passing the little stalls where people had things to trade, however, she forgot her discomfort.

"I didn't know there were places this big!" Gennah exclaimed, looking all around. The size of the place helped her to hope that the chances of meeting Ator were perhaps less than she had feared, and she relaxed a bit. "Don't they have a market building?" she asked.

It's further on," Da-nid replied. "It's not nearly large enough for all the people with things for trading."

"Oh, look!" cried Ashannah, stopping to inspect them. "Here's some shovels and hatchets and knives."

"I know another place with copper and bronze things where I can get a better bargain," whispered En-dor. "They're better made, too. It would be good, though, to get the shovel soon, so we don't have so many things to carry around."

Then they began passing places where people were trading food. Both women were amazed at the variety. There were fruits, roots and nuts they had never seen before.

"We should get a little food to take with us on our trip home," Ashannah suggested.

"You're right," replied En-dor, "but it would be better to do that last so we're not carrying food around with all of these other things."

He led them into a small side path, where they came to a place with many more copper and bronze items than the first place they had seen. Before they got close, En-dor told Gennah and Da-nid to stay back with the travois, while he and Ashannah took off the things they wanted to trade for the shovel.

"If they see all that we have with us, they may ask more for the shovel," he advised. The women were impressed with his knowledge of trading, and Gennah was relieved that Da-nid would be with her while they waited. Nevertheless she was becoming uneasy, noticing how men looked at her red hair. Red hair seemed to be a rarity here, as it was at home. She wished that she had a cloth to tie over it, which she noticed that most of the women were doing. While they were waiting, she found a small cloth among their things and tied it around her head. Da-nid sighed with relief.

When Ashannah and En-dor arrived at the metal vendor's stall, he advised, "You pick out which shovel you would like, Ashannah, but let me do the bargaining."

It didn't take Ashannah long to choose the shovel she wanted. It was somewhat larger and stronger than the one they already owned. It took

En-dor and the trader half of a hand's span of the sun's journey to come to an agreement over the shovel. Ashannah admired the way En-dor bargained with the metal worker. He even managed to have a few of their things left over.

After they had finished bargaining, the metal worker brought out two clay cups, one for himself and one for En-dor. Ashannah would have enjoyed something to drink, herself, but after she smelled the fermentation of the beverage, she was glad he hadn't offered her any. Finally they were able to join Gennah and Da-nid and return to the main road.

"There's some water for everyone just up the road," said En-dor. "I know you're all thirsty."

The water source turned out to be a spring box, something like Ashannah's, but larger. They watched a woman and two children approach the spring box and drink directly from it. Ashannah and Gennah wondered if they would be able to see themselves in it. When they weren't able, they noticed that the sun had gone behind some clouds.

As they got closer to the building where trading was done, it became both more crowded and much noisier. It was uncomfortable having strangers brush against them, although they realized it could not be helped. Playing children would almost knock them over as they chased each other in their games. En-dor suggested that they take up their former positions.

Gennah looked at the baskets and cloths set up for trading and wanted to inspect them more closely, as well as to speak with the weavers.

As if sensing her desires, En-dor suggested, "If you want to look around in there, we can after we get the cart. The people who make carts are down by the seashore. They're next to the boat makers so they can share tools."

Since neither Gennah nor Ashannah had ever seen a boat before, much less a large body of water, they were eager to go there, although the stench of rotting fish became almost unbearable.

When they finally arrived, they realized right away why the odor was so strong. Apparently the fishermen cleaned their catches right on the shore, leaving the entrails there until the tide came in to wash them out. Their amazement at the vast expanse of the sea helped them forget the odor. It was difficult to see where the sea ended and the sky began. At least they understood the sound they had been hearing, when they saw the breakers crashing along the shore line.

As they approached the cart maker, they could see only one other cart besides the one he was working on. When En-dor told him they were interested in acquiring a cart, he stood up to look them over, wiping the sweat from his forehead as he did so. En-dor, Da-nid and the two women did the same thing. The very air seemed filled with particles of water.

"Well it seems like every one else is having the same idea as you. I just can't keep up with it all," the cart maker complained, but they could sense that he was actually quite pleased with the situation.

"I guess if you have enough to trade for it, you could have the one I just finished last night. But even though it is small, I don't know if you have enough." He was already eyeing the bundles on the travois. "It takes a lot of work to make one of these."

At once, Gennah spoke up, "Well, it takes a lot of work to make baskets and shawls and cloths, as well." Then she saw En-dor looking at her and understood that he wanted to do the talking.

"You make really fine carts," En-dor said to placate him, although he hadn't seen many carts to compare with these.

"Well," the cart maker drawled, suspecting En-dor was flattering him, "good enough that people want them."

Although the cart was smaller than the few they had seen, Gennah and Ashannah were eager to have it.

"Let's see what you have to trade for it," the cart maker said, coming to the point. He didn't seem to be impressed with the baskets and bundles of herbs and spices, but when he came across the finely woven shawl, he picked it up and said with a grudging appreciation, "I can see that a lot of work was put into this. Is it the only one you have?"

"We have more cloth, but not as finely woven as this," Gennah admitted

He looked over some of the other pieces and took out three more, thus indicating that the four pieces would satisfy him. Since they had thought he would take all of their things, the women readily agreed, perhaps too soon for En-dor's liking.

"Perhaps you would like to see a larger one I am working on with a bronze body." They followed him around the shed where they could see it. Both of the women's eyes grew round with appreciation. "You could have one like this for four more of those finely woven shawls," he offered.

En-dor was quick to speak up this time. "Three shawls like this one should be worth this cart. It takes a lot of work to spin such fine thread, and of course it takes much longer to weave."

Both of the women were surprised and pleased with his perception. "But we wouldn't be able to finish three more until next spring," Gennah said.

"Well, I'll be making more carts like this one. If you say so, I'll have one ready for you next spring."

Chapter Eight

With great satisfaction, Ashannah and Gennah packed their remaining items in the new vehicle. The cart maker offered to take care of the travois, because he believed he could use the heavier branches for handles. Just as they were about to turn away, however, Gennah cried out, pointing to the sea, "What's that on the water? Is it an animal? A huge fish? Or … what?"

They all turned to look where she was pointing, and the cart maker began to laugh. "It's none of those things, lady! Just watch a little longer. You're in for a surprise!"

Ashannah exclaimed, "Why, it's moving! It's coming towards us! And there are people sitting and standing around … around …what is that?"

"It's a sail," the cart maker informed her. "It's what makes it move. That is, the sail catches the wind, and that moves the whole boat and whatever is on it."

"But how are they staying on top of the water like that?" she wanted to know.

"Because they're on a raft, that's how," the cart maker answered, amused. "Haven't you ever seen one before?"

"Why, no!" the two women exclaimed together.

As the huge raft came close to the shore, they could make out the balsa logs, as well as the people sitting on them. A man standing at the back of the raft, was pushing a stick around in the water. The women gradually figured out that he was guiding the boat in this way.

"And what if there's no wind?" Gennah asked.

"Then they have to row, and that's much harder," Da-nid explained.

As if they had heard Gennah and Da-nid, some of the men on the raft picked up long sticks, went over to the edge of the boat and began to dip the sticks into the water. The boat seemed to move much faster with this help.

As the raft got closer, Ashannah cried out, "Look at those huge baskets and ... and bundles! Are they made of wood?"

When no one came up with an answer, Gennah exclaimed, "Just think of riding on top of the water like that!" The two women continued to stand there, amazed by what they were seeing.

When the raft lurched to a stop, the rowers threw down their oars, jumped over the side into the shallow water and pushed the raft up onto the shore.

Other men came out from a building, nearby, pushing empty carts. Together, all of the men loaded the baskets and wooden bundles from the raft onto the carts and wheeled the loaded carts to the building in which they stored the supplies. After the raft was emptied, some of the men pushed it further up on the shore. Then they all headed for the city.

"Would it be all right if we went up closer to see the raft better?" Ashannah asked.

"I'll go with you," offered the cart maker. "I used to make boats and I came here on a raft, just like this one."

When the women, En-dor, Da-nid and the cart maker got up closer, Gennah cried out, "Why, it's made of wood! They've tied the trunks of trees together!"

"That's right, lady," the cart maker affirmed. "At one time, those logs were the trunks of balsam trees. We don't have any of those trees around here. Balsam makes the best rafts, because the wood is light and floats good on the water." He walked over and picked up an oar. "The oars are made of harder wood." They noticed that the oars had been cut to be larger at the end that went into the water."And the ... the sail is made from a very heavy cloth!" Ashannah cried out.

"How did they ever weave something that large?" Gennah exclaimed as she walked over to examine the sail more closely. "Oh, I see now! They have stitched many pieces together!"

"There are even larger boats made out of one tree trunk," the cart maker continued. "We don't have trees that big around here, either. On those boats, they have slaves to row them."

The two women had never heard of slaves, but before they could question him, Da-nid asked, "Was it boats like this that the men from the north came in?"

"That's right, and I was one of those men," the cart maker affirmed proudly.

All four of them looked at him fearfully, but apparently he had no idea that the women were Virgins of the Goddess, nor that En-dor and Da-nid were believers.

Quickly, En-dor spoke up, "We had better get our cart and go back to town." Gennah and Ashannah picked up the handles of the cart, soon discovering that one of them could easily manage it, even though it was almost half full with their remaining items.

"This cart is really wonderful, Ashannah!" Gennah said. "It's so much easier than dragging the branches. Just think how it will be when we have the other cart, as well! But I'm afraid I was being foolish to think I can spin and weave three fine shawls in one sun cycle."

"Gennah, I'm sure I can learn to spin cotton and linen fine enough. I'll begin working on it as soon as we get home," promised Ashannah. "Wouldn't that help?"

"Of course it would," Gennah readily agreed, "But you'll be busy with gardening and foraging."

"Not so much," Ashannah replied. "The garden is all in and there isn't a lot of foraging for another moon's cycle. And it will be easier to watch over our little girl while I'm spinning, than when I'm gardening or foraging. She's getting to be pretty heavy. But just think! She's crawling! It won't be long and she'll be walking!"

"You know, Ashannah," Gennah interrupted, "there's another small cloth for you to tie around your head. I notice that nearly all of the women, here, are wearing something over their hair. I also notice that some men are staring at your shiny black curls."

"Really?" Ashannah asked, astonished. She hadn't even noticed. As soon as they got to the market building, Gennah got out the cloth, and Ashannah put it on.

As they prepared to enter, En-dor whispered, "Remember, let Da-nid and me go first, so that people will think that you are our wives."

The two women fought back feelings of resentment, knowing his advice was sound.

"I'd like to look at some of the cloth and then go see some of the basket weavers," Gennah whispered back.

"Why don't I stay here with Da-nid and the cart," Ashannah offered. "It would really be hard pushing the cart around in that crowd."

When Gennah examined the cloths on display, she saw that none were as finely woven as her shawl. She quickly understood why the cart maker was so interested in having more. Then her nose informed her that she was approaching some wool. Since she hadn't learned to spin the wool as evenly as she would have liked, she admired the superiority of the woolen cloths on display. She noticed a woman who was spinning some wool, while waiting for business to come her way. Somehow the spinner was pulling harder on the fibers, to smooth out the natural tangles before it reached the spindle. Gennah closely watched the woman's fingers, until she thought she understood how she was doing it. She wondered if she would dare ask her to let her try, but quickly decided not to, since she could tell the woman was already nervous by her close scrutiny.

Just then, the spinner noticed the huge basket Gennah was carrying. "Is that your basket?" she asked. "Are you interested in trading it? I mean, maybe for some nice wool?" She leaned over and pulled some raw wool from a basket at her side.

Gennah looked over at En-dor. She wasn't sure if she should do the bargaining.

"You know more about these things than I do," En-dor said, but he was relieved that she had deferred to him.

"I would like to trade this basket for some wool," Gennah said. "How much would you give me for it? Enough to fill it?"

"If I fill my basket with your wool," here the woman hesitated, "then how would I keep the basket and not the wool, too? You surely wouldn't want me to keep both!" She laughed at the predicament.

"I have another basket almost like this one," Gennah hastily replied. Handing the basket to En-dor, she said, "I'll go get it."

Ashannah was delighted when she learned Gennah was getting some wool. After Gennah returned to the wool weaver's stall, En-dor took the basket and began stuffing it with wool. Gennah could tell that the spinner wanted to put it in herself, but didn't have the nerve to take it from the man. Gennah wanted to stop En-dor, but she knew a wife wouldn't show such independence with the man who owned her. And, *here,* she was supposed to be his wife. Gennah thanked the woman, who at least seemed pleased with her new basket.

"I'm ready to go, now," Gennah announced.

After they rejoined Ashannah and Da-nid, En-dor said, "If we're going to get some food, we should do it now. We ought to be returning to Al-Labah soon." They went directly to the food stalls and were admiring the many things being offered, when Gennah felt the tiny hairs on the back of her neck prickle. She turned around and was shocked to see Ator glaring at her. She had forgotten all about him!

When Ator saw that the red-haired woman was, indeed, Gennah, he snarled and lunged for her. She screamed, and, as one, Ashannah, Da-nid and En-dor turned and leaped in front of Gennah, warding off the snarling Ator.

"Get out of my way!" he screamed. "She's nothing but a whore!"

"She's a Vir … "Ashannah began.

"She is my wife!" En-dor interrupted.

Ator stood as tall as his naturally short stature allowed and looked En-dor in the eye. "I don't believe you!" he shouted.

"You might as well," En-dor calmly replied. "There are others here to back me up."

When Ator saw the size of Da-nid, he spat, turned on his heel and lost himself in the crowd. A few bystanders had watched with interest and then turned away, disappointed that the confrontation had been so short. No one else disputed En-dor's claim.

Both Ashannah and Gennah were hardly able to concentrate on the trading of Ashannah's herbs and spices for food, but the merchants quickly appreciated their fine quality and they were able to get all the food they could carry, much of it being things that they had never tasted before.

They were especially intrigued with a large yellow fruit which the vendor called an apple. He had them taste some pieces of dried apple, and they saw right away how much sweeter the pieces were than the fresh fruit, which actually wasn't so sweet.

"Be sure to save the seeds for planting. Those apples come off a nice shady tree," the vendor advised them. Ashannah was excited, anticipating having trees with fruit like this on them. The women of Al-Rah had gathered berries and dried them, with much the same result, but she had never before seen fruit this large.

They were barely out of Tel Phar, when Gennah lost the precarious hold she had on her self control and began to sob. Since it was late in the afternoon, there were few travelers on the road. Nevertheless, En-dor and Da-nid were concerned when Ashannah gathered Gennah in her arms to comfort her. They stood around the two women, trying to hide them, when finally Da-nid spoke, "I understand why you are crying, Gennah, but please try to let us continue on before it gets dark."

"You could be putting us in danger," En-dor pleaded. Gennah struggled to pull herself together and the two women resolutely resumed walking down the road. The men put themselves in the lead and no one spoke again.

"Look at the size of that cart!" Ashannah suddenly cried out, breaking the silence. "Why, it has two wheels!"

As they came closer to the strange vehicle, they watched in awe as they saw a man even larger than Da-nid pulling the cart by grasping handles coming from each side. The load was clearly much too heavy for him. They could see his muscles straining with the weight, and his lips were pulled back, exposing his teeth. They noticed a huge scar forming some kind of pattern across his shoulders, and underneath that they saw numerous cuts all down his back to his waist. Some of these latter were still bleeding.

"What did he do to deserve that?" Ashannah cried out, tears filling her eyes.

"You'd better keep your woman in line!" growled a burly man, armed with a whip, who was walking behind the cart. Although she had never seen a whip before, Ashannah understood, at once, how the man pulling the cart had received the cuts on his back.

"C'mon, Ashannah!" En-dor called out. "It is none of our affair!"

Tears also filled Gennah's eyes, when En-dor told them to move on. He looked very angry, but Ashannah knew that he was really afraid. After they were well out of the hearing of the strange pair, Da-nid whispered, "He's a captive from a battle!" Neither of the women knew what a battle nor a captive was. En-dor seemed reluctant to talk about it, and told Da-nid to wait until they were off the main road before he explained it to them. They continued on in glum silence until they came to the turnoff for Al-Labah.

"I guess you won't need me anymore, En-dor," Da-nid said, the explanation forgotten. He quickly turned and began his way back to Tel Phar. He was clearly afraid, also.

"It was truly a horrible sight," En-dor said, his voice husky. "A battle is when two groups of men fight each other with bows and arrows and all kinds of spears and hatchets and things I've never even seen. It's usually over a piece of land. I've never seen one and hope I never do! If some of the men on the losing side are still alive, they become slaves for the winners. As you saw, a slave is treated very badly. This is the first one I've ever seen!"

"And that's who the cart maker said pulled the oars on the larger boats!" Ashannah exclaimed.

"I'm afraid you're right," En-dor sadly agreed. Ashannah and Gennah stared at him in shock. They had not even appreciated the cart, which had been about three times as large as the one they hoped to obtain the following spring, They were aware that En-dor was as shocked as they. The three of them began walking towards Al-Labah in complete silence.

When the little village of Virgins came into view, En-dor informed them that he would return by the forest after spending one more day in Tel Phar. Then he turned to begin his way back to the city.

The women of Al-Labah began to rejoice with Ashannah and Gennah over their new cart, but quickly saw that they were extremely upset. Some of the children came running up, and, seeing the food, wanted to eat right away. Their mothers chased them away, promising to eat later, when the woman who had been caring for Elissa came forward. "Your girl is a fine baby," she said, as she handed Elissa over to Ashannah.

Elissa began crowing happily at being returned to her mother, but Ashannah began to sob at the same time that she offered the baby one of her milk-laden breasts.

"Have ... have you ever seen a slave?" she blurted out through her tears.

Before anyone could answer, she continued. "It was his eyes!" she exclaimed. "They ... they had no light in them!"

"Yes," Gennah said, "you're right. There was no light in his eyes! It was as though he was dead, even though he was walking!"

"And the eyes of the man with the whip were worse," Ashannah continued. "They were like knives that could cut right through you!"

The women from Al-Labah quickly gathered around the two travelers to comfort them. None of them had ever seen a slave, although some had heard of them.

In the meantime, the children were, again, being drawn to the cart loaded with food. They were especially drawn to the apples, which they had never seen before. Ashannah gave out all but three, instructing the children to save the seeds and to bring them to her when they were finished eating.

As the children brought back the seeds, Ashannah's heart went out to a little girl, close to menarche, with wavy black hair and a wide smile, reminding her of herself. As the child poured the seeds into Ashannah's hand, the woman sensed that she wanted something.

"What is your name, little one?" she inquired.

The girl suddenly became shy and started to run off, but then came back and whispered into Ashannah's ear, "Could … could I please have a seed?"

"Only if you tell me your name," Ashannah insisted, smiling.

"It's … it's Flora." The child continued whispering.

"What a lovely name!" Ashannah said, as she poured the seeds back into Flora's hand. "You're going to save and plant them, aren't you?"

"Oh, yes," the child answered. "They make big trees, don't they?"

"I've never seen them, but that's what the man at the market told me."

"Then I'm going to plant them at the back of our garden, so the men who come through the forest, can't see us working there."

The sun was finishing its setting when the two travelers realized how tired they were. Tornah observed this and suggested they retire to their hut. She promised that they would have an especially fine feast during the sun's next journey.

The two women lay close to one another with Elissa in between. They needed to comfort one another, after the ominous events of the day.

The sun had traveled several hand spans by the time Gennah, Ashannah and Elissa came out of the hut the next day. "We would probably still be in there sleeping, if Elissa hadn't become hungry," Ashannah said, rueful of the daylight they had lost.

"Well, today might not be as exciting as yesterday, but it will certainly be more peaceful," Gennah remarked, with some irony.

The two women walked over to the stream that ran beside Al-Labah to wash up. Gennah put Elissa down on her blanket, and the little girl promptly pushed herself up and crawled off of it.

"Look at how strong she's gotten!" Ashannah exclaimed. "That one will be walking soon, you can be sure!"

"And she's going to be something to watch out for," Gennah laughed, as Elissa made right for the stream. Gennah picked her up and then splashed a little water on her. Elissa definitely didn't like the iciness of the water and was content to sit on her blanket and watch her mothers as they bathed.

"What's that!" Gennah screamed, as she heard a crackling sound from the forest. She grabbed for Ashannah, and Elissa began to cry. Ashannah pushed away from Gennah and ran over and picked up her baby. Gennah stared hard at the forest, but saw nothing, nor did she hear any more unusual sounds.

"I thought ... I thought it was Ator!" Gennah said with a trembling voice, as she waded out of the stream.

"I thought so, too," Ashannah agreed, "But now I don't think so. I don't believe he followed us here with Da-nid spending the rest of the day with us, and how else would he know where we are."

"Well, he might figure it out that we would spend some time in Al-Labah," Gennah said.

"He might," Ashannah agreed, again peering into the forest, as she tried to comfort Elissa at the same time. "I guess we can't know for sure that he didn't, so let's go back to the village, where we'll be safer."

They went over by the central fire pit to make some porridge. They saw Leenah approaching, and Gennah whispered, "Let's not trouble the women about Ator."

The golden-haired woman came up to them very excited. "Tornah says we are to have a great feast, tonight. I'm baking some emmer buns. Could I have a few of those good herbs of yours, Ashannah?"

"We traded most of the herbs for food, but I'll go see if there's some left over" Ashannah went to the cart and found just enough sage for Leenah's batch. She watched as Leenah poured out the emmer mixture on baking rocks, similar to hers at home. Then she asked Leenah if she could grind some of the grains she had gotten at the market to use on the trip home. As she ground the grains, she noticed how low Leenah's supply of grains was and poured a little from her own supply into Leenah's storage jar.

During the afternoon, both Gennah and Ashannah were kept busy chasing after Elissa, who was celebrating her new mobility with much vigor. This helped keep their minds off Ator, but they both often glanced furtively over at the forest or down the path from the main road. They sighed with relief as the sun began to set. There had been no sign of him.

The women of Al-Labah began gathering around the central fire pit, carrying the food they had prepared during the day. Someone had built a huge bonfire, and as soon as it was almost dark, Tornah lit it. The smoke from the fire drove away the small stinging insects and flies, and the women all settled themselves to enjoy the evening.

After everyone was comfortably full, a woman named Solah began to sing a humorous song about two women, struggling to get along with each other, early in their relationship. There was a little chorus that all the women sang in between the verses, along with much laughter. Ashannah had never heard anyone sing except at religious festivals in or near the temple. She loved Solah's song and knew she would soon be making up some of her own.

Early the next morning, Ashannah was awakened by En-dor's low whistle. She could tell he was nearby. She woke up Gennah and Elissa, relieved they were packed and ready to go.

It was barely light, but they quickly made out En-dor's form in the forest at the back of the village.

"I slept just a little ways from here," he explained, "so we can get on the main road before there are many others to see us come out from Al-Labah. We can't go through the forest with the cart, so I think we should start right out and eat later. The fewer people who notice the path leading here, the better for Al-Labah."

The women quickly agreed and led the way through the village, since none of the women seemed to be up yet. Just as they were passing the temple, Tornah came out. "May you be blessed by Ninlil and Inanna," she said, "and have a safe journey to Al-Rah. Being so far from Tel Phar, it must be very peaceful there," she concluded wistfully.

"It is most of the time," Gennah replied. She didn't mention being raped by Ator in Et-Ray.

"Any of you would be most welcome to come to Al-Rah, either for a visit or to live there," Ashannah invited.

Tornah was visibly pleased and looking directly into Ashannah's eyes, said, "You may well see some of us there in the sun cycles to come."

The women embraced, and Ashannah, carrying Elissa, and Gennah, pushing the cart, hurried to catch up with En-dor, who, after adding a potter's wheel and a few other things to what was already in the cart, began pushing it towards the main road.

With the help of the cart and their own eagerness to be as far away from Tel Phar as possible, they made the trip back in four journeys of the sun.

When they finally arrived in Et-Ray, after asking En-dor to stop by the following spring to pick up the shawls, they also requested that he do the transaction, so they wouldn't have to return to Tel Phar. He agreed readily, understanding why they didn't want to go back there. Also, he knew he would be safer without them.

At first, Ashannah and Gennah considered remaining in Et-Ray for the night, but when they realized they could get to Al-Rah before dark, they decided to continue on. The sun was just setting when the little conical buildings of the Virgins' homes came into view. Just as it had when they had arrived at Al-Labah, the light made the little houses appear to be made with new copper. The two women did not even try to hide the tears of joy running down their cheeks, as they saw Kasha and Orana coming out to meet them. The rest of the Virgins were not far behind. Before their mothers could exclaim over the new cart, Ashannah cried out, "Oh, Mama! Wait until you see what Elissa can do!"

Chapter Nine

After Elissa showed her grandmothers her ability to crawl and Kasha and Orana at least got a glimpse of the new cart, the two weary travelers were free to walk through Al-Rah towards their own home. In spite of the semidarkness, Ashannah noticed that a hole was being dug in the side of the same hill where their home was.

"Look, Gennah," she cried out in consternation as she pointed to the site, "doesn't it look like someone is starting to build a house like ours?"

"Why, I think you're right, Ashannah!" Gennah exclaimed. "And they must have used our shovel to do it!

"Yah, they must have gone to our house, while we were away, and taken the shovel!" They had been gone less than a moon's cycle, but now it seemed they had been gone for much longer. It was obvious the builders had studied their construction very closely. Then Ashannah became aware of the negative feelings seeing the site had stirred up in her.

"Why are we angry that they used our shovel, Gennah?" she asked. "Even though we traded for it, is it really ours?"

"But we *made* the things we traded for it, Ashannah," Gennah answered with some impatience. She drew in her breath and continued in a more subdued manner. "But ... well, I guess anyone in the village should be able to use it. After all, we weren't using it.

The very next day they learned that Grenda and Mirah were building the new home. Hazel-eyed Grenda, with red glints in her light brown hair and freckles scattered across her nose, was around Gennah's age. Gray-eyed Mirah, with her chestnut colored hair, was a sun cycle older. They had become partners shortly before Grenda gave birth to Leah.

"I'm going over to see if I can help Grenda and Mirah," Ashannah told Gennah, later that day. When she arrived at the site, she could see the marks from the shovel, where they had dug out the back wall of their house. They had even begun supporting it with stones from the river and had begun building up the soil for their garden, buttressing the lower end with stones in the same manner she had. However, they were not any place near the site when she arrived.

"Perhaps, they're out collecting branches for the front of the house," she mused, wondering if they had borrowed the hatchet, as well. When she returned home, she discovered that the shovel was there, but the hatchet was gone.

"They weren't there," Ashannah said to Gennah, "but since the hatchet is gone, I guess they're out collecting branches."

"When they see the new shovel, they'll probably wish they had waited," Gennah observed. "It's much larger and the work would have gone much faster."

"That's right," Ashannah agreed, grinning. "And they probably don't even realize we're back."

With that, Elissa woke up and declared herself hungry in the usual infant manner. Since she had begun to crawl, Ashannah was considering feeding her porridge, along with her nursing. When she put the first bite into the baby's mouth, the child was surprised at the difference and spit it out. Her mother put a smaller amount on her finger and tried again, pushing it further back on the baby's tongue. Elissa choked a little and again tried to expel the food, but it went down her throat, instead. The two women laughed at the surprised look on her face.

"Want to try another bite?" Ashannah coaxed. Elissa ate a few more bites but then suddenly made a lunge for her mother's breast.

"That girl knows what she wants!" chuckled Gennah.

The following morning, Ashannah went over, again, to the new site and found Grenda and Mirah putting up the frame on the front of their home. They were startled by her approach, and before she could even greet them, Grenda asked, "Are you looking for the hatchet? I mean we … we were using it to get branches for our house. We … we didn't know you were back."

"It's all right, Grenda," Ashannah assured the stocky woman with muscular arms. "I just came over to see how you're doing. You've done a lot while we were away. It looks good. Wait until you see the new shovel we got in Tel Phar. And the new cart is truly wonderful! They're both down by the garden."

Ashannah followed Grenda and Mirah as they rushed down to the garden. Neither of them had even seen a wheel before, much less a cart. Ashannah demonstrated how to use the cart, and she could almost see them thinking of ways they would use it. She smiled to herself, as she realized that she and Gennah had never considered that the cart would be theirs.

"But shouldn't the shovel have a handle on it, like the other one?" Mirah asked.

"You make your own handle," Ashannah explained. "The hatchet and a knife help a lot. Since you've got the hatchet, anyway, maybe you'd like to make the handle for this shovel. See these little loops. You have to make the handle so it fits tight in them."

"Oh, I see!" Mirah cried out. "Yes, I'd like to make the handle. In fact, one of the branches we got for our house will be just right, I'm sure. We can get another one for the house," she quickly assured Grenda.

A few days later, Ashannah took Gennah over to see the new house. They had completed the frame.

"Have you planted your garden, yet?" Gennah asked.

"Oh, Gennah," Grenda wailed. "We didn't think to look for a spring! We're closer to the stream than you are, but it would still be a lot of work to haul enough water clear up here, even with the new cart. Maybe we'll just have to be satisfied with using the village garden."

"Have you looked good for a spring?" Ashannah asked. "It doesn't have to be real close as long as it's uphill from the garden. You can dig a trench to carry the water to your garden."

"Maybe we could look farther up the hill," Mirah cried out. "We've already put in a lot of work on this garden!"

"That's right," Ashannah agreed. "If you want, I'll help you look. Want to come, too, Gennah?"

The four women and two little girls went up the hill searching for a trickle of water or even a damp place on the ground, which could indicate the presence of a spring. Leah, Grenda's little girl, was walking by now, although it was difficult for her to keep up with the women. Finally, Grenda picked her up and carried her, but she wasn't too grateful and struggled to get down. Grenda found a level spot and told her to stay there and play with Elissa.

"But she can't even walk!" Leah complained.

"You'd be surprised how fast she can crawl, though," Gennah laughingly protested.

"Anyway, I want you to stay right here, while we look for water," Grenda ordered, not being at all certain that Leah would obey. Gennah was about to offer to stay with the children, when Ashannah cried out from further up the hill.

"I've found one! I've found a spring!"

Gennah picked up Elissa and followed the others. Leah toddled after them as fast as she could. They all looked at the little trickle of water coming out of the ground, and Mirah, and Grenda expressed their relief at finding it. Ashannah showed them how to dig a hole in which to store the water, advising them to line it with rocks, as she had.

"You're lucky!" she exclaimed. "You can use the cart to bring the rocks up. I had to carry mine, a couple at a time. But I guess you know how that is. You had to do it that way for the walls of your house and garden!"

A few days before Ninlil's harvest festival and around the completion of Elissa's first sun cycle, the little girl took her first steps. By the day of the feast, she was able to walk across their hut without assistance. Leah became more interested in playing with her, although she wasn't always patient enough to wait for her to catch up. They were quite a contrast to each other, Leah having the light brown hair and hazel eyes of her mother and Elissa having wavy black hair and dark brown eyes like Ashannah.

The spring and summer had been unusually dry, and they weren't going to have extra food or herbs for trading. Fortunately, Ashannah had planted the apple seeds close by the stream and was able to water them frequently. By Ninlil's feast, some of them had sprouted, so she built little bamboo fences around each one to keep the rabbits or deer from foraging them.

It was around this time that Fenn came through with more wool. Since he was more interested in Gennah's baskets than in food, they were able to make a trade. Along with the wool she had obtained in Tel Phar, Gennah decided she could make a shawl of wool, as well as one of cotton and another of linen. By then, Ashannah was spinning cotton and flax fine enough to use for the shawls, and Gennah, herself, had discovered how to spin the wool fine and even. It looked as if they would be able to have the three shawls done by spring.

When En-dor came by Et-Ray the following spring, Rootha went to get Ashannah and Gennah to let them know he was ready to return to Tel Phar. The women were letting him take the small cart, in this way returning his favor of bargaining their shawls for the large cart. He had plenty of things to put in it, as he was hoping to obtain a small cart for Et-Toll. Because Eetoh was going with him, he thought they could manage the three carts on the return trip by putting one of the smaller ones in the larger cart.

The two traders had been in Tel Phar only a few days, when the problem of returning with the three carts was more easily solved. Leenah and Estah of Al-Labah approached them and asked if they could go back to Et-Ray with them. With Tornah's encouragement, they had decided to move to Al-Rah. When the men agreed and told the women about the extra cart, Leenah cried out, "Now I'll be able to take my potter's wheel!"

A half a moon cycle later, En-dor and Eetoh showed up in Et-Ray with three carts and two strange women. Fortunately, Ashannah and Gennah happened to be in Et-Ray working on baskets. They were thrilled when Estah and Leenah told them they wanted to live in Al-Rah. Eetoh hung around, keeping the conversation going, even though En-dor was obviously impatient to continue on to Et-Toll. Ashannah sensed that the younger man wanted to speak with her, but she was eager to take Leenah and Estah to Al-Rah. Suddenly, terror struck her heart as she wondered if somehow, Eetoh had guessed that he was Elissa's father. But how could he? He had never seen her, and even if he had, the baby didn't bear any of his physical characteristics, unless you looked closely at her eyes. They slanted up at the corners in the same way as his. Not even En-dor knew who Elissa's father was.

Ashannah drew Eetoh aside and told him when she had temple duty next. "Could we talk then?" she asked. This satisfied him, and he went on with his father.

As Gennah, Ashannah and the two women from Al-Labah prepared to leave for Al-Rah, Ashannah suddenly realized that she had never spoken with Kasha about the possibility of some of the women from Al-Labah coming to Al-Rah to live. She wondered if Kasha and the others would want these women, whom they had never met, to join their village?

Ashannah was temporarily distracted from this concern, as she and Gennah gave their full attention to their new cart with its shiny metal box.

When they became aware that the two travelers were quite tired, Gennah suggested that they leave at once for Al-Rah, so Estah and Leenah could eat and rest and they could show the new cart to the rest of the women.

As they approached Al-Rah, Ashannah went on ahead, so that she could tell Kasha about the new women. The more she thought about it, the more certain she was that they would be welcome. They could move into some of the huts left by women who had moved to Et-Ray. Nevertheless, she breathed a sigh of relief when she found Kasha in her hut.

"Mother Kasha! Two women from Al-Labah are here! They want to live with us in Al-Rah. When we left Al-Labah, last spring, I … I told Tornah that any who wished could come to Al-Rah to live. We got to know Leenah and Estah well and like them very much."

"I'm certain that if you and Gennah like them, we all will," Kasha assured her.

"Oh, and Mother," Ashannah continued, "Leenah is a potter and brought a wheel with her. Won't it be nice having a potter right here in Al-Rah, again?"

"Yes, it will, and I think I hear them arriving right now."

Ashannah and Kasha went out to meet the new women, and the High Priestess greeted them warmly. Then she exclaimed over the fine new cart with its beautiful bronze basket. "Well, I think you must feel that all the work you did last winter was worth it," Kasha said.

"Truly spoken," Ashannah and Gennah replied.

"Look," Gennah said, "here come Mama and Elissa." Elissa was running circles around Orana, until she saw her mother.

"Mama! Mama! Is that the new cart?" She was torn between wanting to hug her mother and inspecting the cart. This time the cart won. She ran over and tried to pick up the handles, but since Leenah's and Estah's things were still in it, she couldn't budge it. Then she became embarrassed and ran over and hid her face in her mother's tunic.

"That's not the little girl, who was just learning to crawl the last time I saw her!" exclaimed Leenah.

"Why, I believe it is!" Estah replied, laughing.

"Hasn't she grown?" Ashannah asked proudly. "Do you remember Leenah and Estah, Elissa?"

Obviously the child did not, but she squirmed out of her mother's arms and went over and gave each woman a hug.

Ashannah and Gennah found two empty huts in fairly good repair for the two travelers and afterwards went to each woman in the village to tell of their arrival and announce a feast in their honor that night. Every woman in Al-Rah was at the feast, and it felt as if Leenah and Estah had been a part of the village for a long time.

The following day, Ashannah and Gennah helped the new women with some minor repairs on their huts and then took them over to see their new home. As Ashannah was relating how the stones helped keep the house cooler in the summer and warmer in the winter, Estah's brown eyes grew round with admiration. "Oh, I'd love to build a house like this one!" she said. "And to have a little garden of my own! Wouldn't you love to live in a house like this, Leenah?"

"Grenda and Mirah have just finished building one quite similar," Ashannah told them. "You will need to find a good spot on a hillside and one close to a water supply for the garden."

"The huts you've provided for us will do fine for now,"Leenah spoke up. "I want to begin working on some pots. I got some good ideas from Angah while we were in Et-Ray. She told me of a place nearby to get some good clay."

"I know the place," Ashannah assured her. "I'll take you to it as soon as you're ready. In the mean time, Estah, I'll show you some places to forage and, if you wish, you can help me in my garden until you find your plot."

"Thanks Ashannah!" Estah said, flashing her a big smile. She had been disappointed that Leenah had wanted to wait awhile before building a house. With the trees being so different here," she continued,'I'm sure there are many things to forage here that I don't even know about

As Ashannah approached the temple on the night she had arranged to meet Eetoh, she became more and more concerned as to what he wanted to tell her. She felt certain he didn't know about Elissa. She even hoped he wouldn't come. Hearing someone enter, she watched as Eetoh entered and bowed to the icon of Inanna.

He came over to where Ashannah was waiting and said, "Can we sit outside, Ashannah? It's you I want to commune with, not Inanna!"

If she was put off by his irreverence, Ashannah didn't let on. They found a comfortable spot behind the temple. There was no moon, yet, but the stars seemed especially bright in the night sky. Eetoh sat down very close to Ashannah and tried to put an arm around her, but she pulled away.

"Just tell me what … what you want, Eetoh, … what you are thinking."

"I love you, Ashannah," he answered, looking directly into her eyes. She could see that he meant it. She was not expecting this at all. The only people who had said these words to her were her mother and Gennah.

She quickly lowered her eyes, not knowing how to respond. Then she lowered her head, as well, because tears of frustration were filling her eyes. A part of her wanted to return the compliment, but she knew it was just because she did not want to hurt him. She knew her feelings for him were not the same as her feelings for Gennah although she liked him very much. She finally looked up, but still could think of nothing to say.

"I … I guess you … you don't feel the same way," he stammered, his voice trembling with disappointment.

By then, tears were freely running down Ashannah's cheeks. "Oh, Eetoh, I do like you very much. I have many fond memories of our days together when we were children. You have always been kind and gentle with me in the temple. But … but …"

"Then come and live with me in Et-Toll, Ashannah!" Eetoh interrupted. "It's not nearly as big as Et-Ray. Why, you could have your own garden, and I would never disturb you when you're in it," he promised.

Ashannah had to smile at the memories these words brought up, but she still had to say, "Oh, Eetoh, that isn't it! I have a lover! We have been together for over two sun cycles! Gennah is my partner."

"So … so it's true!" he gasped. "You Virgins do take lovers among yourselves!"

"Why, yes, of course we do!" she answered. "Surely you must have noticed, when you were living among us!"

'Gennah will never give you any children!" he blurted out. "Don't you want to have a baby, Ashannah?"

Fear gripped Ashannah's heart. She would not lie to him, but she was also certain that she should not tell him she had a child by him. "I do have a daughter, Eetoh. Surely, En-dor must have told you."

"That's right, he did. I guess I forgot. He said she looks just like you." Tears of frustration were now filling his eyes. "Do you even know who her father is?"

"What is a *father*?" Ashannah asked, even though by now, she had a good idea.

"The man who gave you his seed, so that you could have a baby!" he shouted. "That isn't the only way you can have a baby," Ashannah said, as calmly as she could. She knew that while the statement was true, she had said it to distract him, so she wouldn't have to answer his question directly.

"What! Are you trying to tell me that you can have a baby without a man's seed? Everyone knows better than that, Ashannah! Even the animals have to mate in order to have their young!"

Ashannah did not answer. She finally got up and began to go back inside the temple.

"We men know that sometimes you Virgins couple with us in the temple and then never tell us that you've had our child!" he cried out.

Ashannah turned back and admitted, "That is true, Eetoh. That is how you were conceived and born, is it not? But sometimes we conceive even though we have not coupled in the temple," she insisted.

"It's not fair, Ashannah! It's not fair when you don't tell us when you've had a child by us! At least, Thesta finally told En-dor, so that he could come and get me and show me how to be a man, how to live among men!"

Ashannah's heart was pounding so hard that she wondered how he couldn't hear it. Nevertheless, she looked directly into Eetoh's eyes and said, "If I were to have a boy child, I would do the same, Eetoh!"

"There are men and women in Et-Ray and in Et-Toll and even in Et-Bann, who live together with both boy and girl children. It is a good way, Ashannah! It is the way I want to live!"

"Then I hope you will be able to live that way, if that is what you want, but I am a Virgin of Inanna, and that is the way I want to live!"

With that, Eetoh turned and ran from the temple back towards Et-Ray. Ashannah slowly entered the temple to finish her duty for the night, but she was very troubled over the exchange with Eetoh. She was astonished at what he had said. the women of Al-Rah had always believed that men did not want to be bothered with children There had been some men who had even refused to take their own male child. But apparently, some of the men wanted to be … fathers, even when the child was a girl! She reluctantly came to the conclusion that not all men were the same.

Chapter Ten

"I don't know if we have been unfair, Ashannah. Perhaps we have by not understanding men very well. As you, I truly thought that all men were not interested in children. But now we know that some of them are. I am unfamiliar with the word "father". I hardly know what it means, other than that a father is the man whose seed helps a woman conceive a child, as Eetoh explained to you. But now I think that men have more meaning for the word than that. It is like our word "mother". It means much more than a woman who gives birth to a child."

Kasha was seated on a low stool in her hut, and Ashannah was sitting at her feet, as they had often sat together when Ashannah was still sharing her mother's home. After the meeting with Eetoh, Ashannah had been very troubled by her conversation with him and was even more distressed by the anger with which he had left. She couldn't bring herself to speak of it to Gennah. Yet, it bothered her to such a degree that she had to speak of it to someone. After several tortuous days, Ashannah had sought out Kasha to share the experience and the fears it had brought up.

Now she responded to Kasha's musings. "I wonder what the fathers in Et-Ray and Et-Toll do with their children? They can't nurse them! What would they do with them while they were off hunting or trading?"

"Eetoh didn't say fathers took care of their children by themselves, Ashannah. The woman would still have to be the one to feed the baby, at least for the first sun cycle."

"I guess that you mean the father would ***help*** the mother raise their child. If you really loved the man, it would be good to have help. I have Gennah, but how did you take care of me all by yourself, Mother?"

Kasha's eyes clouded over with tears. Ashannah was astonished.

"When you were born, I, too, had a lover, Ashannah. Her name was Neelah. She took on a terrible fever and died before you finished your first sun cycle. No matter what potions I gave her or the many things I tried to do for her, it didn't help." Now Kasha began to cry freely.

"Oh, Mama! ... I didn't know!" exclaimed Ashannah, rushing over and throwing her arms around her mother.

Kasha wiped away her tears and said, "I was very sad, indeed, Ashannah, but I still had you. For that I was very grateful."

"Oh, Mama, I love you so much!" the daughter said, holding her mother closer.

After awhile, Ashannah continued the conversation. "If Eetoh hadn't been so angry, Mother, I wouldn't be afraid. But he was very angry and ... and I am afraid!"

"There are changes going on, which I do not understand, Ashannah. Like the things you told us were taking place in Tel Phar and how it is affecting the Virgins in the village of Al-Labah. The changes in Et-Ray are not as ... as bad as they are in Tel Phar, but changes there are, and I don't know how long before ..."

"Oh, Mama! Don't say it! Surely things will never get as bad in Et-Ray as they are in Tel Phar."

"I just wish ... I just wish we understood men better," Kasha sighed. "Well, it looks as if we're going to have plenty of chances to do just that, but I don't think it's going to be easy. We must trust that the Goddess will give us the wisdom to know what to say to them, when we need it."

Ashannah left her mother's home, not feeling as comforted as she had hoped.

Later that summer, just after the women of Al-Rah had celebrated Ninlil's harvest feast, Leenah found the time to get her potter's wheel set up. Elissa, who had just begun her third sun cycle, watched her every move, and, when it was assembled, asked if she could turn it. Leenah showed her how to push it from the side. After a bit, Elissa was able to keep it spinning at a steady rate, laughing all the while.

"Do you want to go with me and get some clay?" Leenah asked. "We can go to your mother's garden to get the little cart and tell her where you are."

"Oh, yes, Leenah" the child answered. "I'd like that!"

When they got there, Ashannah was turning the soil she had recently harvested.

"Mama, Mama! May I go with Leenah to get some clay?" Elissa asked, while she gave her mother a hug. "I can spin her wheel, Mama! I really can!"

"Why, that's wonderful, Baby! Maybe I'll go along. My back is saying I've had enough of this work!"

Leenah got the cart and a shovel and the three of them walked through the village, turning off just before they arrived at the temple. Then they followed the path leading to the stream where the bed of clay was.

It had been a dry summer after an equally dry winter, and the clay was hard and didn't dig up easily.

"Would it help if we broke it up with a hatchet, first?" Ashannah suggested.

"It might," Leenah replied, "but I think the best thing would be to get it wet somehow.?

"Maybe if we went nearer to the stream bed, we could find some that would still be damp. Goddess! The creek is really low!" Ashannah exclaimed, as they drew nearer. They soon discovered that the damp clay nearer the stream bed was mixed with too much sand.

"Let's just take these few pieces we've broken off," Leenah said. "I'll wrap them in a wet cloth, and maybe after a few days, we can work with it. In the meantime, I think we'll just have to wait until it rains to get a good supply. I'm sorry, Elissa," she added, seeing the disappointment on the child's face. "Come over to my house in a few days and we'll make a little pot. We won't be able to use the wheel, but you'll see how easy it is to make a little pot just your size."

Several days later, when Elissa went down to Leenah's hut to see if the clay was ready, Leenah started out by showing her how to form a small patty on a smooth rock for the base of the pot.

"Why, it looks just like an emmer bun," Elissa said.

"But it wouldn't taste like one," Leenah warned.

Then she showed the child how to make little "worms" from the clay.

"Do you think Mama would like some of these in her garden?" the little girl laughed, knowing the answer already.

"Somehow I don't believe these "worms" would do the garden much good," Leenah replied. "And, anyway, we're going to use them to make a pot. Just watch."

The woman carefully pulled one of the "worms" from the rock and arranged it around the edge of the patty. It didn't quite go all the way around.

"What are you going to do now?" the curious child wanted to know. Without answering, Leenah picked up another coil and very carefully placed it on the very end of the coil already on the patty, pinched the two together and finished going around the patty and on up on top of part of the first coil.

Elissa's eyes grew large with sudden understanding. "Ooooh, I see, now!" she cried. "We're going to need lots of "***worms***" to make a whole pot."

"Well, we might need a few more," Leenah admitted. "Do you want to try and put the next *one* on?" she invited. "Here, I'll help you."

"Oh, I can do it," Elissa said, only to find that it wasn't as easy as it had looked. She ended up needing quite a bit of help and Leenah sensed that she was getting fatigued from frustration.

"I know another way to make a pot," Leenah suggested, rolling up a couple of pieces of clay, about the size of one of her thumb joints. After placing them on the edge of the rock, she put her thumb in her mouth to wet it.

"Now take your thumb like this and push it down right there," she instructed. Elissa wet her thumb in the same way and poked it into the clay as Leenah had done.

"Be careful not to push too hard," Leenah warned. "You don't want to go clear through. It's a little tricky getting your thumb out, but if you got it wet enough, you'll be able to do it," Leenah said as she carefully pulled the clay off her thumb. Elissa had a little more difficulty getting her thumb out, but finally managed to pull it out without doing too much damage to the sides of the tiny pot.

"And there, you have a little pot, already!" Leenah exclaimed, patting the sides into a smooth shape. Elissa was delighted with these little pots and wanted to take them to show her mother.

"It would be better to wait for them to dry," Leenah advised. "When they're wet like this, it's easy for them to lose their shape. After your pot is dry, you may show it to your mother. When we've got enough pots, we'll dig a pit, put some wood in the bottom and place the pots on the wood. Then we'll put wood all around the pots, light the wood and keep the fire burning until our pots are well baked."

Elissa was disappointed, and asked, "But won't the pots burn?"

"Oh, no" Leenah quickly assured her. "It will make them hard and shiny."

Elissa finally agreed to leave the pots with Leenah. She watched the potter work on the coil pot awhile longer and then decided she had had enough of making pots for the day.

The previous winter had given Al-Rah very little rain, and the Virgins hadn't had any during the summer. It wasn't only the clay that was suffering from the lack of rain. Ashannah noticed with dismay that her spring hole was not filling up as fast as she was using the water. She had put fewer plants in her garden but was still not sure of having enough water for them.

It was quite late in the fall when they had their first rain, but it rained steadily for three days. Leenah wasn't too surprised when she went to the clay bed, to find Elissa already there, with her friend Leah. The two little girls were covered from head to toe with soft, oozy clay. Leenah started laughing as soon as she saw them.

"If you weren't so very lively," she said as she greeted them, "I would have thought you were two clay girls. I can hardly tell who you really are!"

"We came to get some clay for you," Elissa started to explain, "but… but …"

"But you started having so much fun, you forgot," Leenah finished for her. "I think you had better go clean yourselves off in the stream, first, and then if you still want to help, you may."

The children were back in no time, eager to help get some clay, so that they could watch Leenah use her wheel. Although they had gotten themselves and their tunics fairly clean, there was still quite a bit of clay in their hair, but Leenah chose to ignore it for the time being. They dug out several large chunks of clay and put them in the cart and took them to her hut. Elissa and Leah looked on, fascinated, as she pounded the air out of the clay. Finally it was time for her to use the wheel.

Elissa and Leah watched, wide eyed, as Leenah swung her long golden hair back, sat down before her wheel, threw on a glob of clay and began turning the wheel with one of her feet. She cupped her hands around the glob and in a short while, had a lovely new pot.

"Ooooh," exclaimed Elissa. "That's a lot easier than making a pot out of *worms*."

Leenah laughed, as she, again, swept back her hair and said, "It is a lot faster, but it's not faster or easier until you learn how to do it. It's actually easier, at first, to make coil pots, believe me." As she spoke, she began cutting away the extra clay at the bottom of the pot she had just made.

"Do you think I'll ever learn?" Elissa asked wistfully, remembering how hard it had been, even with the worms, when she had tried a few moon cycles ago.

"Yes, I'm sure you will, if you really want to and work hard at it. I'll be glad to help you, since we've got plenty of clay," Leenah promised. "Now I think we had better go back down to the stream, and I'll help you get the clay out of your hair."

Elissa reached up and felt her hair, which was matted and sticky with clay.

"Ooooh, thanks, Leenah. I guess we'd better."

"Do I have clay in my hair, too?" Leah wanted to know, as she also felt her head.

It seemed to take longer to get the clay out of their hair than it had to collect some, pound out the air and make a pot. They were finally able to get it all out, but only after many rinsings.

With the earth being soft once more, Leenah and Estah began to work on their hillside house. They had found a spot about half way between Grenda's and Ashannah's, with a good spring close by. The carts and shovels were so helpful that they believed they would be able to finish it before the weather got cold.

The next spring, Eetoh and En-dor returned from their trading in Tel Phar with six women and two girls from Al-Labah. When the travelers arrived in Et-Ray, no one from Al-Rah was there. Since four of the women wanted to make their homes in Al-Rah, Angah offered to take them. They unloaded the things belonging to Fannah and Deenah and their two girls from one of the carts. Fannah was a basket weaver, and Deenah was learning to weave cloth. They wished to remain in Et-Ray close to the market. Rootha offered to help them find places to live.

Sarah, Gannah, Minah and Flora followed Angah as she lead them out on the path to Al-Rah. They hadn't gone far, when Angah noticed the women were having trouble keeping up with her, and she slowed her pace. She wondered what had made six women with two children all leave Al-Labah at the same time.

When the four women saw the roofs of the huts of Al-Rah, tears of joy filled their eyes and they began to walk faster.

"Ashannah! Gennah! Leenah! Estah!" Angah called out. "Come and see who is here!"

Kasha heard the shouting and came right out to discover the cause.

"Kasha, here are four more women from Al-Labah, who want to make their homes with you in Al-Rah," Angah announced.

"Who will be left in Al-Labah, if you all move to Al-Rah?" Kasha asked, smiling.

All at once, the four women burst out sobbing, as if they had been holding back their tears for a long time. The High Priestess was astounded.

"There … there is no longer an … an Al-Labah!" Flora finally gasped.

"Angah," Kasha said, "You had better go get Leenah and Estah. They will want to hear this."

"Oh, yes," the wiry woman, Gannah, agreed, her voice raspier than ever. "And … and Ashannah and Gennah, too, if they are near."

Angah hurried over to the hillside dwellings to get the women. It did not take long to find them, and they came, at once, to see their friends.

Leenah arrived first. "Why are you crying so?" she asked, as she tried, unsuccessfully, to take all four of them into her arms. Ashannah, Gennah and Estah were right behind, and everyone listened intently as they told their tale.

"A little over a hand's span of sun journeys ago, a large group of men from Tel Phar came to Al-Labah," Flora began. "They came through the forest, but they were not our friends. We were all relieved to see that they were not carrying knives or spears, and one of them was dressed like a high priestess, ready to celebrate a feast in the temple. If we had not been so terrified, we might have laughed at the way he looked."

"I did laugh," admitted Minah, "but not for long."

"The man dressed in the robe told us to go get Tornah, at once," Flora continued. "He said he had important things to say to her."

"We didn't like the way he was ordering us about, but although they didn't have weapons, we were afraid. Sarah went to get Tornah. It seemed to take a very long time for her to come, but as soon as we saw her, we understood why. She had changed into her most festive robes, which were much lovelier than the ones the man was wearing. She looked beautiful and strong as she walked up to him. He didn't even bow to her, but stood there, rudely staring at her. And she ... she just stared right back. She was not afraid!"

As the others were reminded of Tornah's courage, they quickly wiped away their tears and stopped crying. Ashannah was amazed at the way the little girl, Flora, who had asked her for apple seeds only two sun cycles ago, had matured. She could imagine how difficult it must have been for her to leave her fledgling apple trees.

Sarah took up the story. "But then, he ... he began to say terrible things about us. We hardly understood what he was saying, but we knew he thought we were ... very bad! But Tornah just continued to stare at him, as if to prove that he was wrong about us. He grew even angrier, telling her that she was being disrespectful.

"Do you know who I am?" he asked her." Here, Sarah lowered her voice in an attempt to mimic him. His self-importance was evident in her tone. "I am Gan-dor Tel Phar, the High Priest, in the service of Enlil, the creator of us all."

"And I am Tornah Al-Labah," Flora continued the story, taking the role of the High Priestess. Looking him straight in the eye, she said, "I am the High Priestess of the temple of Ninlil in Al-Labah, where you now stand. And as far as I know, your temple to Enlil in Tel Phar, was first the temple of Ninlil and had been so for many sun cycles before you were even born!"

"Gan-dor became very red and actually seemed embarrassed by her words, because he knew she spoke the truth." Sarah continued, evidently enjoying the memory of it. Again, she assumed her voice for Gan-dor. 'Ninlil is an abomination and should be destroyed off the earth!' he shouted. 'And also her priestesses and virgins who are, in truth, whores!'"

"The men, who had come with him, all gathered closer around him," Sarah continued in the rough voice. "You and your whores defile our land! We will give you one hand of sun journeys to leave this village, which we will then destroy, down to the very ground! Do not try to stop us! Your knives and shovels will not save you from our bows and arrows and spears! And we are many more than you!"

"With that, they all turned and went back into the forest and Tel Phar." Gannah ended, her voice even raspier than before, from held back tears. The others began to cry with angry choking sobs.

Finally, Minah was able to go on with the story. "Tornah stood straight and tall until they were out of sight, but she knew there was not much we could do. She sent for our sybil, Cal-dah, who began to prepare her potions right away." Then Minah seemed unable to go on, although she was not crying. By then, none of the women were crying, but no one else took up the story. They were all simply staring, as if they still couldn't believe what had taken place. Kasha was shaken at the tale and wanted to hear the rest of it, but she could see that the women were about to collapse.

"Ashannah, go make some of the tea for sleeping! These women need to rest more than anything else! We can hear more of their story during the sun's next journey."

Chapter Eleven

Tornah shivered against the predawn chill. It was the morning after Gan-dor's visit to Al-Labah. She knew her shaking was from fear, as well as from the cold. As she slowly picked her way along the lightly marked path, running through the forest between Al-Labah and Tel Phar, she wondered if her disguise, as a peddler woman, would be enough to keep her from being recognized.

All through the night, she had struggled to come up with a plan for getting the crones to a safe haven. She had reluctantly come to the realization that Tel Phar was probably as far as the ancients could travel, so she determined to go there and find a suitable place, as soon as it was light enough for her to pick out the trail.

It had been many sun cycles since she had been in Tel Phar, and as she entered the outskirts, nothing was familiar. This was because it had expanded so much, but she was unaware of this. She walked through the crowds as unobtrusively as possible, saying nothing, but taking in everything. Perspiration broke out all over her body as she began to fear she had made a mistake coming here. How had she ever expected to be able to find a safe place for three old women right in the shadow of the enemy? It was some comfort that no one seemed to notice her.

She stopped short when she noticed two men, who looked familiar, standing apart from the crowds. At least she was sure the short, wiry man with hardly any hair on his head was Sa-dor, a believer in Ninlil and a friend to her Virgins. She approached him with caution, since the other man, who was very tall, muscular and quite dark, was not familiar to her.

"Sa-dor?" she said, keeping her voice as low as possible.

Upon hearing her, the small man jumped and exclaimed, "Tornah! What are you doing here in Tel Phar?"

Tornah quickly put a hand over his mouth before he would give her away. She put her face close to his and whispered, "I need to speak with you alone. It is very urgent!"

"I know!" he exclaimed. "I have just heard that Gan-dor wants to destroy Al-Labah!" Again, Tornah put one of her hands over his mouth, not wanting the other man to overhear their conversation.

"Da-nid is a good friend, Tornah, and can probably help you better than I can," he said in a quieter voice.

"Are you Tornah, the High Priestess of Al-Labah?" Da-nid whispered in awe.

"I am," she replied. "But I do not think it is safe for me to be known here."

The three of them went even further from the crowds, and Tornah told them what had occurred the previous day. "We have three crones, who simply are not able to make a long journey," she explained. "Would you know of a place, here, where they could stay, and be safe? Actually, I will want to remain here with them to be sure they have enough food." She had just come to this decision. The men stood in silence, thinking over her request.

Finally, Da-nid spoke up. "My mother has a place with extra space where you might stay. Of course, I will have to ask her. I am certain she will feel it is a privilege to aid the Virgins of Ninlil. But where are the rest going?"

"Well some of them want to move to Al-Rah where Leenah and Estah have already moved."

"Ninlil be blessed!" Da-nid exclaimed. "Endor and Eetoh are here and will be returning to their home soon. They will be glad to accompany your Virgins."

Tornah breathed a sigh of relief.

The day after the women from Al-Labah had arrived in Al-Rah was clear and sunny, and even the birds seemed to be celebrating their arrival. Perhaps this helped to raise everyone's spirits, as the women of Al-Rah cleaned and repaired the two huts where Leenah and Estah had lived before they built their hillside home. These were the only available huts for the four women from Al-Labah. Two adult women in one hut would be crowded, but with the mild weather, they would not have to be inside much.

Later, all of the women gathered around the central fire pit to hear the rest of the story.

"Our Sibyl, Cal-dah, prepared and drank her potion, foretelling exactly what Gan-dor had threatened," Sarah continued. "We realized that we definitely had to leave Al-Labah, in order to escape the wrath of the men from Tel Phar. The problem was where to go. At first, we were determined to stay together, but we soon saw that would only delay our leaving and we didn't have much time."

"Six of us and two children wanted to come here," Minah continued, "but that was too long a trip for the three crones, and some of the others simply didn't want to go so far away. These women finally chose to go to Tel Dann, a small fishing village to the sunrise of Tel Phar. There is very little trading done there, and the people live simply, as we do. We felt certain that the people there would help the women build new homes.

There was a long silence as the women fought to control the tears that were pushing at their eyelids. It was Flora who finally managed to go on with the story, although her voice was trembling.

"That still left the three old women, who didn't even feel able to make the trip to Tel Dann. Early the next morning, Tornah disguised herself as a peddler woman and went to Tel Phar to see if some of our friends there could help find a place for the crones to live."

"She wouldn't even let one of us go with her," Gannah interrupted. "She was afraid that more than one strange woman would draw too much attention. All we could do was to pray for her success, while we went ahead and prepared for our various journeys."

"Thanks to Ninlil," Sarah went on, "she met up with two men who were our friends and believed in Ninlil. She learned that the crones could live with the mother of one of them, who had plenty of extra space. Tornah was able to arrange for it and return to us during the same journey of the sun. Da-nid and Sa-dor promised to come in two more journeys of the sun to help them make the trip to Tel Phar They also informed her that En-dor and Eetoh were in Tel Phar, and would be returning to Et-Ray in the next sun's journey."

"Then Tornah told us that she was going to remain with the crones to make certain they would have enough food and clothing, since they wouldn't be able to have a garden and were too old to spin and weave enough for trading. Then she urged those of us who wished to go to Al-Rah to prepare to leave with En-dor and Eetoh. and thus have their protection. Since that meant we would be leaving the next day, the women going to Tel Dann promised us that they would stay until Tornah and the crones were ready to leave."

"Because we had so much further to go," Gannah explained, "they were able to persuade us, but leaving them was one of the hardest things I've ever done! We ... we worry about Tornah and the crones the most!" Again, she burst into tears, and the others did also.

Kasha and the rest of the women of Al-Rah were filled with a great sadness as they listened to the stories and were quick to console the weeping women, letting them know they were most welcome to live in their village. They promised to help build two more huts as soon as possible, but when Flora and Minah, who were lovers, saw the hillside homes, they wanted to build one like them. Both of them were good at building, and Ashannah and the others were eager to help them. That would leave the two huts free for Gannah and Sarah. With three carts and many shovels now available, along with the many helping hands of the villagers, they were able to finish the hew home shortly after the spring feast of Inanna.

Later in the summer when the women of Al-Rah were celebrating the early harvest festival of Ninlil, Kasha looked at the many faces of the women now living in Al-Rah. It certainly seemed like old times. It was the presence of so many children that pleased her most. Besides Zolah, who had almost reached menarche, and Elissa and Leah, there was the boy Ran-dell, just a little younger than Elissa. Beylah had just told her that she had gone four moon cycles without bleeding.

"So," the high priestess thought, "there are still a few men coming to temple." However, this news caused the High Priestess some concern, since Beylah had just finished her thirteenth sun cycle, and she wondered if the young girl was ready for such responsibility. She was a sweet girl, but seemed younger than most for her age. Even Zolah, who was a sun cycle younger, seemed more mature. Kasha consoled herself with the knowledge that, even though Zolah and Beylah were more like sisters than lovers, Zolah would probably help her friend care for the baby.

By evening, Deenah, Fannah and their daughters, as well as Angah and Rootha, had journeyed from Et-Ray to join in the celebration, and Kasha rejoiced because everyone seemed so contented. However, she herself kept having feelings of foreboding. For some time, the hairs on the nape of her neck would suddenly prickle, for no reason she could think of. She would turn to see if someone was looking at her, but would see no one.

One afternoon, shortly after the feast, as Kasha was sifting some of her dried herbs into a basket, she saw her granddaughter running down hill towards her hut.

"Gramma! Gramma! See what I made!" As Elissa ran up to her grandmother, she held out her hands. Kasha could see there was something in them, but couldn't make out what it was. "Lookee! Lookee!" the child went on, "I made it all by myself!"

Kasha took the clay object from Elissa's hands, so she could see it better.

"Why, it's a bowl!" she exclaimed. It was small and somewhat misshapen, but a bowl, nonetheless. "You truly made it by yourself?"

"Well, Leenah helped me some, but it was mostly me!" the little girl confessed.

"It is truly beautiful, Elissa," the grandmother praised, surprised to have tears suddenly spring up into her eyes.

"Do you really think so, Gramma? Would you like to have it?"

"Why, I'd be delighted, little one. But ... but I think it would hold just the right amount of cooked barley for you. I would probably still be hungry if I ate my barley from it."

"Well, all right," Elissa replied, taking it back with relief. "I'm going to show it to Mama and Gennah, now."

As Kasha watched the little girl run up to her home on the hillside, her tears began to flow copiously.

"What's the matter with you, old lady!" she growled to herself. "Why would you feel sad when you have a beautiful grand daughter like that?" She couldn't answer her own question, but the feelings of sadness remained. She seemed unaware of the feelings, deeper down, feelings of dread for which she had no explanation.

When Eetoh and En-dor came through Et-Ray the following spring, there were no other travelers with them, but they had news of Tornah and the ancients, who had been living in Tel Phar.

"Old Wilma died shortly after they moved into the house," En-dor began. "She found it impossible not to grieve for Al-Labah and especially for her daughter and granddaughter, who were living in Tel Dann."

"Poor Wilma," Deenah sighed, along with Fannah.

"Well, now I have some better news," En-dor continued. "A group of men and women from Tel Dann came up to Tel Phar to ask Tornah to come and establish a new Al-Labah near them. At first, Tornah refused, not wanting to leave the two remaining crones."

"So what did they do?" asked Deenah.

"The men offered to make two traveling chairs in which to carry the crones. The chairs were made of a wooden seat with a leg going down at each corner and handles on each side, extending out the front and back, for the men to use for carrying it. They wove a stiff back rest and put little handles on each side for the crone to hold on with. In this way four men could carry both crones all the way to Tel Dann."

"At first, Tornah thought the trip would still be too difficult for the women, but the crones, themselves, begged her to let them try. Neither of them were at all happy living in Tel Phar.

It took several days to make the trip, but the crones survived it, and when they arrived in Tel Dann, they discovered the others had already begun the new temple and the huts for the new Al-Labah.

Deenah and Fannah were very relieved when they heard this and set out for Al-Rah, at once, to tell the women there. They had a big feast that night to celebrate the news, and Leah and Elissa were happy to have Meldah and Nella to play with.

It was Ashannah's night for duty in the temple. Fewer and fewer men were coming to find ecstasy with the Goddess. Ashannah became lost in her reverie with Inanna and was startled when she saw a man already bowing to the image. She had been unaware that anyone had entered the temple. Seeing that it was Eetoh, she breathed a sigh of relief and then fear fluttered around her heart when she recalled their last encounter. She waited for him to approach.

"Ah!" he said. "I thought you were sleeping."

Hearing the smile in his voice, she relaxed and blushed, because he had come so near the truth. Then he grew very serious. "Ashannah, listen to me. It is very dangerous for you to be in the temple by yourself … and you need to be very watchful."

"What … what do you mean?" she asked.

"I know that I was very angry with you, the last time we met … and not only with you, but with all the Virgins. But still … I know that you are a good woman, that all of you are."

He paused, and Ashannah said, "Thank you Eetoh. I was very sad to have made you so angry." She didn't say that she had been frightened, as well. "We do not mean to be unfair in our dealings with you … men."

"I know, Ashannah, I know! Listen to me! Some of the men of Et-Ray and even Et-Toll and Et-Bann are talking like the men of Tel Phar. They are saying that we, men, and the wives of those men who have them, should stop giving homage to the Goddess and give it to Enlil, instead. They say that coming to the temples of the Goddesses weakens our spirits, makes us less than men. They claim we should not enjoy ecstasy until we take a wife. They speak of all of you as being wicked and become very angry when any of us try to speak in your favor. But I … I want you to know that I know what they say is false."

"May Inanna bless you, Eetoh!" Ashannah exclaimed.

"Oh, Ashannah, I'm afraid for you … for all of you! Thesta, Kasha, even Gennah!" A faint smile formed on his lips.

Ashannah broke in, "If you hear that they're coming to Al-Rah …"

"Of course, I'll come and tell you," he assured her.

Ashannah was filled with a great affection and trust for her old friend. She knew it was time to tell him that he was the father of Elissa.

"Eetoh, I … I have something to tell you. I hope it will make you happy."

Eetoh was surprised she could think of anyone's happiness after what he had just told her. He felt hope rising in his heart. "What is it, Ashannah?"

"It's … you … you are Elissa's father!" Seeing the doubt on his face, she went on to assure him. "You are the only one I have … . I have finished the act with, in order to conceive."

He looked long and deeply into her eyes. "Then … then why won't you become my wife?"

She hadn't expected this response. She looked back directly into his eyes and answered, "Because I love Gennah with all of my heart, and also I wish to remain a Virgin of Inanna" Again, fear gripped her stomach, as she wondered if he would become angry again.

Eetoh perceived without a doubt that she was speaking honestly. He hung his head and remained silent for a long time. Finally, he looked at her and asked, "May I see her?"

"At dawn, I will get her."

As the first predawn light appeared in the east, Ashannah left the temple and walked slowly up the hill to her home. How would she explain to Elissa that she had a father? That her father wished to see her and speak with her? How, when none of the other children of Al-Rah had fathers. Here, she corrected herself. None of the other children of Al-rah ***knew*** of their fathers.

When Eetoh saw the two of them approaching the temple, his heart leaped with a thud into his throat. What would he say to this beautiful little girl? She surely looked like her mother. But shouldn't there be something of himself in her, he wondered.

Elissa walked right up to the stranger. "Hello, Eetoh," she said shyly. "I … I know that you are my father." Neither of them knew entirely what this meant to the other.

When Eetoh didn't respond right away, Ashannah said, "Look at her eyes, Eetoh." He did and saw, to his amazement, that while her eyes were brown like her mother's, they slanted up at the corners like his.

Eetoh held out his arms and Elissa ran to receive his hug. Right away, Elissa felt completely at home in his arms. He was no longer a stranger.

Ashannah and Elissa returned home with light hearts, but later in the day, Ashannah became troubled when she remembered Eetoh's message from the night before. She wanted to speak of it to Gennah, but although it had been more than four sun cycles since Ator had forced himself on her partner and over two sun cycles since he had threatened her in Tel Phar, Ashannah felt that if she told her what Eetoh had said, she would be most upset. Again, Ashannah went to Kasha, instead.

"Ashannah, I'm so glad that Eetoh is no longer angry and also remains so loyal to us," Kasha said, when Ashannah had finished. "I suppose En-dor feels the same way. You know that En-dor is Eetoh's father."

"Yes, Mama, I know, and I am certain that he, too, is loyal to us." Here she paused. Just as Kasha was about to speak, Ashannah broke in. "Mama, do you know who my father is?"

Kasha looked carefully into Ashannah's eyes. She had been waiting for this question for many sun cycles.

"My daughter, you have no father. I swear by Inanna that you came directly from her with no help from a man. I had never finished the act with a man in or out of the temple, when I discovered that I was pregnant with you. Old Clara assured me that you had, indeed, come directly from the Goddess."

"But … but I'm just like everyone else!" Ashannah cried out in shock. The women believed that a child coming straight from the Goddess was special, indeed."Be that as it may, you have no father," Kasha insisted. "But my daughter," she quickly continued, wishing to change the subject, "I think it was most wise of you to let Eetoh see Elissa. Did he notice her eyes?"

Although she dreaded it, Ashannah knew she had to tell her mother of Eetoh's warning. After she finished telling her, the two of them held each other in fear and silence for a long, long time.

At Inanna's feast the following spring, the women from Et-Ray came, bringing Nella and Meldah. Elissa and Leah were so happy to see them that they begged their mothers to move to Al-Rah so they could play together all of the time.

At the ritual, Ashannah had on a new, finely woven linen robe, which Gennah had made for her the previous winter. She had decorated it with shells and feathers. Ashannah sang with especial fervor, from being happy in her new robe, but even more from hoping that Inanna would hear her prayers and protect her Virgins.

After the rituals, Kasha left with Elissa, Leah, Meldah and Nella and took the little girls up to the spring in back of Ashannah's house, where they had a little party of their own, although it didn't last through the night. The four of them ended up sleeping in Ashannah's and Gennah's home.

Back at the women's circle, Ashannah and Gennah began dancing together as they had for the past five springs.

"You are truly most beautiful, tonight!" Gennah murmured in Ashannah's ear.

"Thanks to you, my dearest," Ashannah whispered and drew Gennah closer to her. "And you, too, seem especially blessed by Inanna, tonight."

As each one felt the fluid movement of the other's body, without saying a thing they danced over to the forest to find their favorite trysting place. They took their time stroking each other's hair and gazing into each other's eyes, until passion took over and they were soon bathed in ecstasy.

At dawn, Ashannah awoke first, still feeling euphoric from the evening before. Then a feeling of terror swept over her as she remembered Eetoh's warning. She began to wonder what might take place in the near future, and thought she might be making a mistake not to warn Gennah and the other women, as well.

"But I did tell Mama, and isn't it up to her to tell the others?" she reasoned to herself. Just then, Gennah stirred, smiling in her sleep, and Ashannah couldn't resist bending over her and kissing her tenderly. As Gennah responded, she kissed her with great passion, holding her tightly, as if this might be the last time.

The summer harvest feast of Ninlil seemed especially bountiful, partly because there were so many more women in Al-Rah, as well as more gardens than usual. Lulled by this seeming well being of Al-Rah, Ashannah forgot Eetoh's warning for days at a time. Elissa had finished her fourth sun cycle, astonishing everyone with her ability to learn. She was calling herself a potter and loved showing her efforts to any who would take the time to look at them. Even more, she loved giving them away. As she would work on a cup or a bowl for some particular woman she would try to imagine what would please her.

Kasha chose to remain silent about the threat of danger, but she couldn't help noticing a change in the behavior of the Sibyl, Orana. She was becoming irritable and kept herself apart from the other women.

One evening, when the women were sitting around the fire singing and telling stories, Kasha was relieved when she saw Orana find a place in the circle. But suddenly the woman got up, exclaiming, "You'd better enjoy yourselves while you can!" Then she ran from the gathering. The women sat in stunned silence as they watched her depart.

Kasha told the women to continue their singing and followed Orana into the forest. The waning moon had just begun to rise, so she found her easily. Orana was sitting rigidly on a rock by the side of the stream.

"What is it, my friend?" Kasha asked as she approached her.

Startled, Orana quickly got up from the rock, almost falling into the water. Kasha steadied her and asked again, "Is an Oracle trying to get through, my dear?"

"I … I really don't know," Orana answered with a trembling voice. "Something is trying to get out of me. Sometimes I feel as if I'm going to burst! But I haven't been given a message. It seems as if something is right on the edge of my mind, but it doesn't quite come through. And for some reason, I am afraid … deeply afraid, Kasha!"

"Then I wonder if it isn't time for you to prepare a potion and assist the Oracle in that way."

"Yes, Kasha," she agreed. "But … I am so afraid!"

"You fix the potion, and I will stay with you when you have drunk it," the High Priestess promised.

"As you always have, and I thank you, Kasha. I'll prepare the potion, and I should be ready to give an Oracle in a hand's span of sun journeys."

Back at the fire, Ashannah continued to lead the song as she watched Kasha follow Orana into the forest. The words of warning Eetoh had given her came rushing back into her consciousness with such force that the effort it took to concentrate on the song made tears sting her eyes. She knew that the best thing she could do, for the moment, was to keep the women singing. She was relieved when they got right back into the song, which they had sung quite often before. They seemed to want to forget Orana's outburst as much as she did.

Nevertheless, early the next morning, she sought out Kasha.

"All I can tell you, Ashannah," Kasha said, "is that Orana will be giving us an oracle in a hand's span of sun journeys. Perhaps you and I have some idea what she will prophesy, but then again, we may not. It will be good to get guidance from Inanna. This is what I have been waiting for."

"Yes, Mother Kasha," responded Ashannah, "we surely need guidance from the Goddess."

The women from Al-Rah were not at all surprised when word got around that Orana would be giving an Oracle. Fear filled all of their hearts, just from the little she had said at the fire circle.

On the appointed day, the women gathered in front of the temple, waiting for Orana and Kasha. The two women finally appeared, coming from Orana's hut. Kasha led, followed by the Sibyl, who was carrying a large cup high above her head. They were both dressed in beautifully decorated robes. The rustle of little shells, which they had strung around their ankles and wrists, accompanied them. The others followed them into the temple. The tapers around the wall had been lit, and it comforted the Virgins to see the paintings of their friends, the Goddesses.

Kasha went up to the front where the statue of Inanna stood and began to sing a litany in her praise. The women responded with fervor, perhaps hoping they could thus dispel any evil messages the Oracle might send them. After the litany was finished, Kasha stepped back, giving her place to Orana.

Orana put the cup directly in front of Inanna and bowed low in obeisance to the Goddess. Then she took a sip of the potion, which from the expression on her face must have been extremely bitter. She inhaled deeply, quickly lifted the goblet and drank its contents to the last drop.

The silence that ensued was thunderous, as the beat of each woman's heart drummed in her ears. The very air seemed charged with their unspecified fears and expectations. Orana, herself, was finding it difficult to breathe. Her mind continued to be blank. Would the Oracle never speak? She felt as if she were suffocating. Lights began to dance before her eyes until, finally, she saw a large and powerful woman form out of them. She opened her mouth as wide as she could, to let the Oracle out.

Gennah had slunk to the periphery of the temple, as usual. She had watched, as the skin of her mother's face seemed to shrink and pull itself tightly around her skull. She gasped as Orana's eyes rolled back in her head and her mouth opened wide, to allow the Oracle to speak through her. Gennah simply could not look at her. This could not be her mother! She closed her eyes as tightly as she could.

"Oh, you women of Al-Rah! You Virgins of Inanna! Listen carefully to the message I have to give you," the Oracle began. "Grief and oppression will come among you, walk with you, shrivel your hearts, cut off your breathing, but, in spite of this, you will cry out with pain!"

‘"You will call out for deliverance and for the freedom you have enjoyed until now. This first part of my Oracle will be true for all women, all over the earth."

The women could only stand in silence, wholly stunned by the message. Then as they understood more, they began to moan and weep. The Oracle made Orana stand and face the Virgins to make her position stronger. "Hush!" she continued. "Your crying will not stop anything. It is happening and will continue to happen for many cycles of the sun."

"Within the coming sun cycle, you, Virgins of Al-Rah, and some of the women from Et-Ray will be forced to give up everything you hold dear. You will be filled with fear and sorrow, confusion and misunderstandings, but you will find unsuspected strengths within yourselves."

"Yes, grief and oppression will be upon you. You will feel that Inanna, Ninlil and all the Goddesses have abandoned you. You will find yourselves completely at the mercy of the man. Truly it is the ***man*** who will oppress you, take away your freedom and life as you have known it. Hear my message and attend, oh you Virgins of the Goddess!"

The vision disappeared before the gaze of Orana, who then slumped, unconscious, to the floor. As she had promised, Kasha took Orana into her arms, crooning to her, as her own tears fell upon the Sibyl's shoulders.

As Kasha knelt, holding the inert body of Orana, she glanced up to see Ashannah kneeling at the side of the statue of Inanna. Her arms were outstretched, her mouth was slightly open and her eyes unfocused.

`"Oh, my daughter!" Kasha exclaimed, "Are you receiving an Oracle of your own?"

Chapter Twelve

Because everyone was watching Orana as she drank the potion, no one noticed that Ashannah had slipped over to the side of Inanna's image. Almost at once she was lifted up into that golden haze with which she was so familiar. The haze parted, and there was Inanna, a living, breathing Inanna, much more beautiful than the image of clay. The Goddess looked directly into Ashannah's eyes with such love that the Virgin was totally captivated, hearing nothing of the Oracle terrifying the other women. Inanna also had a message for the Virgins of Al-Rah.

As soon as Kasha noticed her daughter in trance, Ashannah returned fully to the temple environs. She stood and faced the women to deliver Inanna's message.

"Virgins of Al-Rah, my sisters! I have just seen Inanna, and I know that she truly loves us. I have also heard her, and I know that she will aid us in protecting our children. Our lives are going to change in ways we cannot imagine. Some men, most men, will be seeking power over us and will seem to attain it. But I also know that there are some men who remain faithful to the Goddess, at risk to their own lives. Not all men wish domination over us."

"These trials will strengthen us if we remain firm in our faith in Inanna. She will not allow us to be totally under the sway of these power-hungry men. Whatever happens to us in the near future and down many cycles of the sun, we must always believe in her and she will be there for us."

Then Ashannah began singing:

"Blessed be our Mother, Inanna."

"Blessed Be!" the women replied.

"Blessed be Inanna, who loves us," Ashannah continued.

"Blessed be!" the others responded.

"Blessed be Inanna, who guides us."

"Blessed be!"

"Blessed be Inanna, who is with us, wherever we go!"

Blessed be!"

"Blessed is our loving, caring Mother, Inanna, now and forever!"

"So be it! So be it!"

Ashannah was inspired by the enthusiasm of the women's responses and noted that even Orana had recovered and seemed to be uplifted by Inanna's message.

In a few days the women were living their lives much as usual, at least outwardly. They couldn't forget that Inanna had agreed with the Oracle that their lives were going to change, but until the challenge came, it seemed best to live each journey of the sun as fully as possible. Neither the Oracle nor Inanna had given them specific instructions as to how to prepare for the future.

As the sun journeys continued to grow shorter and colder, the women decided it was time to chink the temple walls for the winter. As usual, they made a celebration of this task. Anyone who was able to help did, even Elissa, Leah and Ran-dell. Beforehand, they had prepared a feast for the end of the day, and as they worked, they were dreaming of sitting around the fire that evening, eating, singing and telling stories.

Ashannah thought it would make the task go faster if they sang some of her humor songs while they worked. The women of Al-Labah had also taught them some of their songs. As they worked, sang and looked forward to the evening, life seemed good. The Oracle's predictions were momentarily forgotten.

The sun was setting quickly as a few of the women were filling in the last holes. They felt a quick change in the temperature, and some of them left to light the fire and put out the food. Then, suddenly, the peace of the evening was shattered by the shrill cries of a man.

"Thesta! Ashannah! Kasha! Gennah! It's happening! They're coming! They're truly coming! They'll be here by sunrise!"

Ashannah was on the peak of the roof, filling in the last chink, when she recognized Eetoh's voice. She slid down the roof, shocked by his message, even though he had warned her this might happen. Everyone in the village came running, but Ashannah was the first to reach him. She saw that in spite of the evening chill, sweat was running down his face, and his clothing was limp with the dampness of it. He must have run the entire distance from Et-Ray. He collapsed at Ashannah's feet, and she heard sobs along with his gasps for breath. She sent Elissa for some water.

By the time most of the women had gathered around, he was able to speak.

"Gan-dor ... Gan-dor came to Et-Ray!" He stopped to get his breath, take a sip of water and form his thoughts. "He is an evil man, Ashannah! When he speaks of how vile you, Virgins, are, his face distorts, his mouth twists around, he shows his teeth like an attacking animal. Yet I can see the gleam of pleasure in his eyes as he raves. He might hate you, but he gets pleasure from describing your ... your ... what does he call them? Your sins! Your sins are all the wicked and evil things you are supposed to do! The wickedness he says you are! I don't see how the men can believe him, but many of them do! They believe him, because of the power he promises them if they worship Enlil and get rid of you Virgins!"

"And ... and I have seen the way some of the men treat their wives! I don't blame you for not wanting to be a man's wife! They treat their wives like men treat their slaves! And Gan-dor upholds them in this. He says it is fitting punishment for the evil that is in every woman, Virgin or not! But I can see that he is the evil one!"

"Are you certain they will wait until morning, Eetoh?" Kasha asked, when he paused for breath.

"Tonight they are drinking barley juice. You know! The kind that makes a man crazy! But they believe it makes them strong. I think it makes them forget the terrible things they do!"

At this, some of the women began to cry out, wailing out their fear and wondering what to do.

Kasha climbed up on the pile of wood by the central fire pit. "Women! Women! Stop your crying at once! Listen to me!" Because the crying continued, she screamed again, "Listen to me! We must act quickly! We need to gather as many of our things as possible and leave here tonight, so that these men will find an empty village when they arrive here in the morning!"

"But we can't just leave our homes!"

"What will happen to our gardens?"

"How can we see if we travel at night?"

"What will happen to the temple ... to Inanna?"

"How will we protect ourselves from wild animals?"

"What will happen to my baby?" Beyla cried out. Elsa had been born barely two moon cycles ago.

Kasha felt overwhelmed by their responses, some of which seemed foolish to her, while others were very real problems that they had to face.

Ashannah called out, "Mother! Since the food is prepared, we should all try to eat what we can. It may be the last chance we have for awhile. Then we can carefully pack what is left. As we eat, we can think of what else we must do."

"Well spoken, my daughter. We shall do as she suggests," she ordered.

"We are fortunate in that the moon has just begun to wane," Ashannah continued, while the others began to eat. "By the time we have eaten, there will be light for us to see by, light that will last through the night."

Kasha insisted that Eetoh join them for the meal. "Will you help us make our plans?" she requested. "Only a few of us have traveled farther than Et-Ray." He quickly promised that he would help as much as possible. He realized that if he didn't they wouldn't get very far on their journey.

They had barely settled down by the fire pit, when they heard women's voices coming from the road to Et-Ray. Five women and the two little girls, Nella and Meldah, appeared trundling two loaded carts and carrying all they could. Angah ran up to Kasha. "May we come with you?" she begged. "Now that we've seen Gan-dor, we would all rather be Virgins with you ... even if it means dying with you . . than to become slaves of a man!" She began to weep as she clung to the High Priestess.

Kasha put her arms around the weeping woman, saying, "Of course, you may come with us! None of us knows what the future holds, but at least we will have each other, and most of all, we will have our freedom! We are certainly as one, in wanting that!"

Leenah and Estah were relieved to see Fannah and Deenah among them, and Gennah went up and embraced her old teacher, Rootha. Elissa and Leah were quick to run up and hug Nella and Meldah. The children were excited rather than afraid of the trip that lay ahead and did better than the women at eating. After awhile, some of the women began leaving the fire.

Kasha cried out, "Wait! We must plan together!"

"Mother Kasha!" Eetoh cried out. "May I make a suggestion?"

"Please do," she replied and then turned and faced the women. "As most of you know, Eetoh was raised in this village. Thesta is his mother, and he has remained a good friend to Ashannah. He risked his life to come and warn us about Gan-dor. I know we can trust him. I believe that Inanna has sent him to help us."

"Thank you, Mother Kasha," Eetoh said and began. "I will lead you upstream and on up the mountain. On the other side, I have heard there is a fertile valley where no one lives. I have not been there myself, but I am quite sure you would be safe there. As to getting there ... well, it will not be easy, but I will help you as much as I am able. As you can see, the moon is just rising. We should try to leave before it has traveled one more span of a hand, because with the infant and so many children, along with four carts, our traveling will be slow."

As he seated himself, Ashannah rose and said, "We should put the potter's wheels, the shovels, hatchets and weaving looms in the big cart. As for clothes, put on all that you have, your summer tunics underneath your winter coats and leggings. Wear a blanket over it all to keep warm. We will put any extra blankets in one of the smaller carts. Fill the other carts with baskets of food. If you don't have a child, carry whatever you are able. Since there is not much to forage this late in the fall, we must take as much food, as possible."

"Well spoken, my daughter!" Kasha said as she stood beside her. "Do as she says and do it quickly!" Suddenly Kasha remembered Orana's prediction that Ashannah would lead them over a mountain.

The women mobilized themselves to organize their belongings as Ashannah had suggested. They were ready to leave before the moon had traveled a full hand's span.

Eetoh led them to the sunrise side of the creek, where there was a natural trail to follow. Kasha and Orana stayed near the front, just behind their guide. Ashannah followed, pushing the large cart with the implements in it. Gennah and Elissa were right behind her. Mirah and Leah came next, followed by Grenda with one of the smaller carts. The remainder of the women took up the last part of the procession, ending with Estah pulling the last cart and Rootha and Angah dragging branches in order to erase their tracks, as Eetoh had instructed.

Adrenaline continued to flow in the women's veins, and no one noticed how high the moon had climbed, until Eetoh stopped to tell them that they were going to quit following the stream and begin to climb the mountain. The moonlight revealed a rather wide path, probably made by winter storms and animals coming to drink at the stream. The strong light from the moon enabled them to see and avoid large rocks on the path. After a time the path became more and more rocky, and the women began to envy Eetoh with his leather foot coverings, which went halfway up his calves.

The man gradually became aware of the little grunts of surprise and pain as sharp points penetrated even toughened flesh. He recalled with horror that the women of Al-rah never wore foot protection, as he had never worn any until he went to live with En-dor and began traveling and hunting. He realized that the women would not be able to go much farther, with the path becoming rockier at each step.

Just as he was coming to this conclusion, the predawn light sifted through the trees, surprising him. He could hardly believe they had been walking the entire night. To his right, the soft light suddenly revealed a small clearing. It would be the perfect place to stop and rest and to figure out what to do about all those bare feet. They were most grateful when Eetoh told them to prepare resting places for the day. After eating a little, that is just what they did. When night fell, they arranged themselves as before, to continue with the trip.

After several hands of the moon passed, Eetoh felt he could no longer command them to continue the painful trek. He desperately looked around and suddenly saw a large meadow to his right. He could hardly believe his eyes, wondering why he hadn't noticed it right away.

"It must be a gift from Inanna," he said to himself, as he stopped to tell the women of the plan, which was, even then, quickly forming in his mind.

By then, the women were not only feeling their sore feet, but a great fatigue was weighing down on their muscles. When Eetoh halted and pointed out the meadow, they were more than willing to stop and rest. However, he had to warn them that it would be dangerous to build fires. He thought it quite possible that the men in Al-Rah might see the smoke and guess where the women had fled. He didn't mention that if he were discovered with them, his life would be in certain danger for having helped them escape, but he was aware of it, nonetheless.

Kasha instructed them to take the extra blankets for warmth and also to lie close to each other for the same purpose. Ashannah suggested that they gather pine needles from the floor of the surrounding forest to cushion their bodies as well as helping to keep them warm. Then she made a bed for Eetoh and made certain that he got one of the extra blankets. He was embarrassed and grateful at the same time. He didn't think he would be able to sleep, as he was becoming more and more aware of the weight of the responsibility he had taken on. In spite of his worries, he fell asleep before the sun reached the tops of the trees.

Ashannah gasped as her body wrenched itself, waking her. Floods of memories from the preceding night poured into her mind. She thought it must be a nightmare and shook her head to flick it away. She reluctantly opened her eyes and found the meadow of her dreams displayed in all its firm reality. Then she recalled Orana's oracle from years before, that she would be leading the women of Al-Rah over a mountain to a new village.

"Goddess help us! It's happening!" She sat up, orienting herself to the meadow and the women sleeping there. It seemed that she was the first to awaken. She was shocked to see that the sun had only a few more hand spans before setting. Then she saw Grenda twisting in her blankets and rubbing her eyes. Ashannah got up quickly and went over to her.

"Greetings, my sister. May Inanna bless and keep you!" she said.

"Oh, Ashannah! It can't be true!" Grenda groaned. "Our beautiful little homes ... our gardens ... what will happen to them?"

"But we are alive and well enough, Grenda! It is life that is important!" Ashannah asserted, taking her friend into her arms.

Grenda shed a few tears and then pushed herself away. "You are right, Ashannah. We are still alive. Inanna does love us, to have sent Eetoh to warn us that the men were coming to destroy us."

By then, a sleepy Leah sat up and held out her arms to her mother. Grenda embraced her, almost fiercely. "For you, my dearest! For you, I will live out each journey of the sun as it comes!"

Other women were beginning to wake up, and after giving several more her message of hope, Ashannah saw that Kasha was going around doing the same thing. She returned to where she had left Gennah and Elissa. Gennah was awake, holding Elissa tightly in her arms. The child was looking around wide-eyed at the strange surroundings. When she saw Ashannah, she asked, "Mama, where are we?"

"In a lovely meadow on our way to our new home," her mother replied.

"Our new home?" both Gennah and Elissa asked.

"Yes," Ashannah replied with firmness. "We are on the way to find a new village, perhaps even more beautiful than Al-Rah. It will certainly be safer!" As understanding reached Gennah and Elissa, the three of them embraced tightly.

Ashannah saw that Kasha was speaking with Eetoh. They seemed to come to an agreement and got up together and approached the women.

"I want each of you to find something to eat from the carts," Kasha instructed. "We must eat enough to keep up our strength. Bring your food here and listen to Eetoh while you eat. He has important things to tell us, if we are to survive."

Ashannah didn't feel very hungry, but she knew that what her mother advised was wise.

"Wait here," she said to Gennah and Elissa. "I'll get something for the three of us." Fortunately, there were quite a few emmer buns from the night before. She took three of them and returned to her lover and child.

When everyone had settled themselves, Eetoh stood up before them. "I know that there is a fertile valley on the other side of this mountain, where no one else is living," he began. "It would be a good place for you to establish your new village. Getting there before the winter storms start is not possible. In fact, without protection for your feet, I don't see how you can go any further. Yet it is not safe for you to remain here." The women all murmured their assent.

"I have thought this over carefully," he continued. "I'm afraid that you are not going to like what I am going to say to you next."

The women simply stared at him, ready for anything. Certainly nothing he could say would be worse than what they had already gone through.

"You can see the fine, sturdy coverings on my feet," he continued, holding up one foot for all to see. "They are called boots and ... and they are made from the skins of deer, mountain goats and mountain lions." The women remained silent, but their eyes widened as the significance of what he was saying began to become clear to them. "Yes, you have to kill these animals in order to get their hides or skins." He paused once more. Murmurs of protest reached his ears. Ashannah said nothing, but stared at him intently, letting him know she did not like what she was hearing.

Kasha quickly arose and said, "Listen to him! He is right! We cannot go any farther without protection for our feet. If we tried to make boots from our blankets, they would not last a day. Besides we need the blankets for warmth." As the women stopped their murmuring, Kasha looked over at Eetoh, who continued.

"I know that you have a great reverence for life in all things. I, who was raised by you, also have this reverence for life. But I have come to understand that there are times when we must ask the animals' permission to provide us with food, and, in this case, clothing, as well. Yes, food, also. The food you have brought will not last the winter without being supplemented. You know that foraging becomes more and more sparse as the winter moons go by. And you may well have to spend the winter in a higher place, where foraging is even more scarce. It seems to me that at least for this winter, and until you establish another village with a garden, you will have to learn to eat the flesh of animals and use their skins for boots." He heard some grumbling, but no one challenged him.

"One way we show reverence for animals we … we must kill … and who provide us with their flesh and hides, is not to throw away anything. So, we will eat the meat and use the hides for footwear. Certain tools can be made from their bones and especially from the horns on their heads. We can dry the roasted meat so that it will be available during times when you are traveling and unable to hunt. Also, during the middle of winter it is difficult to find animals, so we should dry as much meat as possible."

Again, his words were met with silence, but there was no murmuring this time. The women were obviously trying to accept what he said. After a long pause, Eetoh said, "We still have a problem. When I realized that most of the men of Et-Ray, Et-Toll and Et-Bann were planning to destroy Al-Rah, I left right away to warn you, so that you could get away. The only hunting tools I have with me are a couple of slingshots, which I always carry with me. All we can kill with these are rabbits, which would only provide a little meat and perhaps provide boots for the smaller children. Still, it is a beginning. If there are any of you who will come with me now and learn to use the slingshots, we could probably get a few rabbits before dark. The rest of you should gather wood to keep fires going throughout the night, for warmth and to keep wild animals away."

He paused for breath and to see what effect his words were having. No one said anything, so he continued. "Tonight I will show some of you how to cook the meat and tomorrow will teach others of you how to scrape and stretch the skins. Later in the day, I will try to find suitable wood to make a bow and some arrows, so that we can kill some deer."

The women continued to stare at him in silence. He couldn't help noticing Ashannah, who seemed to be glaring at him, as if to say, "You ask us not only to eat the meat and wear the hides, but to join in the killing, too!" Eetoh stared right back, and finally her common sense told her that what he requested was necessary. She lowered her eyes in assent, but apparently could not volunteer to learn to use a sling- shot. He was wondering if anyone would do so, when Gannah stepped forward. Gannah was a small woman, but she was very quick and seemed to have an endless supply of energy.

"I will go with you," she said huskily.

"And I will, also," Thesta said, stepping up beside her son. "I just hope I can be fast enough."

The three of them left for the edge of the meadow, Eetoh showing the women how to walk in such a way as not to frighten their prey. After they were out of sight, the others began to gather wood.

The women set two fires around which they would sleep that night. They were beginning to wonder if it was dark enough to light them. The sun had set, but there was still some light lingering. It was also getting noticeably colder.

Just then Eetoh, Gannah and Thesta returned with a string of rabbits. At once, Ashannah walked over to congratulate the hunters. With that encouragement, Gannah admitted she had hit two of them. Thesta had killed one, and Eetoh had obtained four. He told them he thought it was safe to light the fires and settled down to take care of the rabbits. Ashannah watched closely while Eetoh skinned the rabbits so that the hides would remain as intact as possible. Then he stripped most of the meat from the bones. Ashannah was repulsed. Tears smarted her eyes, but she was determined to overcome her feelings. She realized that Eetoh had been right in saying that they would need to eat meat in order to survive the winter. She could see from the determined set of their jaws that Thesta and Gannah felt the same as she did.

A little later some of the women put hot stones into two baskets filled with water, to which they would add grains and roots. Eetoh suggested that they put some of the meat in the stew. He thought it would be easier for them to eat the meat mixed with food they were used to. They agreed with a minimum of reluctance. Ashannah dug out some of her herbs and liberally scattered them over the stews, hoping in this way to lessen the flavor of the blood.

While the stew was simmering, Eetoh quickly fashioned a spit on which to roast the remaining flesh. He explained that he would dry this to eat later.

The women sat in silence, obediently eating the food which did not please them. But they did eat it, knowing it would keep them alive until they ... Their thoughts ended there. The future seemed so vague and far away.

After eating, they continued sitting around the fire, talking and planning. "We might have to remain here for at least two hands of sun journeys," Eetoh conjectured. He had figured out that the number of adult women was three hands plus three and the number of children was one hand plus one. Only the two girls from Et-Ray were older than Elissa and Leah but only by two or three sun cycles. The boy, Ran dell, was close to two sun cycles younger, and Elsa had barely seen two moon cycles.

"I imagine it will take that long to train some of you to be hunters and others of you to learn to make boots for everyone," he stated. "During that time we can also dry a large supply of meat. For now, I'll use the hide of one of the rabbits to make two more slingshots. That way, four of you could hunt for rabbits, while I make a bow and some arrows, so we can hunt for deer."

Eetoh found himself perspiring heavily as he relayed these plans. Even though no one was saying anything, he could feel their resistance. He could only hope that they would soon realize that what he was suggesting was necessary. Still no one else offered to learn to hunt.

Eetoh found it harder and harder to breathe and wanted to shout out that he couldn't do it all by himself. After what seemed endless waiting, Mirah spoke up, saying she would try to learn. Sarah agreed to try, also. Eetoh let out a sigh of relief.

"I think I can learn to make boots, if you will let me look closely at yours, Eetoh." Gennah offered.

"I have never made any," he admitted, "but I know they use sharp splinters of bone with a hole in one end to punch through the hide and draw intestines or strips of sinew through, in order to fasten the pieces together." He wanted Gennah to know that he appreciated her effort to show her willingness to help

Before anyone else could say anything, they all gasped as the figure of a man came running from the path they had taken to arrive at the meadow. Someone screamed. Eetoh rose, at once, calling out so that all could hear, "My father!"

"En-dor!" Ashannah echoed, as she also got up to greet him. They were all quick to see the bows and arrows showing behind his shoulders.

Kasha also got up saying, "May Inanna be blessed for sending you to us."

En-dor acknowledged their greetings. Kasha led him into the circle, and someone brought him a bowl of the stew. He gratefully accepted the food, relishing each bite. Then he was ready to tell his story.

"When I heard the men of Et-Toll making their plans to join the men of Et-Ray in the destruction of Al-Rah, I looked around for Eetoh. I knew he would be very upset, and I was afraid of what he might do. As soon as I discovered that he was nowhere in Et-Toll, I realized that he had wisely left to warn you, without saying anything. I ran to our hut and saw that he hadn't taken his bow and arrows. I added them to my own and set out for Et-Ray. By the time I got there, the men had been drinking barley juice, and while they were bragging about all the terrible things they were going to do, none of them was even able to walk to Al-Rah. Then Gan-dor appeared and began shouting at them to stop drinking and to get some sleep, so that they would be able to carry out his plans in the morning."

"By this time the moon was high, and I slipped away and easily found your abandoned village. I remained there until the dawn's light would reveal your trail to me. I could see the efforts you had made to hide your path, but because of the darkness, you weren't entirely successful. That was fortunate for me, but I knew I had better complete the job you had begun, so that Gan-dor and his men would be unable to follow you, as I had."

"I have spent most of this day hiding your tracks and then finding you after the trail became rocky. I am sure they will not be able to discover how you left. They will probably just give up and satisfy themselves with destroying your village."

At these words, the eyes of every woman present filled with tears. A few wept aloud. Ashannah got up, tears running freely down her own cheeks. "My sisters," she began. "I grieve with you for our beloved Al-Rah. We worked hard to make it beautiful. It was our way of expressing our love for each other, for our Mother Earth and for Inanna. But Inanna has not abandoned us. She has given us life over death, by sending us Eetoh and En-dor to guide us to a new life. We must learn their lessons well and work hard to find our way to a new Al-Rah. Surely we will be wiser and stronger women from this experience. For now, we must try to sleep, so that tomorrow we can continue to learn from our guides."

"Well spoken, my daughter," Kasha cried out, "and so be it."

"So be it," the Virgins responded, as one.

CHAPTER THIRTEEN

The sun had just begun its journey across the sky, when Ashannah, Gennah and Elissa woke up to the sound of the birds and squirrels in the trees at the edge of the meadow, already seeking food.

"There must not be much water near here," Gennah observed. I haven't heard anything like a creek or a river."

"And if we're going to be here awhile, we'll surely have to find some water and soon," Ashannah responded.

The three of them got up as quietly as they could, and, taking a couple shovels, went in search of a spring.

Eetoh saw them disappear into the woods and wondered what they were doing. Surely they weren't about to go hunting for rabbits! He stretched and saw that En-dor was up, checking out the arrows he had brought. This reminded Eetoh that he wouldn't have to make a bow and arrows, at least, not right away. He greeted his father and sat down by him, much relieved that some of the burden of teaching the Virgins how to hunt and care for themselves while traveling had been taken from his shoulders.

"Did you notice, my father, that not one of the women, nor any of the children have any covering for their feet?"

"I hadn't noticed," En-dor admitted, "but I'm not surprised. I remember how, over three sun cycles ago, Gennah and Ashannah walked all the way to Tel Phar without any. But then we were traveling on smooth roads and much-used paths. The last part of this journey must have been very painful for them."

"It was," Eetoh agreed, "and though they didn't complain, I knew we would have to make a bow and some arrows during this sun's journey in order to kill some deer, so we could make boots for them. They will also need dried meat to get them through the winter. Thanks to you, we can begin to hunt at once."

Just as Eetoh began telling En-dor of the discussion about hunting, eating meat and making boots, Kasha arrived with some cooked barley that had dried berries mixed in it.

"May Inanna bless you, Kasha!" En-dor exclaimed. "I didn't expect to be eating this good."

"When Eetoh told us the men wouldn't be coming until morning, we had time to bring a few things with us in our carts. However, we realize that the food we brought will not last us very long. I think Gannah, Thesta, Mirah and Sarah are looking for you right now, Eetoh, to go hunting for rabbits."

As the four women approached, Eetoh said, "We'll have to scrape some of the rabbit skins first, so that I can make more slingshots. Also, now that we have two bows and two quivers of arrows, someone should go with En-dor to learn how to hunt for deer."

By then everyone was awake, and Eetoh spoke his request so that all might hear. Realizing that killing deer was inevitable, Leenah and Estah had discussed it between themselves and volunteered right away. En-dor was satisfied that both of them should come with him. He noted with relief that they were taller and more muscular than many of the women. As soon as they finished eating, the three of them went down to the far end of the meadow, where he could show the two women how to shoot the arrows without endangering the lives of the others.

Eetoh, his mother, Thesta, Mirah and Sarah began scraping the rabbit skins with their knives. After a little, Eetoh said, "Mine is good enough to make slingshots. While I do that, you should keep working on yours. They have to be entirely clean for making boots."

Kasha came up and asked, "Has anyone seen Ashannah, Gennah or Elissa?"

"I saw them go into the woods with some shovels before anyone else was up," Eetoh answered.

Kasha was visibly relieved. "I hope they are looking for water," she said. "I'm afraid there isn't any nearby."

"I was wondering what they were doing," Eetoh commented. "But if they were looking for water, wouldn't they have been carrying jars?"

"We didn't bring any large jars," Kasha replied. "They are heavy and break easily. But Rootha's baskets are tight enough to hold water for some time."

"I'm sure all they had with them were some shovels," Eetoh insisted.

"Then I think I'll get Orana and Rootha and see if we can't find some water," Kasha said.

Just then Ashannah, Gennah and Elissa came out from the forest. Their tunics were wet, so it wasn't surprising when Elissa called out, "We found a nice big spring! And we dug a hole for the water and put some rocks in it and … and …"

"And now we need to find some empty baskets and bring some water to the meadow," Ashannah finished for her.

"I was just going to look for some water myself," exclaimed Kasha. "Let's get some more women and some of Rootha's baskets and all go get some water."

Eetoh had felt embarrassed for Ashannah because she hadn't been able to get up the courage to kill, even for necessary food and clothing. He realized that water was most important and also noticed how prompt Ashannah was in recognizing the needs of the group. He remembered how she had given the women encouragement as soon as they had awakened the day before, and again in the evening, she had been quick to bolster their spirits. As he watched her wavy black hair bounce with energy, along with the admiration he had been feeling, came the old feelings of desire, which he tried to quell at once. He didn't even consider going with them, because he felt he wouldn't have been welcome. His old childhood feelings of alienation returned, along with the jealousy he felt towards Gennah.

"My father! My father!" Elissa was calling as she ran towards him. He knew she was imitating the way he addressed En-dor. His heart filled with joy, and he spontaneously opened his arms to receive her. His happiness was such that it brought tears to his eyes.

"My father, are you crying?" Elissa asked, somewhat surprised.

"Not really," he answered, hastily wiping his eyes. "It's just that … that you make me so very happy."

"You make me happy, too, my father!"

"I'm just about finished with these slingshots. Would you like to go hunting with us?" he invited.

He watched as her face fell and she replied, "I … I would like to be with you, but … but (she sucked in her breath) I don't want to kill any rabbits!"

"Well, in that, she is just like her mother," he thought. "Anyway, she wouldn't have the strength for it." As Eetoh sat down to complete the last slingshot, Elissa came closer to watch the process.

"How … how do you use it?" she wanted to know.

Eetoh pulled the last knot and, picking up a stone, stood up, showed her how to load the stone into the sling, pulled back his arm, swung it around several times and finally, with a flick of his wrist, released the stone far into the woods.

Elissa's eyes opened wide with amazement. "Ooooooh! I would like to do that!" she exclaimed. "But I still don't want … don't want …"

"Don't want to kill any rabbits," Eetoh finished for her. "Well maybe when you get hungry enough, you will change your mind," he added brusquely.

Tears came quickly to Elissa's eyes, as she realized she had somehow made him angry. Seeing this, Eetoh quickly assured her, "Besides you're not even strong enough, yet. Now I have to go with Thesta, Gannah, Mirah and Sarah, so that we can get some rabbits for our stew tonight. Some day I'll make you a little slingshot and show you how to use it. You … you won't have to use it to kill rabbits until you are ready."

"I would like that, my father," the child replied, giving him one of her widest smiles. Again, Eetoh's heart leapt with joy. The smile was her mother's, but he noticed how her eyes crinkled up at the corners, like his. He hugged Elissa and then led the rabbit hunters into the woods.

After Ashannah, Gennah and their mothers had filled the baskets with water at the spring and had taken them into camp, Gennah noticed Orana going off into the woods by herself. Something urged her to follow. Orana didn't go far. She came to a large boulder and sat on it, groaning as she did so. Then she stretched out her legs and began to rub and squeeze them.

"Mama, are you all right?" Gennah asked, as she approached her mother. She saw tears brimming in the eyes of the older woman.

Orana sat up straight and hastily wiped her eyes. "Yes, yes, daughter. I'm just not used to walking so much."

"You shouldn't have helped us with the water," Gennah remonstrated.

Orana quickly changed the subject. "We were blessed to find such a fine meadow with a spring close by. If we need to, we can stay here for quite awhile." She moved over, making room for Gennah to sit beside her.

"Oh, Mama! I already miss our little homes, and I'm sure you do, too!" Gennah exclaimed, as she sat down.

Orana looked closely into Gennah's eyes. "I do, indeed, daughter. Still, we were fortunate to get away safely. And … well, … there were also many sad memories for us in Al-Rah …" As she said that, she looked away.

Gennah was stricken with guilt, knowing that some times she had been the cause of these sad memories. "Oh, Mama! I'm sorry I … I was sometimes … not always a good daughter." Gennah began to cry softly.

Orana put her arms around her and said quickly, "We are … quite different from one another, Gennah. Sometimes I'm afraid I was not such a good mother. I wanted, so much for you to carry on … with the work of my mother and then my own …"

"But, Mama! I do not possess your powers!" Gennah cried out, the old feelings of frustration filling her heart.

"I know … I know, now, Gennah and I am truly sorry for …"

"Well, you more than made up for everything by your kindness to me after … after Ator …"

"That was a terrible time for you, my daughter. I am still filled with anger that we couldn't seem to do anything about it!"

"But you helped so much in my healing, Mama! And you helped Ashannah and me build our beautiful little house …" Here, Gennah began weeping over the loss of her home.

Orana sat silently for a time, her arm still around Gennah. Gennah's sobs subsided and then she suddenly burst out, "And sometimes I was ashamed to be your daughter! Oh, Mama! Now I am truly ashamed of myself! If we had listened more carefully to the Oracle …"

"Really, Gennah. None of us knew what to do! But … well … I hope that, now, you and I can be friends!"

"Oh, yes, Mama! I want that more than anything!"Gennah replied, returning Orana's embrace.

When Eetoh and the four women returned that afternoon with a long string of rabbits, he saw that Gennah was laboriously cutting a rabbit skin into pieces for a small pair of boots.

Gennah looked up at him and said, "Scraping these skins has really dulled our knives. I can hardly cut this."

"Here, you can use my knife, and I'll try to sharpen yours," he offered. "If we were near the Great Sea, you could use shells to scrape the hides. Scraping deer hides will dull your knives even more." He paused while he thought it over. "But after we have killed a deer," he said with enthusiasm, "the breast bones and ribs will make good scrapers."

"Your knife is making this much easier," Gennah said. "I think we should wait until we have some deer bones, before we do any more scraping."

"You're right, Gennah," he replied. "But I think I can sharpen your knife so that it will be as good as before." He took a piece of shale out of his tunic belt and sat down to work on her knife, while the women began stripping the meat from the rabbits.

After she finished cutting out the pieces for the small boots, Gennah found that she could splinter the leg bones of a rabbit and fashion a needle, as Eetoh had described to her. Finally, she cut some narrow strips of skin to stitch the pieces together.

"Who are you making those for?" Eetoh asked.

"For the boy, Ran-dell," she answered. "He has been walking for awhile, but the night we came here, his mother, Beleendah, had to carry him at times. I thought that the rabbit skins would last him fairly well. Later, we can make him some boots of deer hide."

"I had not noticed there was a boy among you," Eetoh said, with surprise.

"Well, he has scarcely finished two sun cycles," she explained, "and stays close to his mother."

"Is he the only boy ... like I was?" Eetoh wanted to know.

"Ummm ... yes, he is," Gennah admitted.

Eetoh continued working on Gennah's knife in silence, as, again, feelings of loneliness, from his childhood, welled up in him.

Ashannah and Elissa came over to them, Elissa sitting on one side of him and Ashannah on the other.

"Can you show me how to do that, Eetoh?" Ashannah asked. "My knife is also dull from scraping the rabbit skins."

"This is the only piece of shale I have, Ashannah, but I can show you and then you can use the shale to sharpen yours."

As the four of them sat there working, Eetoh felt very united with them and wondered why it couldn't always be this way. Elissa, however, soon became bored and went off to find Leah.

Kasha and Orana were setting the fires for the evening when En-dor, Leenah and Estah came out of the forest, dragging a travois with a buck fastened to it. It had taken them the entire sun's journey to make the catch, fashion a travois and drag it back to the meadow. It was obvious that all of them were exhausted.

Eetoh went over immediately to take care of skinning the deer, while Kasha searched out some food for the three hunters. It was still too early to light the fires and make a stew. Ashannah went over to Eetoh, in order to learn how to do the skinning. Again, he admired her for doing something he knew was very distasteful. He was just beginning to enjoy working with her, when desire filled his loins.

"I can't be around her much longer," he said to himself. When it became too dark to work more, he excused himself and went over to sit by En-dor.

"My son, what is it?" En-dor asked, sensing that something was disturbing him.

"I still love Ashannah, want her with all my heart," Eetoh replied, misery filling his voice.

En-dor did not answer right away. Finally, he said, "I do not believe she would ever leave Gennah, my son. They seem very happy together."

"I know! I know!" Eetoh agreed, but he was stung that it was so obvious. He looked at his father, saying, "I do not know how much longer I can stay here!"

En-dor understood right away. Again, he thought awhile before responding. "It is the whole village of women you must think of, Eetoh. They still need our help very much."

"I know, my father. I will try my best."

It wasn't until they had been in the meadow for four more sun journeys that some of the deer hides were ready to be transformed into boots. But when Gennah went to cut the pieces, she soon discovered that their knives wouldn't do the job. She saw that Eetoh was leaving with En-dor, Leenah and Estah, hoping to get more deer, bucks preferably, to add to the one Gennah was trying to cut and an old doe they had also killed. Just as the hunters were about to enter the forest, she ran up to them, saying, "I have been trying for almost a hand's span of the sun's journey to cut the buck's hide so that I can begin making boots. Our knives simply won't cut through, and the more I work at it, the worse it becomes."

"I'm sorry I didn't notice before," En-dor said. "I guess I've been too busy with the hunting. I know that your knives will not cut the hides, but I have something that will. He rummaged around in the belt holding his tunic closed and finally drew out something, carefully wrapped in a piece of linen cloth. "This is a stone that isn't found around here. They are found by the mountains that spit fire. I traded for it in Tel Phar, many sun cycles ago. It is called obsidian, and if you look closely, you can see that a sharp edge has been worked into it. I am sure it will cut the hides."

As she took it, Gennah barely pricked one of her fingers with the edge and it began to bleed. "Well!" she gasped. "I can see that it is truly sharp! If that's all it takes to cut my skin, I'm certain it will cut the buck's hide easily."

Before the hunters started out for the woods, Gennah had the hunters press their feet in some mud so that she could determine the size of boot needed by each. Since they were going out in the forest so much, she felt they should have the first boots. By the end of the day, Mirah, Gennah, Ashannah and Kasha had made boots for all six women, who were hunters.

When the deer hunters returned that evening, pulling two bucks on two travois, Ashannah, Gennah, Orana and Kasha offered to work through the night, roasting the meat to be dried, since they couldn't have fires during the day. It was then that En-dor showed them how to catch the fat dripping off the meat to make candles, similar to the ones in the temple, which had been made from beeswax.

Early the next morning, En-dor told the women that Eetoh had left for Al-Rah to see if any men were still there. Then they would know if they had to remain cautious about building fires during the day. No one suspected that Eetoh needed to be apart from Ashannah for a time.

As Eetoh stealthily approached Al-Rah, his heart constricted when he saw the battered remains of the little huts that had been the homes of so many women. Tears flashed in his eyes, as he picked out the space where the little hut had stood that he and Thesta had lived in for the first ten sun cycles of his life.

He wept openly when he saw the place where the temple had been. It was especially meaningful to him because it was there that he had made love with Ashannah and where Elissa had been conceived.

Believing that no one was around, Eetoh was about to enter the clearing when he saw a man walking down from the spring above Ashannah's hut. It was only then he noticed that her hut was intact and smoke was coming out of the hole at the top. Rage filled him, that a man had taken over her house for his own. He saw the rock image of Inanna standing in her garden. He knew the man probably didn't realize it signified Inanna. It took all of his will power not to run over and order the man to leave, at once. As his eyes cleared, he saw smoke coming from the other huts built on the hillside. Now he was certain that it had been wise not to build fires in the meadow during the day.

He watched as a woman emerged from another of the homes, and, for some reason, his rage became so strong as to be unbearable. He couldn't believe that a woman would take over a dwelling of a Virgin of Inanna! When he saw a dog come out after the woman, his heart leaped into his throat. Quickly, he slipped back into the forest, praying that the animal would not pick up his scent. Dogs were a rarity in Et-Ray, Et-Toll and Et-Bann, but they were becoming more and more common. He knew that, unlike other animals, when a dog picked up a strange scent, it would begin making a sharp sound, thus warning its owners that a stranger was around.

Eetoh slipped down to the stream and began wading in it, hoping to take away any scent of his presence, but the water was so cold that he had to go back to the land. He took a zigzagging trail, rather than the path by the edge of the stream, hoping this would confuse the dog. After a time, he decided it was safe to go back to the path and, thus, hasten his return to the meadow.

It was just dawn when Eetoh arrived at the meadow. He figured out that a hand's span plus one of sun journeys had gone by since he first led the women to the meadow. He stood quietly as he watched Ashannah and three other women carefully put out a fire, stretch and crawl under their blankets to rest, after a night spent roasting meat and scraping hides.

Next, he noticed En-dor stretching and then standing up, preparing to meet the coming sun's journey. Not wanting to startle his father, nor wake the women still sleeping, he slowly approached on tiptoe. "I wish to speak with you, my father," he whispered.

En-dor nodded towards the woods, and they walked over together. "Welcome back, my son," En-dor said, sitting under a tree. Eetoh joined him.

"Al-Rah is almost totally ruined," Eetoh announced, his voice breaking as he remembered the sight. "There is nothing left where the temple was standing. I don't know what they did with all that shale, with the roof, with the statue of Inanna."

En-dor remained silent, as he imagined the scene his son was describing.

"I was just about to go closer, when I saw a man coming down to

Ashannah's hut from the spring above it. All four of the hillside huts are unharmed and there are people living in them!"

En-dor looked closely at his son, but although he could tell Eetoh was quite upset, he still had nothing to say.

"My father," Eetoh began again, "I saw a ... a woman come out from one of them!"

En-dor felt Eetoh's anguish and decided it was time to speak. "Eetoh, it is hard to understand the ways of these people. However, it is good that you thought of not building fires here, during the day. I believe that we must continue this."

"I agree, but it is getting colder and colder each day. How much longer can we ... can *they* ... keep themselves warm just by working hard?"

En-dor chose to ignore the change in reference which Eetoh had made. "My son, I have a plan."

"I am listening, my father."

"By the end of this sun's journey, more than half of the women will have boots. We killed another buck while you were gone, and if we ... *you* can obtain still another one this journey of the sun, there should be enough hide to make boots for the rest. I do not know if we ... if *they* can carry all of the meat we have roasted and dried."

Eetoh noticed the care with which En-dor chose his words and his heart began to beat faster. Was his father thinking that the two of them would leave the women soon? To his surprise, he found his feelings were confused about it. Were the women really ready to fend for themselves, he wondered. "What are your plans, my father?" he asked.

"While you go hunting today with Leenah and Estah, I will go on up the mountain with two women of their choosing." He stopped and smiled. "Two of the women with boots, of course."

Eetoh smiled back, but said nothing.

"We will be seeking a new place for them to stay, but only for a night or so. They must travel quickly, now, in order to find a shelter for the winter. I do not believe it would be safe for them to stay on this side of the mountain. They need to go over the top of this ridge and find a suitable place on the other side. I have heard that there are large caves over there. One or two of these might shelter them for the winter. In the meantime, I will teach the two women who go with me to mark the trail, so that they can return and lead the first group to the new shelter."

"If some of the women still do not have boots, they will have to remain here until theirs are finished. They can send two women back along the marked trail to lead the rest to the new shelter. I truly believe they should move on as quickly as possible."

"As for us, after I have shown them how to mark a trail, we will have shown them enough to be on their own. They can improve their skills without us. I thought we could leave our bows and arrows with them. We will have more time to make ourselves new ones. Perhaps, in the next sun's journey, you can show them how to make arrows. It will probably be the sun's journey after that, before I will return with the two women. What do you think of my plan, my son?"

"Have you told the women of this plan, my father?" Eetoh asked.

Chapter Fourteen

Early that morning, all but the women who had worked during the night, were up, scraping hides and cutting and sewing boots They were so intent on their work, there was hardly any conversation. The sound of scraping and the twittering of the birds in the nearby forest was all that could be heard. As Eetoh watched them, he could tell that the women realized how urgent their situation was.

"I believe that the Virgins are ready to hear of your plan, my father," Eetoh commented.

En-dor continued to sit in silence, which made Eetoh restless. He wanted to leave with Leenah and Estah to hunt, but didn't think he should until they had heard En-dor's plan.

"Are you waiting until the others wake up?" he finally asked.

"Everyone should know of it," En-dor answered. "I hope they do not sleep much longer, however."

As though she had heard him, Ashannah sat up, rubbing her eyes. "Umm, my eyes sting. I don't think it is very good to work by the light of a fire." She got up, stretched and went over to one of the baskets of water and splashed some in her eyes. Seeing En-dor and Eetoh, she greeted them. "Do you think we will be ready to move on after four more journeys of the sun?" she asked. "It is getting colder and colder," she added, shivering and pulling her blanket more tightly.

"Well, Eetoh, I believe you're right. They are ready to hear my plan," En-dor said. Then he spoke directly to Ashannah. "I think that some of you should leave before then."

Ashannah was surprised. "You mean we ... we wouldn't stay together?"

"I have a plan for everyone to hear," he replied.

With that, Ashannah told Kasha what En-dor wished and went over to wake up those who were still sleeping.

After En-dor described his plan, the women sat in silence. Finally, Orana spoke up. "I don't see why we can't just stay here," she said. "This is a fine meadow and we have a water supply nearby. Couldn't we make shelters from poles and deer hides? Some of us still do not have boots and I, for one, do not look forward to climbing that mountain during the winter, even with boots."

"That sounds good to me," Thesta agreed.

"But mother," Eetoh interrupted. "I told you I saw men living in Al-Rah. If they see smoke on the mountain, they might come looking to see who is making the fires. They might even guess that it is you women of Al-Rah. I believe that they are very angry that you got away."

"There can't be many of them, if they destroyed all but the four hill-side huts," Orana argued.

"Do you want to fight with them?" Eetoh cried out. "Besides they could send for more men from Et-Ray."

Ashannah stood up and spoke in a loud and commanding voice, similar to the one Orana used when she was giving an oracle. "I had a strange dream, last night, although I wasn't sleeping. It seemed as if it came out of the fire."

Orana sat down and the others waited to hear the dream, sensing that it would contain an important message for their future.

"Inanna suddenly appeared before me right out of the flames," Ashannah continued. "She didn't speak to me, but beckoned for me to follow her into the woods. Somehow, part of me stayed by the fire, turning the spit, while another part of me followed her. Even though it was very dark, she found a path, and I went after her. The climbing was steep, and I was having trouble breathing, but she continued on. I had to struggle hard to keep up with her. Just when I thought I could go no farther, she stopped and pointed ahead. In spite of the darkness, I saw a large rock leaning out of the side of the mountain."

"This is your next stop," she instructed. "The overhang will give you some protection from the wind and cold." Then she disappeared, and I was back here, sitting by the fire, as if nothing had happened. In fact, I wondered afterward if it had happened or if I had simply dreamed it. I am not certain, even now."

En-dor spoke up, at once. "I believe Inanna showed you the next place for a shelter. You should be one of the women to go with me."

"I will watch out for Elissa," Kasha volunteered.

"Then I, too, will go with Ashannah,"Gennah announced. Eetoh felt pangs of jealousy arise in his heart, but kept them to himself. He wanted this ordeal to be over with, but he didn't want Ashannah to leave. He wanted to be near her for every bit of the time they had left together.

He stood up, saying to Leenah and Estah, "We should go hunt for that one more deer we need." They quickly gathered their bows and arrows and left.

En-dor told Ashannah and Gennah to get two blankets each and instructed them how to fold them so that they could pack some dried meat and other things in them. He demonstrated how to tie the packs to their backs, all the while outfitting himself in the same manner. Finally, he told them to each get a hatchet. While the two women put on their boots, En-dor filled a deer bladder with water, tied the opening and fastened it to his belt. He fashioned two more for Ashannah and Gennah. When Gennah and Ashannah got the hatchets, and fastened the containers of water to their belts, they were ready to follow En-dor up the mountain.

As they climbed, the firs and cedars became thicker and they could see less and less of the sky. After a short time, En-dor stopped, and taking one of the hatchets, he cut a notch in a cedar tree by the path. The women inhaled its pungent odor with pleasure. They watched carefully as he made the notch point in the direction they were taking.

"We will do this every so often, so that we'll be able to find our way back to the meadow. There are many trails made by water and animals, and it is easy to take a wrong one, if you haven't marked the trail," he warned.

The climb quickly grew steep and the forest much thicker. The trail narrowed and began to intersect with others, as En-dor had foretold. They took turns notching trees. After a time, Ashannah said, "It is just like it was in the dream. It's getting harder and harder to breathe!"

"Yes, En-dor," agreed Gennah, "it is getting harder to breathe."

"For some reason, it gets like that when you climb high in the mountains," En-dor said. "Let's rest awhile, but not for too long." He unfastened his bag of water and sat on a rock to rest. The women noticed that he was breathing with difficulty, too, and were happy to refresh themselves.

After a bit, he stood up. "We can walk slower, but we should try to go on. The days are getting quite short, and the sun has already traveled two hand spans since we left the meadow."

Ashannah and Gennah stood up and followed him up the trail, which was becoming so rocky that it was difficult to keep their footing, even with boots. Then En-dor began to zigzag, making it easier. The notching of the trees became more important, and they had to stop and do it more often.

When they stopped to rest again, En-dor decided that they should eat a little of the dried meat. "It will give us energy," he promised.

The two women hadn't yet eaten meat that wasn't mixed in a stew of vegetables. As Gennah ate, she felt more energetic. On the other hand, Ashannah struggled to eat several bites, washing it down with water, and then waited to feel the energy. She didn't feel any different, but said nothing.

"I liked the fish we ate on the trip to Tel Phar better," she finally said.

"Well there aren't any streams nearby, so the dried meat will have to do," En-dor replied with some impatience. He noted Ashannah's silence as she forced herself to eat a few more bites, but he could tell she was disgusted by the expression on her face.

"We need to travel on if we're going to find the rock in Ashannah's dream before dark," he finally stated, as he wrapped the meat and put it back in his pack. He continued the zigzagging, and the women carefully notched the trees at each turn. After a time, he suddenly stopped and pointing ahead, exclaimed, "Look up there! Do you see that large rock? It looks like it's hanging out from the mountain."

They continued on a few paces, staring at the rock. Finally, as the rock came into full view, Ashannah cried out, "It is the rock in my dream!" Since the sun had almost set, they felt fortunate that it was so close. They would scarcely have enough light to gather sufficient wood to keep a fire burning through the night. As they entered the overhang, they gratefully felt the warmth from the huge rock, which had absorbed some of the heat during the day. Later, as they were sitting, huddled by the fire, as far back in the overhang as possible, Ashannah commented, "The overhang does protect us from the wind and the rock will pick up some of the heat from our fire, but still, there is not enough room here for everyone."

"That's right," Gennah agreed. "I don't believe more than half of us could get in here. And if you were on the edges, you would hardly be protected at all."

"But you do need to begin leaving the meadow and getting up and over onto the other side of the mountain, before the snows come," En-dor reminded them. "I suggest that you bring up half of the women, and then you and Gennah should go ahead and look for the next shelter, no more than a day in advance. In the meantime, two other women could go back to the meadow for the rest, who ought to have boots by then. Meanwhile you would have returned here to take the first group up to the next shelter. Do you understand what I am saying?"

"I ...I think I do," Ashannah replied. "I ... guess that we just have to believe that Inanna will lead us to another shelter, no more than a day's journey from here."

"Look how she has taken care of you so far," En-dor reminded her.

"You're right, En-dor!" both women exclaimed, and Ashannah added, "Inanna said that it would be by faith in her that we would survive these changes in our lives."

"And she does that, by showing you the strengths you have in yourselves to meet each challenge," En-dor pointed out.

Both women were surprised by his insight. Just two hands of days ago, they would never have thought they could learn to hunt, much less to prepare meat and hides so that they would have food and also have protection for their feet.

Gennah sat there, puzzling over En-dor's instructions, and finally asked. "I believe you said that just Ashannah and I would be finding the next shelter. Does that mean you and Eetoh will be leaving us?"

Ashannah had not picked up on that and was astounded. En-dor was relieved that Gennah had noticed it, but he didn't know how to respond and sat there awhile staring into the fire. He wanted them to feel certain that they were ready to care for themselves without them and to understand how dangerous it was for Eetoh and himself to remain with them much longer.

Finally, he was ready to speak. "Eetoh and I have taught you all that you need to know in order to continue on. Hunting, preparing the meat and the skins will become easier the more that you do it, as will making the trails. Some day you will begin a new village like Al-Rah. A village with gardens, a beautiful temple and homes. Like Al-Rah, it will be a village of Virgins."

"Eetoh and I are traders. We would not feel that we really belonged in the new Al-Rah, just as my son never felt that he belonged in the old Al-Rah."

As En-dor spoke these words, Ashannah's eyes stung. She knew they were true, but she wished, somehow, that could change, too. "Eetoh and Elissa are just getting to know and love one another. I feel that has been a good thing," she said.

"So do I," agreed En-dor. "But that does not really take care of the other problem. Perhaps, someday, we will be able to find you on the other side of the mountain and begin trading for you again and ... somehow ... to come to know and love one another in new ways." His eyes were glistening now, and tears were freely running down the cheeks of the two women.

"Already, Eetoh and I are going to have to think of how to explain our absence from Et-Toll for so long," En-dor continued. "This is not the season for trading. The men with Gan-dor have probably been wondering how you knew to leave Al-Rah before they got there. If they ever realize that Eetoh and I helped you ...

Both women stopped crying, at once, as they realized the risk the two men had taken for them.

"May Inanna bless you both, En-dor, for your goodness to us, and may she protect you from harm when you return to your home," Ashannah said.

En-dor smiled and replied, "Thank you, Ashannah. I have great faith that Inanna protects the men who believe in her and respect her Virgins."

Because she hadn't had much sleep the night before, Ashannah took the last watch. After En-dor awakened her, she built up the fire to a good blaze and rested against the back wall of the overhang. Their conversation with En-dor the previous evening came back to her. She felt sad that the two men would be leaving them. She knew that Elissa, especially, would miss Eetoh. The two of them had grown quite close during their time in the meadow. She felt good that she had finally told Eetoh he was Elissa's father, and she was glad that they would have some time together during these last days.

Then again, as she was staring into the fire, she saw Inanna rise up out of the flames, smiling at her with great tenderness and beckoning her to follow. This time Ashannah didn't hesitate, knowing that a part of her would remain behind to tend the fire.

Inanna rose up over the trees, as if flying like a bird, but without wings. Ashannah felt herself lift off the ground in order to follow her. She wondered briefly why she wasn't cold away from the warmth of the fire. Traveling this way, it was no time at all when Inanna was pointing out another overhang to her. She looked back and could see the fire she had just left., which would aid her to return. This also gave her the general direction they would need to take in order to arrive at the next overhang. It, too, would accommodate only about half the women, but that no longer seemed a problem. Then, suddenly, she was seated back by the fire, and Inanna was nowhere to be seen. Ashannah knew she wouldn't forget how the new shelter looked, nor what direction to take to get there.

As soon as the dawn presented its light through the trees, Ashannah awoke Gennah and En-dor and told them of her vision. They all blessed Inanna, quickly ate the meat Ashannah had warmed for them on the rocks by the fire, and began the return trip to the meadow.

Because it was downhill and the trail was already marked, they arrived there just a little after the sun had reached its zenith. This assured Ashannah that, even with two of the carts and some of the children, the first group should be able to get to the new shelter in one of the sun's journeys.

As they came into the meadow, Ashannah could see that most of the women were seated around Eetoh, who was showing them how to make arrows. Elissa was seated right next to him, as was the boy, Ran-dell. Then the little girl spotted her mother and ran over to her, shouting, "Mama! Mama! Lookee what Eetoh made me!" Ashannah took the little slingshot to inspect it. "He showed me how to use it, too," the delighted child continued. "But I don't have to kill rabbits with it until I'm ready! He said so, Mama."

Ashannah looked over at Eetoh and smiled her gratitude, not realizing her smile was sending arrows into his heart. Then she saw that Leenah, Estah and Mirah were busy scraping the hide of the buck they had recently killed, with the meat drying nearby. She realized that they could leave with the first group the following morning. The thought that they would finally be traveling towards their new home blocked out the pain of Eetoh and En-dor leaving them. In fact, Ashannah found herself quite excited with the prospect, looking forward to seeking out the shelter she had been shown the night before.

The women in the meadow were surprised to see the travelers returning so early and gathered around them to hear about their adventures. Eetoh remained where he had been seated. and En-dor quietly went over and sat beside him.

Ashannah stood by the fire pit and announced, "We found the shelter I saw in my dream. It is only large enough for about half of us, so those who already have boots will begin the trip, while the rest stay here and finish boots for the others. After Gennah and I have taken the first group to the shelter, we will continue up the mountain to find the next shelter, which Inanna showed me last night. In the meantime, two other women will return here to lead the rest of you to the first shelter."

"Blessed be Inanna and the care she is showing us!" the women cried out.

"So, who would like to be the first to leave?"

"I would still like to remain in the meadow," Orana called out. "Nor do I see why those of us who wish to, cannot stay here."

"Oh, Mama!" Gennah exclaimed. "We told you why that is not possible." She went over and sat by her mother. No one spoke of wanting to remain with her.

"I will want to stay with the remaining women," Kasha announced. "You might as well stay with me, Orana," she invited.

"I, too, will remain," Thesta spoke up. "The three of us do not have boots yet, anyway. But we will need at least two of you who are young and strong, to push the last of the carts."

"I do not have boots yet, and I can help with the carts," Flora offered.

"Leenah and I can finish the boots and also help with the carts," Estah said.

Beleendah spoke up, "I would like to stay here with Ran-dell as long as possible."

Finally, Deenah and Fannah agreed to remain, along with Nella and Meldah.

"Blessed be Inanna," Eetoh whispered to En-dor, but there were tears in his eyes. "I will miss little Elissa ... and, of course, I will miss Ashannah, too. Actually, I will miss all of them."

"So will I, my son," En-dor agreed, "but you know our life leads us on a different path."

"Yes, my father, and a part of me is eager to get started."

"I thought that perhaps we could leave as soon as the waning moon comes up, which will be shortly before dawn."

"That seems like a good plan, my father." Eetoh's voice broke from the strain of wanting very much to return to his life as a trader, yet wanting at least as much, if not more, to remain with his little family.

Ashannah and Gennah spent the rest of the day showing the women of the first group how to make packs out of their blankets, and then they each filled them with as much of the dried meat as possible. En-dor had been right. They had more meat than they could possibly carry in the carts. They were so busy that they didn't notice how the two men kept apart from them.

Chapter Fifteen

Ashannah awoke with a jolt. At first, she thought someone had shaken her, but Gennah and Elissa were sound asleep, and it was absolutely quiet in the rest of the camp. She shivered again and realized that it was definitely getting colder in the early mornings. She could barely see a line of light in the east and knew it would be awhile before the sun would rise enough to give them warmth.

Suddenly she knew what had awakened her. Half of them would be leaving for the overhang she, Gennah and En-dor had found the day before. They were finally starting out in search of their new home. They had been working towards this goal for close to two handsful of days, yet, now that the time was here, she was afraid as well as excited.

'She knew it was necessary for them to break up into two groups, but she was very uncomfortable about it. Also, En-dor and Eetoh would be leaving them. She understood that the two men had already endangered their own lives by remaining with them this long, but she couldn't help wondering if she and the rest of the women were entirely ready to fend for themselves. She was amazed at how much they had learned in such a short time, but …

She carefully raised up on her elbows, so she wouldn't wake Gennah and Elissa, and looked over at the men's little camp on the edge of the forest. Quickly she pushed her arms out straight, in order to see better. The camp was gone. She edged out from under the blankets, pulled on her jacket and boots and ran over. There were the two bows and two quivers of arrows which En-dor had promised to leave for them. Then she noticed how they had carefully removed all traces of their fire pit. Apparently the two men had left without saying good-bye. She could understand why they had chosen to do this, but ... but what about Elissa?

She picked up the bows and quivers of arrows and walked back to the central fire pit in the women's camp. Sarah, bundled tightly in a couple of blankets, was dozing by the coals. She had taken the last watch. Ashannah put down the weapons and gratefully picked up one of the warm pieces of venison Sarah had thoughtfully placed on some hot rocks amidst the coals. As she chewed it, she realized that her repugnance for meat had all but vanished.

Sarah's head jerked up as she realized that she was not alone. "Ashannah!" she exclaimed. "Here, get inside these blankets with me. It's really cold!"

"They ... they're gone!"Ashannah sputtered, as she took Sarah up on her offer. "The men ... have left! I understand why, but ..."

"Well, I don't!" Sarah cried out. "How are we going to get along without them?"

"Sarah, En-dor explained to us yesterday how dangerous it has been for them to stay away from Et-Toll for so long, right after we were found missing from Al-Rah. If the other men find out that they warned us, it would mean their very lives would be in danger."

"So why couldn't they just stay with us ... live with us? Why would they want to go back with those wicked men, anyway?"

"Because our kind of life isn't theirs. They are traders. That's what they like to do."

Ashannah hadn't noticed that Gennah and Elissa had come over to join them by the fire, so she was startled when Elissa asked, "Who likes to trade? Who are you talking about?"

"En-dor and ... and Eetoh, little one. They are on their way back to their home in Et-Toll," Ashannah reluctantly replied.

Elissa turned to look towards the men's camp and could see there was nothing there.

"Maybe ... maybe they've just gone out into the forest hunting!"

"They have rubbed out their fire pit, baby. Besides, En-dor told us yesterday, why it was necessary for them to get back home as soon as possible. If Gan-dor's men realize that they helped us get away from Al-Rah, they would kill them."

Elissa stared at her mother in disbelief. "Would ... would my father leave me without saying good-bye?" she asked as tears welled in her eyes.

"En-dor promised they would find our new village later and come and trade for us again," Ashannah assured her.

Elissa crawled inside the blanket with her mother and, burying her face between Ashannah's breasts, sobbed out her sorrow.

After the other women had awakened and had come over by the fire to eat a little of the warmed meat, Ashannah reminded them that the first group should be leaving for the overhang as soon as possible. The sun had just risen and they would soon be feeling its warmth.

When they finally started out, Ashannah began singing the litany to Inanna. The women remaining in the meadow joined in the responses with the others, until they couldn't hear the invocations any longer. Soon the travelers became too winded to continue singing.

Zolah stayed by Beyla to share in carrying little Elsa. Gennah had given them a small woolen blanket to keep the baby warm. She showed them how to fashion it into a sling, so they could carry her, leaving their arms free.

Ashannah's eyes moistened when she noticed that, inside her belt, Elissa was carrying the little sling shot that Eetoh had made. She watched as the little girl would surreptitiously stroke it, as if to assure herself of Eetoh's love.

Grenda and Mirah, who had been pushing the two carts, struggled harder and harder as they climbed the rough trail. Along with the rest of the women, they were relieved when Ashannah suggested they stop, rest and refresh themselves with food and a little water. When she started up again and began taking the zigzagging trail, they found it much easier. She showed them how to look for the trail markers, which pointed the way.

"Look! Look through there!" she suddenly called out, when the overhang first came into view. The women cheered and felt new energy rise within them. Ashannah warned them that the overhang was not as close as it looked; nevertheless, just seeing it encouraged them to continue on.

The sun still had over a hand's span to travel before setting, when they finally reached the shelter. They quickly took off their packs and began gathering firewood for warmth through the night. As soon as the fire was going well, they began warming up some of the food they had brought with them. There didn't seem to be any water to make a stew. As they were eating, Ashannah spoke of her plans for the following day.

"Tomorrow, Gennah and I will go in search of the next shelter. After another sun's journey, two of you should go back to the meadow, and the next day, bring the others on to the next shelter, so that this one will be free for the rest of the women."

"If you find a new shelter," someone grumbled.

"We will find a shelter," Ashannah firmly replied. "I have already seen it. Who would like to return to the meadow to bring the rest here?" Estah and Leenah volunteered at once.

"Do you understand that you should wait until the next sun's journey before you go get them? That way, Gennah and I can come back for this group and be gone by the time you arrive with them." The two women nodded in the affirmative. Then Ashannah asked if another woman would volunteer to go with her and Gennah, so that they could have three watches during the night.

"But I'll be with you!" Elissa cried out.

"Oh, baby," Ashannah exclaimed, "you wouldn't be able to stay awake."

Before Elissa could reply, Gannah spoke up, offering to go along. By then, the women were finished eating and were more than ready to sleep.

The following morning, when Ashannah, Gennah and Gannah began preparing to leave, Elissa also gathered up her slingshot and pack.

"Listen, my little one," Ashannah said, "we will be making a new trail and we really don't know how soon we'll find the next shelter. It would be best for you to stay here."

Having just lost her father, Elissa couldn't bear the thought of not being with her mothers. She ran over to Ashannah, clinging to her legs. "Please, Mama! Please let me go with you!"

Grenda came over and put a hand on the child's shoulder. "But wouldn't you like to stay with Leah?" she invited. "I'll make her a little sling shot like yours and the two of you can practice using them."

The suggestion was appealing, and Elissa didn't want to hurt Leah's feelings by refusing, but she didn't let go of her mother.

"Please, Elissa!" Leah pleaded. "We could have so much fun practicing together. And just think how good we'll be when your mothers come back."

Elissa slowly pulled away from her mother and went inside the shelter, so she wouldn't have to watch Ashannah leave. Leah was right behind her, and Grenda began looking for a small piece of rabbit skin for the new slingshot, before the women were completely out of sight.

With Gennah and Gannah close behind, Ashannah started off in the direction she remembered from her vision. She believed their goal lay just a little to the mossy sides of the trees from the shelter they had just left. The trail she chose to follow began going downhill and since the slope was gradual, she didn't have to zigzag. Also there were fewer rocks, and the earth was packed hard.

"This trail will surely be easier for those pushing the carts," Gennah commented, as she marked another tree with her hatchet.

"Yes," agreed Ashannah, "but I hope I'm going in the right direction. It seems strange to be going downhill, yet I feel we are getting closer to the shelter."

A little later, Gannah cried out, "We're probably going the right way, Ashannah. Look ahead. We're going to start climbing again, soon."

Ashannah saw that Gannah was right. As they approached the oncoming hill, she thought she saw the shelter for a moment.

"What a relief," she sighed. "Yes, I believe we are going the right way."

As they began to climb, the slope was so steep they had to zigzag, and it became quite rocky, as it had been before. The trees began to become more scarce, and Gannah wondered aloud, "I hope there are enough trees to mark the trail."

"Well, if there aren't, we'll just have to think of another way," Ashannah replied, and then she shouted, "Look! Look up through those trees! That's it! We'll be there before long."

The trail quickly became very steep, and no matter how much Ashannah zigzagged, it was very difficult climbing. "It might take two women to manage a cart here," Gannah said, panting.

"Whew, it probably will," Gennah agreed. "But at least it isn't much farther." Nonetheless, it took them another hand's span of the sun's journey to get there.

"I hope we can make it in one journey with the whole group," Ashannah said, as she began to take off her pack. "But wait! I think I hear running water nearby. We could surely use some, since there wasn't any at the last shelter." She began walking towards the sound, the others following. They soon discovered a small stream, sufficiently deep to fill their bodas.

"It'll be good to have a stew again," Gannah remarked. They drank some of the water and rested a little. Then Gennah suggested, "Let's begin gathering wood, while it's still light. Maybe we can gather enough so that when we come with the next group, we won't have to, or at least not as much."

They realized that, even though the last stretch of their journey had been quite strenuous, on the whole it had been less tiresome than the previous trip, and they were able to gather a good supply of wood.

After enjoying some stew, Ashannah took the first watch. She hoped for another vision from Inanna, but one wasn't forthcoming.

When Estah and Leenah returned to the meadow two more sun journeys later, they could feel the relief and joy of the women. They got tight hugs and saw tears in more than one woman's eyes. Even Orana seemed ready to continue on. Best of all, they learned that everyone had boots, and they could begin the trip to the overhang the next day.

The following morning, Estah suggested that every woman carry at least two bodas of water, since there was no supply at the shelter. Then they set out with light hearts, thinking of soon being reunited with the others. They forgot that the women of the first group would have left for the next shelter by the time they got there.

When they reached the zigzagging trail and Leenah stopped to rest, Kasha noticed how pale Orana was. She asked her how she felt and Orana replied, "My legs are hurting very much. Even after the walk we took the night we left Al-Rah, they ached. That's why I didn't want to leave the meadow!" Orana began to weep quietly.

Kasha got out some of the grease she had saved from the meat and rubbed some onto Orana's legs."That does make them feel better, thank you, Kasha. But I know we need to go on if we're to reach the shelter before nightfall." Having said this, she struggled to stand up. It was obvious to all the women how painful it was for her.

Because she was carrying Ran-dell part of the time, Beleendah had found herself a sturdy stick and suggested that Orana use one, too. It didn't take long to find one, and Orana found that it helped quite a bit and felt able to continue on.

Estah and Leenah cried out for joy when the shelter finally came into view. All of them felt better on seeing their goal. Sarah and Minah took over pushing the carts, and everyone put out more effort, so they would reach the shelter before nightfall. Kasha could see that Orana was struggling to keep up, so she found her a second stick. It didn't help much, but at least Orana knew that Kasha cared.

When they finally arrived at the overhang, the first thing Kasha did was to gather pine needles to make a comfortable bed for Orana, while the others set and lit fires and prepared some stew. After Kasha elevated the Oracle's feet, she massaged her legs and feet until Orana went to sleep. Kasha was relieved that they would rest for a whole day and another night before going on to the next shelter.

After the day of rest, they set out once more. Somehow Orana managed to stay with them but she was obviously in great pain.

Gannah's prediction that it would take two women to manage the carts on the steep incline approaching the second shelter proved to be true. In fact, sometimes three women were involved, in order to keep the carts from tipping over. It took them well over a hand's span of the sun's journey to make that last stretch of the trip, and all of the women of the first group were exhausted by the time they arrived at the shelter. They were relieved to find plenty of firewood already gathered.

Because Ashannah had concentrated on keeping to the trail, she hadn't done much helping with the carts, so she prepared the stew and took the first watch.

Gennah offered to take the first watch with her, but Ashannah could see how fatigued her partner was and knew that Elissa would not sleep well without one of them near her. She also believed that if someone were nearby, she wouldn't receive a vision to guide them to their next destination. In spite of this precaution, Inanna did not come to her. She was somewhat troubled by this, but decided that a day of rest would be good.

When Gannah relieved her of the watch, she was glad to curl up around Gennah and Elissa and was soon asleep. Just before the sun rose, she had a very vivid dream of a huge cave. Upon awaking, she realized she had seen their winter shelter. Did that mean they were near the ridge of the mountain? No particular direction had been given her.

When she got up and looked out beyond the shelter, she saw a light dusting of snow on the ground. However, the sky was now clear, and the sunlight made small rainbows on the snow. In spite of this, the sight of the snow struck terror in Ashannah's heart. She knew she wouldn't rest for the day, as she had planned. Neither of the shelters would provide enough protection from a heavy snow or continuous cold weather. She sought out Gennah and Gannah and asked them if they would go with her to seek the cave she had seen in her dream.

Since she hadn't any idea as to the route she should take, she climbed up on top of the rock that had sheltered them for the night, in order to get an overview of their surroundings.

The first thing she saw was a sheer drop-off quite close to the shelter. She was surprised that none of them had noticed it before, but quickly realized it wouldn't be visible from underneath the overhang. It came to her that it might be easy to walk off the edge, if one didn't know it was there. She breathed a sigh of relief that the small stream was on the opposite side of the shelter. Suddenly she felt nauseous with dread, as she looked out and beyond the cliff. Was it a premonition? Ashannah swallowed several times, thus relieving the nausea, and dismissed the forewarning at the same time she decided that it was not the direction to take to the cave.

She turned around in order to look uphill to determine if they were close to the summit. She saw that the trees became more and more sparse and also noticed a kind of path, probably made by running water. She saw that by following it they would come to what looked like the summit of the mountain.

Ashannah climbed back down under the shelter and told the others what she had seen, warning them not to go near the drop-off, even to collect wood.

Gennah and Gannah had already begun packing, putting in as much food as they could possibly carry. She told the others not to be concerned if they hadn't returned by the following evening. From her dream, she determined that their next shelter would be the cave, where they would spend the winter. They would, therefore, continue looking until they found it. She assured them that it would be found soon.

She asked Rootha and Angah to go back to the first shelter to tell the others, so they wouldn't feel abandoned or worry that something had happened to the first group. Then she led Gennah and Gannah onto the new trail. By now, Elissa understood the seriousness of their situation and didn't offer any opposition.

The three women soon saw that there were not enough trees to mark the trail, so that it could be accurately followed. Gannah devised a plan of making a pile of rocks in the shape of an arrow, pointing the way. When Gennah suggested that the rocks would be covered by snow in a heavy storm, Ashannah reminded her that they had better be finished using the trail before a great storm arose.

"Besides, can you think of another way to mark the trail?" Gannah asked. "This is also going to take longer than notching trees, but it seems to be the only way." Both Gennah and Ashannah had to agree, and they continued on.

When they finally arrived at what had seemed to be the ridge, they saw that the slope on the other side only went down for a short distance and that there was another hill looming ahead. They wondered what was beyond that. The slope down was slight, and they were able to go directly to the hill facing them. The incline was steeper than the downward slope, so Ashannah led them at a slight angle, making the climb easier. When they finally reached the summit, they were totally amazed at what they saw.

CHAPTER SIXTEEN

It was the vastness of the expansive valley, that presented itself to the three women, which held them enthralled. Far across, they could make out seven mountain ranges, the higher ones and those farthest away being lavender. The next range was darker, tending to purple. The purple deepened into indigo, which in turn developed into a deep green, the green of the myriad conifers of the mountainside nearest them.

They noticed narrow trails of yellow, which were hardly recognizable as being alders and willows with frost bitten leaves, following along the veins of tributaries, leading far down to what appeared to them a narrow silver ribbon, running along the floor of the valley. In truth,as they would learn much later, the ribbon was a wide river, which became turbulent in the spring, as the winter snows melted and ran down- stream to the home river.

The women's eyes widened as they looked upon the beauty of their future home. It was Ashannah who finally broke the silence.

"Let her be known as Al-Rah Montah, the dwelling of the Goddess between the great mountains."

"So be it," replied Gennah and Gannah. "Blessed are we to be a part of such a beautiful gift from Inanna."

"Truly spoken," agreed Ashannah.

They were filled with feelings of deepest loyalty to Al-Rah Montah, as if it had been the home of their mothers and of their mothers' mothers and the mothers of those mothers. Or perhaps they realized, on a deeper level, that they would become the ancient mothers of generations to come.

Again Ashannah spoke up. "You can see how many sun journeys it will take for us to get to the floor of this valley. There was a little snow on the ground early this morning. We will not be able to reach our final home before the heavy snows. Now we must seek out the cave of my dream, which will give us shelter from the snows and winds of winter."

She began to lead the others down a winding path. Gannah and Gennah hastily scraped piles of rocks together to point out the way for the trips to come. After nearly a hand's span of the sun's journey, the conifers had become thick enough that they could begin marking the trail by notching trees. They had gone nearly another hand's span when Ashannah went up to an especially large cedar to mark it with a notch. She approached it from the downhill side, she herself facing uphill and looking back from where they had just walked. "Gennah! Gannah! Look! We've passed by the cave! There it is!" she exclaimed, pointing uphill.

The two women turned and looked where she indicated. The sun's light made the edges of the gaping mouth a bright orange, but it was probably the dark shadow of the interior that they saw first, because it was such a contrast.

"You can see it will be large enough for all of us," she continued.

"Yes," Gennah replied, awe filling her voice. "It is truly huge!"

"We need to return to the last tree we marked and approach the cave from there," Ashannah said as she began walking back up the trail. When they found the marked tree, they put rocks across the trail and elongated the notch to show that a sharp turn towards the mossy sides of the trees would take them to the cave.

As they came closer to the cave, Ashannah noticed a musky smell, which told her the cave was probably already occupied. She turned and whispered to the others. "Do you smell it? I think some animal has already made the cave its home. Well, this is the cave I saw in my dream, so we must think of a way to let it know it needs to find another place. After all, a smaller cave would suffice for it."

"But do we know there is only one animal in there?" Gannah asked.

"I guess we don't," Ashannah admitted. "So, now what do we do?"

"It could be some bears or some mountain lions," Gennah whispered, her fear making her voice tremble.

"And we didn't even bring a bow and some arrows," Gannah said ruefully.

"I think we can get it to leave without killing it," Ashannah said. "Listen, I have a plan. Let's gather some dry brush and lots of tinder. Then we can go very quietly to the mouth of the cave and set a small fire. After it is going good, we can put some green branches on top to make it smoke. I don't think it, or they, would want to stay in a smoky cave."

"That sounds like a good plan," said Gannah, "but what do we do when they come out? They'll probably be angry and attack us."

"I'm afraid you're right," Ashannah agreed.

"If we leave as soon as the green branches catch fire," Gennah suggested, "we can run uphill. Since there is a slight breeze coming downhill, I don't think they will smell us. At least I hope not."

"Good for you, Gennah! I'm sure that will work!" Ashannah exclaimed.

They quickly gathered brush, tinder and green branches and, as quietly as possible, walked to the mouth of the cave. Fortunately, the floor of the cave was a smooth rock, which would keep the fire from spreading. Gannah pointed to some droppings on the floor, which further testified to an occupant.

They stood and listened a little before venturing farther in. When they didn't hear anything, Ashannah led the way in as far as she hoped was necessary. They set the fire, which caught quickly. Before they put on any green branches, they heard a low roar come from the back of the cave.

"Go on!" Ashannah yelled. "I'll get the smoke going and join you! Go! Go!" Gennah and Gannah were so surprised by the tone of her voice, they did as she said, without arguing.

Ashannah peered into the darkness as she waited for the fire to get a good start. She saw nothing, but a second growl came from the cave's depths. She quickly threw on the green branches and ran from the cave.

After she had climbed a fair amount, she turned and saw smoke billowing out of the mouth of the cave. Then a mountain lion, followed by two half-grown cubs rushed out. The lioness stopped and sniffed in the direction Ashannah was hiding. Ashannah's heart leaped into her throat. Just then, a cloud of smoke assailed the lioness and she rushed down the hill, the cubs following close behind. Ashannah let out a sigh of relief, but didn't move.

The three women remained where they were hiding for some time. Finally, Ashannah felt it was safe to approach the cave. When Gennah and Gannah saw her, they joined her.

The water they had left in their bodas was hardly enough to put the fire out, but it sufficed so that they were able to finish by stamping it out.

"Another good use for boots," Ashannah said grinning.

While Gennah and Ashannah began gathering wood for the night, Gannah took their empty bodas and went in search of water. She found a small stream nearby and filled the bodas. When she returned to the cave, she noticed much filth in the back of it and knowing it came from the droppings of the lioness, she went to get a large cedar branch, in order to sweep it out.

When Ashannah and Gennah returned, they made a fire and got food out from their packs.

"Come and eat with us, Gannah," Ashannah invited. "You've got most of the dirt out and we can finish cleaning it in the morning. Since I told the women we might not be back by tomorrow evening, I would like to stay here for a sun's journey. We can finish cleaning the cave and look for some roots and even some dried berries. I feel certain we'll be able to find some, since no one has been foraging here but animals. We haven't much left besides the dried meat."

The following sun's journey, Ashannah climbed up the hill behind the cave, to get a good look at their surroundings. She was relieved to see that there were no steep cliffs, like the one by the second overhang. Downhill from the cave, she spotted a small meadow and thought they might be able to find roots and dried berries there.

She returned and helped finish cleaning out the floor of the cave while telling the others of the meadow she had seen. They took their emptied blankets and were able to fill them with plump roots and a few berries.

"Won't the others enjoy the fine stew we'll be able to make with these roots and berries!" Gannah observed.

"So will I!' Ashannah laughed. "It's too bad we don't have a basket so we can make a stew tonight, but we can enjoy some of them raw."

They spent the rest of the day gathering wood. Gannah suggested they stack the wood in front of the cave, thus forming a wall to protect them from the wind. Later, Gennah came across a good deposit of shale and hurried to tell the others. "When we've got the carts here, we can take the shale up by the cave and build a wall of it in front of the wood. That way, we'll still be protected as we use up the wood."

"And it will remind us of the temple in Al-Rah," Ashannah said wistfully.

The next morning, when they arrived at the summit of the mountain on their way back to the second overhang, they stopped again to look out over the vast valley, that was to be their home.

"Just seeing this gives me the energy to push on," Gennah said.

"And I think it will give energy to the rest, also," Gannah added.

"Then let's go on, so the others can see it, too," Ashannah said, as she started down the other side.

Because the trail was already marked, there were still several hand spans of the sun's journey left when they walked into the camp. The women were not only relieved to see them, but were delighted with the roots to enliven the evening's stew.

While they were eating, seated around the fire, the women listened eagerly as Ashannah described the beautiful valley that was to be their home. Everyone loved the name Al-Rah Montah.

Later, as they were preparing to sleep, Ashannah asked Gennah if she would like to go with her to get the women waiting back at the first overhang. "Gannah can take these women to the winter cave and we will be reunited with our mothers," she explained. "We can rest there for a day and then take them to the second overhang and finally join the others in the new cave."

The joy they felt making these plans, led to an embrace and a few furtive kisses, the first they had indulged in for some time.

"And what's going on over there?" Grenda asked, laughing.

Elissa ran over by them, calling out, "I want a kiss, too!"

Ultimately, everyone joined in a little love celebration for having found their winter home.

Before the sun rose the next morning, they were all ready to go on their respective ways, Gannah leading the first group to the cave and Gennah and Ashannah going back to get the others. Again, Elissa wanted to go with her mothers.

"Don't you want to see the new winter home?" Ashannah asked, somewhat surprised.

"I can wait," the little girl insisted. "You've already marked the trail, and I want to see Gramma Kasha and Gramma Orana."

Because the difficult incline was going downhill on their return and they didn't have to notch trees, Ashannah, Gennah and Elissa arrived at the first overhang just a little before the sun reached its zenith. They were greeted with tight hugs and joyfully tearful eyes. These women had been waiting at the first overhang for four sun journeys. Ashannah suddenly realized how difficult it must have been not even knowing if a second shelter had been found .

Kasha told Gennah about Orana's legs, and when she went to massage her mother's legs that night, she found there were swollen blood vessels under the skin and in two places they had burst through. The next morning, Kasha carefully bandaged Orana's legs before she put her leggings on. Orana made a great effort not to show how much pain she felt, as they walked out of camp. Ashannah led the way and Gennah and Elissa stayed back with Orana. They were grateful for the long downward slope at the beginning of the trail.

When they ultimately arrived at the steep incline, while most of the women struggled with the two carts, Kasha slipped back to help Gennah with Orana. Although the sibyl didn't complain, several times tears ran down her cheeks from the pain. Often, they simply had to stop and let her rest.

"Oh, my dears," she finally said, "I'm so sorry to cause you so much trouble. Maybe you should just go on without me! It's getting dark and the others must already be there!"

"That's right," Gennah said, trying to sound cheerful. "They'll probably have the stew cooked and ready to eat by the time we arrive."

As the sky grew darker it was becoming more difficult to keep to the trail, Ashannah came to help. "The women are preparing the stew, and there's just a little farther to go," she assured them. "Even though the moon is new, there's still enough light to see the notches in the trees."

When they finally arrived, Kasha took Orana's leggings off and found two more places the veins had burst through the skin. Ashannah promised that they would remain at the overhang another day so that Orana could rest, but she shivered as she remembered the light snow that had been on the ground again that morning.

Orana ate a little and then seemed to fall asleep. When no one was looking, she drew some dried leaves from the little bag she wore around her neck, mixed it in with the rest of her stew and after eating that, fell into a deep sleep a few minutes later.

Just as she awoke the following morning, Orana heard Ashannah warning the women about the sharp drop off north of the camp. Orana was filled with dread and excitement as a plan formed in her mind.

It didn't take long for the women to replenish the wood supply for the coming night, so Ashannah had plenty of opportunity to describe the beautiful valley that was awaiting them, as well as the large cave where they would spend the winter.

While the others were absorbed, listening to Ashannah, Orana struggled to her feet, got the two walking sticks and hobbled, unnoticed, from the overhang. Just as Kasha became aware that Orana wasn't among them and was getting up to go find her, a piercing shriek riveted the healer to the spot, as it ricocheted back and forth between the walls of the chasm. Kasha guessed, at once, what had happened, but ran with the others towards the sound, praying that her hunch was wrong.

Ashannah yelled out, "Don't go too fast! Look out for the cliff!"

When Gennah realized that her mother wasn't in the cave, she also guessed what had occurred. "Mama! Mama! Where are you?" she screamed, as she ran towards the drop-off. As the truth became clearer, Gennah ran faster and faster, passing up everyone else. "Mama! Mama!" she continued to scream. Even though Ashannah had longer legs, she was barely able to overtake Gennah. She grabbed hold of her, dragging her to a stop.

"Let me go, Ashannah!" Gennah screamed, as she struggled to be free.

"I'm just trying to slow you down, Gennah!" Ashannah yelled. "I'll ... I'll go with you, but we've got to be careful! You ...you don't want to leave me and Elissa, do you?"

"Oh, Ashannah, do you think she did it on purpose?" Gennah sobbed.

"I don't know," Ashannah replied. "Let's go see if we can ... if she needs help, or something!"

By the time the two women had come to the cliff's edge, the other women had caught up with them. The first thing they saw was one of Orana's walking sticks leaning precariously over the edge. There was no sign of the other one. Gennah ran over, picked up the stick and hugged it to herself, crying hysterically. "Oh, Mama! Mama!"

Ashannah took her in her arms, letting her grieve. Neither of them could look over the edge.

"Do you see anything?" Grenda asked cautiously.

"N ... no," Mirah answered, as she looked from side to side. "I can't see anything besides the cliff and the trees below."

"Are you sure?" Gennah asked and stepped over to the cliff edge to look for herself. "It would be terrible, if she's still alive and … and needs help!"

In the meantime, Kasha had heard the cries of Elissa, Leah, and Randell. She went up to Ashannah and said, "I'm going to take the children back to the overhang. I can hear them crying in the forest. You stay with Gennah."

"Oh, thanks, Mama!" Ashannah said, somewhat aghast that she had forgotten about Elissa. Then, she, too, began to search the area beneath the cliff. None of the women could see anything.

"Somehow, I have to get down there and find her," Gennah said. "Even … even if she's dead!" She began to run towards the sunset. The cliff seemed to end there, and a gradual downward slope began.

"Wait, Gennah!" Ashannah shouted. "I'll go with you, but let me get a hatchet first. It won't help if we get lost!"

"Let me go with you, too," offered Sarah. "You might need me to help … to help …"

"Thanks, Sarah." Ashannah said. "You're probably right. We may need your help. Why don't you go with Gennah, while I get a hatchet."

"I'm coming, too!" Thesta spoke up.

"Thanks. Thanks, Thesta," Ashannah murmured, glad for the support. When she saw some of the others preparing to come along, she said, "That should be enough of us. The rest of you should go back to camp. Would someone tell Kasha what we're doing?"

Ashannah quickly found a hatchet and turned to catch up with Gennah, Thesta and Sarah. She went up to Gennah and took one of her hands. "We'll find her if it takes the rest of the sun's journey," she promised. "The sun hasn't' even reached its zenith."

Her heart lurched when she happened to look up and saw some vultures circling lower and lower, down into the gorge, beneath the cliff. She didn't say anything, but hastily directed them towards where the birds seemed to be headed. They finally reached the tree line.

"It's … it's going to be hard to find her, if she's somewhere in the trees!" Gennah gasped, slowing down. Wondering how Ashannah seemed to know where she was going, Gennah followed. Then she inadvertently looked up and saw the circling birds. "Hurry!" she shouted as she started to run. "We don't have much time!"

Giving the hatchet to Thesta, Ashannah ran to catch up. "I want to be with you … when we find her!"

Gennah slowed down a little, but continued to run forward. When Ashannah caught up with her, they both slowed down, so that they could search carefully. The vultures were right overhead.

Suddenly Gennah screamed, as she pointed. "There she is!" She stopped so fast, Ashannah ran into her.

Ashannah quickly followed Gennah's pointing finger. Orana's body was caught on the lower branches of an oak tree. She could see blood dripping on the ground.

"Let me go first, Gennah," Ashannah insisted. "I don't believe she is alive, though."

Gennah fell to her knees sobbing, unable to look anymore, or to go closer. Sarah went on with Ashannah, while Thesta remained with the sobbing Gennah.

"Call me if you need me," she cried out.

When Ashannah and Sarah approached Orana, they could see that her body was almost completely severed in half from the force of the fall. She was most certainly dead. Ashannah reached up to pull Orana down by her legs, but stopped when she realized that she might pull her completely apart. Sarah began to climb the tree.

"Stand right under her, Ashannah, and I'll try to lift her off the branch."

Ashannah did as Sarah asked, holding out her arms. Sarah eased Orana off the branch, and Ashannah caught her, falling to her knees from the weight. By then, Gennah was running over towards them.

"Oh, Mama! Poor, poor Mama!" she sobbed as she reached for her mother's body. Sarah climbed down out of the tree and Thesta came over to help.

"At least we got her before those … those awful birds!" Thesta gasped.

"We need to … to decide …" Ashannah couldn't finish the sentence.

"Well, go find it!" Gennah cried out. Ashannah eased the body entirely into Gennah's arms and, with the others, began looking for some kind of hole or overhang, where they could put the body and then cover it with earth and rocks. Sarah saw one first. She pointed to a small cavity beneath an overhang with loose dirt and rocks close by, as if a small rock slide had fallen from the top.

"Blessed be Inanna!" Ashannah gasped, as she ran up to it. "It's just right!"

"It's ... it's not going to be easy to get her here," Thesta pointed out.

"We'll do it, though," Ashannah insisted. "It won't be easy to get her anywhere the way ... the way she ..."

"We'll do it though," Sarah repeated, and they went back to where Gennah was still cradling her mother in her arms.

The four of them got on one side of Orana's body and slipped their arms under her back. In this way they were able to carry her over to the cavity without doing further damage to her body. They carefully laid her out in the bottom of the cavity and began to cover it with loose earth and rocks. Gennah was, by now, dry-eyed, wholly concentrated on protecting her mother's body from the vultures.

When they finished, Ashannah led them in singing the song to Inanna, asking the Goddess to take her daughter, Orana, into her earthy bosom. Gennah was not crying, but she was unable to join in the singing. When they finished, Gennah thanked them and they began the return to the camp. On the way, they found a small stream which enabled them to wash the blood from their tunics.

Later in the day, Thesta led the rest of the women down to the grave, where they also sang the song. Gennah, Ashannah and Elissa remained in the camp, comforting each other.

"Oh, Ashannah, what would I do without my little family?" Gennah said.

That night as Ashannah lay with Elissa on one side and Gennah on the other, waiting for the blessing of sleep, she thought, "This is our first loss, since we had to leave Al-Rah. Will there be more?"

CHAPTER SEVENTEEN

"I … I just can't believe it, Ashannah," Gennah gasped early the next morning, shortly after they had awakened. "I can 't believe that Mama's not here with us … that she's dead!"

Ashannah looked deeply into Gennah's eyes and wondered if she had slept at all. She couldn't really think of a comforting thing to say, so she simply put her arms around her beloved, and together, they wept.

"We were just beginning to get closer, Ashannah," Gennah finally continued. "Not like you and Kasha, but we were getting closer."

"I know, Gennah," Ashannah agreed. "I know you were getting close, and it was very beautiful."

"Really? You could tell?

"Oh, yes," Ashannah instantly replied. "It was truly a blessing."

"So why did she … oh, why?" Gennah began to weep, once more.

"She was in a lot of pain, Gennah," Ashannah offered. "And … and I think she was afraid of holding us back … of keeping us from reaching the winter shelter in time."

"But we were so close!" Gennah burst out. "But … I think you're right. Remember when she told us to leave her on the trail? Oh, you weren't there! Just before you came to get us, she said, "Why don't you just leave me here and go on?"

"And she knew we would never do that," Ashannah said, holding Gennah closer.

Just then, Elissa woke up, asking as she rubbed her eyes, "Where … where are we?"

"We're on our way to our new home," Ashannah reminded her.

In a trembling voice, Elissa asked, "And Gramma Orana ... where ... where is she?"

Before either woman could think of what to say, Kasha came up with a bowl of steaming barley. "If we're going to our new home today, she said, "we should eat a good meal first." She handed the bowl to Ashannah, although it was meant for all three of them.

Ashannah glanced out of the overhang and gasped, "Is that snow on the ground, again?" She could see that it was more than a light covering, as before.

"Yes, it is," Kasha answered. "Thanks to Inanna, it isn't deep, but it is snow. It isn't snowing now, though, and it looks as if the sky is clearing."

"Gennah, ... do you think ... you can ... can ..."

"Of course, I can. If Mama ..." Here she interrupted herself. "Let's eat and get ready!

All of the women were unusually quiet, almost listless as they prepared to continue on to the cave. Ashannah didn't even consider starting up a song to make them feel better. But she had hopes that when they saw Al-Rah Montah, their energy would be at least partially restored.

By the time they were approaching the ridge of the mountain, the snow had all but disappeared. When they crested the ridge, every woman there gasped at the beauty which lay before them. Across the way, the highest peaks were covered with a sparkling layer of snow.

"Why, it is beautiful, truly beautiful!" Kasha cried out. "It is truly Al-Rah Montah!"

When Ashannah felt that their spirits were filled with the beauty of it all, she spoke up. "You can see that it will take many sun journeys to get down to the floor of this valley. And winter is already here. But as I told you, we have found a huge cave we can all live in until spring. Let us give thanks to Inanna and continue on."

She began singing the litany of praise to Inanna, and she could tell that the women's spirits had been lifted, by the way they sang the responses. Much to her relief and joy, she heard Gennah joining in.

They had barely begun to descend the mountain, when Gannah came running up the trail towards them.

"Wait!" she called out. "Let me show you how to manage the carts going down hill."

They waited until she came up to them. "Oh, Ashannah! Kasha! I'm afraid that we lost one of the little carts!" she wailed. "They are much harder to control going downhill," she explained. "We didn't exactly lose it, but it got away from us and crashed into a tree. We were able to save most of the provisions, but the cart, itself, is badly damaged."

No one spoke, not even Kasha. They realized how serious it was to lose one of the carts. They would never be able to replace it, now.

"Anyway," Gannah finally continued, "We discovered that if we turned the cart around and the person taking it got in front of it and pulled it, rather than pushing it, she could control it with her body, like this." Gannah walked up to one of the carts and demonstrated.

When they were passing by the remains of the broken cart, Ashannah went over to see if she could fix it. She didn't want to delay the journey to the cave, however, and decided to come back for it later. She doubted that they could fix it, but she knew the milled wood would be of some use to them.

When they finally arrived at the cave, there was a big feast waiting for them, a stew generously enhanced with herbs, roots and grains.

The women began hugging each other, laughing and talking, rejoicing at being together again.

Kasha clapped her hands to get their attention. "My sisters, please listen! I have something very sad to tell you. Orana is no longer with us. She chose to … she was afraid to hold us back and … and … "

"And what, Mother Kasha?" Gannah broke in.

Gennah stood up to finish telling them.

"The blood in my mother's legs was breaking through the skin. She was in great pain and finding it more and more difficult to walk. Rather than holding us back and perhaps making us all be caught by the heavy winter snows, she chose to … chose to throw herself off that cliff near the second overhang." Here Gennah began to sob.

The women of the first group stood there, gaping, unable to believe what they were hearing. Those who had been there began sobbing with Gennah, and soon everyone was grieving together.

Finally, Ashannah was able to speak. "We found her. We found her and buried her well, to protect her from the vultures."

Stifling the urge to begin weeping again, she started singing the song to Inanna, begging the Goddess to take her daughter, Orana, into her bosom. Soon the cave was filled with the voices of the women, as each joined in.

Filled with grief and shock, they now found it difficult to eat the stew they had prepared. Ashannah noticed all the work that had been done by the first group while waiting for the others to arrive. She stood and spoke out. "I can see all the work you've been doing. You've got over half the wall of wood up and you've begun the wall of shale."

The women were glad to be appreciated, as well as to have their minds taken off the tragedy, and they began to eat a little.

That night, while she was waiting to go to sleep, Ashannah heard Gennah sobbing softly. She curled around her and began stroking her hair and shoulders, crooning softly into her ears.

"Isn't Gramma Orana coming back?" Elissa asked.

The two women were startled, thinking the child had fallen asleep. Gennah took the little girl into her arms and answered, "No, Elissa, Gramma Orana isn't coming aback. But she truly wanted us to take care of each other."

The next morning before it was light, the women sleeping where there was no wall as yet, found their feet and legs covered with snow. Ashannah built a fire so they could warm themselves, and some of the others tried to sweep out the snow, but it kept blowing back in. Fortunately, with the dawn it stopped. The women quickly pulled on their boots and worked most of the day, finishing the wall of stacked wood. Grenda took half a deer hide left over from making boots and hung it over the small opening they had left to get in and out of the cave.

After building a fire by which to dry the blankets in which they had wrapped themselves, as well as their boots, they prepared the only meal of the day. They were so exhausted that as soon as they were finished eating they quickly fell asleep.

Kasha and Thesta kept the fires going until the boots were nearly dry. As they were sitting there, Thesta let out her feelings of anxiety. "Oh, Kasha, can we live like this for a whole winter? I even wonder if we have enough food."

"Thesta. we have to believe that Inanna will show us how to care for ourselves until we are able to leave here for Al-Rah Montah. I do not see how we'll do this for the whole season either, but for tonight we will keep the fires going, so that we will have warmth and dry clothing for tomorrow. And tomorrow, we must believe that we will do what we must for that day, and in this manner, work it out, day by day."

"Well, I guess you're right. What else can we do? If nothing else, my faith in Inanna will grow."

Thesta, I firmly believe that there are many things for us to learn from this. We have already learned so much. We have learned to kill animals, in order to have food and protection with their skins. We can mark trails and protect ourselves from the weather with whatever means we find" Kasha paused. "Perhaps, not all of us will arrive at Al-Rah Montah. One of us ... has already ... left us. May her spirit be united with Inanna's."

"So be it," whispered Thesta.

The women were pleasantly surprised when they awoke the next morning, to find how warm the cave was. But when they went to put on their boots, they discovered they had stiffened so much, it was impossible to put them on. Ashannah finally got hers on, but it was very painful to walk on them. With great determination, she hobbled o the doorway and looked out.

"Well, we won't have to worry about getting water," she announced. "It's right here at our door." She kicked off her boots and quicklly walked barefooted a few yards from the cave to relieve herself, even though it was still snowing. While the others followed her example, she got one of Rootha's tightly woven baskets and filled it with snow.

The women quickly built a fire in order to warm their feet and heat some stones to melt the snow. Ashannah found a rock and began pounding on her boots, hoping to soften them.

"En-dor told me that we really weren't preparing the skins in the right way," she explained. "After scraping the hides, we should have stretched them and then soaked them in oil from the insides of the bark of oak trees. They should soak in this for an entire sun's cycle, but we just didn't have the time."

When she had softened one of her boots a little, Ashannah began to pull on it this way and that, hoping to stretch it back into something of its original shape. The other women began to work on their boots in the same way.

"Are we going to have to do this every time they get wet?" Sarah asked.

"Well, there's not much else we can do," Angah laughed. "For instance, even though I have my potter's wheel, I don't have clay, and even if I did, I could hardly build a kiln in here to fire my pots." Ashannah laughed along with her, as did the others, but it was because it seemed better to laugh than to cry.

By that time the snow in the basket had melted, so they brewed some tea and cooked some barley and emmer. After they had eaten and had begun, again, to work on their boots, Ashannah began singing one of her humorous songs. Everyone joined in, making up new verses as they went along.

The sun had just passed its zenith when they tired of working on their boots, especially since they were making little progress. They had even lost energy for singing. Gannah looked again and announced that it was snowing harder than before.

As the women looked at each other, they began to feel that they were being forced together in a space that was growing smaller by the moment. Little ripples of panic began to flow through each woman. Suddenly Gennah stood up. The force of her action riveted everyone's attention on her.

"I think we are all scared of spending the winter together in such a small space," she began. There were murmurs of assent and a few nervous giggles. "We are used to living alone or with a child or at most with one other adult and child, and now we are sharing one space with four hands of women …" Here, Gennah gulped and corrected herself, tears filling her eyes as she did so. "three hands of women plus four fingers … and a hand plus one finger of children." The women and children remained silent, while she fought to control herself.

"We were not given much choice in the decisions we were forced to make so quickly. Basically, we chose life over death and freedom over something like slavery, which Ashannah and I have described to you. Is life and freedom worth all of the things we have suffered so far?" Again, her voice broke, and tears filled the eyes of every woman in the cave.

"I have lost … lost my Mama and the whole tribe has … has lost its sibyl and some of you have lost a dear friend." She looked over at Kasha, who was crying silently.

"Is life and the freedom to live it as we wish … and as we have been taught by our mothers, and their mothers and … and many mothers going back before our memories … is this life of ours worth this pain and the other pains we will probably be suffering before we reach Al-Rah Montah? Four sun cycles ago, I had a taste of slavery, myself. A man forced me … forced me and … hurt me. I still cannot bear the thought of doing duty in the temple." Gennah smiled, in spite of herself, as she realized she had no reason to worry about this for some time. "I would love to have a child, someday, but unless Inanna sends me one without the help of a man …" Some of the women were weeping in sympathy. All of them were giving her their entire attention.

"When I think of Ashannah and Elissa and when I think of all of you, my sisters, and when I remember the beautiful valley, where, together, we will build Al-Rah Montah ... I am ready to go on, whatever it takes!" Ashannah got right up and hugged her beloved while the others cried out their allegiance. Elissa ran over and tried to hug both her mothers, at once. Ashannah gave her a tight squeeze and then began a very simple song, which she accented by clapping her hands in a stirring rhythm.

Al-Rah Montah, we are coming!
Al-Rah Montah, we are coming!
May Inanna bless you,
May Inanna bless us all.
Al-Rah Montah, we are coming!

Soon the cave was overflowing with the voices of the women, singing the simple but stirring song, expressing their loyalty and their hopes and their dreams.

"It has stopped snowing! It has stopped snowing! And it's beautiful! The snow is beautiful! It makes everything look wonderful!" Angah cried out, as she ran back into the cave early the following morning. As the women began to rush toward the opening, she called out a warning, laughing at the same time, "But it's cold all the same! It's so-o-o-o co-o-o-ld!"

Her warning slowed down the exodus a bit, but everyone was eager to see the sky again, and to breathe in some fresh air. Some stopped to put on their somewhat softened boots, but many ran out in their bare feet. They didn't stay long, however. Angah was right. It was cold!

After they had built some fires and had some tea and cooked emmer, they all put on their boots and wrapped themselves in blankets, so that they could go out and appreciate the beauty of the winter day. They hadn't been out long, when Elissa came running up to Ashannah to show her a tiny goddess she had made from the snow.

"I don't think it's Inanna, though. It's so little!" she stated, disappointment coloring the tone of her voice. "Oh, I don't know who she is, but isn't she beautiful?" A smile wiped out the disappointment.

"Well, she is certainly some goddess," Ashannah said, laughing. The other children began making little goddesses, and finally the women got together to make a huge Inanna, amidst a lot of laughing and throwing snow at each other.

As their boots soaked up the moisture, they softened again, but their feet also got very cold, and reluctantly, they returned to the cave. Nevertheless, the little outing had lifted their spirits. Ashannah came up with the idea of stretching their boots before they dried. She also suggested that they not put their boots so close to the fires, so they would dry more slowly and perhaps not shrink so much and, possibly, not get so hard.

The next day, when the women went to put their boots on they had to admit that the pain which they inflicted on their feet, made the boots worthless. Angah came up with a plan of cutting the boots down to where they would just protect the soles of their feet. She went on to suggest that they pierce holes in the edges, through which to put bindings. With these, they would tie the leather soles to their feet and ankles.

Ashannah got out the obsidian and cut out the soles of her boots as Angah had instructed. Then she cut in slits for the binding, found some leather thongs, slipped them through the slits and tied them to her feet. It would work! The others began working on their boots. With only one piece of obsidian, it was a slow process.

In the meantime, Ashannah went outside to see how they would work in the snow. She quickly discovered that the new boots did not offer much protection from the wet and the cold. She went back inside with the news, and Mirah suggested cutting one of the wool blankets in wide strips and wrapping their feet and ankles in those, before tying on the modified boot.

With this improvement in their footwear, Ashannah and Gennah took the large cart up to where the broken cart was. They could see that it would take a long time to repair. They took it apart, packed it in the large cart and pulled it down to the cave. It was almost dark when they returned.

As the days went by, their food supply got lower and lower. One day, when it was clear outside, Gannah and Minah wrapped their feet in wool, laced on the leather soles and took their slingshots, hoping to find some rabbits. Just before sunset, they came back carrying between them two hands of rabbits and some hard little berries they found still clinging to some bushes. They knew the berries would give a nice flavor to the morning's mush and also stretch out their supply of grain, which was getting low.

The next day, Leenah and Estah took the bows and arrows and left to see if they could find a deer. When they came back, wet and shivering, they had nothing but a few more berries. They found no recent traces of any large game.

As time went on, it became more and more difficult to find rabbits, and when they did, the meat on them was sparse. The supply of grain and dried meat was disappearing rapidly. They made many trips to the meadow and usually found something to forage, but even that source of food finally gave out. They began to eat only once a day, carefully rationing out equal amounts to each. Even the children got the regular amount, as the women realized they needed more for growing. Some of the women were sharing their small portions with Beyla, whose supply of milk was getting less and less. The hungry cries of the baby became anguished and pierced the heart of every woman there. The women began asking Ashannah why Inanna wasn't sending her any more messages. All she could do was to tell them to continue to have faith in the Goddess, but she spent hours begging Inanna for a message, either from the flames of the nightly fires or in a dream. None was forthcoming. The only encouraging signs were that the days were getting noticeably longer and a little warmer.

The women were getting more and more listless from discouragement and lack of nourishment. One afternoon Ashannah took a walk up the mound lying directly over the cave. As she looked across the valley at Al-Rah Montah, hoping to receive inspiration and perhaps a message from Inanna, she noticed that the snow was melting on the lower elevations, even though there was still much on the peaks of the mountains. It gradually dawned on her that it must be the same on the mountain where they were. Slowly she reasoned that if it were warmer down below, then there might be more food there as well. Thanking Inanna for the insight, she rushed down to the cave and got Gennah, Gannah, Mirah, Estah and Leenah.

"I've been noticing that the snow across the valley has been melting on the lower parts of the mountains," she began. "In fact, it is almost all gone except towards the tops. Don't you think that's probably true on our mountain? I'm certain that Inanna helped me to realize this and that it is so. I think that if we go down a ways we will find the snow gone and the spring plants beginning to grow. We would probably find some food, both new plants and animals coming out of their winter sleep." The women agreed with her, at once, and made plans to leave the following day.

That evening, as the women ate the last of their grains, along with some dried meat, Ashannah shared their plans with them.

"Blessed be Inanna for showing you the way!" exclaimed Kasha, and the others joined in. Once again, hope sprang into their hearts.

However, when Ashannah went outside to relieve herself the next morning, it was snowing so hard, she could barely see more than the width of two persons ahead. The flakes were heavy with moisture, which was a sure sign of spring, but the snow didn't let up until evening and the women were unable to go search for food. The cave was silent, but palpable with the women's unspoken fears, and their newfound hope waned rapidly

During the night the cries of little Elsa became weaker and weaker and were finally silenced forever. When Beylah was forced to realize that her baby would never cry again, she cried out, "Oh, no, she can't be dead! No, Inanna wouldn't let that happen!" Kasha ran over to Beylah, noticing that she was holding on to the baby tighter than before. The High Priestess curled herself around the two of them, as Beyla continued to sob. Some of the other women were sobbing also. Kasha remained curled around them, until finally the young woman fell asleep and the cave became absolutely silent..

CHAPTER EIGHTEEN

The next morning Ashannah arose as soon as she saw a dim light coming through the crack near the top of the cave. She hurried over to the entrance and saw that it was no longer snowing. She could see remnants of stars in a clear sky. She could also tell it was very cold. Nonetheless, she went around and awakened Gennah, Gannah, Mirah, Estah and Leenah, told them to put on their inadequate boots, wrap themselves in blankets and prepare to leave. "Cold or no cold," she said grimly, "we will all be returning to Inanna's bosom if we don't get some food! Take any spare blankets you can find to bring the food back in."

"Wow! Here's some dried meat in this blanket!" cried out Mirah, holding it aloft as if she had caught an entire deer.

"Well, at least we can put it in some water for flavor," remarked Gannah.

"It's enough to make a somewhat nourishing broth," Kasha said, "but since you're going hunting, perhaps you should take it."

"No, mother, I'm sure we're going to come across some food. You need it here."

With that the six women departed, plodding resolutely through the deep, wet snow, marking the trees as they went, although they left a clearer trail in the snow.

About the time the sun had reached its zenith, the snow had all but disappeared. It was definitely warmer. Gannah killed a rabbit, tucked it in her belt, and they continued down the mountain for another hand's span of the sun's journey. The women were getting weak from lack of nourishment, so when Leenah added another rabbit to their cache, they stopped to build a fire and roast their fresh supply, of meat, meager as it was.

As they were guiltily gnawing on the bones, remembering the hungry women back in the cave, Ashannah happened to look back up the mountain and saw a small cave.

"Look!" she cried out. "There's a little cave back up there! I believe we had better go over there and spend the night. It's too late to make it back home before dark. I just hope it's empty!"

They found the cave unoccupied, and since there were a few hand spans of light left, Gannah, Minah, Leenah and Estah went hunting, while Ashannah and Gennah cleaned the cave out and gathered pine needles and wood. When they had finished with these chores and the hunters had not yet returned, the two women went out looking for roots and berries. Just as they found some mushrooms under the roots of a fallen oak, they heard Leenah and Estah shouting that they had downed a deer. They quickly gathered up the mushrooms and went to help. When they found that Gannah and Minah were already there and the four of them were busy taking off the hide, Ashannah suggested that she and Gennah make a travois so they could drag the carcass back to the small cave and, on the following day, up the mountain to the women in the winter cave.

It took the rest of the afternoon to get the deer fastened to the travois and back to the small cave. They roasted the mushrooms with some of the meat and had a grand feast.

The following morning, Ashannah, Gennah, Gannah and Minah began to get ready to make the trip back to the cave of waiting women. The travois, with more than half the deer meat tied to it, would be a heavy pull.

"I guess we didn't have enough faith to bring a cart with us," Gannah groaned. They also planned to carry a few of the roots they had been able to gather, since the ground was softer at the lower altitude.

Leenah and Estah were to remain at the small cave, in order to try for another deer. They had decided that after the women had gained some strength, they would bring some of them down to the cave, where the snow was nearly gone and food was more plentiful. It would give everyone more space.

Just as the four of them were about to leave, Gannah shouted, "Look! Look up there! Isn't that another cave?"

The others followed her pointing finger, and saw the gaping mouth of a cave, somewhat larger than the one where they had spent the night. They all began climbing towards it, when Ashannah cried out, "I'm afraid this one is occupied. I can smell something from here."

"So can I," groaned Gannah. "But the two caves together will give us all shelter for a while and we won't have to separate."

"You're right, Gannah," Ashannah said with new hope resounding in her voice, "but we've really got to get back to the others with some food."

"Yes, you do," Leenah agreed, "but Estah and I can probably get the … whatever it is … out of the cave, like we got the lioness and her cubs out of the big cave. The rest of you go on up with the food. We'll have both caves ready by the time you come back with everyone."

"That sounds wonderful!" Gennah said, with tears of joy streaming down her cheeks. "But are you sure that just the two of you can do it?"

"I don't see why not!" Leenah exclaimed, laughing. "We're not going to carry it …or them … out!"

It took Ashannah, Gennah, Minah and Gannah most of the rest of the day to get back to the big cave, dragging the travois with the heavy load of meat. The waiting women wept with joy on seeing their companions with food.

The women prepared a hearty stew with the roots, mushrooms and meat, but Kasha had them drink some of the broth before eating solid food, believing they might become ill if they put the heavy, rich food directly into their empty stomachs. By the following day, everyone was enjoying the stew and feeling much more energetic. That is, everyone but Beyla. She sat leaning against the cave wall, still holding the body of her child, still wrapped in the tiny blanket, to her breast.

Kasha sat down beside her with a bowl of broth and finally persuaded her to drink a little. The odor of the decomposing child was almost more than the High Priestess could bear, but Beyla seemed unaware of it.

"Now, my dear, it is time for you to let go of Elsa and allow her to return to Inanna's bosom."

"No! No! I can't Kasha! I can't put her in the cold ground!" The young woman began to sob hysterically and clung tighter to the little body. This outburst caused the other children to begin crying.

"We don't have to put her in the ground, Beyla," Kasha said. "Now listen to me." Beyla stopped sobbing somewhat and Kasha continued. "I have found a deep crevice in the back of the cave, where we can make a little bed for her and lay her in it. Come with me and I'll show you."

Beyla was so weak, by then, she could hardly get up, especially clinging to the little body at the same time. Kasha sucked in her breath and reluctantly took the body and led Beyla back into the cave. The other children looked on, mouths agape, but stopped their crying. The odor of the dead infant kept them from approaching.

"See, I have already gathered some pine needles for you to prepare a little bed for her," Kasha said when they had reached the crevice.

Beyla stared wide-eyed at Kasha, but finally stooped down to arrange the pine needles. Kasha handed the little body to the woman, hoping she wouldn't cling to it again. For a brief moment, Kasha thought Beyla was going to press it to her bosom, but, as if noticing for the first time how grotesque it had become, she carefully placed it in the crevice and then ran, sobbing, from the cave. Ashannah ran out after her.

Kasha remained behind to close the crevice with rocks.

Some time later, Ashannah returned with Beyla and persuaded her to drink more of the broth. That night while everyone was preparing to sleep, Kasha lay down beside Beyla and took her in her arms. The young woman began to moan and finally, to weep. Soon, every women there was weeping with her, and after a time, all were able to relax into a healing slumber.

When the women awoke the next morning, Beyla seemed as ready as the others to begin the trip down the mountain to the awaiting shelters. The promise of food gave them the strength they needed. Gannah, Gennah and Minah easily managed the three remaining carts, since they were much lighter than they had been on the trip up the mountain.

After the others had left with the travois and deer, Estah and Leenah began to gather wood in order to smoke out the inhabitant of the second cave. As they set and lit the fire, they heard nothing. Then Leenah threw on some of the green branches, and they waited for the smoke to form and fill the cave.

Without warning, a black and exceedingly angry bear rushed out at them, snarling ferociously. They both ran from the cave, Leenah running towards the sunrise and Estah in the opposite direction. It was Estah the bear chose to pursue.

"Climb a tree, Estah!" Leenah screamed, as she saw the enraged bear gaining on her partner. As Estah leaped for a low hanging branch of an oak tree, she felt a sharp pain in her left leg. Ignoring it, she began to climb as fast as she could. After she had gone for several feet, when she reached for the next branch, it tore away from the trunk, unable to bear her weight. She lost her balance and started to fall back, but her feet were firmly placed on the lower branch and she was able to grab the trunk and regain her equilibrium. It was then she saw blood streaming from a gash on the calf of her left leg. The bear's claw had ripped through her winter leggings. The smell of her blood seemed to give the bear added energy, and it leaped and caught hold of the same branch she had used to get in the tree.

"Can bears climb trees?" she asked herself in astonishment, as she watched the animal do just that. The animal was less agile than she, which slowed it down some, but it gradually climbed closer. Since she could not climb any farther, knowing the higher branches could not bear her weight, she was about to scream, when she watched as the branch the bear was clinging to gave way under the strain of its weight. It clung precariously to the trunk for a few seconds, but was finally forced to let go and crash to the ground, where it lay, stunned by the fall.

In the meantime, Leenah had also climbed a tree for protection. She had watched, horrified, as the animal gained on Estah. She, too, had not known bears could climb trees. She gasped in relief as she saw it fall to the ground. Both women remained on their respective perches, wondering how long it would remain unconscious. Or was it dead?

Just as Estah had decided that it must be dead, the bear began to moan and stretch. She watched, fascinated and terrified, as it struggled to its feet, slowly shook its head, as if clearing its sight, and ambled back towards the cave. It had either forgotten about her or had had enough of tree climbing.

Fortunately. the fire in the cave had continued to burn and smoke was still pouring out of the mouth. The bear slowly turned from the cave and went downhill, perhaps in search of food or to seek out another place to finish its hibernation.

Leenah and Estah remained in their respective trees until they felt certain the animal was not going to return. Estah finally slid down her tree, because her leg was throbbing and was very painful, and she was weak from loss of blood. Leenah climbed out of her tree and ran over to help. Estah's leg was no longer bleeding so profusely, but the wound was visibly throbbing.

Leenah found a sturdy stick for her partner to lean on and finally was able to get her to stand. They walked slowly over to the cave, and by the time they got there the fire had died down. They knew by then that they would not be able to go back to the other cave, even though it was where their food was and would have been more comfortable, since it had been cleaned out.

Leenah carefully slid Estah to the floor of the cave, as far away from the ashes as she could get. She gathered some pine needles for Estah to lay on, putting more under the injured leg. By then, both of their throats were burning with thirst. Leenah went over to the other cave to get their bodas of water and some of the meat. After they had both slaked their thirst, Leenah found herself trembling from fatigue and from the horror of their narrow escape. She lay down beside Estah, and soon they were both asleep.

The sun was just past its high point, when Leenah was awakened by her partner's moans. When she saw that Estah was still sleeping, she hurried over to the other cave to retrieve their bows and arrows, blankets and the remains of the deer.

When she returned, Estah was awake, only to find she couldn't move without causing the leg to bleed again. Leenah made her as comfortable as she could and then gathered some firewood and slowly roasted the liver from the deer. She sensed that it would help build up Estah's blood supply.

After eating, Leenah gathered more wood and made up another bed for the two of them as far back in the cave as she could, so they would keep warm. By stooping over and putting her arms under Estah's armpits and on around her chest, she was able to drag her to the new bed without causing her leg to bleed again.

Leenah stayed awake as long as she could, tending the fire to discourage any night predators from coming into the cave. She finally fell asleep by the fire, then awakened because she was shivering from the cold. She started up the fire, threw on more wood. and groggily crawled back by Estah. Inanna would just have to keep watch for them, she thought, as she rapidly fell asleep again.

The sun had traveled several hand spans, when Estah was awakened by the throbbing in her leg. She looked down and saw that the wound was swollen with pus. Fine red lines were radiating from it. "I wish Kasha were here," she moaned. "She would know what to do with it. I feel hot all over!"

Leenah got up and washed Estah's face in cold water, meanwhile studying the leg and trying to decide what to do for it. "We need to get the yellow stuff out somehow," she finally stated. She built a small fire and held the blade of her knife in it, until it glowed. She waited for it to cool and then went over to Estah.

"What ... what are you going to do?" Estah asked fearfully.

"I'm just going to make a small cut, so that the poison can run out. I've seen Kasha do it. It will stop the throbbing, and your leg will heal." She quickly made a small slit in the wound, before Estah could object.

As the pus ran out, Estah exclaimed, "You're right, Leenah. It feels better already!" She leaned down to wipe her leg. Leenah swiped her hand away, explaining, "I need to find something to clean it with. I should have gotten something, before I cut it." She pulled her tunic out from her leggings and ripped a piece off the edge. She washed the small rag out as well as she could and wiped Estah's leg.

"I'm doing this all backwards!" she groaned. "I should have pressed out as much poison as possible, first." She gently pressed more pus from the wound, rinsed out the cloth and wiped Estah's leg once more.

"That does feel good, Leenah," Estah sighed. "I didn't know you were such a fine healer."

"Well, I'm glad it feels better," Leenah replied. "I've never done this before, but I have watched Kasha a few times. Now, Kasha would put something on the wound and cover it, but I don't know what. I probably wouldn't be able to find it, even if I knew. I hope they'll get here tomorrow, so she can take care of it."

"Leenah, I'm about ready to burst, if you know what I mean!" Estah groaned.

"Now that you've said it, so am I," Leenah said. "Wait until I get back, can you?

We'll have to think of a way, so that you don't have to move much." Leenah left, after removing Estah's clothes as gently as possible, and rearranged the pine needles so that the leg would be raised, as before.

I'm going to take these clothes to the stream and wash them out, Estah. I'll be right back," she promised.

When Leenah returned, she examined her lover's leg. With the pus mostly gone, it looked much better than before, but the little red lines seemed to have extended themselves. She didn't know what that meant, but doubted that it was a good sign. She didn't say anything to Estah and hoped she wouldn't notice.

Even though the two women had planned to go hunting while they were waiting for the others to arrive, Leenah chose to stay close to Estah.

In the afternoon, she left only long enough to find some tubers and berries for their evening meal. Later, she was able to assist Estah out of the cave to relieve herself, without any noticeable damage to the wound. When Estah finally observed the progress of the red lines and asked Leenah about them, she answered honestly.

"I wish they weren't there, Estah, but I really don't know what they mean - whether they are good or bad. It still looks better than when we woke up this morning. How does it feel?"

"It's not throbbing like it was, but it feels hot, like someone is holding a burning stick next to it."

"I'll put some cold water on this cloth and lay it on the wound," Leenah offered. "Maybe that will help." It helped as long as the cloth was wet, but after it dried out, the wound would start to burn again.

Again, Leenah stayed up as long as she could to keep the fire going, but sleep finally took over, as before. The last thing she remembered was praying fervently to Inanna that the others would arrive the next day.

During the following afternoon, at Estah's insistence, Leenah took her bow and arrows and went out to try and bring down a deer. She didn't go far from the cave, not only because she wanted to hear if Estah called for help, but also because she knew she wouldn't be able to drag a carcass very far by herself.

Just as the sun was about to set, a huge buck appeared on a knoll uphill from where she was standing. The light of the setting sun made his coat the color of new copper. There was a breeze blowing downhill into Leenah's face, so she knew that he would not become aware of her, unless she made a noise. A lump filled her throat, as she admired his beauty and dignity. She truly did not want to kill him, but the thought of the hungry women, hopefully on their way, helped her to raise her bow and take careful aim. She held her breath, only letting it out after she released the arrow. The buck must have heard the arrow approaching, because it moved its head, putting it right in line with the speeding arrow. It went through one of his eyes and lodged itself into the brain, killing him instantly.

Tears filled Leenah's eyes, as she watched him crash majestically to the ground. Then, before she started over to where he lay, she heard the shouts of women calling Estah and herself.

"Oh, Goddess! Oh, Inanna, thank you!" she cried out as she ran towards the first cave. "We're over here!" she shouted. "I'm coming! I'm coming!"

Ashannah was the first to reach her. "So you were able to get the other cave?" she asked, as she embraced her friend.

"We got it, but the bear living in it clawed Estah's leg! Kasha should see it, as soon as possible. I did what I could, but it needs more care. I didn't know what to do to draw out all the poison. Or, maybe you would know," Leenah added, as she remembered that Ashannah was learning to be a healer, like her mother.

"Kasha has some healing herbs in her blanket. You go ahead and tell her about it, while I go take a look at it."

As soon as Leenah saw Kasha, she called out, "Kasha, a bear clawed Estah's leg, and she needs your help. I didn't know how to get all the poison out!"

Kasha turned to Thesta, saying, "Have the women choose which cave they wish to stay in and start to unpack." Then Leenah guided her to the other cave.

"I didn't know bears could climb trees," she commented, after Leenah told her what had happened. "But then I've never seen many bears, at all!"

"I think it was weak from its winter sleep," Leenah explained. "Otherwise . . I ... don't know ... We didn't even have our bows and arrows with us. I don't know what would've happened if the branch hadn't broken."

"The wound is healing well, but obviously not all of the poison is out of it," Ashannah informed her mother, as soon as Kasha entered the cave. "I'm afraid you'll have to open it before you put a poultice on it."

You're right, daughter," Kasha replied as she inspected the wound. "Could you build a fire?"

Leenah started to help Ashannah with the fire, when she remembered the buck she had just shot. "Just before I heard your shouts, I had killed a big buck," she said. "Perhaps I should get some women to help me drag it over here, before it gets dark."

"Of course, Leenah," Ashannah said. "Kasha and I can care for Estah, now. You did a fine job, with what you knew," she assured her.

As soon as Ashannah had the fire going, she heated up her knife. "Now gather yourself into Inanna's embrace, Estah," she instructed, after her knife had cooled some. "This is going to hurt a little, but there is definitely still some poison in there, which we have to get out."

Kasha deftly cut through the wound, and immediately pussy blood ran out. She placed a small cloth on it and rummaged around in her bag, looking for some wild onion and plantain. She had discovered that the two together made a strong drawing poultice. She mixed them together with water in a very small rock mortar, and after crushing them into a paste, she placed it right on the wound, then covered it with a large cloth, which she loosely secured with strips of cotton.

"Let's lower your leg a little, so that the new blood can get to it," she advised. Just then, the women who had chosen to stay in the second cave arrived. They quickly built up the small fire and soon had a stew brewing for the evening meal. Most of the women were helping Leenah with her kill, since the sun had already set. They dragged it into the cave just as the last of the dusk faded away.

After eating, the women skinned the buck by the light of the fire and hung most of the meat on a tripod to be dried.

As Leenah lay down by Estah, later in the evening, she was grateful that there were plenty of others to keep the fire burning throughout the night. She knew that the smell of the carcass would most likely draw predators to the cave.

Chapter Nineteen

"My leg isn't hot!" Estah exclaimed, when she awoke the following morning. Seeing that she was awake, Kasha came over to see how the young woman was doing. Twice during the night she had changed the poultice.

"Good! The red lines are fading, as I expected," Kasha said. "After you've peed, I'm going to put on another poultice. I think you should stay off the leg, as much as possible, for the next few days."

Estah groaned at the thought of so much inactivity, but promised the healer she would do as she requested.

When Angah announced that she was going to look for some clay, Ashannah sputtered, "But Angah, this isn't where we're going to settle! As soon as Estah is ready, we should begin our trip down the mountain to Al-Rah Montah. I hope to get a garden in this spring!"

Angah laughed heartily and said, "Well, it would be nice to eat something besides meat and berries!"

"Why don't some of us go on to find the next resting place?" Gannah suggested. "It will take at least a day to find one, another to come back and another before we would all start out. Estah will be ready by then, won't she?"

"Well, she might. At least, soon after," Kasha replied. "I want to keep a poultice on her leg until the red lines are entirely gone."

"Why don't we go tomorrow, Gannah?" Ashannah asked. "Gennah, would you like to go?

Gennah replied at once, "Oh, yes! Very much."

"One more person should be enough," Ashannah continued. Minah volunteered, at once.

"Today, I'd like to finish scraping the two new hides," Ashannah said. "Maybe someone could get some oak bark and we could begin tanning them, so we can make really good boots for next winter. We could roll them up with the bark inside, while we're traveling. I'd like to try, anyway."

"That sounds good, Ashannah," Gannah agreed. "C'mon, Minah, let's go see if we can find some oak bark."

"Just take a little from each tree," Kasha advised. "The sap is just coming up and if you pull away too much bark from one tree, it wouldn't get up to the leaves."

"The best thing would be to try to find a fallen tree," Ashannah said. "Then you can take all you want from one tree. It would have to be one that has fallen recently, though. The sap shouldn't be dried out."

"We'll try to find one, then," Minah agreed. The two women got some hatchets, emptied one of the small carts, and went searching for a fallen oak.

Gennah persuaded Beyla and Zolah to help scrape the deer hides, along with Leenah and Ashannah. They sat near Estah, so she could join in the conversation.

Kasha went searching for medicinal herbs to replenish her supply, and Fannah and Deenah took the children to search for tubers, berries and mushrooms. Except for small bags of emmer and barley which Ashannah had hidden for planting, there were absolutely no grains for buns or to put in their stews. Even if they came upon some wild emmer plants, it wouldn't be ready to harvest for several moon cycles.

When the women all gathered together that evening in the warmth of the cave to enjoy a meal, their spirits were much revived from having been able to do constructive things and not being forced to remain in the caves all day.

The next morning, when they awoke, it was sleeting outside. It continued well into the day. Ashannah and the other women who had planned to go with her were forced to wait another day. Kasha was silently relieved that Estah would thus gain more time to heal.

"Look at those two overhangs over where the sun sets!" Minah shouted. "Do you think they would provide enough protection for all of us for a night or two?"

"Well, one of them will surely give the four of us protection for tonight," Ashannah answered, obviously relieved by the discovery.

After coming closer to the two overhangs, they determined that they would offer enough shelter for at least one night.

Although they had been walking steadily since early morning they had been slowed down by the continuous breaking of the straps holding on their foot protectors. They had been forced to stop, gather grasses and weave them into straps, since they hadn't brought any leather along.

"Before we start out again, everyone should have a supply of straps," Gennah observed.

"We'll have to use some of the new hides, if everyone is to have a supply," Minah added.

"We can use the skin on the bellies," Ashannah suggested. "It is thin and soft and easy to cut into narrow strips."

"C'mon, Gannah," Minah said. "Let's go get a few rabbits before dark, so we can make some straps to get us back tomorrow. Too bad we didn't bring the obsidian, but maybe we can cut the rabbit skins with our knives. I don't think we'd have to bother scraping them."

Soon after Gennah and Ashannah had prepared their sleeping spaces and had gathered wood for the night, Minah and Gannah returned with a hand of rabbits. They quickly skinned them and put the flesh over the fire to roast. They stretched out the skins and pegged them to the ground, hoping they would remain pliable.

"Gannah, why don't you and Minah go bring the others down here, while Gennah and I go seek out the next shelter. By the time you get back with the others, we should have returned. Then we can lead the way to whatever shelter we find," Ashannah suggested.

"That sounds all right to me," Gannah answered, "but I think you and Gennah should go get the others. Gannah and I can get more rabbits for new straps. I doubt if these last more than a sun's journey, maybe not that long. We can also replenish our food supply that way."

Ashannah blushed over the fact that she could still not bring herself to kill, even a rabbit. "I guess you're right," she murmured. "Well, Elissa will be happy to see us." After saying that, she curled around Gennah, and Minah wrapped herself in a blanket, while Gannah prepared to take the first watch.

The following morning, they discovered that cutting straps with their knives was difficult, and that delayed an early start. However, the sun was still several hand spans from its meridian when they were finally ready to start out on their respective ways. In the meantime, Ashannah had climbed on the top of the highest overhang to see if she could determine how many more days it would take to get to the bottom of the valley.

"It's hard to tell," she reported to the others, "but I think it will take close to a handful of sun's journeys of steady walking, to get there. That means close to two hands of days before we will actually arrive."

"After spending most of the winter in a cave, that doesn't sound bad at all!" exclaimed Gannah. "Let's go!"

When Ashannah and Gennah arrived back at the caves, the waiting women cried out in fear. "Where's Minah?"

"And Gannah?"

"Did something happen to them?"

"Did one of them get hurt?"

"No! No!" Ashannah quickly assured them. "We found two small overhangs that will shelter us for a night. It will be crowded though, so they went on to see if they could find something for the next night."

Elissa ran up to her mothers, crying out, "I'm sure glad you came back and Minah and Gannah went on to find the next place!"

Ashannah caught her little girl up into her arms, saying, "I thought you'd be glad to see us, little one! Are we about ready to eat? I'm really hungry!"

While they were eating, Gennah came up with a plan to get Estah down to the overhangs. "The small amount of food we have will easily fit in the small carts, along with the two deer hides. We can divide the looms and potters' wheels among us, and with three women managing it, Estah can ride down in the big cart."

"You don't mean it, do you?" Estah wailed.

'That's a wonderful idea, Gennah," Kasha broke in. "The red lines are gone, but the wound is large and not entirely healed. It could easily break open again. You really must do it, Estah."

Ashannah was about to point out that they would have to leave the broken cart behind, but realized in time, that it would not be good to bring that up at the present. They could store it carefully in the back of one of the caves, and she and Gennah could come back for it later.

Leenah, Grenda and Mirah volunteered to manage the big cart with Estah in it. They made it seem like a game, although it was very much of a challenge.

The next sun's journey, when they were ready to leave, Leenah got in between the two handles, using her body to steady the cart. Grenda and Mirah each took a handle and told Estah to climb in. There was a lot of giggling and false starts, but they were finally able to begin moving down the trail in a fairly steady manner.

When Ashannah told them that she thought they would be at Al-Rah Montah in two hands of sun journeys, they all cheered and began singing:

Al-Rah Montah we are coming! etc.

In the meantime, Rootha had noticed that Beyla was somewhat withdrawn again, and she got Angah to walk with the younger woman and herself, to help keep up a steady conversation. Finally, Beyla interrupted them, crying out, "How am I going to have another baby, if there aren't any men close to Al-Rah Montah?"

The two older women looked away so Beyla wouldn't see their smiles.

"I'm sure if you want another child, so much, Beyla, Inanna will find a way," Angah said.

"Maybe she doesn't want me to have a baby!" the young woman moaned.

"If she doesn't," Rootha retorted quickly, "then there's nothing any of us can do about it, but I am certain that isn't the way it is. Inanna loves children. She will have to provide a way for all of you young women, or we will finally not have a village!"

The three women walked on in silence, as each tried to think of how Inanna would solve such a serious problem, but, at least, Beyla no longer felt alone in her predicament.

When they arrived at the two overhangs, they found that Gannah and Minah had already returned. "We found a large cave almost a sun's journey from here," Gannah announced. "We could start out in the morning."

The women could quickly see how limited the overhangs were and thought Gannah's suggestion a good one. One of the problems was that they had cut up most of the blankets for footwear, and while it was warmer at these lower levels, it still got quite cold at night. The overhangs would not offer as much protection as the caves. They set about gathering enough wood, so that they could have two fires in each overhang.

Ashannah was relieved to hear that a cave would be their next stop. It would not only be warmer, but would be comfortable enough to remain a few days, while they replenished their food supply, which was, again, becoming quite low.

No one got much sleep that night because of the cold. In spite of their fatigue, they were all feeling anxious to start out on the trail, leading them closer and closer to Al-Rah Montah, as well as the promised cave for the coming night.

Kasha bound up Estah's leg, so that she could start out walking on her own. The women who had trundled her the day before were definitely tired. After they had traveled two hand spans of the sun's journey, Estah felt something trickling down her injured leg. She knew the wound had opened. She didn't say anything until her leg began to ache and the trickle increased.

"Now don't cry, Estah," Kasha said. "We know you are doing the best you can." The healer quickly unbound the leg and saw that the wound had, indeed, broken open, but she was encouraged to see that had happened in only one place. At once, three women volunteered to manage the large cart with Estah in it. Kasha loosely bound the leg and elevated it, after Estah had climbed in.

By the time they reached the cave, everyone was utterly exhausted. Ashannah realized that they should not try to travel two days in a row, again.

"It will be better to arrive at Al-Rah Montah a little later, ready to begin building our new homes, rather than arriving there half sick with weariness," Kasha agreed.

The sun was already half way to its meridian before the women awoke the following day. Gannah, Thesta and Minah went out hunting for rabbits, and Beyla and Zolah volunteered to go with Leenah in search of a deer. By the middle of the afternoon, the rabbit hunters came home with almost two hands of rabbits. On the other hand, the deer hunters returned to the camp just before sunset without having seen any deer. A few of the others had found some berries and some of the ferns with the curly tips, tasting like almonds, as well as some mushrooms.

"We went mostly downhill and towards the sunrise in our search, today," Leenah said. "Tomorrow we'll go towards the sunset. I think there might be a stream, where the deer would go for water."

That night, when Ashannah was keeping watch, she had a vision of two large caves, from which she could hear the roar of a huge river. She ran over and carefully wakened Gennah. "Inanna has just shown me Al-Rah Montah!" she whispered, tears of gratitude glistening her eyes. It was the first vision she had received since before they reached the winter cave. Ashannah was able to describe the caves in detail, and she related how it was not possible to see the far bank of the river, because it was so wide. "There are many beautiful trees from which to build our homes," she continued. "And Inanna showed me how to catch fish with little loosely woven baskets. Won't that be a nice change from rabbit and deer meat?"

The following morning, Ashannah described her vision to the rest of the women, and everyone felt a surge of energy. The day was spent gathering food, and in the middle of the afternoon, the deer hunters came in search of help to drag in a kill. It was next to impossible for Kasha to keep Estah in the camp. While the young woman's wound had closed nicely, Kasha thought it would break open easily with a minimum of strain.

Ashannah, Gennah, Gannah and Minah didn't take a watch that night, because they planned to go ahead the next day in search of the next camp. However, when they awoke the next morning it was drizzling rain, and by the time they had eaten and gotten their packs together, it was raining too hard to start out. Beyla and Zolah, who were becoming enthusiastic hunters, had planned to go hunting with Leenah in hopes of securing another deer. Both the hunters and the trailblazers ended up scraping the hide of the deer they had dragged in the day before.

Ashannah thought that three hides would be barely enough to furnish everyone with boots for the following winter, so she hoped they would get another deer, soon. That would ensure that they would have enough food to get to the bottom of the valley, and everyone would have boots, when they were needed.

When the sun began its journey the following day, it revealed a cloudless sky, and the four women prepared for their trip in search of their next shelter. They had to go slowly, at first, because the ground was slick from the rain of the previous day. As the sun dried the ground, they were able to go faster, but in spite of that, by the time there was only about a hand's span of light left, they still hadn't found a shelter, even one that would afford them protection for the night.

Gannah found five bay trees, growing in a circle. The branches overhead would offer some protection if it began to rain, but it wouldn't offer them much defense from the cold. While they were trying to determine if it would be safe to build a fire in the middle of the trees, Minah called out, "Look! Look over there!" They followed her pointing finger and saw an overhang, down and towards the setting sun.

"Blessed be Inanna!" Ashannah said. "That will be plenty of protection for us tonight. Perhaps we'll find something more, tomorrow." Secretly, she hoped Inanna would give her another vision, during her watch.

As the women approached the overhang, something urged Ashannah to walk on past it. She was still within sight of it, when she looked back up the hill and saw a small cave. The cave and the overhang would provide the entire group with enough shelter for two nights. Suddenly she realized that Inanna had more than one way of guiding her, and she fell to her knees and thanked the Goddess.

The sun had set, so they quickly gathered wood, prepared a meal and stayed under the overhang for the night. When the rising sun shone directly into the overhang the following morning, Ashannah threw an arm over her eyes in an attempt to sleep longer. Gennah rolled over onto her stomach with the same purpose in mind.

"Wake up, you lazy women!" Minah cried out, laughing. "We have lots to do today. Remember, we are getting closer and closer to Al-Rah Montah!" That reminder gave the others the energy to get up, relieve themselves and eat the warm pieces of meat, Minah had put on the hot rocks surrounding the fire.

"Well, I guess we might as well go see if the cave is occupied, Ashannah said. "If it is, I think we should all work together getting whatever is in there, out. We don't want someone else getting clawed." The rest agreed and began approaching the cave cautiously.

"I don't smell anything," Gannah said, sniffing the air.

"Neither do I," Minah affirmed and hastened her approach.

"Be careful, though," Ashannah called out, but she didn't smell anything either, nor did she feel any presence. She caught up with Gannah and Minah, who had stopped a few yards from the cave's mouth.

As Gennah joined them, she whispered, "Listen, I have a plan. Instead of smoking it out, let's all gather some rocks. Three of you should spread out a good distance from the cave, ready to throw your rocks. I'll stay here and throw my rocks in the cave. If there is something in there and it charges out at me, I'll run uphill and the rest of you pelt it with rocks, until it turns and runs downhill." When no one said anything, she asked impatiently, "Well, don't you think it'll work?"

"It seems dangerous to me," Ashannah replied, "but maybe it is better than the ways we've done it before. Why don't you let me stay and throw the first rocks?"

"Because you're about to lose a strap on one of your feet," Gennah laughed. They finally agreed to her plan and began gathering an arsenal of rocks. After Gennah saw that they were ready, she began pelting rocks into the cave. Nothing happened. When she bent over to pick up more rocks, Ashannah yelled, "Don't do that! Something could rush out and get you when you aren't looking!"

Fortunately, nothing like that happened. Since she had already picked up a few rocks, Gennah threw them into the corners of the cave, being careful to remain ready to run. Still, nothing happened.

Ashannah, Gannah and Minah cautiously came up by Gennah. Together, the four of them walked up to the mouth of the cave. As they entered, their noses were assailed by a musty odor they hadn't noticed before. As one, they stopped where they were. Just then, the sun came out from behind a cloud, and since it was still low in the sky, it lit up the entire cave. They could see that it was empty, but there was debris all over the floor.

"I guess this cave was occupied until recently," Ashannah observed. "The season for the long winter sleep must be over, at least down this far."

"Since we're just about out of food," Gannah suggested, "Why don't you and Gennah go back for the others, and Minah and I can catch some rabbits and clean out the cave?"

Again, Ashannah felt chagrined for not being able to hunt, but she didn't argue. She and Gennah walked back to the overhang, collected their hatchets and began walking back up the trail. That evening, as they approached the large cave, they noticed how the setting sun made the trees, the bushes and even the waiting women appear as shining new copper. They also discovered that Leenah, Beyla and Zolah had brought in another buck. The hide was almost entirely scraped, and someone had already gathered some oak bark. They had two fires going, in order to dry the meat. Over by the side of the cave, Ashannah saw many roots and the nutty flavored fern tips.

"You've really been working hard," she exclaimed with admiration, and as they sat around the fire eating the delicious stew, she continued, "We found an overhang and a cave down the mountain. Do you think we could start out in the morning?"

"Estah's leg is looking very good, now," Kasha said. "I don't see why we couldn't."

"You mean that I can walk, don't you?" Estah asked.

"I think you'll be all right walking," Kasha assured her.

"Those of us keeping watch can probably finish scraping this hide," Rootha remarked.

"So we will leave in the morning, then," Ashannah stated and shouted,

"Al-Rah Montah, we are coming!"

Al-Rah Montah, we are coming!" the rest responded.

Two days later, Ashannah climbed up on top of the overhang, where she was able to get a good view of the valley.

She ran down to the others and announced, "You know, I think we are closer to the bottom of the valley than I thought!" Then she began to laugh and shouted, "In fact, I believe we can be down there in another journey of the sun! The river running through the valley is truly huge!"

The women and children ran up on top of the overhang to see for themselves. When they saw how close the river was, they began laughing and shouting, and as soon as they had returned beneath the overhang, Ashannah began singing:

Al-Rah Montah we are coming!
The others responded with alacrity.
Al-Rah Montah we are coming!
May Inanna bless you!
May Inanna bless us all!
Al-Rah Montah we are coming!

It was all Kasha could do to keep them from leaving at once.

Chapter Twenty

As the women approached the floor of the valley, they became aware of a roaring sound, which gradually increased in intensity as they continued down the mountain. They began to slow their pace and to look at each other fearfully. Finally, Ashannah recognized what it was, from her dream.

"It's the sound of the water rushing down the river!" she cried excitedly. The women relaxed and walked unhesitatingly towards the sound, because now it meant they were getting close to their new home.

On impulse, Ashannah began running down the mountain, in her eagerness to see if what lay at the bottom corresponded with her dream. When she arrived at the bank of the great river, she gasped at the size of it. Although she could easily see the towering mountains across the way, she could not actually make out the shore on the other side. Only the Great Sea she had seen in Tel-Phar, was a larger body of water.

"Why, boats could go on this water!" she exclaimed to herself.

Then she turned around to search out the caves she had seen in the dream. She saw nothing but the mountainside of trees, through which she had approached the river. Intuitively, she began walking along the bank towards the sunset, or as she would later notice, downstream. She quickly came to a wide bend, which, after she had completed the turn, showed her the caves of her vision. They were quite a distance from the shore, and the land between was slightly sloping and rocky.

"Blessed be Inanna!" she cried out, and quickly retraced her steps, so that she could show the others the site of the village-to-be. She heard the women exclaiming over the size of the river, when Elissa caught sight of her and ran towards her, screaming, "Mama! Mama! I thought you had fallen into the river! Oh, Mama! I'm so glad to see you!"

Seeing the terror in the little girl's eyes, as well as copious tears, she swept her up in her arms, holding her tight. "I'm all right, little one," she consoled. "I was looking for our new home. And I've found it! Blessed be Inanna!"

Then she shouted to the others, "I've found Al-Rah Montah! Come and see! It's up this way!"

Still carrying Elissa, she walked around the bend and pointed up to the caves. She noted that they would offer much more space than the large cave they had wintered in. By then Elissa was squirming to get down, so she could run along beside her mother.

By the time they reached the nearest of the caves, which was also the largest, they were all quite winded, and forgetting that it might be occupied, they walked right in. Fortunately, there was nothing there, although it had probably sheltered some animals a short time ago, as it was quite littered.

"Where are the carts?" Ashannah asked, suddenly noticing that none of the women had them. Three shamefaced women quickly confessed that when she had begun running down the mountain, they had left the carts behind, so they could keep up with her. "I would have done the same thing," she assured them, "but we'd better go get them right away, since one of them has the makings of our supper in it!"

The three women were happy to redeem themselves and, with several others, began retracing their steps to the place where they had left the carts. Several others went over to the second cave and found it was also unoccupied. A few of them began sweeping out the caves, while others went in search of wood. Still others took some of Rootha's baskets to go to the river to get water for the evening's stew. Then Zolah noticed a stream, a little to the sunrise of the caves, running down to the river. This gave them a closer water supply, and it was clearer.

By the time the women returned with the carts, Kasha had started a fire and was heating stones to put in one of the water baskets to make a stew. Later, as they sat around the fire eating, the women began discussing how they would choose which of the two caves they wished to live in.

"This doesn't mean we can't change our minds, later," Kasha assured them.

"Aren't we going to build little houses?" Elissa asked. No one answered. Certainly, no one was in a hurry to do this.

Finally, Ashannah yawned and stood up to go over to the other cave, as did Gennah, Elissa, Grenda, Mirah and Leah. Leenah and Estah also gathered up their things, preparing to leave with them, when Beyla decided to come along, even though Zolah preferred to remain in the larger cave. Ashannah looked over at Kasha, who smiled enigmatically and shook her head, choosing to remain where she was. Ashannah wondered what that smile meant.

The following day, the women cut saplings to make frames for the fronts of the caves, thus extending them and providing protection from the wind, rain and cold. They wove in smaller branches and long grasses, as they had on the walls of their small huts in Al-Rah. This likeness made the children less homesick.

Two hands of days later, Ashannah and Gennah came back with the news that they had found a large meadow with wild emmer growing in it. "The plants are small, as you would expect, for this time of year," Ashannah explained. "Probably the grains will be smaller than what we had in Al-Rah, but when we plant the seeds I saved from there in with them, we'll get both large and small grains this year. By next year, they should all be fairly large."

She didn't mention they had also found a small cave uphill from the field of emmer. As soon as she and Gennah saw it, they knew they wanted to build a home for themselves and Elissa, similar to their hillside home in Al-Rah. This one would be somewhat larger and offer even more warmth in the winter and coolness in the summer. There would be plenty of room for Gennah's looms and baskets, as well as for Ashannah's herbs and Elissa's little pots.

The stream that ran to the sunrise side of the caves, also ran by the emmer meadow and the new cave, so they would not have to find a spring and construct a spring box. Elissa reminded them that this meant they wouldn't have a place to see themselves, but the two women were only too glad to be saved the extra work.

Soon after that, Rootha announced she had found a field of hemp. It was growing almost a hand's span of the sun's journey towards the sunset from Al-Rah Montah, but she reminded them that hemp was light and they could carry quite a bit in one of the carts. When some of them began planning a trip to gather it, she reminded them that they would have to wait for it to mature before they could begin weaving it into mats for their floors and doorways.

Kasha and Thesta found a small meadow which would be good for the village garden. They named the stream which ran by it after Ninlil, to ensure good harvests. The couldn't find any bamboo to make a fence for the garden, so they decided to use the alders at one edge of the meadow for part of the fence, by weaving small branches between them. It took a handful of days to cut saplings to go around the rest of the garden and another two hands of days to make a loosely woven, but firm, barrier against rabbits and deer.

For this reason, by the time Inanna's feast came, Ashannah and Gennah hadn't even begun working on their own home, but they shared the discovery of the small cave with the four women who had built hillside homes in Al-Rah, thinking they might want to search out similar caves.

Mirah and Grenda found a small cave almost directly above the two large caves. It was too far from Ninlil's Creek to water their garden, but they found a small spring nearby, which delighted the children, because now they would have a place to go to look at themselves.

Leenah and Estah found a small cave on the other side of Ninlil's Creek. By Inanna's feast, however, all they had done was to make a path through the creek, by rolling a row of large boulders across.

Gennah and Rootha went searching for some grasses to replace the well-worn baskets they had used on the trip. They found some uphill from Mirah and Grenda's cave, and Gennah found a small field of flax nearby.

Ashannah began thinking of the damaged cart they had left in one of the caves, coming down the mountain. The many projects they were working on for their very survival were all that deterred her from going after it. One evening, when the women living in the smaller cave were eating supper, Ashannah said, "I wish there was some way to bring the broken cart down here, without taking six sun journeys to do it."

"I think we could do it in four journeys, Ashannah," Estah said. "We would have to take a cart along to bring the broken one back in, but we could use it to carry food for the trip up, and if Leenah and I went, we could catch rabbits and forage on the trip back down. Besides, it's warm enough now that we wouldn't have to find a cave or shelter for the night and could keep traveling longer. Also, if there aren't any children along, we could go faster." Estah looked over at Elissa and Leah, expecting a reaction, but the two of them were so busy playing, they hadn't heard.

"I really hate to be away from Elissa so long," Ashannah broke in. "We were separated a lot on our way down here."

"I feel the same way," Grenda said, "and I wasn't away from Leah nearly as much as you were from Elissa."

"But it would be good if we could get the cart fairly soon," Gennah observed.

"So why don't Estah and I go get it?" Leenah volunteered. "I'll ask Minah and Gannah to go along."

"If we went in a day or two, we could even be back in time for Inanna's feast," Estah added.

"Do you really want to do this?" Ashannah asked, looking directly into Estah's eyes.

"I'm not real eager to do more traveling so soon," Estah admitted, "but we could use that cart or the wood from it. Yes, I'm willing to go. We probably won't meet up with a bear, anyway," she added smiling.

Minah and Gannah also agreed to go, and the four of them set out on the trail. Four sun journeys later, they returned, as Estah had foretold.

"It turned out that the box of the cart was in fairly good condition. It had been somewhat loose at the front end, but Gannah had been able to knock it back together with the blunt side of her hatchet. The wheel, however, had received the brunt of the blow, and the copper rim with the spikes was twisted and had torn off in several places. Besides that, the copper pinning had ripped loose from the three planks. Since there were still many other things they wanted to finish by Inanna's feast, they decided to store it in the back of the cave.

By Inanna's feast, they had the garden fenced and planted, and Ashannah and Gennah had sown the emmer seeds from Al-Rah right in with the wild emmer. Ashannah helped Gennah plant cotton seeds that she had brought from Al-Rah on the south side of the emmer field, and on the sunrise side, Grenda and Estah planted the barley seeds Ashannah had saved. They began looking for stones suitable for grinding the grains, even though it would be three more moon cycles, around the feast of Ninlil, before the grains would be ready.

The day before Inanna's feast, Ashannah remembered her vision in which Inanna had shown her how to fish with loosely woven basket-like things. She described them to Gennah, who tried making one from hemp. As soon as she had finished it, she showed it to Ashannah.

"That's it! That's what I saw in my dream … except … except …"

"Except what?" Gennah interrupted impatiently.

"Well, there was some kind of … something stiff going around the top to keep it open, like this," Ashannah continued, forming her hands into a circle, "and whatever it was, it came out into a handle."

"Hummm," Gennah mused, as she tried to visualize Ashannah's description. "I can see why it would be good to have something stiff holding it open so the fish could swim in easily … and yes, a handle would make it possible for the person not to be so close to the fish, as to scare them away. But what could we use?"

Ashannah was turning the net in her hands, thinking, when she excitedly turned to Gennah, exclaiming, "Gennah, have you noticed those graceful trees by the side of the river, where it bends? I don't know what they're called, but the branches must be very flexible. You can tell by the way they bend from only the slightest breeze."

"Yes, I have noticed them. Let's go see if they're strong enough. I think they might be just right!"

The two women rushed over to the small grove of willows. They noticed the leaves were similar to bamboo leaves, but the stems were much thinner and more flexible. Gennah pointed out how the branches were thicker where they came out from the tree trunk and would work as a handle. They ended up twisting two of the branches together for sturdiness.

It didn't take long to make four of the baskets, nor did it take much longer to persuade Leenah and Estah to try their luck at fishing, since they were eager for something different to eat.

That evening, they wrapped their catch in maple leaves, as there didn't seem to be any catalpa trees on this side of the mountain. Then they placed the bundles on coals, as they had seen En-dor do on the trip to Tel Phar. There was barely enough for each woman to have half a fish, but it was enough that everyone knew they wanted more.

Before the feast, when they usually would have had a ceremony in honor of Inanna in her temple, they simply gathered around the fire and sang her litany. "We don't even have a statue to give her honor," Angah complained. "I would make one, but we would need a temple to keep it in. Maybe we could find another stone one, like the one you had in your garden in Al-Rah, Ashannah."

"Most of us living in the small cave are going to build hillside homes, now that the gardens are planted," Ashannah replied. "Don't you think the small cave would make a fine temple, Kasha?"

"It would indeed, my daughter," Kasha replied. "What do the rest of you think?"

"It would be the quickest way to have a temple," Gannah agreed. "Maybe later we can build a larger one."

Beyla was wondering what men would come to this temple, but she didn't say anything out loud.

"While you're building your homes," Angah interjected, "I'll be thinking about a statue. I haven't found any really good clay yet, but I'm still looking."

Elissa, Leah and I found some really fine clay, just yesterday," Leenah spoke up, "It's pretty far up Ninlil's Creek, but at least we'll be coming downhill when we bring it home."

"Could we … could Leenah and Leah and I … could we help with the statue?" Elissa stammered.

"I'm sure it would be a more beautiful statue if we all work on it," Angah said. "Would you want to help, Leenah?"

"I really would, Angah, thank you," Leenah readily replied.

After the women ate the fish, along with some tubers and mushrooms, Ashannah began shaking some little shell bracelets that she had managed to protect during the journey. Out came some drums and bamboo flutes. The rest of the women clapped their hands, preparing for the dancing.

After a time, Ashannah danced over to where Gennah was sitting, swaying and smiling suggestively. When Gennah got up to join her, she said, "How often have we done this on Inanna's feast? Why, I do believe this makes it one hand plus two fingers! Remember the first time? You were so beautiful, but you're even more beautiful now!"

"How can I resist you, when you talk to me like that?" Ashannah laughed. They danced closer and closer to each other, letting the rhythms of the drums guide the swaying of their bodies.

"We'll have to find a good place to make love," Gennah murmured, as she rested her head on one of Ashannah's shoulders.

"So we will," Ashannah replied, still giving herself up to the drumming. She was contented holding her beloved close, feeling her body undulate against her own. "Oh, Gennah! Here we are in Al-Rah Montah, at last!" she cried out. "And still together and loving one another more and more!"

"Yes, beloved," Gennah murmured, as she began to croon a little tune.

Ashannah saw a circle of bay trees and slowly led their dancing in that direction. When they arrived, she asked, "Do you think this nice little nest will do?"

For an answer, Gennah pulled Ashannah between two of the trees. They quickly settled themselves on the bed of leaves, gazing steadily into each other's eyes, stroking each other's bodies, tasting each other's skin, as if it were the first time. Gennah began sucking the fingers on one of Ashannah's hands, making smacking noises and grinning widely.

"You like them, huh?" Ashannah laughed. "How would you like to suck some other place?"

"Did you have some place in mind?" Gennah asked.

Ashannah laughed and proffered one of her breasts with her free hand.

"Now that does look like it would be very suckable," Gennah chuckled, as she moved in. Ashannah put one of her legs over Gennah's hips, as if to capture her, so she could continue sucking forever. Gennah got so enthusiastic that Ashannah had to push her away. The redhead slid down directly to her lover's mons, her tongue wiggling back and forth in Ashannah's bushy, tightly curled pubic hairs, as she sought out her clitoris.

Ashannah screamed from the intensity of it, thrusting for more. She found Gennah's clitoris with one of her hands and began rubbing it, until they were both screaming towards a grand climax. Afterwards, they lay there, their bodies entwined, feeling totally fulfilled. Ultimately, they fell asleep, breathing as one.

Ashannah hadn't noticed that Kasha and Thesta were dancing together, in much the same manner. Grenda and Mirah were also enthralled in an embrace, and no one thought to send Elissa and Leah to bed. The two of them began imitating the dancing of the women. Their undulations sent them into spasms of laughter from the tickling sensation they felt. They fell to the ground, imitating the screams of the women, until they finally lost energy for it and became bored. They got up and took themselves off to bed, wondering how their mothers could go on and on …

A few evenings later, while the women of the smaller cave were sitting around their fire, Estah came up with a plan for building their homes. "Since all of us here want to build homes from hillside caves," she began, "I was thinking that if we got together and worked on one house at a time, we would be finished with the three of them faster than if each couple worked on their own."

"They will be a little different from our houses in Al-Rah. Because of the caves, we won't have to dig out the backs of the houses, but at least on the place Ashannah and I found, we are going to have to build up the earth in front of the cave, before we begin the frame."

"Yes," Ashannah agreed. "It's going to be the opposite of what we did in Al-Rah. I thought we could begin by leveling off a place for our garden and use that dirt for building the ground up in front of the cave."

"We're going to have to do the same thing," Estah said. "The earth in front of our cave slopes downhill, too."

"And ours is the same way," Grenda said.

"I believe you're right, Estah!" Ashannah exclaimed. "It would be much faster if we all helped each other, at least with digging out the level places for our gardens and hauling that dirt over to the fronts of the caves."

"I think it would also help if we all worked on bracing the earth in front of the caves with stones," Mirah continued.

"These houses are going to be larger than the ones we had in Al-Rah," Leenah observed. "Wouldn't it also help if we all went out together to cut the saplings for the frames in front of the caves and help set them up. Then we could each do our own weaving in of the grasses."

The women were very excited now, imagining the quick construction of their homes.

"I ... I wish I had a partner," Beyla said, quietly, from where she sat.

The others were instantly embarrassed for having ignored her, as she sat there listening to them.

Perhaps we can find a cave and build a house for you, too," Ashannah quickly offered.

"I don't think I'd like to live alone," Beyla replied. "There will probably be room for me in the other cave. I moved in with you, to be near the little girls."

"I like living with you, Beyla," Elissa spoke up.

"Me, too!" Leah cried out. "You might as well stay here, until we get the houses built."

"Well, thanks, I'd like to," Beyla said, obviously pleased.

"And when we move into our new houses," Elissa added, "you can come and play with us as often as you want."

"I probably will," Beyla assured them, laughing heartily.

Ashannah hurried down to the river, where she saw Kasha beating out some tunics. It seemed as if she hadn't had a good talk with her mother since they had arrived in Al-Rah Montah. Perhaps it was because they weren't living together and were both so busy with the many projects involved in building a new village.

"Mama, how are you?" Ashannah asked, as she approached the busy woman. Kasha was somewhat startled, as she hadn't noticed her daughter's approach. She stood up and stretched out her arms.

"It seems a very long time since I've seen you!" Kasha exclaimed.

"I know, Mama," Ashannah agreed. "Have you chosen a place to build your new home?"

"Well, daughter, it seems that most of us in the big cave don't want to live alone again! We've gotten used to being with each other, I guess."

"That will make a big difference in how the village will look!" Ashannah cried out.

"It will make more changes than just looks!" Kasha foretold smiling. "Like those of you building hillside homes, we are finding it's easier and quicker to do things together, rather than by ourselves."

Ashannah envied her mother's closeness with the other women. "I know what you mean," she responded. "Everyone will be, somehow closer, too."

Kasha could hear the envy in Ashannah's voice. "I think we need to build a central fire pit, so that we can have more suppers all together," she suggested. "Would you like to help me with one, tomorrow?"

"I'd like that, Mama."

"For now, let me wring out these clothes, and then let's find a place where we can sit down and talk. I have some things to tell you, daughter."

Ashannah began helping her mother with the clothing, and together they hung them on bushes to dry. Then Kasha led them over to a big oak, where they could lean back on its trunk as they talked.

When Ashannah glanced over at her mother, she saw Kasha looking at her, smiling broadly. "First of all, I want you to know that it has been a long time since I have been so happy."

"I can see that, Mama," Ashannah agreed, but her heart began beating rapidly.

"Thesta and I have ... have become very close."

"Oh!" Ashannah gasped. "I guess I did see you dancing together at Inanna's feast." Ashannah didn't know why she felt like crying, but she knew she felt sad, as well as happy, for her mother.

"I know you are happy for me, Ashannah," Kasha said, as she looked deeply into her daughter's eyes. "If you are also sad, perhaps it is because you are no longer the only one filling my heart. But you are there, my daughter, very much there!"

With that, Ashannah burst out sobbing and let her mother hold her, as she had often done in the past. Finally, Ashannah was able to speak. "I understand, Mama. It's like Gennah and Elissa being in my heart ... along with you!"

"And you will always have a very special place in my heart, Ashannah, as my beloved daughter."

"Oh Mama, thank you! You'll always have a special place in my heart, too."

After sitting together in companionable silence for a time, Kasha finally got up. "So, I'll meet you here in the morning. Don't you think right over there would be a good place for the village fire pit?" she asked, as she pointed to a clearing.

Ashannah got up and quickly agreed about the location. "I'll help you gather your clothes, Mama," she offered.

"Why, thank you, Ashannah, I'd like that."

Some days before Ninlil's feast, the three couples and two little girls, who had been living in the smaller cave, had moved into their hillside homes. Beyla was enthusiastically received by the women in the large cave. Everyone in the village gathered together to transform the smaller cave into a temple. They plastered down the walls, so that later they could paint pictures on them.

Angah and Leenah, together with Elissa and Leah, had been working steadily on a clay figure of Inanna. They had built a little hut near the new temple, to protect the statue, while they worked on it. After they had completed the shaping of it, they built a huge fire from the hut and other wood, so it would harden. Elissa and Leah could be heard all over the village, as they shouted with joy when, later, they brushed away the ashes. Then they rubbed the figure down with pieces of wool, which gave it a nice sheen.

As she watched them working, Gennah couldn't help wondering if they would ever get more wool for weaving. Nearly all of the blankets had been cut up for their feet, and there wasn't enough wool left to spin anything.

Suddenly, they all heard Ashannah shouting that the emmer was ready for harvesting. "We'll have emmer buns for Ninlil's feast!" she cried out. Every woman and child came at once, ready to begin the harvest. They had already cleared off a space for a threshing floor near the meadow.

A team of five women went along three rows, holding the stalks tight, cutting through them with their knives. They were followed by a second team of twice as many women, working in couples. One woman would grasp a bundle of emmer, and another woman would bind it with hemp. The last group picked up the bundles and carried them over to the threshing floor, where they loosened the hemp and scattered the sheaves, layer after layer. The children began jumping on the stalks, in order to separate the wheat from the chaff.

When the first team had finished cutting the stalks, they began scooping the grain and chaff onto loosely woven pieces of hemp, which they held over storage baskets to receive the grain. The chaff remained on top. They carefully poured the chaff into holes in the ground. It would be used to nurture the soil for the next crop.

They finished about a third of the field that day and worked most of the next, in order to complete the task. The loaded baskets were heavy, so they used carts to take the grain to the large cave, where they stored it in the back, far from moisture.

The following day, individual women were up early, grinding grain, and by the time the sun had reached its zenith, they were mixing the grain with water and herbs and putting patties of the mixture on rocks, to bake in the sun. That evening the feast in honor of Ninlil was celebrated, thanking her for the emmer and for the berries and other wild edibles, as well. Not a piece of deer or rabbit was seen roasting. However, they had caught enough fish to set aside one of the fires for baking them on coals.

Peace and contentment settled over the village. The barley was harvested, as well as cotton and flax. Perhaps the most valuable lesson they had learned from their new life was the benefit of working together.

When the temple was not in use for special rituals, couples, especially those living in the large cave, used it for lovemaking. If there was concern about the continuation of the village without the help of men, they did not speak of it.

One afternoon, each woman in the village suddenly stopped what she was doing, as she heard the cries of Elissa and Leah. "A man! A man! There's a man coming!" Obviously the children were terrified, and fear gripped the heart of every woman there.

Chapter Twenty-one

Ashannah took Elissa into her arms, saying, "Did you say *one* man is coming?"

"Yes, Mama, and he has a gray beard and a big stick!"

"And long, gray hair, too!" Leah quickly added.

By that time Kasha had come up, and as she heard the girls' description, she said, "Even though he has a big stick, I think we can manage this." She started walking downstream, in the direction the girls had come from. Ashannah, Gennah and the rest followed closely. It wasn't long until they all saw him, just as the children had described. The women and children slowed to a halt, and he did the same. He dropped his stick and raised his arms and only then began to walk slowly towards the women. Even though they could see that he wore a knife in his belt, he seemed to be clearly indicating that he meant them no harm. Many of them were also wearing little knives in their belts for convenience.

When he began to speak, however, they were astonished that they were unable to understand him. When he realized this, he stopped speaking and pointing to himself, he repeated his name several times. "Moshe! I am Moshe! Moshe!"

Kasha pointed to herself and repeated her name in like manner. "I am Kasha! Kasha!"

Moshe pointed downstream, saying, "I live downstream, one hand of the sun's journey from here." The indication of the time and the distance were enough like their words that the women understood.

"Do you live with others?" Kasha asked.

He spread out his hands as he shook his head negatively. They knew he didn't understand the question.

"Do you live in a village?" Kasha asked.

Apparently he understood the word for village. He shook his head up and down, excitedly.

Kasha pointed to the women and children surrounding her and said, "This is my village."

"Are there no men in your village?" he asked, pointing to himself when he said the word men.

They understood all too well what he asked, but hesitated to answer. Little Ran-dell stepped forward. "I am a ***men***," he said proudly, using the same word Moshe had.

Moshe laughed and the women laughed with him, since his laugh was not scornful. "You are a ***man***," he corrected, pointing to Ran-dell.

Ran-dell looked puzzled, not hearing the difference.

"I live in a village with no women," he said slowly, hoping they would understand. He had pointed to Kasha when he said the word for woman.

Ashannah thought she heard a negative before the word, "women", so she repeated his words in the form of a question. "There are no (she shook her head negatively) women in your village?"

He vigorously shook his head in the affirmative, laughing at the same time. "Yes, there are no women in my village!"

The women laughed also, but they were fearful, upon learning that there was a village made up entirely of men, so nearby. Moshe sensed their fear and tried to assure them. "We honor the Goddess Inanna and her Virgins."

The women understood Inanna, and by his demeanor they knew what he was trying to tell them. They relaxed visibly, and Kasha spoke up, "I am a High Priestess of Inanna."

Moshe's face brightened. "You are going to build a temple, soon?"

They understood his word for temple and guessed at the rest, but Kasha wondered how he knew they had no temple, as yet.

"We watched, as you made your way down the mountain in the spring," he informed them. This time ***mountain*** and ***spring*** were the only words they understood. They stood there, looking at each other and then at him. Kasha shook her shoulders and head, letting him know they had not understood.

Moshe again pointed downstream towards his village and said, "There is a man in my village who will be able to talk to you."

The women understood the first phrase, but not the second. "There is a man in your village ...' Ashannah repeated and then paused, shaking her head and shoulders.

Moshe repeated again, "There is a man in our village, who speaks ..." Here he put his fingers close to Ashannah's mouth and drew them away from it.

"Yes! Yes!" she cried out, shaking her head affirmatively. "I understand!" and turning to the others, she said, "There is a man in his village who speaks as we do."

"He is A-bel. Early in the sun's next journey, I will bring him here."

"Early in the sun's next journey, we will be here," Kasha assured him. Then she turned to the women. "If they live so close to us, we should get to know them." The women all nodded their heads in agreement, and Moshe turned downstream towards his village. The women turned back towards Al-Rah Montah.

"I used to be a trader and have been to Tel Phar many times. That is how I know your speech," A-bel explained, early the next morning. A-bel was somewhat younger than Moshe, but he, too, was careful to act in a non-threatening manner.

Kasha did not explain that neither she, nor any of the other women had realized that there were people, who spoke differently. "May Inanna bless you for coming to help us understand each other," she said, simply.

"It is a privilege," he said, as he bowed low, showing that he knew and respected her status as High Priestess. "During the winter, we heard of the destruction of Al-Rah, but we did not know you had been able to avoid your enemies. According to their stories, they had successfully annihilated every last one of you. This spring, when we caught glimpses of you coming down the mountain, we guessed that somehow you escaped. We did not make ourselves known to you at once, because we imagined that you would not be pleased with our presence. But, be assured, we are peaceful men, who honor Inanna and Ninlil. In fact, we came to this valley, because we did not like the warlike ways of the men from the north. Nor did we wish to give our hearts to their warlike gods."

"I am certain that Inanna and Ninlil have blessed you for your loyalty," Kasha replied.

"That is true," he agreed. "They have already blessed us, and we consider your coming to our valley another blessing. We finally decided to send Moshe to you, so that you would not be frightened, if one of you did happen to meet up with him. Also, we would like to know if ... if you are ... (he coughed with embarrassment) if you are going to build a temple."

"It is indeed a blessing for us, as well, that there are men nearby, whom we can trust enough to offer our services," Kasha replied.

Here, Moshe spoke up and A-bel translated for him. "If you would like, we would be happy to build a temple for this purpose. Some of us have been in the valley for close to three sun cycles and probably have more time to give to this."

"Yes, we are very busy getting ready for the coming winter. Our shelters are built, but besides harvesting, we need to gather wood and make warm clothing," Kasha said. "But we have always built our own temples, so I must give this some thought."

"Perhaps we can help you in other ways," Moshe offered through A-bel. "We have a large flock of sheep and have some fine wool to give you for warmer clothing. The winters are colder here than they are in Al-Rah. Are you familiar with wool?"

Kasha turned to Gennah, who spoke up, "We have been weaving wool for three sun cycles, and I have been wondering how we could find more. We cut up our wool blankets to protect our feet during our journey down the mountain."

"Thanks to Ninlil, we had a good harvest of emmer and barley," Ashannah said. "Perhaps we could give you some grain for some wool."

"Ah," replied A-bel. "We have not had much success in growing emmer. The yield is sparse and the grains are very small. We have not even tried to grow barley." Then he told Moshe what had been said.

"We also need help in making good boots for our feet," Gennah said.

"We have men who could help you with that," A-bel promised.

"It seems we are going to help each other in many ways," Kasha broke in. "If I could show you some things necessary for a proper temple and we could find a place that would be convenient for both of our villages, I do not see why you couldn't begin building it as soon as you wish."

"Blessings upon you, Kasha!" both men cried out.

"For now, we will go get some wool, so you can begin spinning and weaving," A-bel stated.

"And we will bring grain for you," Ashannah promised. "We have carts to help with this, but we don't have baskets to spare."

"Our baskets are not the best," laughed A-bel. "But they are good enough to hold grain. We will bring baskets, and we also have some carts."

During the exchange of grain for wool, Gannah mentioned the cart that had been damaged on the trip down the mountain.

"We have a fine metal worker in our village," A-bel said. "If you bring the pieces of the wheel and the metal binding, I'm sure he'll be able to fix it. Shall we meet again on the next sun's journey for this purpose?"

"If that is agreeable to you," Kasha continued, "I will also come to talk more about the new temple."

Through A-bel, Moshe replied, "If you would show us what you want and we can find a good place for it, perhaps we can begin digging it out before the ground gets too hard."

"So it is agreed that some of us will meet here just after the sun begins its next journey?" Kasha asked.

"It is agreed," A-bel answered.

On the way back to Al-Rah Montah, Angah laughed and said, "I can hardly wait to tell Beyla we're going to have a temple soon."

The next day, Kasha and Moshe found a good site for the temple about half way between the two villages. There was an unspoken agreement that the men would stay away from Al-Rah Montah and the women would stay clear of the men's village. They hadn't even shared the names of their respective villages.

By the time the first snow fell in the valley, the women had woven enough blankets for the entire village and were working on winter shawls of the same material.

One day, while Ashannah was spinning some of the wool and Gennah was working on a pair of leggings, the weaver suggested, "Now that the new temple is almost finished, perhaps we can start making Kasha a new robe. The trip over the mountain left her temple robe in shreds."

"That's a good idea, Gennah. We could surprise her with it!"

"Since the winters are so much colder here, why don't we make her one of wool?" Gennah suggested. "You are getting better and better at spinning it, and I'd love to weave it. Then, later, we could make another one of linen."

"She'll love it, Gennah!" Ashannah exclaimed. "Oh, Gennah, Al-Rah Montah is turning out to be wonderful! I love our home, and it's large enough for my herbs and potions and for both your looms and even room for your rushes and baskets!"

"And for Elissa's little pots!" They laughed with joy and soon ended up in each other's arms. ...

By the Longest Night, the men and a few of the women had finished the hole for the temple, as well as the shale wall. The men had already discovered a shale deposit near their village. The women were pleased that it was going to look very much like the old temple in Al-Rah, although the new one was somewhat larger. The evening was mild enough that they built a fire in the center of the temple and celebrated their first feast there, even though there were stars shining overhead. Kasha was resplendent in her new woolen robe, decorated with some clay beads that Elissa had made.

It was during the festival that the women discovered that there were only two hands of men living in their village, nor were there any young boys living with them. However, Ashannah noticed with pleasure how gentle the men were with the children of Al-Rah Montah.

Kasha began the ceremony by chanting the litany to Inanna, and after a few of the invocations, the men were able to join in the responses. Their enthusiasm added to the joy of everyone there.

Then Ashannah sang the invocations to the directions, and Kasha purified everyone with smoke from burning sage. Kasha felt chagrined that they had never before shared these rituals with men. But these men had proven themselves to be trustworthy in respecting these sacred rites.

After raising the cone of power, the men and women embraced each other and were ready to begin feasting. Outside the temple, the men had begun roasting some mutton earlier in the afternoon. The women had brought a good supply of emmer buns and a rabbit stew brimming with vegetables and grains from their harvests. As they ate together, both men and women began to relax and to share stories of their lives.

While Gennah and Ashannah were sitting together eating, Da-nid came over and sat by them. At first, they couldn't remember where they had seen him before."I'm Da-nid," he said. "Remember? I was with you when you got your first cart in Tel-Phar."

"Oh, now I remember!" Ashannah exclaimed. "You were with us when we passed that poor man … that slave."

"Yes, I'm afraid so," Da-nid replied solemnly. "I am truly glad to no longer be living in Tel-Phar. I was happy to help Tornah of Al-Labah find a dwelling until she and the crones went to Tel Dann. I didn't like leaving my mother, but when Gan-dor began to seriously hunt down those of us who remained faithful to Ninlil, I felt blessed when my friend, A-bel, told me about this village."

"It seems that A-bel makes friends easily," Gennah said, smiling and nodding towards A-bel and Beyla, who were seated across from them.

"If Beyla is a Virgin of Inanna, I am sure A-bel will respect it," Da-nid said, somewhat stiffly, wanting to reassure the women.

"She has been a Virgin of Inanna, at least until now," Ashannah laughed. "We do not have to be Virgins for all of our lives. If we give ourselves to one man, we lose the temple privileges of Virgins, but if later we wish to leave that man, or he dies, we may return and, again, consecrate ourselves to Inanna." This statement made Da-nid distinctly uncomfortable.

"The men of Et-Huyuk do not think it is good for men and women to live together," he stammered.

Gennah and Ashannah were amazed. Finally, Gennah offered to explain their position. "The women of Al-Rah Montah prefer living with other women, but sometimes a woman will change her mind and wish to live elsewhere with a man."

"But there is no other place for them to live, near here," Da-nid objected.

"We really do not know that they have that in mind,"Ashannah broke in, laughing. "They do seem to like each other very much, though."

Da-nid had become so uncomfortable that he got up to leave, saying, "It would not be good for one of our leaders to go off with a woman."

After he had gone some way, Ashannah said, "Well, now we know the name of their village, and they know ours. We can surely rest in peace that not one of them will force himself on any of us, but their rules seem very strict."

In the meantime, A-bel was saying to Beyla, "I have never seen a woman as beautiful as you. You … you seem … like the Goddess!"

These words definitely pleased Beyla. The possibility of giving up her virginity did not enter her mind. "It will be good when we have finished the new temple," she said, blushing deeply.

The celebration and the feast made the men and women realize how much they had benefited from each other, and they made plans about additional ways they could help each other. The temple would serve as the meeting place, where they could come together and trade or make plans for future projects. Only two hands of days later, the builders had the roof on the temple completed, and the women began taking turns for temple duty. However, the ground had become too hard to make the plaster for the walls or to chink the roof, so the nightly rendezvous had to stop, because without the added insulation the temple became quite cold. Nonetheless, they had apparently met long enough for Beyla to conceive, as she began to swell long before the women resumed temple duty in the spring.

It was during this coldest time of the year, when Ashannah happened to be walking upstream one clear afternoon, in search of hemp with which to make more mats for their floors. She was startled to hear a crashing sound coming from up the mountain, on the very path they had come down the previous spring. Her heart beat rapidly, as she tried to determine what had caused the noise. It seemed strange that an animal would come this close to the village at this time of year. The sound continued briefly, and then all was silent.

Then she heard a much different sound, but coming from the same direction. Her heart leaped in her throat, as she realized it was the rasping sound of a man struggling to breathe. Her heart beat even more wildly. She was certain it was not one of the men from Et-Huyuk. One of them would not be on this side of Al-Rah Montah.

She gasped when she distinctly heard a cry for help. Had he seen her, she wondered. She started to run back to Al-Rah Montah for help, but reconsidered when he cried out again. She quickly realized that he would hardly be able to injure her, and if she delayed helping him, she might be too late. Also, there was a slight familiarity in the sound of his voice.

She quickly walked over to where she had heard his cries, her heart beating harder and harder, until she could hardly breathe. Soon after she entered the forest, she saw him leaning against the trunk of a large oak. Again, there was something very familiar about him, although she couldn't recognize him from where she was. As she advanced, she saw that his clothing was in rags, hardly enough to protect him from the cold, and she could see bruises all over his body. Then she saw the sandy- colored hair and the turned-up eyes.

"Eetoh! Eetoh, is it you?" she shouted. He turned his head towards the sound of her voice, but she could see that his eyes were glazed. Then he slumped to the ground. "Eetoh, it's me! It's Ashannah!" She ran up and knelt down beside him and took his face between her hands. "Eetoh, don't you know me? It's … it's Ashannah!"

Finally, she saw his eyes focus on her. His mouth began to tremble, and tears filled his eyes. "Ashannah! It *is* you! Oh, blessed be Inanna! Oh Ashannah … they killed him! They killed my father!" With that, he fell into unconsciousness.

Chapter Twenty-two

After she had tried to revive Eetoh with no success, Ashannah took off the wool blanket she had wrapped around herself and laid it over him. Then she ran back to Al-Rah Montah to get help. It was cold, and no women were out and about. Ashannah ran into the larger cave, crying out, "It's Eetoh! Eetoh is here! But he is injured. He fell at my feet."

Thesta leaped up, saying, "My son? My son is here?"

"Oh, Thesta, before he fell he said they had killed En-dor!"

"Who killed En-dor?" Thesta asked.

"*They* … *they* killed him! Gan-dor's men, I guess! But I couldn't get him to wake up … Eetoh, I mean! And the clothes he is wearing are not enough to keep him warm. I covered him with my blanket, but I need help to get him inside a warm place! He's way back on the path we came down the mountain on."

Ashannah headed for the doorway with Thesta right behind her. Kasha grabbed her bag of herbs and a couple blankets. "There's a travois right outside the cave," she said. "Some of us can carry him on that."

At once, Minah, Gannah and Deenah got up to help. No one had forgotten that Eetoh and En-dor had saved their lives. They stopped to pick up the travois and quickly caught up with the others.

Ashannah led the way, as fast as she could, without actually running, so that Thesta, Kasha and the women with the travois could keep up. When they arrived where Ashannah had left him, they found him still unconscious. Kasha held a strong smelling mixture of pennyroyal and oil up to his nose. His breathing was shallow, but the pungent odor revived him. When he saw his mother bending over him, a light came into his eyes and then died away.

"Oh, Mama! I didn't have any place else to go! I know I don't belong with you and ... and the other Virgins, but they were going to kill me and ... and I guess I want to live ... even if I don't belong anywhere!"

"Eetoh!" Thesta shouted, "You saved our lives, and we know that's why they want to kill you! Now it is our turn to help you!"

Eetoh turned his face away, as if the future was too much to think about. Seeing this, Ashannah cried out, "Eetoh, there is a place for you! There is a small village of men in this valley. Like you, they came here to get away from the evil men from the north. After you have healed, I know they would be happy to have you join them!"

Eetoh looked at Ashannah as if he couldn't quite believe her.

"Eetoh, you are welcome to stay with us as long as you wish," Kasha assured him. The injured man looked at Kasha and then fell back into unconsciousness. He simply didn't have the energy to take it all in.

The women struggled to get Eetoh on the travois, without much success. They could see the cuts and bruises all over his body, and Kasha didn't want to injure him further. "Let me try the pennyroyal, again," she said. She held the mixture to his nose, and once more he revived enough to roll over onto the travois.

When Thesta and the four younger women started to lift him, the branches made a cracking sound, warning them that his weight was too much. Kasha put her arms under his back, and this extra support helped keep the branches intact. Even so, the village was barely in sight when the women had to put him down, because his weight had become too much for them.

Kasha again applied the pennyroyal to see if he could possibly walk the rest of the way to the cave with assistance. "Blessed be Inanna!" Kasha exclaimed, as Eetoh regained consciousness. With a woman at each side, he was able to stumble to the cave. Ashannah saw his clenched jaws and the beads of perspiration form on his forehead from the effort.

Kasha hurried on ahead to prepare a bed of pine needles close to the fire. The others were barely able to get him inside the cave and down on the bed. Seeing that his skin was blue from the cold, Kasha had them wrap some hot stones in cloth and put them next to his body. Then she covered him with several woolen blankets.

Thesta remained close by him, while Ashannah went home to get

Gennah and Elissa. By the time she returned with them, he was conscious enough that Kasha and Thesta were able to prop him up, in order to get some hot broth into his stomach.

"My father!" Elissa cried out, as she ran over to him.

"My little Elissa!" he responded, as tears ran down his cheeks. He put his arms out to hug her.

"I'm so glad you're here," she said, as she snuggled into his arms. It felt so good having someone really want him, that Eetoh was afraid he would break down and sob his heart out. He didn't, only because he was afraid it would frighten Elissa.

"I am so happy to be here with you," he said, as he buried his face in Elissa's abundant hair. He had no control over the tears streaming from his eyes.

Kasha was about to suggest that Elissa allow her father to finish his broth, but quickly decided that the love of the little girl was doing him more good. After a few minutes, Eetoh, began to feel the pangs of hunger.

"You may stay right by me, my daughter, but I need to finish this good broth. It has been a long while since I've had some good, warm food."

As he ate, Elissa wanted to ask him many questions, but she could see that it was very important for him to eat. When he had finished the bowl of broth, he said, "I am going to be here for awhile, so we can visit later. You have made me feel so much better, my little one, but right now I am very tired and need to rest. Can you understand?"

"Oh, yes," the child responded as she climbed off his lap.

For the rest of that day, Kasha kept feeding him broth, and by the next day, he was eating rabbit stew and fresh emmer buns, which Ashannah and Elissa had prepared for him. Finally, Elissa could not wait any longer to ask him where he had been, since he had left them more than a sun's cycle ago.

"I have been on a long and difficult journey, since I last saw you. The men who drove you from your village finally came to realize that En-dor and I had warned you and helped you to to leave Al-Rah before they got there. They were very angry and went to Tel Phar to ask Gan-dor what they should do. We knew they were angry, because they wouldn't talk to us. But we didn't know they wanted to punish us so much so we remained in Et-Toll, trying to live our lives as usual. In the spring, even though we didn't have much to trade, we made the journey to Tel Phar. As soon as we arrived, some men forced us to go to the temple of Enlil, where Gan-dor was waiting for us. He came right out and asked us if we had warned you and helped you to leave. We admitted that we had. Then he asked us if we realized how wrong we had been to help you … and, well, he began calling you all those horrible names they have for you Virgins."

"When he asked us again if we were sorry for what we had done, my father looked him right in the eyes and said, 'We do not believe the Virgins are evil. We still believe that they bring us to ecstasy with the Goddess and, with our help, bring children into Inanna's world. Besides that, they grow good food, weave fine cloth and sturdy baskets and make pots of clay. Also, they understand how to use certain plants to help a person heal. They live their lives and let us live ours. I do not understand why you hate them so!'

"They have weakened your spirits," Gan-dor shouted, "until you are no use to us. You have become as evil as they are!" Then he turned to the men who had dragged us there. "Take them from the temple and let them be stoned to death, when the sun begins its next journey"

"The men took us to a field near the edge of Tel Phar, where some large trees were growing. They tied us to one of the trees, built a huge fire on which to roast some meat, and began drinking barley juice and boasting and singing. After some time, they all fell asleep from drinking so much. Perhaps our tunics had hidden the knives we were wearing in our belts, because they did not take them from us. We were finally able to cut each other loose from the tree, all of the time afraid that we would awaken them. The light from the sun was just beginning to show, when we got loose and crept out of their camp.

"At first we thought of going to Tel Dann, but we didn't want to bring trouble to those people. Instead, we climbed high into the mountains, purposely not following any trails, so they couldn't discover our tracks. All summer long, we kept fishing, hunting and foraging, but always kept moving on, in case they would discover out trail. Then fall came, and we knew we had to find a place to stay for the winter. We found a place above Tel Dann and decided to stay there. One of the men from the village found us and brought us some blankets and hatchets to cut wood.

"I do not believe he told the men from Tel Phar where we were, but somehow, they found us. We heard them coming in time to get away, but they also could hear us and pursued us for a handful of sun's journeys. Again, we were without blankets or tools. I had my slingshots, a knife and a hatchet, but no bow and arrows. After two more days of running from the men, En-dor suggested that we climb high in some trees so they would lose our trail. That afternoon, we watched from above as they tried to figure out what had happened to us. Finally, they went on, ... we thought. En-dor told me to stay where I was, until he had made certain that they had lost us. As he was climbing down, he slipped and fell to the ground. I heard the men, as they came towards the sound. En-dor was unable to move. The men began to kick him, while they shouted and yelled over their victory. Even though he was unable to fight back, they began stabbing him with their knives, screaming and yelling louder and louder. I can still hear them in my head.

"I am ashamed to say that I was as if tied to the tree. I couldn't move nor cry out. I watched in horror as they ... they killed my father." Eetoh broke down and began to sob. Elissa, frightened by the vehemence of his crying, stared at him, as did the rest of the women, but Thesta went over and took him into her arms.

"Oh, my son!" she crooned. "My poor, poor son."

Finally, Eetoh regained control and continued with his story. "When the men were sure that En-dor was dead, they left, going in the direction of Tel Phar. Nevertheless, I stayed up in the tree until just before dark. I gave myself just enough time to bury my father, before night came. I really did not care if they came and got me. I felt truly alone. But something drove me to ... to continue on. Probably, it was my memories of you, my daughter."

At this, Elissa ran up to Eetoh and clung to him.

At first, I stayed high in the mountains, but finally I went back towards Al-Rah, hoping to pick up your trail, so I could find your village. I found your path, just as it began to snow. The shelter you used last winter saved my life. But I had no provisions and had to keep moving, at least by day, when it wasn't snowing too hard. Also, by moving continuously, I kept somewhat warm. And finally, I found you ... or Ashannah found me!"

As he finished, Eetoh looked over at Ashannah with such love and gratitude that she burst into tears and ran from the cave.

After several days of rest, Eetoh began taking walks in order to regain his strength. Thesta showed him the way to the new temple. There, he met Da-nid, who ran up to him saying, "Eetoh! We were afraid you ... that you had been killed."

"I nearly was, Da-nid, and my father ... my father was killed. I am happy to see that you are living in Et-Huyuk. I would like very much to live there, also."

"You are most welcome, my brother," Da-nid replied. "You could go back with me now, if you wish. It must be difficult living with only women."

"They have been most kind to me, Da-nid," Eetoh quickly replied. "My mother and a girl child, who is my daughter, lives among them and all of them helped me regain my strength Nevertheless, I do not belong there with them. I have some things I left back at the cave, where I've been living. Could I meet you here, when the sun next begins its journey, and go to Et-Huyuk, then?"

"I will be here, my brother," Da-nid assured him.

Eetoh was not familiar with the word ***brother*** but assumed it referred to some relationship among men. It made him feel welcome, although he wondered if he would be able to spend time with Elissa. Ashannah had told him that none of the women had ever seen Et-Huyuk. Then she admitted that none of the men had ever been to Al-Rah Montah.

When he brought it up that night, while they were eating, Kasha explained that all of their dealings with each other were done at or near the new temple. "It will be easier, as it gets warmer," she said. "In the meantime, if you wish, you may come here and spend time with your daughter ... and with your mother, as well."

"Thank you, Kasha. As soon as I am a little stronger, I will surely do that."

As soon as the earth thawed in the spring, some of the men and women began plastering the walls of the new temple, as well as chinking the roof. By then, Eetoh was fully recovered and joined in the task. Ashannah would bring Elissa with her, so she could be with her father. Often Leah and Ran-dell would come along, and sometimes Nella and Meldah, as well. Eetoh took an especial interest in Ran-dell, whom he came to regard as a son.

Eetoh made slingshots for all the children, and they became proficient rabbit hunters. Elissa, however, remained like her mother and refused to kill. Now that the women were able to have gardens, again, many of them only ate meat from the animals they killed for the leather.

One afternoon, as they were resting from work, Ashannah asked Eetoh if he liked living in Et-Huyuk.

"My brothers have been very good to me," he replied. "I have been living with Da-nid until we can make the bricks for my home. But I do not understand their strict rules about not living with women. I guess, in that, they are very much like you. At least, they understand their responsibility to Inanna, to help people the earth, and now that you are here, they are looking forward to having sons in their village. If Beyla does not have a boy, they will be very disappointed. But it is A-bel, that I feel sorry for. I know and they know that he and Beyla wish very much to live together. They wander around in the hills every chance they get, to be together. At least, you are accepting of Beyla. Many of the men no longer speak to A-bel. Somehow they feel that he has betrayed them. But they would not be welcome to live together in Al-Rah Montah, either, is that not so?"

Ashannah did not answer, at once. She knew that what she had to say would hurt Eetoh's feelings all over again and take away the last vestiges of any hopes he had of living near her and Elissa.

"I cannot speak for all of the women, but I believe that most of them would rather Al-Rah Montah remain as it is, a village for Virgins of Inanna. However, any woman who wishes to leave the village and live with a man, remains our sister and our friend."

"Perhaps Beyla and A-bel should begin a third village, here, close to the temple," suggested Gennah.

"That's a really good idea, Gennah!" Eetoh cried out. "I wonder if they have thought of that. I, too, would come and live with them, so Elissa could come and visit me in my own home."

"She would like that very much, Eetoh," Ashannah assured him.

"Perhaps you could give them the idea," Gennah suggested smiling.

"Most of the men would be very unhappy with me ... but I think I will anyway," he replied.

Just at that moment, Beyla came over to join them. "I've been practicing throwing stones with slingshots with the children, but they have much more energy than I, especially with my big belly!" She patted her stomach lovingly. "May I join you?"

"We were just talking about you," Ashannah said, laughing.

"You were?" Beyla was obviously curious as to what they had been saying.

"We ... we, uh, ... er ... we were thinking ..." Here Eetoh had to stop.

"Well," Gennah took over, "we think that you and A-bel would like to live together, isn't that so?"

"Oh, yes it is!" Beyla exclaimed. "But what do you think about it? The men are angry with A-bel for spending so much time with me."

"Not me," Eetoh broke in.

"You aren't?" Beyla asked, surprised.

"You know that we virgins have always respected a woman who decides to live with a man," Ashannah reminded her.

"But still ... you ...would not want us to come and live with you in Al-Rah Montah, would you?'

"That's why we were thinking that you and A-bel could start a new village, close to here," Gennah said.

"And I would come and build my home there, too," Eetoh said. "That way, my daughter could come and visit me where I live."

"What a wonderful idea!" Beyla exclaimed. "Actually, A-bel was thinking of going off and living somewhere together, after our baby is born. But I would not want to be far from my family. And who would play with our child?"

"Do you want me to tell A-bel about it?" Eetoh asked, very much excited by the prospect.

"Well, perhaps I should," Beyla said. "The other men would be very upset, if they knew it was your idea."

"Actually, it was Gennah who thought of it," Eetoh pointed out. "But I think it is a good plan, and I would want to come and live with you."

"We would like that very much," she assured him. She looked around to see if any men were standing near by. "We ... A-bel and I are meeting tonight. I will ask him then."

The men of Et-Huyuk made their huts of clay bricks, stabilized with straw and sheep dung. Except for the few who had traveled to Tel Phar, the women of Al-Rah Montah had never seen such dwellings.

As he described them, Eetoh explained to Ashannah that the thick walls also protected the dwellers from the cold of winter and the heat in the summer, even more efficiently than her cave house. When Beyla and A-bel began building their house, just north of the temple, later that spring, Eetoh and some of the women of Al-Rah Montah helped.

First A-bel fashioned some forms from some crudely milled boards. They were a little less than the width of a man's hand and about the length of a person's forearm and half as wide. He fastened them at the corners with copper pinnings and put a band of copper, about the same width as the form, around the entire frame. Finally with a metal tool he called a trowel, he pressed the wet clay firmly into the form. After a time, he was able to pull the form from the hardening brick and begin the process again.

A few days later, the bricks were dry enough to turn on their sides to hasten their drying. In the meantime, they made more bricks. After half a moon's cycle, they had enough bricks to begin building. "I can see how these thick walls would keep the hut warmer in the winter and cooler in the summer," Ashannah observed. "Maybe we could make walls like these for the fronts of our caves. We would have to find a big bed of clay, though."

"It doesn't need to be as fine as the clay used for pots," A-bel explained. "You can test it by making a mud ball, letting it dry and then dropping it. If it doesn't shatter, there is enough clay in the soil to hold it. If it breaks, you need to find soil with more clay in it."

"I don't see why you couldn't make the front walls of your cave homes with the bricks," Eetoh said. "You could even leave the walls of branches and grasses up until the brick wall is finished."

"We could do that with the large caves, as well," Gannah said with excitement.

"We'll help you with your house, first, Eetoh," Ashannah promised.

By the feast of Ninlil, they had finished A-bel and Beyla's house and a smaller one for Eetoh. As they had feared, the men of Et-Huyuk would have nothing to do with the new village, nor with Eetoh or A-bel.

Everyone was shocked, therefore, when Far-min and Yuk-tol declared their intentions to live with Fannah and Deenah and their daughters in the new village.

Chapter Twenty-three

There was such a turbulent reaction among the men of Et-Huyuk, when Farmin and Yuk-tol announced their intention to move to the new village, that Kasha was fearful the friendship between the two original villages would be severed. After these two left the men's village, only a handful plus two men remained. She could understand their consternation. It seemed far more difficult for them to replace their numbers, than for the women.

She arranged to have a meeting with Moshe, in order to discover if the men were blaming the women for this turn of events. When she saw the old man approaching the temple, she was not surprised to see Da-nid with him. Moshe was quickly learning the language of the women, but she could understand why he would want someone he could trust, who was also more fluent with the language.

"May Inanna bless you and keep you safe," she murmured, as she bowed to them.

"And may she bless you also," the two men replied, returning the bow.

They sat themselves around the fire pit on the sunset side of the temple. Although the leaves of the alders and oaks were changing, it was not yet cold enough for them to need a fire.

"We were blessed with another fine harvest," Kasha said. "Does your village have enough grain for the winter?"

"We have already traded wool for your grain," Da-nid replied stiffly. Kasha detected a certain surliness in his voice.

"Moshe quickly added in a more conciliatory tone, "I believe we have sufficient grain, thank you, Kasha."

"Especially with so few men left in our village," Da-nid growled.

Kasha quickly decided to ignore this last remark, but now she knew that at least Da-nid was angry with the women.

"When you first arrived here," Da-nid continued, "I was very happy. And when both of our villages seemed to benefit from each other and you seemed as content to remain apart in Al-Rah Montah, as we were to remain in Et-Huyuk, I was especially pleased." Da-nid paused to consider his words carefully.

Kasha couldn't help breaking in. "When we came over the mountain and down into this valley, we thought there were no other villages here," she said, speaking slowly so Moshe could understand. "You can believe how terrified we were, when our children came running into our village, shouting that they had met a man. When Moshe informed us that there was a village of men, only a hand's span of the sun's journey from here, we were very concerned. But we soon understood that you meant us no harm and that you were even willing to help us prepare for the coming winter. We have been truly grateful for that help."

Moshe was quick to respond. "We, too, have benefited from your gardening skills and are especially grateful for the temple and your services to us."

"But we did not know that some of our men would be leaving our village, in order to live with your women!" Da-nid exploded.

"We did not foresee this either," Kasha calmly replied. "We have also lost women from Al-Rah Montah, although there were more of us to begin with," she conceded.

"We do not believe it is good for men and women to live together!" Da-nid exclaimed.

Although Kasha was puzzled by this statement, she did not try to dissuade them from it, nor even try to find out why they believed this. "Most of the women of Al-Rah Montah prefer living apart from men, but for many sun cycles, now, there have been a few women, who have preferred living with a man."

"But we do not believe that it is good for a man and a woman to live together!" Da-nid repeated vehemently.

"We believe that it causes fighting among the men," Moshe explained. "Sometimes two men will want the same woman and this causes trouble."

"And we also believe that one person should not own another!"Da-nid interjected.

"I am certain that none of the women of Al-Rah Montah would want to belong to another person, man or woman," Kasha quickly replied. "Nor do I believe that Beyla, Fannah or Deenah believe that they are owned by the men they are living with. When a woman decides to live with a man, she gives up her virginity and her temple rights, but these are the only changes in her life."

"How can you allow them to desecrate their virginity in this way?" Da-nid asked.

Kasha did not answer, at once, but continued to look at him, while she considered her reply. "We do not believe that all women are the same or even that they should be," she stated. "If we forced a woman, who wished to live with a man, to remain in the village with us, I am certain her unhappiness would cause even more trouble than ... than the trouble you described among the men."

"But you don't allow her to live in your village with her man!" Da-nid said.

"That is true," Kasha agreed, "but we still remain friends and can spend time together in each other's homes, if we wish. When we were still in Al-Rah, some of the women preferred living in Et-Ray, so they could be near the trading, not so they could live with a man."

The three of them remained silent for a time, wondering where the conversation was leading. Finally, Kasha broke the silence. "I believe that when the men from the north came down and taught that a man should own his woman and even own other men as slaves, that's when trouble began for all of us."

Moshe and Da-nid sat staring at her, trying to take in what she had said. After a time, Moshe spoke. "I begin to see ..."

Da-nid quickly interrupted, "I don't see what that has to do with us! All of us have come to this valley to get away from those men and their teachings!"

"Yes, that is true," Kasha agreed, keeping as calm as she could.

"Listen Da-nid," Moshe said with firmness. "What is important, is that every man or woman can choose to live his or her life in the manner they wish, as long as they do not take away this choice from another."

"I don't know ..." Da-nid grumbled.

"Do you men … sometimes choose to live … with another man?" Kasha asked hesitantly.

"Do you mean that we choose to live together as lovers?" Da-nid asked.

"That's what I mean," Kasha stammered. "Many of us Virgins choose to live that way."

"I have a lover," Da-nid admitted.

"And others of us do, also," Moshe added.

"I believe that most people choose to enrich their lives in this way," Kasha continued.

"I never thought of it in that way," Moshe said.

"Nor I," Da-nid agreed. "But yes, living with a person, who is special to you, does enrich your life."

"And should we be concerned if a man and a woman choose to live this way?" she ventured. "In fact, should we not rejoice that they, too, have found someone to share their joys and sorrows?"

Again, the two men stared at her, as they tried to decide if they agreed with what she said.

"Perhaps, you are right," Moshe finally said.

"I will have to see how it works out with those … those living together in the new village," Da-nid said.

"You have given us much to think about, Kasha," Moshe said, as he and Da-nid got up to return to their village.

Soon after the feast of Ninlil, A-bel came rushing over to Fanah's house. "Beyla is going to have our baby!" he exclaimed, breathlessly, but also with much pride. "Would you please go get Kasha and Ashannah?"

"I'll get Deenah to stay with her, while I go get them," Fannah said, to A-bel's relief.

Beyla was glad to see a woman return with A-bel. She was perspiring freely and the pains were coming more and more frequently. Deenah took charge immediately. "Even though it is warm, A-bel, we will need warm water to clean the baby and its mother."

A-bel was glad to have something useful to do. Just as he finished gathering wood for the fire, they heard a chorus of women's voices singing louder and louder as they approached the new village. Every woman in Al-Rah Montah wanted to share in Beyla's joy at once again being a mother.

Kasha, Ashannah and Gennah went inside the small dwelling. Ashannah and Gennah stooped side by side and offered their thighs for Beyla to sit on, in the meantime, supporting her with their arms. This would leave Kasha free to catch the infant, cut the cord and present Beyla with her baby.

Outside, the rest of the women gathered around the fire A-bel had started and began singing the litany to Inanna. A-bel paced back and forth between the hut and the circle of women. When Beyla's cries became almost more than he could bear, he was grateful for the company of singing women. None of them seemed affected by her cries. In the meantime, Eetoh came over and stood by him, as well as Farmin and Yuk-tol.

With Beyla's final scream, the women stopped singing and looked expectantly towards the entrance of the hut. Shortly, Kasha appeared, exultantly holding out a bloody, but beautiful infant.

"Come and look upon your daughter, A-bel," she invited.

"Will she be all right?" he asked, looking askance at the blood all over the little body.

"Oh, yes," Kasha assured him. "She is whole and entire and very well formed. As soon as Ashannah and Gennah have bathed Beyla, you may come in and be with her. In the meantime, I will clean the baby, so you can see how beautiful she truly is."

When A-bel finally entered his home, he was overcome by the beauty of his beloved, as she nursed their little daughter. "Kasha was right," he said. "She is truly beautiful, and so are you, my love. Have you a name for her?"

"I would like to call her Lorana, in honor of the sybil, Orana," Beyla replied. "She took her own life, so that we could travel on towards Al-Rah Montah before the winter snows caught us unprotected."

The women of the village did not like to repeat names within a generation, because of the confusion it would cause, so they made slight changes in a name, when they wished to show honor to someone.

Since he had heard many stories of their journey over the mountain, A-bel was pleased with the choice. When Gennah heard the name, honoring her mother, she wept with joy.

Elissa had been asleep for some time, as Gennah and Ashannah sat talking around the little fire in their home. Ashannah looked deeply into her beloved's eyes and asked, "So, how has it been … serving in the temple again?"

"Oh, Ashannah, I was terrified, the first time, but Moshe was so kind and gentle and went into ecstasy so quickly, that I felt certain I could do it again."

"And ..." Ashannah prompted.

"And ... well ... it was Da-nid the second time."

"I hope he was gentle."

"He was, Ashannah. He really was, but ... he takes his duty of bringing forth children, very seriously."

"And he insisted on mating with you?"

"He asked me to, Ashannah. He was very understanding, although he was very persistent, too. I asked him to let me think it over and ... and I told him when I would have temple duty next."

"Well, I know we aren't supposed to do that, Gennah, but I doubt if there are many Virgins, who have not done it, at least once."

"I know, I know. Anyway, I thought about it and knew I very much wanted a child of my own. Elissa has been like my own daughter, in many ways, but ..."

"It's not quite the same," Ashannah finished for her.

"No ... no it isn't." Gennah looked carefully into Ashannah's eyes to see if she really understood.

"I would be happy for you to have a daughter of your own, Gennah, and, in a way, to have another daughter, myself." Then Ashannah chuckled, "without going through ... "

Now Gennah began to laugh, too, and took up Ashannah's thought, saying, "Without having to go through the pain! Well, I think I am ready now!"

"You mean you've missed your bleeding time, already!"

"We did mate, but only two nights ago. It's too soon to know, but, really, Ashannah, I don't believe it happened. I couldn't help it. When he went inside me, I got scared and tightened up. I don't think he noticed anything, but ... but, well, I just don't think it happened."

"I think you would know, Gennah."

"I just hope he will want to mate again. I'm a little used to him now, and I'd rather not have to go through it with someone else!"

"Why don't you tell him you would like to try again on the Longest Night."

"If I have bled again by then, I will."

★★★★★

Beleendah pulled her shawl around tighter, as she walked towards the large cave, hoping to find Kasha there. She doubted that the High Priestess would be alone, especially since it was quite a cold afternoon in the middle of the winter. It was not a good time to want to talk to someone privately. It was one of the few times she wished they were living in their own little huts, as they had in Al-Rah.

She entered the cave and found it full of women, as she had expected. However, Kasha was a little apart from the others, sifting dried herbs into little clay jars. She, too had a blanket around her shoulders, since she was some distance from either fire. Beleendah walked over by her. "I would like to speak with you, Kasha," she requested.

"Let me finish with this basil," Kasha replied. After she completed the job, Kasha looked expectantly at Beleendah.

"I am so happy and proud to be a Virgin of Inanna," she began.

Kasha smiled and said, "I know."

"I want with all of my heart to continue being so," the younger woman continued. Kasha remained silent. "But ... but, still ... I would like to go live in the new village, not because I want to live with a man, but because I believer Ran-dell needs to be with some men. Yet, I do not want him to go to Et-Huyuk. He is still too young, and ... and, well, although they respect us Virgins, their ideas about women are strange."

"Their ideas may be changing," Kasha said, "but I agree. Ran-dell is too young to go live with them."

"And now that Meldah and Nella have moved to the new village, there are fewer and fewer children here in Al-Rah Montah. Even Leah and Elissa go there often, to be with Eetoh."

"That seems to be so," Kasha replied.

"So, could I live there in my own house and still be a Virgin of Inanna?"

"I do not see why not, but it is not up to me to say who can live in ... in the new village," the older woman replied. "I hope they give it a name soon!" she interjected laughing and then, continued on. "Also it would be good to have a Virgin living near the temple. Would you like me to go with you to ask the ... the new villagers, if they would allow you to live there, as a Virgin?"

"Oh, yes, Kasha, I would, indeed!"

"Well, I am certain that Eetoh, for one, would be happy to have Ran-dell living there. Shall we go now, Beleendah? Let's each take an extra blanket. It may be almost dark and quite cold by the time we return to Al-Rah Montah.

Thus, it was arranged that when the earth became soft enough in the spring, the new villagers, along with some of the women from Al-Rah Montah, would build a mud brick house for Beleendah and Ran-dell.

"I hope you understand why I am not helping with Beleendah's house, Ashannah," Gennah said, one evening after supper, late in the spring.

"Well, since you haven't said anything, I can only guess," Ashannah answered, smiling.

"I haven't bled for three moon cycles," Gennah announced, her eyes shining like two bright stars.

Chapter Twenty-four

When Eetoh approached Ashannah in the temple, begging her to bear a son for him, Ashannah quickly replied, "Even if I chose to have another child by you, Eetoh, I could not promise that it would be a son!"

"Well, then, Ashannah, if it were another girl, I would still love her."

It was uncommon for a woman of Al-Rah to have more than one child, unless, like Beyla, she lost it in infancy, or if she had twins. Without explaining what seemed self-evident to her, Ashannah continued with her argument. "You should ask another woman, Eetoh. I am certain one of the other women would be happy to bear you a child and, perhaps, even live with you in the new village."

Eetoh flinched and replied, "I could … could never mate with another woman, Ashannah. I still love you and you, alone!" Ashannah looked long into the man's tear-filled eyes as tears of frustration filled her own. "I know I am asking a great deal of you," Eetoh continued, "but please, please, try to bear a son for me!"

"Why a son rather than a daughter?"

"Because I already have a daughter. I love Elissa very much and she loves me, but still, I would also like to have a son."

"Having a daughter is enough for me," Ashannah insisted.

"That is because you are not a man! I am a man and I want another, like me!"

Ashannah looked even deeper in Eetoh's eyes, trying to feel as he did. "I must consider this carefully, Eetoh. You are asking quite a bit of me, and I wonder how Elissa would feel about having a brother … or sister? She will have completed a handful plus two sun cycles by the time he or she would be born. And I have completed four hands plus two sun cycles! I do feel strong, and I still have much energy, but ... well, remember it may be another girl!"

"I've already promised to love her with all my heart, if it is another girl, but, somehow, I am certain it will be a boy."

"That is because you want it so!" Ashannah exclaimed, exasperated. "Besides, I have not decided to do this thing for you." After a brief pause, she told Eetoh when she would be on duty again. "If you come back then, I will have an answer."

As the lunar cycles progressed and the bellies of Ashannah and Gennah grew rounder, Elissa finally figured out what was happening. "Am I going to have two sisters?" she asked.

"Or a brother and a sister," Ashannah offered.

"Or two brothers," Gennah teased, although the thought of having a boy was still quite fearful for her. "There is even a small possibility that one of us would have twins!" Gennah gasped.

"This house is getting smaller and smaller," the little girl observed.

"We can always make it larger, when we add on the mud wall in the front," Ashannah laughed.

"We just might have to do that," Elissa said, in all seriousness.

"Don't you want a little sister?" Ashannah asked, becoming serious, herself.

"I would love to have *one* little sister!" Elissa exclaimed.

"Well, I think your heart is big enough for two," Gennah said.

"But not *three*!" Elissa retorted.

"I think we are getting ahead of ourselves," Ashannah again laughed. "At least, I will be able to catch your baby, when it arrives, Gennah."

"Will I get to help, too?" Elissa asked, her eyes widening with anticipation.

"That would be up to your grandmother, Kasha," Ashannah reminded her daughter.

"I'm going to go ask her, right now!" Elissa shouted, as she ran out of the house.

Beleendah preferred round houses, like the ones in Al-Rah, to the rectangular homes of the new village. She persuaded them to try to build a round house with the bricks. They figured out how to do it as they went along. It ended up looking somewhat like the conical huts of Al-Rah. They built the bricks right up to the smoke hole, so she didn't have to thatch a roof.

By the time they had completed the new house for Beleendah and Ran-dell, they had named the new village El Raspell. With five dwellings, it appeared more like a village. Everyone was invited to attend a feast, in order to celebrate, but of the men from Et Huyuk, only Moshe was there. However, every woman and child from Al-Rah Montah was there.

Ran-dell was excited about living near Eetoh. He had never forgotten the ways Eetoh had made him feel special during the days before the trip over the mountain. Ran-dell's devotion made the older man feel like he had a son already, but he still looked forward to having a son from his own seed.

During the festivities, every time Eetoh looked upon Ashannah's swollen belly, tears of gratitude came to his eyes. He had already chosen a name for his son, but he hadn't told Ashannah, who would have reminded him that the baby might be a girl. He would name the boy after his father, making the slight change required. His son's name would be An-dor.

True to her promise, Ashannah was right by Gennah during her long labor. Thesta and Kasha squatted down for Gennah to sit on their thighs, so Ashannah could catch the baby. Stooping was somewhat difficult for her, since she was in the late stages of her own pregnancy. However, she was able to persevere, because she wanted, so much, to have the honor of catching Gennah's baby. With the encouragement of the women singing outside of their cave home, Gennah was finally able to release her child.

Ashannah joyfully cried out, "It's a girl, my love! Now, you have your very own daughter!" Out of the corner of her eye, Ashannah noticed Elissa flinch at the realization that she hadn't really been considered Gennah's daughter. Ashannah deftly cut and tied the umbilical cord and presented the infant to her mother. Then she hurried over to Elissa.

"Isn't it wonderful to have a new sister, just when you have finished a handful plus two sun cycles?"

"I ... I guess so," Elissa answered, making an effort to seem pleased.

"I think you will enjoy having a baby sister in your home," Ashannah went on. "I never had that pleasure, nor did Gennah."

Elissa looked straight into her mother's eyes. "Just so you don't forget that I am your *true* daughter!"

With that, Ashannah took her little girl into her arms, holding her tight, assuring her how happy she was to have her as her *true* daughter.

"Will *she* be your *true* daughter, too?" Elissa asked, eyeing her mother's swollen stomach.

"If she turns out to be a girl," Ashannah admitted. "But she will also be your *true* sister."

"And what will she be if she's a boy?" Elissa persisted.

"Well first of all, *she* will be *he* and he will be your brother," Ashannah explained.

"Will he be Eetoh's daughter, too?"

"He will be Eetoh's son," Ashannah corrected.

"I think I would like that better," Elissa said.

Ashannah laughed and said, "In that, you are like your father!"

Gennah couldn't think of a name for her daughter right away, but a few days later, she asked Ashannah and Elissa how they liked the name Verda. "That's because her eyes are green. I think it's a beautiful name, don't you?"

Both agreed at once. It looked like the baby would have the red hair of her mother, contrasting beautifully with her skin, which was dark like Da-nid's.

When Da-nid heard that Gennah had given birth to a girl, he was sorely disappointed. Although two more men had come to Et-Huyuk, there were still no young boys there. He had no interest in developing a relationship with his daughter. Since Gennah hadn't been raised with a father, nor had many of the children of Al-Rah known their fathers, his indifference did not bother her. Later, if Verda wished to know who her father was, she would be able to tell her.

One and a half moon cycles after Verda was born, Ashannah began to experience her own birth pangs. By then, the leaves of the maples, oaks and alders were turning to bright reds and golds, and while the nights were getting chilly, the days were still quite warm.

It was the middle of the night when Ashannah's contractions began. Gennah got up and built a fire in their pit. The sun still hadn't begun to show itself, when Gennah finally decided to go get Kasha and Thesta to help with the birth. Ashannah had confided to Thesta that Eetoh was the father of this child, also.

The waning moon gave Gennah the necessary light to find her way to the big cave. As if they had known it was time, the two women were up, dressed and ready to leave for Gennah's and Ashannah's home.

By the time the baby's head was cresting, it was dawn and the rest of the women had come over to help the new infant into the world with their singing. As Gennah caught the infant, she cried out, "Oh, Ashannah! It's ... it's a boy! Will that be all right?"

"Eetoh will be delighted," Ashannah gasped. "And ... and so am I! Thesta, will you go tell Eetoh?" Then she looked over at Gennah. "Would it be all right with you ... if Eetoh comes back with Thesta, to see his son?"

"Of course, my love," Gennah readily replied. "I imagine he even has a name for him. Here, let me have him, so I can have him cleaned up before his father comes. A-bel thought something was wrong with Lorana, when he saw the blood all over her." Ashannah quickly gave up her newborn, wanting Eetoh to be entirely pleased with him.

Elissa was relieved to have a new brother, rather than another sister to share with her mothers. It seemed to her that daughters were closer to their mothers than sons, since they were more alike. She didn't stop to think that sons might be closer with their fathers, by the same reasoning, and that Eetoh might feel closer to his son than he did to her. She was much too preoccupied getting used to the new pronouns and relationships, for this to bother her.

Suddenly they heard Thesta announcing that Eetoh was approaching. The baby was clean and wrapped in a new cotton blanket, sucking hungrily at his mother's breast, when Eetoh stepped inside the little cave home. It was truly getting crowded with two cribs and another child already living there.

"My son!" Eetoh said gently, taking him from Ashannah and lifting him to his shoulder. "Your name shall be An-dor." An-dor was not happy with losing his source of nourishment and let his displeasure be known, at once. Eetoh quickly returned him to his mother, realizing that it would be several sun cycles before he could expect his son to appreciate him.

That winter was exceptionally cold, but Eetoh made certain Ashannah's home was abundantly supplied with wood. With all of the love surrounding them, Verda and An-dor not only survived the harsh winter, but, by the following spring, both were crawling about the little space.

As soon as the earth thawed, Eetoh was busy helping Ashannah and Gennah with the mud wall that would enlarge the front of their house. They soon learned it was better to form the bricks on the level ground, where the clay bed was. Then after the bricks had baked in the sun sufficiently, they could bring them over in a cart to begin the wall. The other women helped, too, because they wanted to learn in order to enlarge their homes and the village temple. Following the example of Beleendah's house, they were able to avoid having thatched roofs.

By Inanna's feast, Ashannah's and Gennah's house was completed, and the two women began helping the others with their houses. With two crawling babies, this was often a challenge, but Elissa took pride in being able to help with her brother and sister and became quite proficient at it. After the two babies began to eat mush, the women would sometimes leave all three children with Eetoh and the women of El Raspell. Beleendah was only too happy to help, as by this time Ran-dell was quite independent.

During the following summer, two new men arrived at Et Huyuk. They had been living in Za-Phir, a somewhat larger seaport, south of Tel Phar. However, since it was farther south, the men from the north had only recently arrived there.

Hel-vid and his partner Ya-ir had known Moshe and A-bel, when they were still living in Za-Phir. When the Kurgans arrived and had begun spreading their teachings and taking over Ninlil's temple, dedicating it to Enlil, Moshe and A-bel came up with the idea of creating a new community of men who still worshipped the Goddesses. They persuaded several men to come with them, but Hel-vid and Ya-ir were traders and were unable to imagine a life without opportunities for trading.

When A-bel returned to Za-Phir several moon cycles later, he could see that the two traders were getting more and more disgusted with the ways of Gan-dor and his followers, so he gave them careful directions to Et-Huyuk, in case they should finally decide to leave the seaport.

Two more sun cycles were to pass, before Hel-vid and Ya-ir came to realize that the seaport was no longer a safe place for them. They packed up their things and set out in search of Et-Huyuk. Both of them had lived almost entirely in Za-Phir, and while they had traveled to Tel Phar via a trading boat, they had never experienced traveling in forests and mountains. After a few days, they were quite lost, and their supplies were running dangerously low. One evening, they reluctantly decided they had better try to return to Za-phir the next day.

Hel-vid busied himself with clearing a space for their fire, while Ya-ir went off to gather wood. Hel-vid was concentrating on pushing aside some branches and brush, when suddenly he heard a sharp whistle as something flew past, very close to his face. Mouth agape, he watched as the missile lodged itself in a nearby tree. With horror, he made out an arrow, still quivering from the impact.

Just then a large, dark man came crashing through the brush, totally shocked to find a man standing there. "By the Goddess, I almost hit you!" he cried out. "I thought you were a deer! Not many people travel in these woods!"

"I guess I can believe that," Hel-vid exclaimed, as he stared hard at the hunter. "I've never been that close to an arrow, before!"

Hearing voices, Ya-ir hurried into the clearing. "What's ... what's happening?" he asked. "Who ... who are you?"

"I am Da-nid of Et-Huyuk," the man answered, before thinking of the possible consequences of revealing the name of their village. The men of Et-Huyuk were very secretive about the existence of their village, not wanting any men from the north to discover them.

Ya-ir burst out, "Et-Huyuk! Praised be Inanna! Do you know the man Moshe or the man A-bel?"

Da-nid was immediately relieved that they knew Moshe and A-bel. "Are you looking for them?" he asked.

"Yes. Don't they live in Et-Huyuk? Is it close by?"

By then Da-nid felt he could trust them. "Yes, they live there and it is quite close."

"Blessed be Inanna for sending you to us ... and for turning your arrow from my head," Hel-vid laughed. "We have been searching for Et-Huyuk for a handful of days and had just decided to return to Za-Phir, although we really don't want to!"

"You have been blessed by the Goddess," Da-nid agreed, "and I will be happy to lead you to Et-Huyuk."

Hel-vid and Ya-ir had been in Et-Huyuk a handful of days when the women of Al-Rah Montah held a feast in celebration of Ninlil's harvest. The men of Et-Huyuk were less angry with the women, especially since their numbers had been increased, and showed up for the festivities. Hel-vid and Ya-ir were very impressed with the quality of Gennah's weavings and Leenah's and Angah's pottery. They promptly praised the women for their craftsmanship, but it was some time later before they approached the women, offering to take their wares for trading in Za-Phir.

"Would you feel safe to be seen in Za-Phir?" Gennah asked.

"We did not speak out about our opinions of the Kurgans," Hel-vid assured her. "Nevertheless, they were beginning to notice that we did not go to the temple, to give honor to Enlil. However, there are many things to trade for in Za-Phir that would make life in our villages easier. We would wait until spring to return there and remain just long enough to do our trading. I believe they would be so fascinated with these fine goods that they wouldn't notice what else we do. We would be very careful that no one would see us leave and follow us here."

"This is something we must consider very carefully," Kasha said.

Gennah was elated with the challenge the trading would bring to her craft. This was also true for the potters and metal workers in all three villages. They spent much of the winter making things for Ya-ir and Hel-vid to trade, in order to obtain things for the villages.

Spring finally arrived and the two men left for Za-Phir with a cart apiece, loaded down with goods. Da-nid and A-bel went with them for added protection from thieves. The latter two did not enter the city, however, because they all agreed that so many strangers would draw too much attention to them.

Everything went well, and Hel-vid and Ya-ir were ready to return to Et-Huyuk after three sun journeys of trading. They left towards dusk, remaining on the main road, leading west out of the seaport, for about a hand's span of the sun's journey. This left them just enough light to make out the landmark designating the path to Et-Huyuk. Unless one was made aware of it, the path to Et-Huyuk was indiscernible. There, they stopped and set up camp, as if they were going to remain there for the night. After dark, Da-nid and A-bel joined them, and they continued on. They were certain they were not being followed.

Chapter Twenty-five

During a return trip to Za-phir, Ya-ir paused to watch carefully, as a woman spun out an unusually shaped vase on her whirling potter's wheel. To him, it looked something like a dolphin standing on its tail, its mouth wide open to receive a bouquet of flowers. Since he saw that she had made others that were similar, he praised their beauty and originality and asked her to make one, while he watched. Pleased with his interest, she did as he requested. Later, Hel-vid came and made a trade for one of the vases.

Ya-ir was especially good at watching potters, weavers and metal workers. Then he would take samples of their work back to the three villages, where he could explain how they were crafted, bringing new ideas and techniques to the artisans. Because of his close observations, he was able to describe the new techniques well enough that the villagers were able to understand and incorporate them into their own work and often, even improve on them.

When the vases first arrived, the potters of Al-Rah Montah and El-Raspell had never seen any before. The clay workers loved both their graceful lines and their function. Soon, both temples were festooned with vases of flowers.

When the vases first arrived, Elissa's hands were not large or strong enough to do much on the wheel. However, by the time she reached ten sun cycles, her hands had matured to where she was able to make pots of many sizes and shapes, which were both durable and practical. In no time she was fashioning products that found their way into the trader's carts.

If Ashannah and Kasha were disappointed that this child, who looked so much like them, did not choose to follow them in their healing and herb craft, they did not express this. As soon as she was making pots, that could be traded, her mother, grandmother and Gennah helped her build a little work hut near home, where she could throw pots and model figurines as much as she pleased. They had already obtained a wheel for her by trading fine linen pieces spun by her mother and woven by Gennah. By the time she had reached two hands plus four sun cycles, she was shaping delicate cups and vases, which were pleasing to the touch, as well as to look at.

Elissa let her strong, tan hands, with their extra long fingers, revel in the feel of the moist, closely packed clay, before she began turning her wheel. Then, slowly, she began pumping the foot pedal, gradually increasing the speed, until the clay was a blur to her eyes. Her hands immediately took over, as she carefully shaped the vase she already saw in her mind.

She leaned back and sighed appreciatively, as she admired the results. If all went well in the firing, this vase would certainly be worthy of a place in Inanna's temple at El-Raspell.

After she scraped away the excess clay around the bottom, she set the vase aside to dry with other pots, cups and vases, until she was ready to do a firing. She was amazed as she noticed, as if for the first time, the number of pieces ready. She cleaned her hands, methodically stretched the muscles of her neck, back, arms and legs and, only then, left her work hut to walk down the slope to the temple, in order to thank the Goddess for the inspiration. She took time to choose a spot for the new vase and then went back out and on down to the river, where there was a large, flat rock, warmed by the sun.

As she lay there, her body eagerly soaking up the warmth from the rock, she listened to the rushing water, and memories of the past few years flowed through her mind.

Years ago, upon discovering that she was too small to throw pots on the wheels, to console herself, she began forming little clay goddesses, much like the one she had made from snow outside the large cave where they had spent the winter. She soon devised little tools that would enable her to form more details on the faces, hands and feet. Everyone was amazed at how beautifully human her goddesses appeared. Their eyes, however, were much larger than human, because, as she explained, goddesses saw so much more.

Elissa interrupted her reverie and sat up, because the hardness of the rock had become uncomfortable. She looked to see where the sun was and decided that she had time to walk to Al-Rah Montah and work awhile on the most recent of her figurines.

First, she hurried back to El-Raspell to the hut where Ran-dell had a forge and was making metal tools. He had learned this trade from the only metal worker in Et-Huyuk. As she approached the man, a lump arose in her throat, as she remembered the day she had told Ashannah and Gennah that she had decided to give up her status as a Virgin of Inanna, so that she could live with Ran-dell in El-Raspell.

After she placed a lingering kiss on Ran-dell's lips, she set out for Al-Rah Montah. Again, memories of the recent past formed in her mind. She had not even begun to bleed, when she told her mother of her affection for Ran-dell. Her mother had looked deeply into her eyes for, what seemed to Elissa, a very long time. Finally, Ashannah spoke. "My daughter, I would not think of trying to dissuade you from doing what your heart directs, but I wish that you would remain here until your moon bleeding begins. After you have received the instruction for the temple rituals, if you still wish to go to El-Raspell and live with Ran-dell, you will have my blessing and Inanna's, as well.

Now, as Elissa strode along the path towards her former home, she remembered how envious she had felt when Leah had begun her moon bleeding. It had been especially difficult, when Inanna's feast had come and Leah got to stay with the women, and she had to return home, alone. Even now, tears stung her eyes, as she recalled how she and Leah had grown apart, even before Leah had begun bleeding.

It hadn't made much difference in their relationship, when Leah had discovered that her own abilities lay in weaving, rather than working with clay. Leah began spending hours with Gennah and learned these skills as quickly as Elissa developed her skills in making pots. They had both been so proud and happy the first time that articles they had made found their way into the carts bound for Za-Phir.

The following spring, when Ya-ir and Hel-vid returned from the trading city, they had a loom for Leah and a potter's wheel for Elissa. Mirah and Grenda helped Leah build a work hut, just as Ashannah and Gennah helped Elissa. That they were spending less time together didn't seem to affect their close friendship. Elissa realized it was when she began spending more and more time in El-Raspell to comfort Eetoh, that the change in their feelings for one another began. Ran-dell, who was living in El Raspell with his mother, became her new friend.

Tears stung Elissa's eyes, as she recalled the morning when she had stumbled upon Leah and Nella in a tight embrace, kissing passionately. They had quickly broken apart when they discovered Elissa staring at them, mouth wide open in shock.

"We ... we love each other!" Leah had finally gasped, blushing furiously.

"Yes! Yes, we do!" Nella added. "We love each other very much!"

In spite of the tears rushing down her cheeks, Elissa had been able to respond, "May the blessings of Inanna be upon both of you!" Then she began to run, aimlessly at first, but finally she realized she was heading for El Raspell. Her breathing became more and more labored, and she had to slow down and walk. She thought to herself, "If I felt that way about anyone, it would be Ran-dell!"

When she arrived at El-Raspell, she went directly to his work place, walked right up to him, looking at him intently, and said, "I love you, Ran-dell!"

Ran-dell did not seem surprised. "I have always loved you, Elissa!" he responded and took her into his arms.

As she felt the heat of his passion rise, she pushed him away, stammering, "I don't think I am ready for that, yet!" Then she had turned and run all the way back to Al-Rah Montah. Again, she felt the deep embarrassment that had filled her at the time.

Not long after, Elissa started to bleed, and the women began instructing her in the ways to bring a man to ecstasy in the temple. As they spoke, she felt a strong pulsing between her legs and knew she was ready to make love with Ran-dell. Now, as she again approached her old home and saw Ashannah outside grinding grain for the evening meal, she ran up to her and gave her mother a tight embrace, thanking her for her acceptance and support in her decision to be with Ran-dell. Ashannah had told Elissa that she believed that such love, whether it was between Virgins, or between two men or between a man and a woman, was a gift from Inanna and was not to be taken lightly. Also, Ashannah knew that Eetoh would receive much comfort with Elissa living in his village.

Kasha, Gennah, Thesta and Ashannah had helped gather her things and went with her to El-Raspell, to make certain that she would be welcome. They were all somewhat astonished when Beleendah, Ran-dell's mother, had broken out laughing heartily, as she put her arms around Elissa. "This will be your home, my daughter. Receive it with joy! Now, I can return to Al-Rah Montah and live in the big cave with the others."

Kasha quickly enfolded the woman in her arms to let her know she was welcome and helped gather her things together to make room for Elissa's. As soon as the women had left for Al-Rah Montah, Elissa and Ran-dell relieved the mutual throbbing in their loins.

Now, many sun cycles later, Elissa separated herself from her mother's arms and went to work in the little hut, nearby. She had decided to keep working on her goddesses near her old home. As she entered the little space, the familiar odor of wet earth assailed her. She knelt in front of her latest creation, carefully lifted off the wet cloth, and looked long at it. Finally she reached for one of her small tools and put little swirls in the goddess' robe. With a slight twist of her wrist, she made them look like little flowers. After some time, she settled back on her heels and again, inspected her work with great intensity. Finally, she got up, walked over to the side and picked up a small pot. Pot in hand, she once more knelt in front of the figurine and shook out a number of minute pieces of mica, and with the help of a tool, carefully placed it in one of the eye sockets. She repeated the same procedure for the other eye, and, again, leaned back on her heels.

"I love you, little goddess," she sighed. With the mica in the eye cavities, it was as if the figure came to life, and she knew it would be hard to separate herself from it when it was time to send it to Za-Phir.

Even though he had inherited his father's sandy-colored hair and upslanting eyes, in every other way, An-dor seemed to be the opposite of Eetoh. And while his wide mouth and ready smile obviously came from his mother, he was not much like her, either, although he seemed to love her dearly and tried hard to please her.

The most difficult thing was that An-dor simply did not care for his father, and the more Eetoh tried to develop a close relationship with him, the more An-dor resisted it. Ashannah did everything she could to encourage the boy to emulate and love his father, but she soon understood that the more efforts she put into this, the more resistance the boy offered. She drew back and even advised Eetoh to let the boy come to love him on his own. But this never happened.

During the family's frequent visits to El-Raspell, An-dor seemed attracted to Da-nid, almost before he was out of his mother's arms. As soon as An-dor was able to walk and speak a little, whenever the leader of Et-Huyuk was present, An-dor would hurry over to him and stay by his side. The tall, muscular man with his regal bearing was irresistible to the youngster. Not having a son of his own, Da-nid was pleased by the evident admiration the little boy had for him, and he began to increase his visits to El-Raspell.

Eetoh could't help noticing the growing relationship his son and Da-nid and was deeply hurt by his son's obvious preference for the other man.

Finally, he realized he was powerless to change this and reluctantly resigned himself to it. It was then that Elissa became aware of her father's sorrow and began to go more often to El-Raspell to comfort him.

Leah could not understand Elissa's devotion to her father, never having had any knowledge of her own father, but, for a time, she made these trips with her friend out of loyalty. However, she often felt unwanted, and, after awhile, she only went to El-Raspell with her own mothers for the festivals or for trading.

When Leah began coming less and less to El-Raspell, Elissa spent more and more time with Ran-dell, who shared her affection for Eetoh. Certainly, Ran-dell seemed more like a brother than An-dor. Ran-dell was also aware that Eetoh was being hurt by An-dor and tried to make it up to him. He would have been proud to be the son of the man who had helped him so much just before the trip over the mountain.

An-dor had only recently completed a handful plus two sun cycles, when he approached his mother and told her he wanted to leave Al-Rah Montah and go live with Da-nid in Et-Huyuk. He carefully explained to his mother, that while he loved her very much, he was now old enough to go live in a men's village, instead of a village of women. Ashannah knew that Da-nid had probably encouraged him in this decision, but she tried one more time to direct her son's loyalty towards his father.

"I can understand why you feel that you would rather be around men instead of women, An-dor, but what about living in El-Raspell, with your own father and the other men living there?"

An-dor shifted uneasily. Finally he looked his mother straight in the eyes and answered, "Because I love Da-nid, and I ***don't*** love Eetoh, even if he is my father. I wish Da-nid were my father. I feel like he is more my father, than Eetoh."

"Eetoh loves you very much," Ashannah pressed on.

"I guess he does," An-dor admitted, shrugging. "But I don't love him. To me, Da-nid is ... is who I want to be like. And if I'm going to be like him, I need to be with him."

Ashannah was surprised at how thoroughly the youngster had thought this out. She returned her son's solemn gaze and finally replied, "I can see that you want this very much, An-dor. I could not keep you here, nor do I wish to. If you must, go live with Da-nid in Et-Huyuk, but please try to be as kind to your real father as you can."

"Why is Eetoh more my real father than Da-nid? It is Da-nid I learn from and who I wish to be like! And Da-nid loves me, too, maybe even more than Eetoh!"

Ashannah's eyes filled with tears, but she had nothing more to say. Finally, An-dor said, "I will try to be nice to Eetoh, but I am leaving for Et-Huyuk when the sun begins its next journey." Then, he gave his mother a quick, but fierce, hug and hurried off.

It was a warm and lovely day when the inhabitants of the three villages began gathering together, near the temple outside El-Raspell, to celebrate the early harvest festival of Ninlil.

Eetoh had just heard that An-dor had moved to Et-Huyuk to live with Da-nid, and he watched from the outskirts of the crowd, as the two of them walked, arm in arm to the center. They climbed up a mound of dirt from the diggings of the temple.

"Hear us, all you men, women and children of Et-Huyuk, El-Raspell and Al- Rah Montah!" Da-nid called out. "An-dor has chosen to live with me in the village of men. Since he is not old enough to live by himself as a man, I now designate him as my son."

Eetoh's mouth flew open in shock and watched, in a daze, as An-dor put his little hands on Da-nid's arms, since he was not tall enough to reach the man's shoulders. Then he stated loudly and clearly for all to hear, "My father!"

How often Eetoh had longed to hear these words from his son. A lump filled his throat as he turned and walked away from the gathering. He walked until he was out of sight and then ran for his hut in El-Raspell. He did not want the others to see the tears running down his cheeks.

Back at the temple, there was a long silence, as the others took in the meaning of the little ritual. An-dor was relieved that Ashannah and Gennah had not arrived, as yet.

He did not see Eetoh returning to El-Raspell, but Elissa and Ran-dell had. After a short time, they also left the festivities and returned to their village to see how Eetoh was faring. As they drew nearer, they heard rasping sobs coming from Eetoh's hut. Then the sobbing gradually ceased.

Elissa cried out, "My father, Ran-dell wishes to speak with you."

After a short time, Eetoh appeared at the door. Ran-dell walked up to him, placed his hands on the older man's shoulders, and said, "My father, please accept me as your true son."

Eetoh saw the love pouring out from Ran-dells's eyes and quickly replied, "My son! My son!" and embraced him.

When Leah and Nella decided they wanted a cave house of their own, this increased the number of dwellings of Al-Rah Montah to seven. Most of the crones, including Kasha, Thesta, and Beleendah, preferred living together in the large cave. Since the five dwellings in El Raspell were clustered together, whereas the hillside cave homes of Al-Rah Montah were not even in sight of each other, El Raspell had more the look of a village. The central fire pit and the small cave temple became important in Al-Rah Montah for community gatherings.

Kasha and Thesta thoroughly enjoyed being grandmothers to Elissa, Verda and An-dor. They felt hurt at An-dor's early independence and obvious preference for the men of Et-Huyuk, but it was Eetoh's pain they sympathized with most. When they arrived at Ninlil's feast with Ashannah, Gennah and Verda and heard what had just transpired, none of them could go up and congratulate Da-nid and An-dor, as the men were doing. They set out the food they had so lovingly prepared, but none of them felt like eating.

When Ashannah noticed that Eetoh was not present, and realized that Elissa and Ran-dell were not there, either, she easily imagined what had happened. After a few minutes, she went to El-Raspell and found the three of them enjoying their own private feast.

Ashannah walked up to Eetoh and stammered, "How ... how are you faring, Eetoh? I ... I just heard what happened."

Eetoh saw the deep concern in her eyes and was happy to stand up and proclaim, "Well, it seems that in one journey of the sun, I lost one son, but gained another. Ran-dell has just chosen me to be his true father, and, of course, I was very happy to receive him, as my true son."

At once, Ran-dell stood up and the two men, again, embraced.

Joyful tears flowed down Ashannah's cheeks as she watched, and Elissa quickly invited her to join them. Soon Gennah, Verda, Kasha and Thesta came along, bringing their own festive dishes.

Almost from birth, Verda had shown that along with the red, tightly curled hair of her mother, she had also inherited the prophetic gifts of her grandmother, Orana. She also had a love for gathering herbs and healing people, which made her close to Ashannah and Kasha, but from the beginning she showed signs of her grandmother's clairvoyance. At first, Gennah resisted this by ignoring the child's gifts, but when she realized that she was isolating herself from her own daughter, she began to help Verda recognize and develop these talents.

Verda always preferred being by herself to playing with Elissa and An-dor, or any of the other children. However, she wasn't entirely reclusive. She loved going with Ashannah and Kasha when they went into the woods to forage, and she spent hours with them in the gardens. Ashannah and Kasha were comfortable with the child's presence and enjoyed teaching her about the healing properties of herbs.

One day, when Ashannah and Verda were working together in the garden by their home, Ashannah said to the child, "If you would rather be playing with An-dor or Lorana, I can easily finish this planting."

Tears filled the little girl's eyes, as she replied, "Oh, 'Shannah, let me stay here with you! I ... I would really rather work in the garden!"

Ashannah remembered the times she would have preferred working in the garden to playing with Eetoh, but she also knew she had benefited from their games.

Then she noticed the tears filling Verda's eyes. "Do they make fun of you, Verda?" she asked.

"They do sometimes. I'm ... I'm different, somehow," and with this, the child began sobbing. Ashannah knew how sensitive and aware Verda was and that she was truly different from the other children. She held the little girl tightly in her arms, comforting her. "You are different, Verda, because you are very special to Inanna. Because she loves you very much, she gave you many wonderful gifts. And I love you, too, and love to have you work with me. Of course, you may stay."

After they had worked in silence for a few minutes, Verda asked, "Does ... Mama like it that I'm different?"

"Your mama loves you, just as you are," Ashannah assured her.

Therefore, when Elissa left for El-Raspell and An-dor went to Et-Huyuk, Verda felt relieved rather than bereft.

The first time that Verda had a strong precognitive vision, it was difficult for Gennah to remain by her. In spite of the little girl's lack of years, she looked so much like Orana had when she delivered an oracle, that Gennah felt the old urge to separate herself, as she had separated herself from her mother, years before.

Ashannah drew her lover and the little girl to her, and the three of them remained this way for some time. The two women hadn't been able to make much sense of the Oracle, but it had left the child exhausted, and they sensed the message held a negative aspect. Verda, however, quickly fell asleep, and she seemed to have forgotten it when she awoke the following morning.

The days were becoming quite short, and in the mornings the women were finding frost on their dwellings. One crisp evening, as Ashannah, Gennah and Verda were sitting around their fire, enjoying its warmth, Ashannah noticed a trancelike look in Verda's eyes, as the child gazed into the flames. The woman quickly realized what was going to happen, as she remembered the visions she had received from the flames of fires, during the flight from Al-Rah. However, she wasn't at all prepared for the message they were to receive.

Suddenly the little girl stood up, raised her arms above her head and described the vision she had received. "I see many men. They are all shiny and they are carrying long, pointy sticks. They are coming here ... here, to the three villages, and they look mean. I don't think they like us!" With that, the child fell forward and began to sob hysterically.

The two women looked at each other in shock, and then Gennah gathered her daughter into her arms to give her comfort. Ashannah stood and, as if she, too, were in a trance, proclaimed, "We cannot keep running! We will not allow them to make us leave our homes again!"

Chapter Twenty-six

Ashannah's heart filled with happiness, when Elissa confided to her that she hadn't bled for three months. Yet, she could hardly have been surprised. Nonetheless, pregnancy was always considered a gift from Inanna, and the two women went together to the small cave temple in Al-Rah Montah to give thanks to the Goddess. They knelt in silent joy before the statue, which the child Elissa had helped to create, and were somewhat startled when they heard someone come in through the opening. As if Inanna, herself, had brought her, it was Kasha who approached them. She, too, was overcome with delight at learning she was to be a great grandmother, a rare happening in those times. The three of them sang Inanna's litany with great fervor, and the old High Priestess hurried back to the large cave to share the news with the other crones.

Ashannah had gradually taken over most of the duties of the High Priestess and even those of the village healer, because of Kasha's increasing infirmities, but the women of both El Raspell and Al-Rah Montah, including Ashannah, still went to Kasha for counsel. Nonetheless, Ashannah and Gennah still had not told the crone about Verda's disturbing vision.

A little later, Nella had more good news to give the women, and there was much rejoicing over the expectations of having a new infant in each village.

Shortly after Verda's disquieting vision, Hel-vid and Ya-ir had made their annual trip to Za-phir without any alarming incidents. This gave Ashannah and Gennah hope that the vision did not apply to the three villages, in spite of the fact that the child had clearly stated that it did. Thus, they made the decision not to frighten the others by disclosing it.

Later, the announcement of the two pregnancies and the general well-being of all three villages helped even them to completely forget about it. However, as winter approached, Verda became increasingly reclusive, somewhat restless and even irritable. It reminded Ashannah of the way Orana had acted just before she had received the warning vision at Al-Rah.

Since Gennah hadn't the gifts necessary to be the Sibyl for the village, Orana had not passed on her knowledge of the powerful potions she made to stimulate and bring about the prophetic visions. Even if she had the formulas, Ashannah would have hesitated to give them to such a young child. Under this pressure, Gennah and Ashannah finally went to Kasha and told her of the vision and of Verda's disturbing behavior. Kasha helped them to comfort and divert Verda in any way she could think of, but she, too, did not want to disturb the rest by sharing the vision.

By the time the traders began gathering their goods for the journey to Za-Phir that spring, Verda was hardly speaking with anyone, and the three women hoped it was a sign that the dangers the vision had described were not imminent. The villagers gathered together at the temple near El Raspell bringing their items for trading, which for the first time filled three carts instead of the usual two. That this would make it necessary for a third person to go into Za-Phir with them wasn't a concern. After all these years, people would hardly recognize Yuk-tol.

The hand of days plus one that it had always taken for the traders to do their business before returning went by without incident. The villagers all came together at the temple in a festive mood, waiting to see what the men would bring back with them. However, Verda's behavior had become increasingly disruptive, so Ashannah, Gennah and Kasha kept themselves apart, trying to comfort the disconsolate child. Since she hadn't received a further vision, they still hoped that the traders would return as usual.

When the women heard the shouts of men coming from the trail to Et-Huyuk, they could barely make out the figures of the two running men and were unable to understand what they were saying. The three women were frozen with fear and could only stand and wait to hear the men's words.

"Soldiers are coming! Soldiers are following us here! They want to destroy our villages!"

At once, Ashannah leaped up on the pile of dirt and screamed, "We cannot let them drive us from our homes again!"

"Where are Hel-vid, Ya-ir and Yuk-tol?" someone else yelled.

"They wouldn't give up the carts!" A-bel managed to get out between his gulps for breath as he ran up to the crowd.

"They are close behind us, though, and because there are so many soldiers, they have to move slower and are even farther behind," Da-nid cried out, and quickly continued, as he hugged An-dor, who had run out to him. "We must arm ourselves with whatever we can find to defend our villages!"

"No!" screamed Ashannah. "That would only anger them! Our small bows and arrows and knives and shovels would be no match for their bows, which are many times larger than ours, and their spears, which they can throw for great distances, would bring death to us!"

"But you said we cannot let them drive us from our homes, again!" someone pointed out.

"That is right!" she yelled back. "We must think of some other way than trying to fight them!"

The others stared at her, waiting for what she had to say. When she didn't continue right away, Da-nid started out for Et-Huyuk crying out, "Well, I would rather die defending our villages than just standing by and watching them be destroyed!"

An-dor ran after Da-nid, grabbed hold of his tunic and shouted, "Wait, my father! Listen to what she has to say!"

After a brief pause, Ashannah came up with a plan. "We will all march together to meet them before they arrive at Et-Huyuk. When we can see them, we will raise our hands high in the air to let them see we are a peaceful people and mean them no harm! We will sing to them of our lives and ... and how could they just destroy us for no cause?"

"But will that alone keep them from destroying us?" someone called out.

"We must believe that Inanna will change their hearts towards us, when they understand we do not wish them any harm," she said. "Truly, it is the only way!"

Kasha and the other women backed her up immediately. Then Moshe, feeble as he was, got up beside Ashannah and shouted to the men. "We must listen to her. She is right! We do not have weapons good enough to defend ourselves against them. Nor do we even know how to fight in such a way! I say to you, our faith in Inanna is all we have! And it will be enough!"

Just then Hel-vid, Ya-ir and Yuk-tol came running up with the loaded carts. They quickly pushed them into the temple for safekeeping while Moshe related Ashannah's plan.

"She is right," Ya-ir conceded. "We would surely be defeated if we try to fight them!"

Da-nid finally saw the wisdom of her plan and ceased trying to dissuade the others. With Ashannah and Da-nid in the lead, the others quickly formed themselves behind the two and began their march down the trail to Et-Huyuk.

As they marched through the men's village, the women saw for the first time the neat little rectangular dwellings made from mud bricks. Then they looked up behind the village, at the beautiful pasture, bright green with the new spring grass, looking even greener by the contrasting white wool of the sheep grazing there. They did not slow down for this, but continued to march resolutely onward.

Soon they came to another meadow cut by a dark swath, which was the path leading to the road to Za-Phir. As Da-nid led them onto it, their eyes were momentarily blinded by a blaze of sunlight on metal. On the far side of the meadow, they made out a group of men holding shields. Beside each man stood an archer. As soon as the soldiers saw the villagers, the archers raised their bows and set their arrows into place.

At once Ashannah raised her arms over her head and began singing,

"We are the children of Inanna,"

Before she could continue, there was a loud horrifying scream coming from among the soldiers. Instantly there was another scream from among the villagers.

"Oh Goddess, I'm having my baby!" Elissa cried out.

Ashannah broke into a cold sweat, realizing she had completely forgotten about Elissa and Nella when she had made the plans for facing their enemy. She immediately turned and ran towards her daughter, seeing Ran-dell beside her looking very helpless. By the time Ashannah reached them, Gennah, Kasha and Thesta arrived on the scene. The women became absorbed in the task at hand, entirely forgetting about the soldiers. Da-nid led the rest in a protective circle around the healers. Soon after, the loud cries of the newborn filled the air.

Across the meadow the jaws of every soldier dropped as they comprehended what was happening. Slowly the raised arms of the archers dropped. Someone gasped, "They have forgotten we are even here, they are so intent on helping the woman bring forth her child! It is the doing of Inanna! We can't just kill them now!" The leader must have agreed, because he barked out orders to that effect. Some men even fell to their knees, praying for forgiveness from the Goddess.

And on the other side of the meadow, the villagers once more raised their voices in song:

We are the children of Inanna
We are a peaceful people
Tending our gardens and sheep
Weaving baskets, forming pots,
Forging our tools for gardening and building homes.
We are the children of Inanna!
We are a peaceful people!

"It is a boy! It is a son for Ran-dell!" Ashannah cried out.

"And a grandson for Eetoh!" Elissa echoed.

Epilogue

He was a little man, that is, short of stature and wiry, but he had become even smaller by the constant drain on his energy from his ever-present desire for revenge. This exceeded his thirst for liquids or even hunger for food. He lost weight, his clothing became loose and ragged, his eyes had sunk back into their sockets.

He had been at the forefront of the men who had traveled to Al-Rah, some years ago, in order to destroy the village and the Virgins living within its borders. When they found it empty, he, especially, was thoroughly enraged.

He returned to the Great Sea and began sailing on cargo boats. He thought traveling to new places and the hard work of loading and unloading supplies would help him forget ...

He did not forget, however, and his desire for revenge continued to consume him. Some years later, when he was staying over in Za-Phir, waiting for a new assignment, he overheard some of Gan-dor's men speaking of a village of Virgins and castaway men, a few days journey from Za-Phir, which they were planning to destroy. At this point, however, they planned to take the inhabitants as slaves, because they were excellent potters, weavers and metal workers. When he heard this, he felt certain that the object of his revenge would be found among them. He decided to sign on with these soldiers, but because he appeared wild and somewhat crazed, they let him come along only to help carry their supplies.

For several days, they marched deeper and deeper into the forests and on into the very mountains to the north and east of Za-Phir. Finally, one day, shortly after the sun had reached its meridian, he suddenly heard the order to halt, which every man did, instantly. He could feel their tension mount, along with his own. He slipped up to the front of the ranks, being careful not to draw attention to himself, and discovered that the forest had come to an abrupt end. The soldiers in front were facing a huge meadow. He carefully looked to his right and to his left, but could see no reason for the halt.

After slipping over to a large oak, he climbed it for about twenty feet, in order to see better. His efforts were quickly rewarded. Almost directly across the meadow he observed a crowd of men, women and children, walking towards him and the battalion of soldiers. When he noted a flash of red hair among them, his heart leaped into his throat, beating so hard that the veins on his neck could be seen pulsing.

Then the little band of people stopped, and he knew they had seen the soldiers. He watched in awe as they lifted their arms, began singing and started walking directly towards them.

As soon as he was able to distinguish Gennah's features, his heartbeats quickened even more, until he thought he would faint. He grabbed onto the tree trunk to keep from falling. Then in a strange manner, he felt the consuming desire for revenge slip away, as he realized that he was still in love with her. He had hardly taken this in, when he heard an order barked and watched, in a daze, as the archers raised their bows and set their arrows.

"I thought they were going to take them as slaves!" he exclaimed to himself and then screamed with all his might, "Noooooooo!" Believing his cry would be ignored, Ator threw himself from the tree, the scream continuing until he hit the ground and was instantly killed.